# enlightenment for idiots

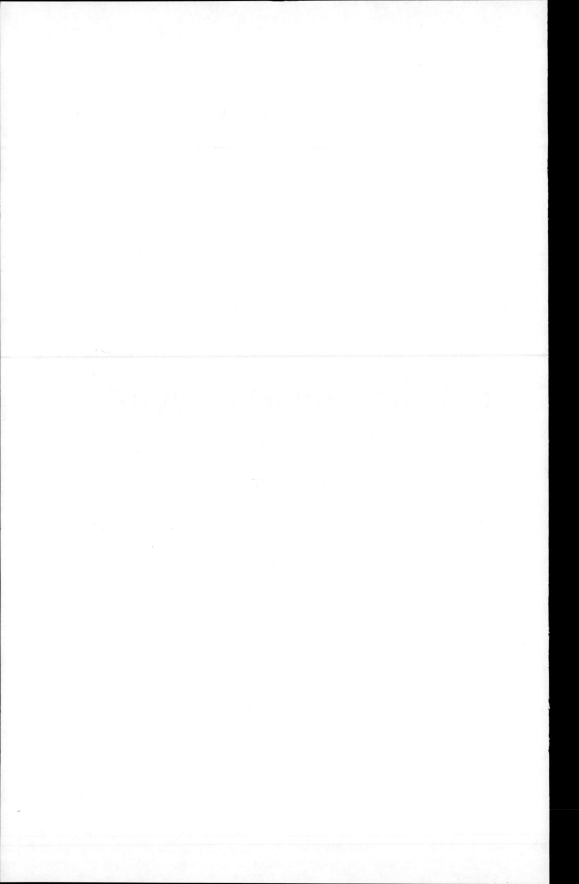

NONFICTION BY ANNE CUSHMAN

*From Here to Nirvana*

# enlightenment

A Novel

# for idiots

Anne Cushman

Shaye Areheart Books
NEW YORK

All rights reserved.
Published in the United States by Shaye Areheart Books, an imprint of the Crown Publishing Group, a division of Random House, Inc., New York.
www.crownpublishing.com

Shaye Areheart Books with colophon is a registered trademark of Random House, Inc.

Library of Congress Cataloging-in-Publication Data

Cushman, Anne.
Enlightenment for idiots : a novel / by Anne Cushman. — 1st ed.
p. cm.
1. Americans—India—Fiction.   2. Pregnant women—Fiction.
3. Yoga—Fiction.   4. India—Fiction.   I. Title.

PS3603.U824E55 2008
813'.6—dc22          2007040268

ISBN 978-0-307-38164-4

Printed in the United States of America

Design by Lynne Amft

10   9   8   7   6   5   4   3   2   1

First Edition

*For Kathleen*

# enlightenment for idiots

# PROLOGUE

*Step on your mat.*

*Let a river of breath sweep your arms overhead and then fold you forward, your spine pouring from your pelvis in a waterfall of muscle and bone.*

*Lie on your back with the soles of your feet together and your knees winged out to the side, your tender belly exposed.*

*Curl on the floor in a fetal position, a seed under frozen earth.*

*Each of these yoga poses will lead inevitably to another, each one blossoming out of the one before in a rippling wave. So where you end up will be, in some way, bound to the place you started. Don't try to separate beginnings from endings. Your last pose will have your first pose buried within it, if you look deeply enough.*

WHEN MY MOTHER was six months pregnant with me, my father walked out the door and never came back. That's pretty much all I know about him; all I need to know, my mother says. She doesn't like to talk about him; the few times I got up the nerve to ask, her face shut down like an iron gate clanging shut. "Not everybody has a daddy," she used to tell me when I came home from preschool and asked where mine was. "Daddies are optional." "He was very young," she'd say when I got older. "We both were. He just wasn't ready to grow up yet."

There were no pictures of him in our scrapbooks or displayed around our home—more precisely, around any of our homes, because we moved every couple of years, trying to find a job or a city or an apartment or a boyfriend that could make my mother happy. But once, snooping around in my mother's wallet trying to find a dollar for a candy bar, I came across a folded snapshot tucked behind an expired library card. There was my mother, impossibly young, standing on a boardwalk by the ocean beside a boy with a crooked grin and a tangle of dark curls exactly like mine. His arm was around her, but he was looking in the other direction, out to sea. She was leaning into him, tiny and blonde. She didn't look anything like me. But even at nine years old, I recognized that her expression was mine: happy but guarded, afraid to lean into the joy and trust it to catch her. Knowing that any minute, it could be snatched away.

I never told her I found the photo. I never told her something else, either: that it isn't true that my father left and never came back. I carry a memory around with me, as creased and hidden as my mother's snapshot. In this memory I am very young—I couldn't be more than three, because we were still living in the studio apartment in Los Angeles where my father had left us. It was the middle of the night. My bed was under a window in a tiny alcove off the kitchen. I woke up from a dream of a field of pumpkins growing bigger and bigger all around me, to the hum of the refrigerator and the tick of the clock and the urgent sense that someone had just been calling my name. I sat up, pulled aside the corner of the curtain, and peeked through the window into pooled moonlight and tree shadows black as spilled ink. My father was standing in the driveway below, looking at the house. Although I'd never seen him, I knew instantly who it was. But I just sat there, hidden in the shadows, watching him look up at the blank eyes of the windows. I had the feeling that if I just pulled back the curtain and stepped into the light where he could see me, he would reach out his arms to me. He would come inside, and he would not be able to go away again. But I didn't move. After a long time, he turned away. He walked to a pickup truck on the other side of the street, got in, and drove off with no lights on.

I NEVER TELL this to anyone. But sometimes I think that this story is the pose that's buried within all the poses that came after.

*The student of hatha yoga should practice in a solitary place, in a temple or a hermitage, an arrow-shot away from rocks, water, and fire. The hermitage should have a small door and no windows. It should be level with the ground and have no holes in the walls. It should be neither too high nor too long, and clean and free from insects. It should be laid daily with cow dung.*

—*Hatha Yoga Pradipika,* ca. AD 1400

# CHAPTER I

MY CELL PHONE RANG at 6:27 a.m., ripping me out of a nightmare in which I was teaching a yoga class wearing only a bra and panties.

"Amanda? Maxine here," snapped a voice that was not the one I was hoping for. Strange how the fantasy—*maybe it's Matt*—could hijack my mind before I was even awake. I squinted blearily at the glowing red numbers on the clock. Oh, damn. I must have slept through my alarm. In exactly thirty-three minutes I was supposed to be at The Blissful Body Yoga Studio, substitute teaching the Monday

Rise and Shine class. The regular teacher had called me late last night, croaking with laryngitis; I knew that I was probably seventh or eighth on her list, but still, for an aspiring yoga teacher, not even certified yet, subbing for this class was a rare honor. And here I had almost slept right through it.

"Oh, hello, Maxine." I tried to sound as professional as possible as I scrambled out of the tangled sheets and began groping around on the floor for my yoga pants. Of course it wasn't Matt; I'd told Matt I never wanted to speak to him again. Maxine was my editor at Bigday Books, the publishers of the For Idiots: Guides to No-Risk Adventure series, which Maxine hoped would put her mark on the publishing industry. Her book contracts were helping me pay my way—barely—through my yoga teacher training, which I was counting on to launch me into a Right Livelihood career in which I never again had to dodge calls from credit card collection agencies. I switched on the overhead, scrunching my eyes against the light. "What can I do for you?"

"I have a very important question for you." That wasn't surprising; all Maxine's questions were very important. And almost all of them came extremely early in the morning. Bigday was based in Manhattan, and Maxine believed that "Pacific standard time" was just another excuse used by California writers to justify their chronic lack of work ethic.

"Lay it on me." I picked up a turquoise camisole and sniffed the underarms.

"Amanda, what do you know about enlightenment?"

"About *what?*" I was pulling the shirt over my head as she spoke; the phone must have slipped. Maxine couldn't have just asked me about enlightenment. I had cranked out two manuscripts for her in the last eighteen months. The first one, *RV Camping for Idiots,* had forced me to spend my entire August traveling in a rented Winnebego from state park to state park, sandwiched each night between families with screaming toddlers watching *Dora the Explorer* on portable televisions. The second one—*The California Winecountry for Idiots*—had been particularly problematic given that I was in the middle of a yoga teacher training program in which the instructor had advocated drinking nothing but lemon water with cayenne and maple syrup. "I'm sorry, I didn't quite catch that."

"En-light-en-ment." Her voice radiated impatience. "I know you're into this whole yoga craze. So tell me: What is enlightenment?"

"Well . . ." 6:31.Would anyone notice if my socks didn't match? "As I understand it, enlightenment is a state of blissful awareness that's not dependent on any external circumstances." I tucked the phone in the crook of my neck and tugged a comb through my hair until it snagged, then gave up. "It's the understanding that you're not separate from anything else in the universe: the trees, the sun, the—"

"Okay, I get it. My question is, is this something that people are looking for?"

"Well, sure, I guess so. Some people, anyway." I grabbed my rolled-up yoga mat and held the phone to my ear as I went down the creaking stairs, speaking softly so as not to wake up my housemate. Ishtar was annoyed enough about living with a writer; she claimed that when I worked my mental vibrations seeped through the wall into her bedroom, disrupting her meditations on global harmony. In retaliation, whenever I sat down at my iBook she had begun playing her tablas and singing hymns to the Earth Goddess with great hostility and volume. "I mean, it's really the whole point of the yoga practice. It's—"

"So where would people go to get it?"

"Oh, I don't think you have to go anywhere." Even I knew that. The books filled two whole rows in my bedside bookshelf, all with the same optimistic message: *Be Here Now; Wherever You Go, There You Are; Present Moment, Wonderful Moment.* "You can find it anywhere, like in the sound of a bell ringing, or a butterfly flapping its—"

"A-man-da??" It was her ominous voice, the one that told me that if I wasn't careful, I'd be working at Starbucks again. "I'm talking about travel that involves No-Risk Adventure."

"Well, if you had to go somewhere—India, I guess. I mean, that's where yoga came from." I grabbed my battered mountain bike from the front hall and wheeled it out the door into a swirl of morning fog mixed with the salty wind off the San Francisco Bay. I groped for a metaphor she would relate to. "It's like going to Paris to buy your clothes, versus just getting them at Target."

"So if we wanted to do a book about this yoga thing that really set us apart from the competitors—something a cut above all this *Yoga for This* and *Yoga for That*—we should send our writer to India to get enlightened. Am I correct?"

I slung my legs over my bike. My ancient Honda had died a few months ago—the engine finally seized up at 185,000 miles—and I hadn't been able to afford a new one. And with my credit cards run up the way they were—charging yoga workshops, teacher trainings, an occasional dose of Xanax—no one would give me a loan. "Yes. I'd say that's correct." If I pedaled hard, I could still be there on time.

"Ah." She sounded supremely satisfied. "So, Amanda. This is my concept. We send you to India. You track down this enlightenment thing, tell our readers all the places they can go to get it. We cover your expenses. When you find it, you come back, and as soon as you write the book, you'll get the rest of the advance."

"Um . . ." I was feeling a bit slow on the uptake. I coasted down the hill, past the rows of Victorians with their windows still shuttered. I'd been dreaming for years of going to India. Was Maxine actually offering to send me there to write . . . to write . . . "What is the book I'm supposed to write, exactly?"

Maxine let out a sigh. "Amanda. Have you not been listening to me? The book is 'Enlightenment for Idiots.' Are you on board with this? Or do I need to find someone else?"

*Yoga is the cessation of the turning of thought.*

—*The Yoga Sutra of Patanjali,* ca. 200 BC

# CHAPTER 2

"INHALING, SWEEEEEP YOUR arms to the side and overhead. Exhaling, *foooold* forward from the hips." I stood at the front of the yoga studio, gazing out at the faces of thirteen students and an intimidating panel of floor-to-ceiling mirrors that reflected their pastel bottoms back at me as they folded into their forward bends. "Let your body ride on the waves of your breath like seaweed on the ocean."

I hoped I didn't sound as nervous as I felt. I'd been in a teacher-training program for almost a year and a half, but I'd only taught a handful of real classes, and I still felt like a fraud whenever I did. I was afraid that the students would be able to see straight through my paper-thin facade of serenity to the realities of my life: a stressed-out twenty-nine-year-old galloping toward thirty with a broken-down car, no savings account, no career, and a kite's tail of failed relationships flapping in the breeze behind her.

"Exhale, step back into Plank Pose. Inhale, opening the heart into Upward Dog." My pretense of peace wasn't helped by the fact that my mind was churning over my conversation with Maxine. *India! I can study yoga with the greatest living masters. I'll live so simply, so spiritually, carrying everything I need in my backpack. But first I have to buy a backpack. And an ultralight travel yoga mat. And some new yoga clothes, something that won't wrinkle, maybe some of those rayon pants with Hindu gods printed on their butts.* "Exhaling, press back to Downward Dog, and take five long, steady breaths. Feel the line of energy from your palms out through your sitting bones." *Wait till I tell Matt. He'll be so jealous. Oh, right, I'm not talking to Matt. I'll get enlightened, then he'll be sorry. He'll want to sleep with me and I'll just smile and say, 'I'll always love you, but I'm really beyond all that now.' Or maybe we will sleep together, just one time. It will be a tantric kind of thing, not just physical.* I pressed into Downward Dog myself to demonstrate, looked back at my thighs, and realized that I had put on my yoga pants inside out. The long seam ran ragged and obvious down the inside of my thigh. There was probably a tag hanging out right above my tailbone.

I HAD STARTED doing yoga almost five years earlier, a couple of years after I graduated from San Francisco State with a BA in Creative Writing, $37,000 in student loan debt, and no discernible job-related skills. I had just moved into a shared house in the lower Haight, where I was writing and rewriting the first three paragraphs of a novel while working a collection of odd jobs—waitress, dog walker, pizza deliverer, nanny—at which I was uniformly mediocre. It was my best friend, Lori, who dragged me to my first yoga class, held in a studio a few blocks away from Golden Gate Park. "It will make you less uptight," she'd told me. "I'm not uptight," I had argued, folding my fingers into my palms so my bitten nails wouldn't show. But because Lori had been for years the sanest person in my life—ever since I walked into my freshman dorm room and found her tucking her sheets into crisp corners on her bed—I went to class with her.

Ropes dangled from metal hooks on one wall. I lay on a hardwood floor with my spine draped over a bolster, my legs strapped together, canvas sandbags weighting my groin. "Draw your tailbone toward your pubic bone," the teacher commanded. "Soften your armpits toward your shoulder blades and draw the inner borders of your shoulder blades down your spine. Let your brain drop down toward the upper palate of your mouth." There was something immensely comforting in the precision of the instructions: a roll call for my body, letting me know that everything was there, reporting to duty.

I began going to class every day, sometimes twice a day. I went to classes in every style: The cautious, precise Iyengar classes, with their arsenal of blocks and straps and sandbags and metal folding chairs to protect students from the perils of a misaligned Triangle Pose. The feel-good Sivananda classes, with candles and incense and Indian kirtans crooning in the background. The Kundalini classes, with a wild-eyed, turbaned teacher who taught us to snort Breath of Fire and churn our bellies like washing machines.

Within about a year, I found my way into the hard-core group: the 7 a.m. Ashtanga class. Six mornings a week I'd ride my bike down the still-empty city streets, ski jacket zipped over my yoga clothes, the wind biting my ears. The studio windows would be closed, the air thick with sandalwood incense, the heat blasting—to simulate the climate in India, said the teacher, a small, stern, incongruously busty woman with military posture and knotted ropes of muscles standing out in her bare arms and legs. We'd step to the front of our mats, draw our palms together at our hearts, and chant in Sanskrit like Hindu priests in jewel-toned workout clothes: *Vande gurunam charanara vinde* . . . Then we'd sweep our arms overhead and swan-dive into our practice, our breath hissing like surf in the backs of our throats.

Our mats grew slick with sweat; the windows fogged with steam.

I wrestled my legs behind my neck, balanced upside down on my forearms with my toes straining toward the crown of my head, dropped back from standing into a punishing backbend, hands groping at my heels. After class, my body tingled, throbbed, and glowed. Sometimes, later, I'd find bruises on my arms and legs from the pressure of bone against flesh. I would sneak glances at them throughout the day with a secret thrill, like bruises left after a night of hot sex.

When I'd been practicing Ashtanga about six months, I noticed a new guy in class. You couldn't help noticing the men, of course—stripped to the waist, their muscles flexing, their skins shining with sweat. Even if I didn't know their names, I knew the intimate territory of their bodies: the smell of their armpits and their breath, the placement of their moles and tattoos, the way their bellies hung over the top of their shorts, whether they powered through the prescribed series like guided missiles or meandered as if they were taking a stroll in the park. This one was more the guided-missile type—thin and wiry, with bands of muscles sliding under his skin. He had dark hair pulled back in a ponytail, a beaklike nose, and lips that pursed into a half kiss when he concentrated. His arms were brown but his chest was pale and hairless, lending him the illusion of vulnerability, like a turtle out of its shell. When he rolled out his mat in the corner next to mine, I could smell his musky sweat, a blend of skunk and lemons.

All that week, we flowed through the series side by side, linked in an intricate, intimate dance. His breath hissed in lockstep with mine. Tattoos of snakes writhed down his arms. After the final chant, we'd both sit quietly, eyes closed. When I'd get up to leave, he would still be sitting there, his torso tapering in a bony V down to his bare legs folded in full Lotus.

That weekend I sat at my usual table at the Bookends Café, drinking a chai and scribbling in my journal. I looked up to see the guy from yoga walking up to my table, wearing a leather jacket, with a Nikon hanging from his neck.

"I need a model for a photo series about a yogini who falls in love with a feral cat," he said, looking me over. "Are you interested?"

"I hate posing for pictures."

"You just have to be yourself." He set the camera down on the table and gestured to the waiter.

"That's the hardest thing of all," I said.

His name was Matt, he told me as I drank another chai and he drank a double espresso. He was a freelance travel photographer for a stock photo house, just in town for a couple of months between gigs. He had just gotten back from six weeks in India. Next month he was off to Bogotá. In between he was shooting a series of artsy calendars distributed by a small press in San Francisco. The yogini cat romance would be one of them: twelve months of an unfolding photo essay, cat pose morphing into cat love with no interruption.

"So is this supposed to reveal the spiritual side of cats?" I asked.

"More like the animal side of yoga. At least the way we do it in America. You don't know yoga at all till you've been to India. This stuff they're doing here—it's just glorified gymnastics."

"So why are you wasting your time with it?" I asked, annoyed.

He grinned at me. "It's a good way to meet girls."

I took another sip of chai, trying to resist being charmed. Outside of yoga class, he didn't strike me as particularly attractive: His face was too craggy, his body too thin, and there was something obscurely unsettling about his pale eyes fringed with dark lashes. "Yeah, yoga classes are full of girls. Most of them are more beautiful than I am. Lots of them do better yoga. Why do you want *me* for this calendar?"

"That's the problem. They're all *too* beautiful. You look at them doing yoga and all you see is their hair and their breasts and their personalities and their designer yoga wear. I need a model who disappears into the poses."

I set my cup down, too hard; chai sloshed over the edge and into the saucer. "So you're saying you chose me because I have no breasts and no personality and bad outfits?"

He tipped back in his chair and regarded me. I realized what was odd about his eyes: One of them was gray and the other was green, giving his face an oddly unbalanced look, as if I were talking to two different people at the same time. "Look. Do you want to do this photo shoot with me, or don't you?"


WE SHOT THE calendar later that week near a pond in Golden Gate Park where the cat liked to hang out—a giant gray tabby named Bigfoot with a tattered ear and a limp, a park cat belonging to everybody, or nobody. He was an uncooperative subject. He'd disappear into underbrush, climb high into redwood branches. Sometimes we sat by the pond for hours, just waiting for him to turn up. A waterfall sluiced down the rocks behind us, drowning out the sound of traffic from a nearby road. The air smelled of damp earth and redwood needles. I brought picnics for us to share—crusty sourdough bread, Stilton and Brie, sweet juicy tangerines. Some days the cat never showed at all. "Couldn't you have found an indoor cat to photograph?" I asked Matt. He looked at me and raised one eyebrow. "What kind of yogini would fall in love with an indoor cat?" he asked.

"What I like about photography," Matt said as we waited for the cat on a park bench by the pond in the long afternoon shadows, "is the way it makes me pay attention to everything. It's a lot like yoga, that way." He held his camera in his lap, his fingers playing with the lens cap. "I mean, here we are, sitting here all day, just studying the movements of a cat. Our whole agenda suspended in favor of his. It's incredibly intimate. I'm closer to that cat right now than I am to anyone in the world."

"Funny to think what a different day we'd be having if you were shooting a calendar about a woman who falls in love with a dog." I picked up a tangerine and began to peel it. "We'd be tramping around through the bushes right now, finding dead things to sniff at. Or throwing a soggy tennis ball up and down a field."

"Well, to start with, I wouldn't be spending the day with you. I'd have cast some other woman. You are definitely a cat person."

"I do like cats." I pulled off a section of tangerine and popped it into my mouth. "There's always something wild about them. You can't entirely domesticate them."

"See? Perfect casting. You're in love with him already."

"I don't fall in love that easily."

He reached out and picked up my hand, began running his hands lightly over the knuckles. "Don't worry. Neither do I."

That night we did the final shoot, me and the cat curled up together on the queen-sized loft bed in Matt's studio apartment in the Mission, where we'd transported Bigfoot in a carrier baited with sautéed chicken livers. To create the effect of candlelight, Matt had hung lights all over the room, screened off in layers of translucent orange plastic—I was astounded at how much light it took to create the illusion of darkness. Just outside the frame, the fringes of the room were filled with rolls of duct tape, reflectors, extra gels. Matt shot in extreme close-up, the camera almost caressing my skin. Bigfoot lolled on the sheets, sated with liver into temporary quiescence.

Looking back later, I found it hard to remember where the photos stopped and the sex began. Although it was our first time together, it was strangely familiar—the rush of our breath in each others ears, the perspiration on our skin, the musky body smell, the way we lay together afterward, spent, our bodies humming. It was almost as intimate as yoga class.

"You really should go to India," he told me, sometime past midnight. We were lying naked in a tangle of sheets, candlelight flickering on our skin. The candle was fixed to a plate on the floor next to his futon; an incense stick was stuck in the melted wax, the same sweet sandalwood we burned in class. "It would change your whole yoga practice."

"Tell me what it's like," I said, just to keep him talking. I wanted to keep him awake with me for as long as possible in this bubble of intimacy, before we collapsed into separate worlds of sleep and woke up in the glare of sunlight to the sour smell of each other's breath and the awkward realization that we didn't really know each other at all.

"I'll show you." He rolled over, grabbed a folder off the floor, and began spilling pictures across the bed. I picked up one: a naked man with matted dreadlocks past his waist, covered with a film of gray powder. His forehead was marked with three orange vertical stripes. A garland of bones hung around his neck.

"This is a sadhu," Matt told me. "It's a yogi who's given up everything—his home, his family, even his name. See that gray powder all over his body? That's ash from a funeral pyre."

"Why does he put it on himself?" I pulled the blankets tighter around my own naked breasts.

"To remind himself that he's going to die." He pushed aside the sadhu and picked up another picture: a tree trunk festooned with orange silk. "And look—this is the Bodhi Tree. I meditated right in this spot, right where the Buddha himself got enlightened. This is an actual leaf from that tree." He reached for a journal lying beside his bed and opened it carefully. Between the pages lay a heart-shaped leaf, dried to translucence, its veins as delicate as a spiderweb. He held it out to me, but I shook my head. I was afraid to touch something so fragile, even when it seemed to be freely offered.

"You can lose yourself in India." He propped himself up on one elbow and began lightly tracing the length of my spine with his fingertips, vertebra by vertebra. "You can become someone else."

That sounded good to me. I rolled toward him.

M ATT WAS RARELY in town for more than a few weeks at a time. He left for months at a stretch: Peru, Turkey, China, Indonesia. He'd come back burned brown from the sun, thin from bouts with foreign intestinal bugs, on fire with a new and consuming topic, and smelling of mosquito repellent, a smell that clung to his skin even after several showers. Even when we'd been lovers for years, we never moved in together. His place was too small, he told me, and it was true: just a one-room studio, a loft bed with his computer and camera equipment tucked underneath. After we made love, he'd go down there again and work late into the night, shaping his digital images, cropping them, highlighting them, polishing them until they were more real than reality itself.

In bed with him, my body hummed with a pleasure so intense it was almost painful. His touch hooked up two loose wires inside me, and I was electrified. The more I had of him, the more I wanted; as if in the very act of satisfying my craving, he was carving a deeper and deeper pit of hunger inside me. He was never around long enough to qualify as a boyfriend, a term he said he hated anyway. "Putting labels on things destroys them," he'd say. But he was never gone long enough for me to write him off. I continued to go out with other guys from time to time, though the relationships rarely went very far—no one could compete with the intensity of my memories of Matt. I assumed he had other lovers, too, though I never asked. For the most part, I was able to tolerate the yearning I felt for him as a kind of background music that threaded through my life. Its very unsatisfactoriness—the sense of always being a little hungry—was what marked it as love.

"I love how nonattached we are," Matt sometimes said. I'd nod: Nonattachment—wasn't that what the spiritual path was supposed to be about? But sometimes when he said it, I'd see myself as an astronaut in a space suit, free-floating high above the green and blue earth, alone in a vast, empty sky.

THE YOGA CLASS I was teaching was winding to a close. The morning light slanted through steamy window panes. The room reeked of sweat, of skin lotion, of intestinal gas, of vanilla candles. "Lie down on your backs and close your eyes," I instructed my students, as I walked among them handing out silky eyebags stuffed with flaxseeds. "Let the weight of your body surrender into the embrace of gravity."

At the front of the room, I lay down with them in Savasana, or Corpse Pose—the little death at the end of practice that's supposed to remind you how little control you ultimately have over anything. But my eyes wouldn't close. I stared up at the squares of off-white acoustic tile, with a tea-colored stain directly overhead from the time the fire sprinklers went on accidentally when a teacher lit too much incense.

I remembered those pictures of Matt's spread out on my bed: the sadhu with the necklace of bone; the cows sleeping by the side of the road; the orange-wrapped Bodhi Tree. They were probably packed away in some storage cell—along with the monks at the Shaolin temple in Japan, the artic penguins flapping across the ice . . . and me, arched in a deep backbend, Bigfoot poised on my belly, his haunches gathered to leap off into space.

The last time Matt and I had seen each other, three months ago, we'd had a terrible fight. I was in his apartment, watching him pack for another trip: to Alaska this time, to shoot a sled dog race. He was folding gray thermal long johns, rolling wool socks into balls. He was ignoring the telephone, which rang, insistently, every ten minutes—

as if, I thought, someone were sitting on the other end of the line watching a clock and saying, *In ten minutes you can try him again.*

"How long do you think you'll be in Alaska?" I asked.

"Probably just a month or so." He stuffed a sleeping bag deep into its nylon sack.

"And when you come back? How long will you be around before you leave again?"

He slipped a glove onto his right hand, flexed the fingers experimentally, then pulled it off. "Actually, I'm not sure if I'll come back here right away," he said. "A friend offered me an apartment in London for a few months. I just have to take care of her fica plant and a couple of Pekinese."

*Don't ask.* But I did. "What friend is that?"

"Her name's Cynthia. No one you know. Just someone I met when I was doing that dolphin shoot in Greece."

*A sleek blonde in a thong bikini lies on a white sand beach, sipping a gin and tonic.* I said nothing.

Matt gave me a sideways grin. "Amanda. She's twenty-five years older than me. She was the dolphin trainer. She really is just a friend."

"I'm sure she is. Otherwise you wouldn't have mentioned her."

He raised an eyebrow. "Is this an issue? Because there are some friends of yours I could grill you about."

The phone rang again, and the answering machine clicked on. I looked at Matt. "Go ahead. Turn up the volume. I dare you."

"Amanda. Stop it."

I walked over to the machine and slid the volume lever up to the top. A man's voice came on: ". . . so anyway, if you want to pick up the memory card, it'll be in the store behind the counter. Just give me a call when you're coming over. See you."

"You see," said Matt, flatly. He stepped to the phone and switched off the ringer. "Okay if I turn this off? Or do you want to keep monitoring my calls?"

Anne Cushman

I sat down on the bed. "Oh Matt, I'm sorry. It's just . . . It's getting really hard to have you coming and going like this. I'm twenty-nine. We've been doing this for almost four years. Do we really want to go on living like college kids the rest of our lives?"

"You've known from the time we met that my work is the most important thing in my life. It's how I know I'm alive. It's how I make a difference in the world. I'm not going to give it up for anyone, not even you."

"I'm not talking about giving anything up. I'm talking about *adding* something."

"So what exactly is it that you want me to add?"

*A diamond ring? My name tattooed on your belly? A promise you'll be here tomorrow?* I didn't say anything.

He sat down on the bed next to me. "Look. Maybe if you had something you cared about as much as I care about photography, you wouldn't need me so badly."

"I do. I have my yoga practice."

"Great. So when you start feeling like this, why don't you go stand on your head or something instead of getting on my case?"

"Okay, fine." I stood up. "There's a class in a half an hour. See you when you get back from London."

"Oh, come on, Amanda." He caught my hand and pulled me down again. "I'm sorry. That didn't come out right." He put his arm around me and pulled me close. "Look. I love you. You know that, right? There's no one else I feel this way about."

"I know. I love you, too." With his touch, I could feel the tight ball of anxiety in the center of my chest begin to relax. Maybe he was right; maybe I was making a big deal out of nothing. Maybe this was just another opportunity to let go of my attachment. Yogis let go of all kinds of things: their clothes, their families, their houses, their past. Maybe my relationship with Matt was a kind of spiritual practice, the modern equivalent of sitting naked in a ring of fire under a blazing sun with a boulder balanced on your head. He kissed my neck and pulled me down onto the bed. My fear began to melt into the familiar dance of skin, hands, and mouth.

With no ring to introduce it, the answering machine clicked on again: a woman's voice, British, very young, choked with rage and tears, as close as if she were sitting on the foot of the bed, watching us. "Goddamn it, Matt. Where the hell are you? Why the *fuck* aren't you calling me back?"

I pulled away. Matt rolled on his back and looked at the ceiling. "Cynthia?" I asked.

Matt didn't look at me. "Cynthia's daughter."


LYING ON MY back in Savasana, I could hear the hum of traffic from the street outside, the clang of a garbage truck backing up. In one corner, a student was gently snoring.

How had my relationship with Matt gone so awry? Like my life, it had teetered on the brink of being something good, then diverged in such tiny increments that I couldn't say exactly when it went off course. I had graduated from college poised for something big that was just about to happen. Suddenly I was almost thirty, and it hadn't happened yet.

I sat up and reached for the small Tibetan bell by my mat, ready to ring it and call my students back to the world again. I took a deep breath, willing my voice to be soothing and steady—as if I'd been lying there communing with my inner light, rather than communing with my screwed-up past.

*Enlightenment for Idiots.* Maybe this book would be the magic portal to the life I really wanted.

# Bound Angle pose
# (Baddha Konasana)

*Sit on the ground and place your soles together, letting your knees fall out to the sides. Clasp your toes with your hands. Drop your heart toward the opening book of your feet.*

*Don't force yourself open. Wait for your unwinding core to invite you in. Release the dense, stubborn tissues that hold you bone to bone. Sense the soft organs that float inside the protective shell of your skeleton. Hear your body start to sing in its ancient language of sensation and emotion. Begin to excavate the relics of memory buried deep in this city of muscle, nerves, and bones.*

*Your body is made of stories. And with every breath, you will learn that the present is made of the past.*

*Life is a pilgrimage. The wise man does not rest by the roadside inns. He marches direct to the domain of eternal bliss, his ultimate destination.*

—Swami Sivananda (1887–1963)

# CHAPTER 3

T HE FIRST STEP in going on a spiritual pilgrimage, as it turns out, is buying a whole lot of very expensive gear.

"Now this backpack," said the salesperson at REI, an aggressively athletic young woman with a blonde ponytail and a baked-on tan, "has a built-in water pouch. You don't even have to take the backpack off to take a drink—you just sip through this retractable straw. And for an additional forty-nine dollars, you can add a filtration system that will remove microbes down to .2 microns."

I was standing in the backpack section, looking at packs: packs with wheels, packs with zip-off daypacks, packs with steel security cables. They had special pockets for water bottles, sunscreens, sunglasses, snacks, iPods, cell phones, rain gear, cosmetics, travel guitars.

I could feel my travel expense budget melting away like a popsicle in the tropical sun. "I mainly just want something very light," I said. "I'm going to have enough to carry already—I'm researching a book."

Her eyes lit up. "This one has a zip-off protective computer shuttle with its own shoulder strap. And there are holes in the back to plug in for Internet access, if you happen to be somewhere your AirPort card doesn't work." She eyed me speculatively. "Have you thought about bringing a satellite phone or a GPS unit?"

"It's not like I'll be climbing Everest." I was starting to feel defensive: *Why wasn't I climbing Everest?* "There are phones at all the ashrams. Even email."

I should know. For the past few weeks I'd been surfing the websites of ashrams that seemed like they were straight from the days of the *Mahabharata,* aside from their Internet access. The sites described swamis who could manifest gold watches out of thin air, bury themselves alive in airtight coffins, stand for days in pits of blazing fire. They described rivers so holy that a dip in their waters washed away generations of bad karma, hills so sacred that a walk around them guaranteed a royal rebirth.

I'd already bought my roundtrip ticket to Delhi, leaving in just over a week. Maxine was in a hurry: She wanted to get the guidebook out in time to catch the yoga wave, before everyone moved on to pole dancing. My head was starting to throb. I stared at my list: Mosquito net. Water bottle. Fanny pack. Passport belt. Suitcase lock. Walking sandals. Hiking boots. Travel yoga mat. Inflatable meditation cushion. Melatonin (for jet lag). Grapefruit seed extract (a guy in my yoga class swore that a few drops of it would kill intestinal bugs). Spirulina ("The hardest thing to get over there is green vegetables that aren't boiled to a pulp, and believe me, you do not want to be eating the salad"). Probiotics capsules. Vaccinations against tetanus, polio, hepatitis. A sleep sack to protect against filthy mattresses. An inflatable Therm-a-Rest pillow. Water purification drops. A water filter.

Earplugs. A face mask. A wide-brimmed sun hat. A rain poncho. In short, hundreds of dollars worth of gear designed to protect me from the place Maxine was spending a couple of thousand more dollars to get me to.

Two days ago, I'd waited in line for two hours at the Indian consulate to get a visa, only to arrive at the counter just as the man with the rubber stamps closed it for his lunch break. *Who takes lunch at 10:30?* "Back in one hour," he informed me cheerfully; but when I returned at exactly 11:35, a note on the door informed me that the office was "closed for Raksha Bandhan." Whatever that was: A meal? A holiday? A ritual? A disease? *Not tonight dear, I've got Raksha Bandhan.*

I could feel the pressure building at the top of my skull. I still hadn't found someone to sublet my room. I hadn't had time to do yoga for a week. My neck muscles were tied into knots and I was having trouble taking a deep breath. And now I was supposed to deliberate the advantages of a teal versus a periwinkle backpack.

"I'll take this one." I grabbed a random pack. "And a mosquito net." I heaved the pack on top of my already heaped shopping cart and pushed it toward the checkout line. If I didn't get out of there fast I was going to punch someone in the face.

It was odd that I found myself working as a travel guide writer, because I'd never really liked to travel. When I was a child, other kids fantasized about flying spaceships to distant galaxies. I fantasized about having a friend that I'd known for more than a year. But my mother's restlessness hurled us up and down the West Coast in search of a place that would make her forget her disappointment in the way her life had turned out. She'd be happy, for a while, in each new home. She'd make gallant gestures toward domesticity—buying huge rolls of contact paper and papering half the kitchen drawers; painting my bedroom "any color you want, sweetie. But please, nothing pastel.

Pastels are so trite." When we moved to San Diego, when I was nine, she bought half a dozen fruit trees, which she brought home in the back of her Toyota hatchback, their root-balls wrapped in muddy brown burlap. "In a few years we'll have homegrown apricots!" she crowed. We spent a happy Saturday afternoon shoveling holes in our front lawn and dropping the saplings into them. But she had neglected to consult a gardener, who undoubtedly would have informed her that June is not the optimal time for planting fruit trees. Within a couple of dry summer months, the trees were dead, their leaves dropping away despite our sporadic attempts at watering them. And with them died my mother's enthusiasm for her secretarial job in a real estate office. By the times the winter rains hit, we were heading north up Route 1 to Santa Cruz, where she planned to finish her undergraduate art degree—a dream that, like most of her visions, never materialized.

Perhaps because of this rootless childhood, I grew up with no sense of direction. I got on northbound buses when I wanted to go south, drove the wrong way up one-way streets. I knew the delicate thread of streets that stretched between familiar destinations—say, the Bookends Café and The Blissful Body. But if I got thrown off course—a detour, some road construction, a wrong turn—I was lost. Coasting down a San Francisco hill on my bike, I was often astounded to see the bay appearing in front of me, with the Golden Gate Bridge rearing up in a place I'd never expected it.

Two years ago I had stumbled into the For Idiots work the way I did all my jobs—randomly. I'd been dog walking for a woman named Patricia, a forty-five-year-old graphic designer from New York City who'd been lured to San Francisco by a romance with an aspiring writer twenty years younger she'd met at publishing conference. She'd moved in with him in an apartment on Russian Hill and gotten him a gig writing guidebooks for her older sister, an editor in Manhattan. But I came home one day from running Patricia's two collies in Golden Gate Park to find her lover in the driveway loading his furniture into a U-Haul. He had decided that he was gay, he told me, and that he would rather be a sculptor than a writer anyway. Upstairs, Patricia was on the phone, trying to appease her sister's wrath by finding someone else to finish off the guidebook he'd been working on, *Sea Kayaking for Idiots*. "Didn't you say you wanted to be a writer?" she'd asked me, the receiver still pressed to her ear.

"Well, yes—but I was thinking more of novels. Poetry, maybe. Or a screenplay. And besides, I get seasick."

"Don't worry," she'd said. "All the research is done. It's just a matter of writing it up." And before I knew it, I was working for Maxine.

LORI WAS WAITING for me in the parking lot in front of REI, sitting behind the wheel of her bright green VW Bug, the trunk already cracked open so I could load my purchases. She'd offered to meet me and give me a ride home so I wouldn't have to lug everything on BART. Normally, I insisted on being self-sufficient, so that the contrast between my life and hers wouldn't be too overpowering, but this time I'd accepted gratefully.

"Tampons," she said as I got into the car. "Don't forget to bring a huge supply of tampons. I hear they're hard to get once you get out of the big cities. And contact lens solution. Oh, and condoms."

"Lori, I'm going to be meditating and practicing yoga in celibate ashrams." I pulled the door shut. "I'm not going to need condoms."

"Famous last words." Lori pulled out of the parking lot. "I remember when you went on an all-women's breast cancer bike-a-thon and ended up needing condoms."

"What was I then, nineteen? I was an idiot."

She pulled up to a light and stopped, looking at me and raising her eyebrows. "And your point is?"

An ayurvedic doctor once told me that my friendship with Lori worked because we were so different that our energies balanced each other out. I was *vata* and *pitta,* he told me—wind and fire—with a wiry frame, flyaway curls, and a tendency to stay up all night worrying about whether I looked stupid when I danced. Lori was *kapha*— earth—with the plump body, cheery temperament, and bossy efficiency of a sparrow.

Our friendship had survived every obstacle imaginable, including the fact that she had been in a committed, monogamous relationship since she was twenty-one. For the past five years, she and Joe had been sharing a one-bedroom apartment in the Sunset, jointly running a small organic landscaping business called New Leaf, their rare conflicts centering around things like where in their tiny backyard to put the compost heap and whose turn it was to enter the receipts into QuickBooks.

Now she reached for the CDs in the flap on her car visor and popped one into the CD player. A Mozart piano concerto began to play, its notes as ordered and efficient as Lori herself. "So. Have you told Matt you're leaving yet?"

"You know I'm not speaking to Matt." I looked out the window. "Besides, he's in London."

"Well, good. Keep it that way. The moment he gets wind of the fact that you're not just sitting here waiting for him, he'll be all over you in a minute."

"I wish it were that simple."

"It *is* that simple." Lori shook her head in exasperation. "When will you ever learn? Guys are simple."

"And when will *you* ever learn? For me, they're not."

This is something that Lori never understood: For me, men were a foreign language that I learned too late in life to be fluent. I grew up as an only child, shy and brainy, a year too young for my grade, with thick-rimmed glasses and a mouthful of silver braces. "Honestly, sometimes I wonder if they switched you in the hospital for someone else's baby," my mother would sigh, shaking her sleek blonde head as she wrestled a comb through my frizzy curls. While the other girls in my junior high were sprouting breasts and dating college lifeguards they told their mothers were sixteen, I was in the library reading *Pride and Prejudice* and fantasizing about Mr. Darcy. In high school, alone at home on a Saturday night, I would imagine that someday I would have a relationship with a blind man, who would love me undistracted by my long nose and unruly hair. I pictured our relationship in intimate detail: the way his fingers would caress my face, the close friendship I would develop with his seeing eye dog.

My first month in college all of that changed. Adopting puppies from the pound, it turned out, was one of Lori's passions. She took one look at her scrawny, anxious roommate and saw a border collie mix who needed a bath and a good brushing. She dragged me to the optometrist for contact lenses; untied my tangle of curls from its tight ponytail and got it cut so it flew in a dark cloud around my face. She taught me which jeans made my hips look slim, which shirts brought out the golden flecks in my brown eyes.

To my astonishment, her remodel worked—although not in quite the way that she had envisioned. Lori had been hoping I would sail into a safe port in the stormy world of romance, like the one she anchored in with Joe. Instead, I began a series of affairs that went nowhere. I collected boyfriends as if my brief, overheated encounters with them could protect me from relapsing into the person I used to be. I went out with an artist, a dancer, a fisherman. For a few weeks I slept with a juggler from the Pickle Family Circus, in the tiny back bedroom of the apartment he shared with a trapezist, a clown, and a pair of equilibre artists who practiced their balancing acts in the kitchen.

I told myself I wanted a serious relationship. But in fact, I mainly dated men with whom there was a built-in limitation: They were leaving town in a few days. They had another girlfriend. They se-cretly preferred men. This way, I had an excuse for keeping them on the other side of an invisible glass wall in my heart—a wall that, for reasons I couldn't quite understand, it felt vitally important to keep in place.

But Matt was different. With Matt, the wall had come down: perhaps because I sensed that ultimately, he was the most unavailable of all of them.

Matt had told me early on that he was philosophically opposed to marriage. "A social convention that's only recently been linked to ro-mantic love," he said, as we lay side by side in bed one Sunday morn-ing. "Through most of history, it had more to do with the transfer of property and inheritance. These days, most of them end in divorce, anyway. And the ones that don't, you can tell just by looking at the people that they don't love each other any more."

"But don't you think there's something beautiful about promis-ing to always be there for someone, no matter what?"

"When you wake up next to someone, do you want it to be be-cause they promised they'd be there, whether they liked it or not? Or because that's where they really want to be?"

When I got to know him a little better, he told me that his earli-est memory was of his father slashing his mother's car tires so she couldn't drive to Tahoe to go skiing with her lover; then his mother breaking his windshield with Matt's stroller before storming off down the sunny Southern California street in her snow boots. Trying to run after her, Matt cut his foot, and his father had to take him to the emer-gency room. He still had the scar, which he showed me; a two-inch white band on the sole of his foot, which hurt when the weather got damp.

Matt divided the rest of his childhood between two homes: his mother's commune in Los Angeles, where she was a pioneer in the swinger's movement and eventually wrote a free-love manual called

*Your First Few Hundred* that landed her on Johnny Carson; and his father's mansion in San Diego, where he spent most of his time with a series of Mexican nannies while his father successfully defended the rights of large oil companies to drill selectively in designated wilderness areas. His father had died of a heart attack when Matt was twenty-two; his mother, now in her sixties, still lived in a nudist community near Las Vegas and on principle still only wore clothes when she left the compound, which meant that Matt met her mainly in restaurants, preferably pricey vegetarian ones.

My marital models weren't much better. My mother had bounced from boyfriend to boyfriend: Sy, a melancholy salesman of high-end hospital equipment; Burt, an unemployed contractor who made blueberry pancakes for us every morning; Jeremy, who owned the Laundromat where we washed our clothes. They all dropped away after a year or so. My mother said it was because they couldn't handle the stress of dating a single mom. But I always suspected it was because they couldn't compete with the memory of my father, whom she had eliminated so rigorously from daily conversation that I knew she must still be in love with him.

But unlike Matt, I still believed in marriage. I believed in it the way, as a child, I had continued to believe in the Easter Bunny long after the evidence had piled up to the contrary.

Only once had I managed to shake off Matt's spell for a little while. It was almost three years ago, when Matt was in Peru shooting photos for a book about ayahuasca, and drinking lots of it. I was getting emails from him every few weeks, ranting about gateways to another universe and how I should meet him there—whether "there" meant Peru or the other universe was always unclear. At the recommendation of my therapist, I had gone to a bookstore to pick up a copy of *Women Who Love Too Much*. I was standing in the self-help section, browsing through it. "Being women who love too much, we operate as though love, attention, and approval don't count unless we are able to extract them from men who, because of their own problems and preoccupations, are unable to give them to us," I read.

Suddenly, the shelves began shaking, books tumbling to the ground in a cascade of suddenly irrelevant advice. Along with the other customers, I bolted out onto the sidewalk and stood there, breathless, waiting to see what happened.

"Just a tremor," said the guy in a business suit standing next to me. He was short, not much taller than me, with receding blond hair and a pleasant, open face. We smiled at each other, caught in the instant, illusory intimacy of people who have escaped disaster together, if only in their imaginations. *The bookshop collapsed to a heap of rubble . . . It took them days to dig us out from under the bricks . . .* "It's probably safe to go back in."

"I don't know. Personally, I'm not willing to risk death to get a book."

When he laughed, I realized that he was younger than I had thought. "Looks like you brought yours with you, just in case." He gestured to the paperback I clutched in my hand. "Do you? Love too much, I mean?"

"Not really too much. But probably too long." Lori always told me that I'd hung onto Matt long after I should have dumped him, the way I kept leftovers sitting in the fridge until they were so disgusting I could throw them away without guilt. I looked at the book he was holding: *The Wine Lover's Guide to Cheese.* His fingers were curled loosely on the cover, nails clipped into perfect half-moons over pink fingertips. "And are you? A wine lover, I mean?"

He laughed again. "No. I'm just trying to upgrade my image."

By the time Tom and I slept together—almost three weeks later— I knew that he was eight years older than me and worked for a software firm in San Jose, designing corporate-training modules with titles like *Work Experience: How to Act So People Think You Have It* and making more money in three months than I made in a couple of years.

He knew that I used to date a photographer, but that that was definitely over.

Lori was supportive but baffled; her desire for me to have a committed relationship—with someone who wasn't Matt—collided with her earth mother distrust of anyone who worked in any industry more high tech than garden supplies.

"Amanda, what are you doing with this guy?" she asked. "He's not your type."

"Meaning, he actually returns my phone calls?" I was rummaging through Lori's closet, looking for something to wear to go out to dinner with him. I held up a dark-green cotton turtleneck. "Meaning he shows up on time for dinner, and gets up in the morning to go to work?"

"Meaning that this is a guy who spends his whole day designing products to help people convince other people to buy things they don't need." Lori was lying flat on her stomach on her bed, chin propped up in her elbows. "You can't wear that, Amanda. It makes your skin look like split pea soup." She got up and went to her closet. "Here, try this. I think he's boring. But if you're going out with him, I want him to think you're the hottest thing in the galaxy."

I held the shirt she had tossed me up to my chest—a sheer red silk blouse with a scooped neckline. "For your information, his latest client was a company that sells surgical supplies." I frowned at my reflection. "I don't know, Lori. I don't want him to be thinking about my boobs the whole time we're talking."

"He'll be thinking about them anyway. And for God's sake, don't even get me started on the medical-industrial complex."

"Do we really have to debate the whole capitalist system? Give me a break, Lori. I thought you'd be pleased that I was with someone respectable."

"I have a bad feeling about this, that's all. I think you're looking for a father figure."

I was silent for a minute, holding the blouse to my chest. *My father's shoes in the back of the coat closet, caked with mud, bigger than any
shoes I have ever seen. My mother had discarded every other trace of him.
But for some reason, she had kept these, as if some part of her believed he
might come back and step into them.*

"This guy is nothing like my father," I told her.

"My point exactly," she said.

Within a month, I was spending almost every night with Tom.
When I forgot my overnight bag one weekend, he suggested that I
move in. I got a part-time job at Doggie Day Care in San Jose, groom-
ing aristocratic salukis, playing fetch with retrievers whose owners
were too busy to throw balls. In the afternoon, I'd come home to his
condo and do yoga on a balcony just big enough for my mat, overlooking a small cement carp pond filled with golden fish. Sometimes,
when he got home from work, I'd still be there, balanced upside
down in a shoulder stand. He'd lean against the sliding glass doors
and look at me. "My little yogini," he'd say fondly, as if I were an exotic animal he'd brought home from the pet store.

Tom had a kitchen filled with white-and-steel appliances: a microwave, an espresso maker, a juicer, an ice cream maker, a pasta maker, a
bread machine, a yogurt maker, a rice cooker with settings for sushi
rice, brown rice, dry rice, wet rice. The manuals were all in a drawer
right under the waffle iron, still in their sealed plastic sheaths. Propped
open on his counter in a plastic cookbook holder was a pristine copy of
*The Tassajara Recipe Book,* whose pages had been open for as long as I'd
known him to a recipe for goat cheese zucchini pizza. I kept meaning to
make it, but I never did. Instead, we went out to dinner almost every
night: Thai, Japanese, Italian, Chinese, Vietnamese, Indian. Every Friday night we rented a video and made love afterward, finishing by
11:00 sharp, so as not to throw off our sleep schedules.

At first, the distance from Matt was a relief. It was a relief to be in
a relationship with someone who would introduce me as his girlfriend,

instead of arguing that the word itself was a demeaning simplification of life's complex relationships; a relief to watch Tom walk out the door in the morning, and not think of him again until he'd walk in the door at night. I emailed Matt and told him I was in a serious relationship, but that I hoped we would always be friends. All he wrote back was a quote from Carlos Castaneda: "All paths are the same, leading nowhere. Therefore pick a path with heart."

Tom proposed to me after I'd been living with him for six months. He proposed over dinner in his favorite Japanese restaurant. The waiter presented the ring on a little cloisonné tray along with two glasses of warm sake and a pair of origami cranes. The ring flashed on my finger, a diamond surrounded by tiny rubies. Doing yoga the next morning, it dug into my hand as I did Downward Dog, a sharp reminder that the shape of my life was going to change forever.

Two days later, I got a manila envelope in the mail, covered with foreign stamps. Inside it, with no note, was a feather, a foot-long flame of crimson and turquoise and gold.

That afternoon, I got out the manual for the bread machine. I poured in the flour, the yeast, the salt. I stood and watched through the glass lid as the moving arms pummeled the dough. I hadn't even gotten flour on my hands. I didn't even realize I was crying until I saw the tears dropping on the granite counter.

I left the ring by the bread machine, with a note wrapped around it. I took the bus back to San Francisco and never came back. By some miracle, there was an opening in my old household; I moved back into my own room gratefully, like putting on a familiar suit of clothes. Two months later, I was in bed with Matt again.


"EARTH TO AMANDA," said Lori now, as we pulled up to the curb in front of my house. She popped open the trunk to her car. "All I do is mention Matt's name, and you're gone for thirty-two blocks."

"I was thinking about Tom, actually."

"Well, that's a little better, but not much. Have you told *him* you're going?"

"He must have gotten the email I sent out. But I didn't hear anything back."

"Yeah, well, that's not surprising. You're his Matt. He's probably got fifteen friends telling him, 'Don't write her back. Whatever you do, don't write her back.'" She leaned over and gave me a hug. "Listen, I've got to run—I'm putting in a bonsai garden over near the Presidio. I'll call you later and we'll set up a time tomorrow for me to help you pack."

"You don't have to do that," I said, getting out of the car and walking around to get my new backpack—bulging with supplies—out of the trunk. It was a ritualistic protest. We both knew she would never let me pack by myself.

As Lori's car pulled away, I unlocked the front door and began to haul my purchases up the narrow stairs, hoping I wouldn't run into either of my housemates. I'd been living with the same two people for almost two years, which was a kind of record for stability in my life. One of them was Ernie, a former Buddhist monk who now sold life insurance for Allstate. He was a stout, balding man in his mid forties who walked with a stiff-legged limp from the cartilage he tore in his left knee on a meditation retreat. At the age at which many successful businessmen are starting to look around at their accumulated wealth and ask, *Is this all there is to life?* Ernie was trying to make up for a youth squandered on spiritual practice by putting as much money as possible into his SEP-IRA.

Unfortunately, so far that didn't appear to be a whole lot; monastic training had not done wonders for his salesmanship. "Remember that everything in life is impermanent," I once overheard him saying to a potential client on the telephone. "Everything that is dear to you will dissolve eventually." A few minutes later, he walked glumly into the kitchen, where I was making a smoothie. "Did you make the sale?" I asked. "They're still thinking about it," he'd said.

My other housemate was Ishtar, a goddess worshipper with a night job answering calls on a phone sex line. Her professional dream was to lead tantra workshops in which she could teach people to have multiple orgasms without ejaculating. The men, that is. The women actually *were* supposed to ejaculate, through some process involving the kundalini energy and the third finger of your left hand. Ishtar had explained it to me repeatedly. But I'd never been able to make it work, myself, and at this point just thinking about trying it made me irritated; just another item to add to the list of personal-growth techniques I was supposed to practice every morning, along with writing down my dreams, doing yoga, meditating, and doing my Bates eye improvement exercises. (If one of those had to go, would I rather be multiply orgasmic or have twenty-thirty vision without corrective lenses?)

I stopped in the kitchen to grab a cold beer from the refrigerator. I popped the top, took a long swig, and then headed for the hall. But at the door to the kitchen, Ernie met me, looking like a worried donkey. "Have you found a subletter yet?"

*No, I haven't even started looking. Give me a break.* "Uh . . . I think I'm close. There's a guy who seems really interested." I took another slug of beer and felt the comforting buzz start to spread through my body. "He's a handyman," I improvised. "A Buddhist, like you. I met him at Whole Foods."

"When do we get to meet him?"

"I'll set up a meeting. Maybe tomorrow night." That would give me time to find someone plausible. I could see myself cruising the aisles, looking for a Buddhist handyman. *Excuse me, I couldn't help noticing your drill and mala beads; would you like to live in my house?*

"Does he have the qualities we want in a roommate?"

"What qualities are those?"

"A couch," said a voice from the stairs. Ishtar walked into the room, wearing a jangle of gold necklaces and a pair of harem pants that made her look like she just walked off the set of *I Dream of Jeannie*. "We want someone who has a couch."

"I was speaking more of spiritual qualities," said Ernie. "Stability, cooperativeness, willingness to communicate, that sort of thing."

"I think it takes a lot of character to acquire furniture," Ishtar said. "Plus a positive, empowered self-image. You really have to see yourself as an adult to go out and buy an actual couch."

"He has a couch," I said. "In fact I think he has a whole matched set of Pottery Barn furniture. Coffee table, couch, rug, drapes, the works. He seemed to really have it together."

They both looked at me blankly, before Ernie asked the obvious: "Then why does he want to live with us?"

In my room, I dropped my packages on the floor, gulped the last of the beer, and flung myself on the unmade bed. Through the window, I could hear the screech of a recycling truck backing up across the street, followed by clanging metal. I was fulfilling the dream of a lifetime. I was preparing to go on a spiritual pilgrimage to India. Why was I in such a foul mood?

Hoping for inspiration, I reached for one of the books on my bedside table, and opened it at random. "Meditation is based on the premise that the natural state of the mind is calm and clear." *Yeah, right.* "It provides a way to train our mind to settle into this state."

The beer was starting to take effect; belching, I could feel myself floating off onto a cloud of spiritual inspiration. *Meditation: there's a fabulous idea! That will get me in the mood to go to India!*

To be honest, I'd never had much luck with meditation. True, I always loved the three or four sweaty, endorphin-buzzed minutes of silent sitting at the end of yoga class, when all thoughts seemed to have been wrung out of my mind like dirty dishwater. When I first started practicing yoga, I had even created a little altar in the corner of my bedroom out of a shawl draped over a TV stand. I picked up a brass Buddha at a garage sale and stocked up on vanilla-scented candles and amber incense at the yoga studio store. I even went online to order a meditation cushion stuffed with buckwheat hulls.

But when it came right down to it, there always seemed to be more compelling things to do than sitting still staring at a candle. And in the chaos of getting ready for my India trip, I'd been tossing my dirty laundry in my meditation corner.

I heaved myself out of bed and began picking my socks off my altar. Damn, where were my matches? I spent five minutes looking for them, finally finding them by the bathtub next to Ishtar's bong. I went back to my room and sat down cross-legged on my cushion. I lit the candle and the incense. I breathed in the sandalwood smoke, the sulfur of the match.

I felt virtuous. I imagined a serene smile on my face. Yes, this trip to India would transform my life. I studied my toes tucked up onto my thigh in half lotus. The other yoga teachers all had brilliantly colored toenails, but I kept forgetting to buy polish. But now my life was back on track. I would meditate thirty minutes every day. I would drink wheatgrass juice. I would bike to Walgreens and get some new nail polish, something red—not a tacky scarlet, a deep burgundy. I saw myself walking up to an ashram, my new backpack on my back, white-tipped Himalayan peaks all around me, my burgundy toenails peeking out of my sandals. I closed my eyes again.

What did they mean, really, by "follow your breath"? Where was I supposed to follow it? *In. Out.* I saw the breath like a piston sliding back and forth. *In. Out.* Or like a . . . no, don't think about that. Maybe I would meet a guy at one of the ashrams, someone really spiritual with a buff yoga body who was just coming off his vows of celibacy.

My knee hurt. I must concentrate harder. I would be like those Tibetan monks who meditate outside in the snow for hours, drying wet blankets with their body heat alone and learning to love their Chinese torturers.

*Brrringgg.* I reflexively started to reach for the phone, then restrained myself. *Brrrinng.* Was I missing my appointment for my hepatitis vaccination? No, that was tomorrow. *Brinngg.* The answering machine clicked on. I heard my own taped voice, which always sounded more uncertain than I imagined it would: "Hi, this is Amanda. When you hear the beep, you know what to do."

The long beep. Then a voice that made my stomach leap:

"Amanda. Hi. I know you probably don't want to talk to me. But I really want to talk to you."

THERE WAS A MEMORY I returned to again and again, when I found myself wondering what I was doing still hanging out with Matt. It was my birthday, a few months after we'd met. He'd driven me up Mount Tamalpais, parked the car by a bluff overlooking Stinson Beach, and told me we were going hang gliding.

"For my birthday present, you're pushing me off a cliff?" Two thousand feet below us, the ocean glittered under a cloudless sky.

"Not pushing. I'm jumping off with you."

"But you know I'm terrified of heights.

"That's why it's the perfect gift."

I'd only agreed because my fear of looking like a coward in front of my new lover was greater than my fear of crashing to a horrible death. But when I was finally airborne—strapped into a tandem hang glider with a bald instructor built like a paratrooper—my terror became so intense that it was indistinguishable from ecstasy. A red-tailed hawk soared below me. My heartbeat pounded in the top of my skull. Every nerve felt electric. I could see the arc of the Golden Gate Bridge, the rocky curve of the coastline thousands of feet below. An updraft spiraled us higher and higher, the earth dropping away. I could see Matt's glider a few hundred feet away, rising and falling on the wind. I swore that if I landed safely, I'd never do such an idiotic thing again. But as we began to ease into our landing, I suddenly wanted the flight to go on forever.

"I'M JUST IN town for a week or two, then I'm off again," said the voice on the answering machine. Lori once told me that when a certain species of bee flaps its wings, it hums at a particular pitch that causes the blossoms on tomato plants to open wide and eject their pollen. This was how Matt's voice hit me. *Don't pick up the phone. Whatever you do, don't pick up the phone.* I opened my eyes and looked at the Buddha on the altar again. He had the right idea, slipping away in the middle of the night when his wife couldn't say a word to him. Did he ever yearn for her, sitting up nights with all those holy men? Suppose when he was meditating under that tree, an answering machine had clicked on nearby and he'd heard a voice: *Sweetheart, I miss you so much, please come home, your son's been asking for you . . .*

"I really felt terrible about how we left things last time. I need to talk to you face-to-face . . ."

What did the Buddha know about passion, anyway? He lived as a monk for most of his life. Why would I listen to his advice?

"Amanda. I know you're there."

*Don't pick up the phone.* I was getting up off the cushion. I was reaching for the phone. I felt the wind pulling me up and out over the ocean, heard the sound of seagulls calling as the earth tilted below.

*My experience is that everything is bliss. But the desire for bliss creates pain. Thus bliss becomes the seed of pain. The entire universe of pain is born of desire.*

—Nisargadatta Maharaj (1897–1981)

# CHAPTER 4

ON'T DO IT. Do *not* get together with him." Lori stepped over a pile of laundry and stood in the center of my room, her hands on her hips, glaring at me. "I'm warning you. That guy is poison for you."

"Come on, Lori." I sat down on the edge of my bed, wondering if inviting her over to help me pack had been such a good idea after all. "It's just a walk on the beach. I'm leaving in a week. How bad can it be?"

"I don't care. It's like an alcoholic saying he's going to stop in at a bar and just order orange juice."

"Well, we're not going to a bar. How much trouble can we get into on a beach in broad daylight?"

"Just promise me you aren't going to bring him back here."

"I won't. I promise. Now can we just get on with the packing?"

She nodded, reluctantly, then began to brighten at the prospect of bringing order to chaos. "Okay. So over here in this corner we'll put all the stuff that's going to India with you. Everything else we're going to pack into boxes. I picked up a bunch of empty ones at Safeway—they're out in the hall. And I got packing tape. And a marker."

"You're a goddess. I don't know how I'd get through life without you."

"You wouldn't. You'd have driven off the road into a ditch a long time ago." She walked to my closet and began pulling clothes down off their hangers. "Grab me a box and I'll start putting these into it."

"Wait. Shouldn't I see if there's anything there I want to bring?" I handed her a box, alarmed.

"What, you're going to wear a velvet miniskirt in Calcutta? You don't even wear it here." She began piling things into my box. "So what time are you meeting him?"

"Actually, in just an hour and a half. I thought we could make a start on things here, then finish it up tomorrow."

She began pulling sweaters down off a shelf. "It's better just to do it all at once. How about this: We'll get started on the packing together, then I'll keep going while you meet with Matt. I'll finish faster without you anyway. You have exactly two hours with him, then meet me back here."

I sat down on the floor next to my backpack and began snipping off the tags on the things I'd bought, trying to look like I was matching her level of activity. "I see what you're trying to do, Lori. What are you, my mother?"

"No." She grabbed a roll of packing tape, pulled it out with a crisp *whirr,* ripped it off, and sealed the first box. "I'm your best friend. And I've picked you up off the floor for this guy too many times."

"Yeah. But I haven't been like that for a long time."

"I know you haven't! Duh! Because you broke up with him!" She was working her way through my bureau now, relentlessly tossing clothes into another box. "I know you've missed him for the last few months. But you've also been happier and more focused on your own life than I've ever seen you. I don't want you to backslide."

"I won't backslide." I looked around at the room, half torn apart, and was struck by how familiar the chaos felt. My mother had heralded each new move with bright excitement—*Guess what, Amanda? I've found us a wonderful new home!*—as if, in these new places, she and I would both become entirely different people. But inside me, there'd be a dropping feeling—my world annihilated, yet again.

"Actually, I really think we should do this in stages," I said to Lori. "Let's find a good stopping point."

"Amanda, we've only just begun. You just want me to leave so you can bring him back here." She sat down next to me on the floor. "You're saying you don't want to sleep with him. But I bet you ten bucks that after he called, you went in the bathroom and shaved your legs, just in case." She leaned over and started tugging on my pants legs teasingly. "I'm right, aren't I? Show me your legs!"

"Keep away from my legs, you freak!" I rolled away and she began chasing me around the room on her hands and knees, both of us laughing, until we collapsed in a pile of unsorted clothes.

"Not just my legs," I admitted. "My bikini line, too."

"Well, don't show me that. And you better not show him, either."

"Okay, okay. I give up. You stay here and pack."

She nodded. "Good. Don't bother taking the bus—you can borrow my car. And by the time you're back, I'll have your whole life boxed up in numbered, labeled boxes."

She leaned over and gave me a hug. "Amanda. Just dump him. You won't be sorry."

HE WAS LATE, of course.

I waited at the edge of the parking lot at Ocean Beach for ten minutes or so, next to a warning sign: DANGER: RIP CURRENTS. PEOPLE SWIMMING AND WADING HAVE DROWNED HERE. Then, not wanting to look like I was waiting for him, I headed down the cement steps to the beach, which stretched flat and almost deserted in both directions. Out to sea, a few surfers were bobbing in the waves in black wet suits, like seals, ignoring the warnings. I sat down on a log, facing the water, and stared out at the waves. Just a few miles inland, at my house, it was sunny and warm, but here it was foggy and cold, a whole different weather system. A sharp wind bit at my cheeks. I hunched my shoulders and wished I had brought a warmer jacket. I heard the crunch of feet on sand behind me and looked around—too quickly— but it was just an older woman, a tangle of gray hair blowing in the wind, head down, shoulders hunched, walking fast.

I ran my fingers through the coarse brown sand, which was littered with seagull feathers and blackened bits of half-burned driftwood, the remnants of past bonfires. I remembered something I'd once told Lori: that sometimes I thought I didn't just want to make love with Matt, I wanted to *become* him—someone who lived untethered, letting the wind carry him into the future without looking back.

Lori had looked at me like she thought I was crazy. "But he's not coming back again and again because you're like him," she'd said. "He's coming back because you're different. You're his taproot, his anchor. You're the only thing that's constant in his life."

About fifty feet away, tossed on the white foam, a guy in a black wet suit glided to the shore on a boogie board. He stood up and stepped out of the water, shaking his head like a puppy, and walked across the sand toward me. I didn't realize who it was until he was just a few feet away.

"The waves were so good, I couldn't resist," he said, grinning at me. He had cut off his ponytail and shaved his head; his skull was glistening with water. He dropped the board on the sand. "Afraid of getting wet?"

"That's the least of my fears," I said. And then I was in his arms, my arms around thick wet rubber, my face against his chest.

"I brought you a board, too," he said. "And a wet suit."

"Matt, you're insane. It's freezing."

"No! It's great once you're in. The waves are unbelievable. Come on. Give it a try."

"But Matt, seriously. I haven't boogie-boarded in years. And besides, we have to talk."

"Then it's been too long. We'll talk afterward, I promise." He grabbed me by the hands. "Come on, Amanda. Look at it this way: We can sit in my truck and argue. At least one of us will yell. At least one of us will cry. Or we can get in the water and have a fabulous time together. Come on. What are you afraid of?"

*Danger. Rip currents.* But I found myself standing behind his truck, pulling off my clothes and wiggling into the tight skin of a wet suit.

He was right, of course. It was fantastic. I had forgotten what it was like to be in that wild rush of water. Again and again we fought our way through the surf, diving under the breaking waves until we were far enough out. Then I'd follow him in, swimming hard toward the shore just ahead of a wave until it swelled up underneath me and I was carried in, water surging under my belly. The cry of the seagulls, the roar of the surf—they drove everything else from my brain, for a while, including the little voices in the back of my mind that were still protesting. *Weren't you going to talk? Why does he have an extra boogie board and a woman's wet suit lying around in the back of his car?*

Afterward, we toweled down in the cold wind, pulled on our clothes, and crawled into the back of his truck under the camper shell. The truck bed was covered with an old futon. I saw a cooler, a camping lantern, a pile of blankets, and a sleeping bag stuffed in a sack.

"Been on the road?" I asked.

"I drove my truck back down from Alaska." He slung a blanket around his shoulders and held out part of it for me, so that I found myself snuggled up against him.

I reached up and touched his skull, lightly, then pulled my hand away. "What's this? Joining a monastery?"

"I'm sure you think that would be good for me. But no. I just got sick of dealing with hair every day. It's just one less thing to take care of."

*Like you're taking care of so much.* I didn't say anything. Under the blanket, his arm slid around me. "Thanks for coming into the water. I really didn't think you would. That's what I love about you: the way you'll go with whatever wild thing is going on with me."

"That's what I love about you," I said. "There's always something wild going on."

There was an awkward silence. The word *love* sat between us like a small animal, unsure of its welcome.

"How have you been?" I asked. My body still felt like I was riding the waves. I shut my eyes and saw water crashing all around.

"Up and down. I finished the Greek dolphin series and exhibited it in a gallery in London, which is good. But only like three people saw it, which is not so good."

I picked at the fringe of the blanket. "Was one of them Cynthia's daughter?"

I felt his body tighten. "That didn't last long. Predictably. And now Cynthia's not so keen on me."

"That's funny. *My* mother's not too keen on you, either."

He reached for my hand under the blanket. "Look. I'm sorry if I hurt your feelings. But that whole thing had nothing to do with you and me. Sometimes other women are just like another country to explore. Or a mountain to climb. It doesn't *mean* anything. It's just another adventure."

I pulled my hand away. "And so what am I? A river to raft? A tree to chop down?"

"You're a whole different story. You should know that by now."

"Exactly what story is that? It would be good to know, so I could start rehearsing my part."

"Amanda. You know you have a place in my heart that no one else does. It's just that there's so much I want to explore out there in the world. I'm nowhere near ready to settle down."

"You say 'settle down' like it's some sort of insult." I slid out from under the blanket. "Boring. Restrictive. That's not what I'm looking for, either."

"So what exactly *are* you looking for?"

"Just—more than we have. What we have isn't a relationship at all. It's more like a semiannual train wreck on acid. I look around afterward and my whole life is in shambles. But boy, the colors look pretty."

"So instead what you want is a safe ride on a commuter train. Punch your ticket, get off, and go to work."

"You're doing it again." It was cold, away from the warmth of his body; I was beginning to shiver. "Can't there be anything in between?"

"There probably is. I just can't figure out how to do it."

"Can't? Or won't?"

He sighed. "I don't want to be the one holding you back from getting what you want in your life. Maybe you're right. Maybe you'd be happier if we did take a break from each other."

"How would I be able to tell?"

"Stop it. Just stop it." He grabbed me by the shoulders. "Look. I love you. I love you like I don't love anybody else. And you love me. What more do we need, really?"

*More,* I wanted to say. *Less.* But then his mouth was on mine, and the water was cresting over us, rough and wild and insistent. *People swimming and wading have died here.* But all I could do was either ride the wave wherever it took me, or go under.


WHEN I GOT BACK to Lori, an hour and a half late, all the boxes were packed and sealed and stacked in a corner of my room. My backpack was out in the hall, packed as well. She had even rolled up my rugs and swept the floor bare. Stripped of all my possessions, the room looked bigger than I remembered, and curiously neutral. It could belong to anybody.

"Wow." I sat down on the edge of my bed.

"All that's left to do is carry away the boxes. Don't worry about the sheets and blankets. I'll come back after you're gone and throw them in the laundry."

"Wow," I said again, stupidly.

She looked at me sharply. "Amanda. You did break up with him, didn't you?"

"We agreed not to have any contact for a year. Not till I come back from India, at least. To give us some time to sort out who we are to each other." His mouth on mine had been insistent, intent. Our bodies had moved together, following a logic all their own. *One last time,* we had agreed. *We'll do this one last time, just to say good-bye.*

"Not even email?"

"Not even email." I wanted Lori to leave, so I could lie down in my empty room on my neatly made bed and cry.

She sat down next to me and gave me a hug. "I'm so proud of you."

# downward-facing dog pose (adho mukha svanasana)

*Kneel on all fours and sweep your pelvis toward the sky. Grow your spine long as your heels root. Let your head dangle, a ripe fruit.*

*A yoga pose is a journey, not a destination. Twine around its structure like a vine around a trellis. Disappear into the velvet darkness between each breath. Some days, you'll pick your way through mossy forests that open into meadows dotted with wild iris. Others, you'll slog through swamps that stink of rotted dreams. Down unmapped streets you'll find jeweled pleasure palaces. In desert vaults you'll uncover ancestral plutonium, its half-life measured in generations.*

*If a pilgrim employs a conveyance, he will lose half of his merit. If he takes advantage of shoes or an umbrella, he will still further reduce his merit. If he carries on business on the way, three-fourths of the merit is gone, and by accepting a gift, he loses all merit.*

—*Vaya Purana*, ca. AD 800

# CHAPTER 5

I WOKE UP with my face pressed into hard, vibrating plastic and my mouth open, drool trickling out the corner. Fragments of a dream still swirled around me: *I'm sitting at a desk addressing wedding invitations. But I can't remember who I'm marrying. Tom? I canceled that one. Matt? I'm not speaking to him. I try to open one of the envelopes to see whose name is in it, but when I rip open the flap, all that falls out is a handful of tiny radish seeds.* The air was humming and throbbing; it was dark except for a little pool of light spilling onto my lap from an overhead socket. My feet were swollen and sweaty, but there was a jet of cold air blasting on my neck. It took me a few seconds to figure out where I was; thirty-three thousand feet in the air, somewhere between San Francisco and Delhi, with my head slumped against the airplane window and my arms clutching my tiny pillow like a teddy bear.

I sat up, blinking and rubbing my aching neck. It felt as if I'd been on this plane for centuries—as if I'd fallen into some *bardo* between lifetimes, just like the Tibetan monk who'd spoken at The Blissful Body fund-raiser had told us about, and when the plane landed I would be reborn as an entirely different person: a sadhu with matted dreadlocks. A courtesan in a silk sari practicing the arts of love from the *Kama Sutra*. Actually, it struck me as strange that you could even get to India by plane. You should have to travel by elephant through a desert. Or you should just sit on your meditation cushion and say the right mantra. Instead here I was in this humming metal tube—where I'd been sitting, now, for almost thirteen hours—with a silent TV screen on the seat-back in front of me playing a rerun of the *Dr. Phil* show.

"Something to drink for you?" The flight attendant was wearing a green silk sari; a red dot glinted between her eyebrows.

"Um . . . just apple juice, please." I took the plastic cup and a small bag of honey-roasted peanuts. My head was throbbing. Lori and my housemates—including the subletter I'd found at the last minute, an aspiring DJ who worked in the meat department at Real Food— had thrown me a going-away party the night before, with take-out Indian food from Bombay Garden and too many bottles of cheap champagne. Sometime past midnight, Lori had handed me a sealed letter, with instructions to read it "when you feel the urge to do something you suspect might be really stupid." Then she had insisted on driving me to the airport to catch my 5:00 a.m. plane. Standing outside the security checkpoint, she had flung her arms around me. "Don't worry. If enlightenment doesn't work out, you can always apply to graduate school."

In the seat next to me, an Indian man in a business suit was tapping away on a laptop, illuminated in a pool of bluish light. Somewhere in the back of the plane, a baby was wailing. In the seat in front of me, a Sikh in a blue turban was watching *The Simpsons*. I was amazed at how many people were on the move—hurtling through the airport, getting on planes and trains and buses, stuffing their belongings into bags and going somewhere else, anywhere else. I thought of my mother, yanking up roots and moving every couple of years. What kind of inner turmoil must she have been in, that tearing our whole life apart again and again had seemed like it might be a solution?

I'D NEVER BEEN able to get my mother to talk to me about my father. What little I knew about him came from my mother's younger sister, my aunt Elsie, whom my mother and I had stayed with in San Antonio, Texas, the long, sweltering summer that I turned twelve. She'd sat on her front porch with me all one evening while my mother was out waitressing, after my three little cousins were in bed, drinking Scotch and regaling me with stories she made me swear never to tell my mother she'd told me.

My mother had been just a few months short of twenty-one years old when she met my father, Aunt Elsie had said: the former homecoming queen of Tumbleweed High School in College Station, charming and wild and ten times smarter than she let the Texas boys guess. She was still living at home at the time—waitressing at Denny's, dating football players at Texas A&M, and sampling and dropping out of random classes at Valley Community College: Poetry. Ceramics. TV Production. Cosmetology. As she served up burgers and fries, she dreamed up ways to get out of Texas, which she told Aunt Elsie about every night as they fell asleep. Maybe she'd be a flight attendant. Maybe she'd write a screenplay. Maybe she'd be a lingerie model. Maybe she'd get a job on a cruise ship.

My father had showed up in Denny's one night and ordered a burger and a chocolate shake—a business school student at UCLA out for a conference on marketing meat at Texas A&M. He asked my mother out for a beer, then another, then another. The next morning, he stayed in bed with her in his hotel room till noon, missing the lecture on new methods for packaging pork. She'd never slept with anyone who didn't have a Texas drawl, and his voice in her ear drove her wild—she told Aunt Elsie it was like making love with a TV anchorman. A week later, he sent her a round-trip ticket to Los Angeles. Snooping through her closet years later, I found the second half of it tucked at the bottom of a shoebox under my birth certificate—her ticket back to a life she didn't want any more.

When she found out she was pregnant with me, two months later, she didn't tell him until it was too late to do anything about it. By then, they were already fighting about everything: the way she left her underwear strewn all over the floor of his studio apartment; the way he stayed out past midnight studying for his final exams at the UCLA library. I was just one more missile they could hurl at each other. One night, she borrowed his bike and rode it down to the library, five months pregnant, ready to give him hell. His carrel was empty, books piled neatly in the corner: *How to Sell Almost Anything to Almost Anyone. The Seven Secrets of Highly Successful People.* She rode all over campus and finally found him in the student center, drinking beer and playing video games with a couple of guys from his personnel management class. When she ripped into him, he saw the future, and it didn't look good.

Two nights after graduation, he packed his suitcase and left while she was bartending at the Coyote Grill. He left her a check for five thousand dollars and no forwarding address.

She could have tracked him down and hit him up for child support. But that wasn't my mother's style. Instead, she tore up his pictures, gave his clothes to the homeless guy on the corner, and cut his memory out of her heart like a piece of cancerous tissue. Being pregnant was a great way to get tips, as it turned out; so was showing off baby pictures. When I was three months old, she enrolled in a cosmetology school that had cheap day care and began dating a divorced father twenty years older than she was who owned a car dealership. She turned her face to the future and sailed on.

When I'd told Matt that I wanted to track down my father, he had scoffed. "Biology isn't destiny," he'd said. "He's not your father. He's just the sperm donor." But Tom had urged me to look up his name in the UCLA online alumni database. And as easy as that, there he was: a real estate developer, living in Seattle with his wife and three children. The alumni magazine didn't show a picture of him. But there was a picture of the kids: two boys and a girl, all in their teens. All with a tangle of dark curly hair, just like mine. All with my olive skin, my long nose.

I wrote him four or five letters, but I never mailed them. Once, I even picked up the phone and dialed his number, but I hung up as it started to ring. My mother and I were just the first trial run of a family that got discarded, like the first batch of pancakes made before the griddle was hot enough. Even worse than never seeing my father would be to see him and have him turn me away.

But every few months, I dreamed about him. In my dreams, he was a voice in the next room, or around a corner. He called on the phone, but when I picked up, the line was dead. He was waiting for me at a train station, but I got off one stop too late, and couldn't find my way back to him.

THE INDIAN MAN in the seat next to me closed his laptop with a click and looked at me. "Let me guess. You're going to India to study yoga."

I pulled out my earplugs. "How did you know?"

"I don't know . . . Maybe it had to do with the stretches you were doing in the aisle by the bathroom." He was somewhere in his midthirties, with pointed features as crisp as his voice, a lilting British-Indian cadence that made everything he said sound more interesting. "Or the om sign tattooed on your bicep. And by the way, I should warn you that wandering through rural India with that arm exposed will get you approximately the same reaction as walking through Louisiana topless with a crucifix tattooed on your breast."

I put my hand over my upper arm, wondering if he was joking. "Do you do yoga, too?"

He laughed. "Are you kidding? I have a friend who's an orthopedic surgeon. Specializes in knees. Every time he hears that someone does yoga, he turns to me and says, 'Oh good! Another payment on my Lexus!' No, I'm going back there to run a software start-up in Bangalore. My wife is coming in a few weeks. She's a doctor. She'll be opening a women's health clinic." He slid his laptop back in its case and slipped it under the seat in front of him. "How about you? What part of India will you be blessing with your yoga rupees?"

"I'll be traveling all over, actually. I'm working on a guidebook about where to find enlightenment."

He laughed again. "Good Lord. So thousands more rich Californians can tramp all over India looking for inner peace. While meanwhile millions of poor Indians are praying to die and be reborn in California." He tore open his package of honey-roasted peanuts and popped a handful in his mouth. "So tell me. Why on earth would someone go to India to practice yoga, when you can find a yoga studio on every corner in San Francisco? Where you can also drink the water without getting dysentery?"

"Because India is the birthplace of yoga! It's the land of the gods. It's where all the sacred texts come from."

"Yes, now that you mention it, I have heard that yoga is making a comeback in India. Particularly since the Indians have discovered that there's an export market for it."

"For an Indian, you're awfully negative about India."

"I'm not negative. I'm an optimist, in fact. I believe that India is going to be the next superpower. And when I say 'power,' I'm not talking about yogic siddhis." He crumpled up the peanut bag and stuck it in the seat pocket in front of him. "But I'm open to being convinced. Tell me more. How are you planning to find your great Indian enlightenment?"

"I'm going to research all the different types of yoga. Hatha yoga, the path of the body; raja yoga, the path of the mind; bhakti yoga, the path of devotion—"

"And what about banka yoga? You've left that out."

"Banka yoga? What's that?"

"That's the yoga of building up a hefty Swiss bank account by ripping off gullible American girls who believe you are an enlightened guru."

I picked up my empty glass of apple juice and began sucking on the ice. "I'm *not* gullible. I'm a *journalist*."

"Of course." He pressed the armrest button and leaned his seat back a little farther. "So you understand that India is a real-world place, with real-world challenges. If they're going to be solved, they're going to be solved by real-world solutions like better engineering and sanitation and birth control, not by gurus spouting moldy texts from a feudal society that died out a couple of thousand years ago. Not to mention the fact that while you Western hippies are traveling around here looking for enlightenment, Indian billionaires are buying up your corporate assets faster than you can say Sun Salutation."

I was starting to get nervous. "So are you saying that my whole book is bogus? Or is it my whole *life* you have a problem with?"

"Look, I'm sorry. I don't mean to give you a hard time. Tell me. I really want to understand. What is it about yoga that appeals to you so much?"

For some reason, it seemed urgent to convince him that I wasn't a flake, as if the success of my whole project depended upon his belief in it. I groped for words. "There's a way I sometimes feel when I'm doing yoga." I'd been inhaling his exhalations for hours; this gave me an illusion of intimacy that was only heightened by the fact that I'd never see him again. "It's a feeling—just for a moment—that I belong somewhere, even if it's just inside my own skin. I want to have that feeling more of the time."

I'd lost him. He didn't say anything for a long time. I stared at the TV screen. A man and a woman, both of them very fat, were sitting in the chairs next to Dr. Phil. Then they were standing by a sink full of dishes with him yelling at her, and a wailing kid wearing nothing but underwear and a Superman cape holding onto her legs. The image cut to a car commercial: a beautiful young woman and a gorgeous guy driving fast down a mountain road. As if, if they drove fast enough, they could elude all that suffering forever.

The Indian man reached in his pocket, pulled out a business card, and handed it to me.

*A. J. Rao, software design*
*159 Mahatma Marg*
*Bangalore, India*
*email: raoji@indiasoft.com*

"Hang onto this," he told me. "If you get into any trouble, you be sure to send me and my wife an email."

*Do thy duty, even if it be humble, rather than another's, even if it be great. To die in one's duty is life; to live in another's is death.*

—Bhagavad Gita, ca. 300 BC

# CHAPTER 6

I SPENT MY FIRST night in India kneeling in front of a toilet in the Harmony Hotel, spewing liquids out of both ends of my gastrointestinal tract.

In between rounds of vomiting, I lay on the gritty bathroom floor, too weak to drag myself to my bed, wondering what had made me so sick. The lettuce on the cheese sandwich in the airport? The banana lassi in the Harmony restaurant? Two pigeons had nested in the ventilator fan; the floor was dotted with their grayish droppings and bits of feathers. The smell of the sewer came up through the toilet, which was just a porcelain bowl in the floor. There was no toilet paper, just a tap and a cup of water. From a courtyard outside came the wail of Hindi film music and the blare of a television show that primarily consisted of explosions and car crashes.

When my stomach subsided, just before dawn, I staggered to my bed, a dingy mattress covered with a single sheet, and lay down with all my clothes on. The overhead fan had a bolt missing: It made a shrill *whine-thump, whine-thump* like an imbalanced washing machine. I fell into a fitful sleep.

A few hours later, a clanging began, as if men were forging steel directly under my bed. It merged with the shriek of recorded chants from a loudspeaker on the roof of a temple down the street. Sitting up in bed, I peered out through the grimy glass and down into a narrow road jammed with autorickshaws—motorized three-wheelers about the size of golf carts, painted bright yellow, belching fumes. The rickshaws were going in both directions, according to no discernible traffic patterns; the whole alley reverberated with the two-toned wail of their horns. There were no sidewalks, so people and bicycles spilled out into the road, bringing traffic to a crawl. The crowd was heaving, shouting, packed shoulder to shoulder; was it some sort of riot, or were they just going to work? A cow stood on the other side of the street, chewing on a newspaper. And there, riding in the back of that rickshaw with the man in the turban . . . Was that a goat he had in his lap? The cow lifted up its tail and a stream of manure fell into the road. A child darted out from a doorway, scooped up the pile of cow dung with a flat shovel, and carried it back inside like a treasure.

Over the whole scene loomed a giant billboard bearing an advertisement for "Minto's, the mint with no hole." "You don't have a hole in your head," proclaimed the billboard. "Why do you want a hole in your mint?"

I flopped back on my bed and stared up at the ceiling—peeling white paint and a large brown stain as if someone had thrown a cup of chai at it. From down the hall, I could hear the sound of someone else retching, and my own stomach heaved in sympathy.

I'd exited the airport late yesterday afternoon, dazed and exhausted, into a crush of bumper-to-bumper traffic. My taxi had crawled down a brand-new freeway, past billboards advertising Reliance cell phones and resort property in the Himalayas. An electronic sign blinked overhead: CONTROL YOUR SPEED, CONTROL YOUR MIND. I'd asked the taxi driver to just drop me off at the popular backpacker area near the train station. But instead he had talked me into coming to the Harmony Hotel, which he swore was run by his cousin, who "is also loving the yoga, just like you."

Where were the restaurants, the stores, the train station, the banks? How did I make a phone call? Who could I call, anyway? To quell my rising panic, I pulled a pen from my bag, looked in vain for a scrap of paper, and began making a list on my palm of things I needed to do: *Cash travelers checks into rupees. Find Internet. Find train station. Buy train tickets.* The list crawled off my hand, up my arm. *Crash* went the machines under my floor, and my whole bed vibrated.

Still queasy, I got up to take a shower in the tiny bathroom. The showerhead sprouted from the wall, spraying water over the sink and floor. *Actually, it's much more ecologically sound to not use toilet paper.* I scrubbed away at my hands with the tiny sliver of graying soap, hoping I wasn't going to throw up again. *Much cleaner, too, really.* I looked in vain for a towel, then dried myself by rolling around on my bedsheets. I pulled on my clothes and went looking for tea.

"Coffee tea bottled water?" asked the waiter. He was the same man who had checked me in at the front desk last night, but now he was wearing a white jacket. "Milk porridge? Toast butter jam?"

I studied the greasy plastic menu. *Veggie cutlets . . . ornge juice . . . curd with muesli . . . Scrampled eggs . . .* I wasn't hungry, but I should probably try to get something down. "Just some plain toast, please."

"Very good." The waiter went through an open door into a tiny kitchen; I saw him take off his jacket, put on an apron, and begin to fill a giant cast-iron pot with water from the sink. I looked around the dining room: four Formica tables and a linoleum floor the color of spilled coffee. I appeared to be the only guest. I continued my list on a scrap of napkin: *Buy Immodium. Find enlightened guru. Breath mints?*

"Breakfast, madame." The waiter set a bowl of oatmeal on the table in front of me, with a pitcher of steaming milk and a little plate of brown sugar.

"Actually, I ordered toast."

"Yes, yes," he said pleasantly. "But today, toast is not coming."

I was too tired to ask why. I sprinkled sugar on the cereal, poured on the steaming milk, and took a bite. It was surprisingly good, hot and sweet, sliding down my throat without too much effort. The waiter was still standing by the table, watching me. "You will be staying here long, madame?" he asked.

I shook my head. "No. I should leave in a couple of days." The table had one leg shorter than the others; it lurched and wobbled every time I clicked my spoon into the bowl, giving the meal an unsteady feeling, as if I were eating aboard a ship.

"Going to where?"

"Rishikesh." I put down my spoon—a few bites was all I was up for—and turned back to my list, in a gesture intended to communicate that the conversation was over.

"Ah! Rishikesh! Rishikesh is yoga capitol of world. Gateway to Himalaya. So many sadhus, yogis, holy men are living in Rishikesh, living on banks of goddess Ganges, eating only air and water and some little bit of chai and biscuits, having the conversations with God and all like that. And also, there is my cousin, who is running very good river-rafting business. You would like to try river rafting?"

"Actually, I'm going to focus on yoga. I'm writing a book about enlightenment."

"I talk to so many Americans, British, Germans studying yoga, they tell to me, 'Vikram'—that is my name—'Vikram, white-water rafting on the bosom of mother Ganges, that is enlightenment itself.'

This is what they are saying to me." He reached into his pocket and pulled out a folded brochure, which he handed to me. "You see here, it describes it all, right here only."

"Could you tell me where I could find a place to change traveler's checks around here? Or somewhere I can connect to the Internet?"

"For shops and Internet, will be necessary to walk a little way, very little way, toward train station. Here, this is not really tourist area."

I looked at him, baffled. "Then why are you running a hotel here?"

"My cousin, downstairs, is running rickshaw repair shop. He offers me the space upstairs, very reasonable rate."

"And the hotel is doing well?"

"Oh, no, madame, as you see, hotel is doing very poorly. Very few guests." He gestured around the empty room.

"But you seem very happy anyway."

Vikram beamed at me. "Oh yes, madame. I am always happy. It is like this: What happens to us in life is for God to decide. But whether to be happy or not—that is our choice."


"HELLO, HELLO, MONEY?"

In the dark, predawn din outside the train station, it took me a few seconds to figure out where the voice was coming from: right around the level of my knees. Weaving my way through the crowd, I looked down to see a boy seated on a battered skateboard, propelling himself after me with his skinny arms. His legs ended in shiny stumps just above the knee. He couldn't have been more than ten years old. "Money, money, chapati?" He gestured with his hand toward his mouth.

I hiked up my shirt to fish around in my money belt, making impossible calculations in my head: How much was enough, given the preposterous gulf of wealth that lay between us? Should I give him my rupees? My traveler's checks? My rings? My backpack? My whole life? I handed him a wad of small bills and tried to trudge on. But suddenly there were children all around me, hands outstretched, plucking at my clothes—"Money, money?" A ragged little girl with a baby in her arms, a boy pointing at a bloody gash on his leg . . . "Hello, hello, one rupee only?" I hesitated, not sure what to do, paralyzed by a bewildering fusion of compassion and irritation. Then I pushed past them, not meeting their eyes, afraid that I would miss my train.

The station platforms were dim and jammed with men, half of whom appeared to be scratching their crotches. My train was supposed to leave in ten minutes, but from which platform? An electronic sign labeled ARRIVALS and DEPARTURES displayed nothing but flashing red lines. An Enquiries and Complaints counter had no one sitting behind it. No one was at the Ladies Only counter, either. I looked around, desperate, and accosted a man in a red uniform with shiny buttons down the front. "Excuse me. Where does the train to Haridwar leave from?"

He wagged his head in a gesture that seemed half yes, half no. "Yes, yes. Haridwar train leaving soon."

"Yes, but where?"

"Five minutes."

I turned to another man. "Haridwar train? Where?"

"Haridwar train. Platform 12."

I was on Platform 1. The straps of my backpack digging into my shoulders, I sprinted up the stairs and along the overpass, pushing my way around porters carrying suitcases on their heads, past whole families camped out on blankets. There was no train at Platform 12. But I did spot an open Assistance counter. A uniformed man sat at a desk behind it, his eyes closed.

"Excuse me." I rapped at the glass window. "When is the Haridwar train going to get here?"

He looked up sleepily. "Haridwar train. Platform 1."

I sprinted back up the stairs and fought my way back through the crowds to Platform 1. Sweat was streaming down my neck. My backpack was the weight of a small elephant. I stepped in the open door of the waiting train and looked in vain for a conductor; instead, I turned to a man seated just inside the door and repeated my mantra: "Haridwar? Is this the Haridwar train?"

He smiled, revealing a mouth with exactly one snaggled tooth hanging down from the top gum. "Yes, madame. This Madras train. Madras is very good city. You are going to Madras?"

"Is your marriage arranged marriage?" asked the Indian woman sitting next to me on the train to Haridwar. The words came out in a rush, as if she had been rehearsing them for the last ten minutes. "Or . . ." Her face flushed and she looked down, as if she were about to ask something risqué, like whether I liked to be handcuffed naked to a bedpost. "Or is it love marriage?"

We were rattling north through mile after mile of crumbling cement slums, tent cities, and garbage dumps—an unrelenting sea of inhabited rubble in which I couldn't tell houses from ruins. The train seats were upholstered in mustard-yellow plastic; the walls were dotted with ads for broadband Internet. My seatmate was a slender young woman in a dark blue sari, hair pulled back in a tight knot at the back of her neck, a golden bindi between her eyebrows. Her name was Anjali, she had told me shyly; she was traveling home to Dehra Dun to visit her mother. I guessed that she was about my age. Squeezed between us, leaning up against her side, was her three-year-old daughter, clutching a dark-haired Barbie in a sari.

"Actually, I'm not married at all," I told her.

Her face registered shock, which she struggled to cover up. "You are how old?"

"Twenty-nine."

She looked down at her daughter, now sleeping, and reflexively pulled her close, as if her mere proximity to me might cause such a fate to swallow her up. "Oh. I am sorry."

A conductor stopped at our seats and offered us breakfast: thermoses of hot English tea, sugar biscuits, a crisp copy of *The Hindu* newspaper. The landscape outside was shifting to fields of sugarcane and smoke-belching sugar refineries. Buffalo carts hauled piles of sugarcane down dirt roads. Cows clustered under groves of eucalyptus. Women in brilliant saris picked through the garbage by the tracks.

"What about you?" I asked Anjali, dipping my biscuit into my tea. "How long have you been married?"

"Seven years. Now I am twenty-eight years old." She continued to stroke her daughter's hair. "This is my second child. Her older brother is at home; I didn't want him to miss the school."

She was stunningly beautiful, as so many of the Indian women seemed to be—radiating a kind of effortless calm, eyes dark pools, olive skin flawless. Despite the dust of the train station, her sari was clean and draped in elegant folds. She looked as if she had never perspired a drop in her life. In comparison, I felt scruffy and disheveled, dressed in the *salwar kameez* I had bought at the market in Delhi yesterday—a pajama-like outfit with baggy pants and a shapeless tunic that hung down to my knees. An Australian woman I met in a chai shop had told me that dressing in Indian clothes would make me less likely to be harassed by men. But my *salwar kameez* was already smudged with dust and sweat, crumpled from the weight of my backpack, which hitched it up awkwardly in the back. I had stored my money and passport in my security belt around my waist, which meant that when I wanted to buy my ticket, I had to hitch up my tunic to my belly button to get out my wad of rupees—thereby attracting stares from every man within eyesight, as if I had paused at the ticket counter in Grand Central station, pulled down my jeans, and begun pulling out hundred-dollar bills from my panties. In the window, I could see the shadowy reflection of my face, strained and splotchy, my hair escaping in frizzy tendrils from my ponytail.

"So your husband is watching your son?"

She laughed again. "Oh no. My husband has very good job with cell phone company. He is working all day. But I live in same house with his mother and father, his brother, and all rest of joint family. My sister-in-law is watching my boy. She has two children also and our children are all like brothers and sisters."

"And how did you meet your husband? Was it . . ."—I tried to remember her phrase—"a love marriage?"

She blushed and looked down again. "Oh no. It was arranged marriage. My mother's cousin was good friend of his mother. She made the introduction."

"So you had never met him before you were married?"

"Oh yes, I had met him. These are modern times! I met him with my mother, and gave the approval. Then we met five, maybe six times before our wedding. Once he invited me out for chai, just the two of us, so we would have time to get to know each other and all like that. But my mother said no. She said, 'You have the rest of your lives to go out together. Why you are wanting to go out now?'"

Across the aisle from me, an Indian man was watching a DVD on a portable player of a giant white-bearded swami standing knee-deep in a rushing river, his arms outstretched in blessing. Anjali and I eyed each other across a gulf of culture. I liked her. In another reality, I imagined, we might have been friends. I tried to envision her in cutoff jeans and a tank top, a tattoo snaking down her spine, lying next to me on the grass at a concert at Golden Gate Park. Or me in a sari, the two of us side by side in a kitchen making chapatis for our husbands' dinner.

"In America," I told her, "we like to get to know each other for a long time before we get married, to find out how well we like each other. Sometimes we even live together first."

She shook her head. "In India, we feel so sorry for Western women. You have to find your own husbands . . . going to bars, even searching on the Internet by yourself." Her inflection made the term *Internet* sound vaguely scandalous. "And then, how can you make a proper choice? Even if someone is getting quite old, like you, you are still inexperienced. Without the help of your mother, how will you know what will make you happy through a whole lifetime?"

I looked out the window. We were flashing through a village of squat mud huts. About twenty feet from the train tracks, an outdoor school was set up under a grove of eucalyptus: rows of desks with children bent over composition books, looking up to wave as the train rushed by.

"Maybe I don't. But I don't think my mother does, either."

Over and over, as I was growing up, I'd sat at our kitchen table with my mother, eating microwaved macaroni and cheese and listening to her talk about her relationships. It was a litany of hope followed by disappointment: how this man had let her down, how that one had betrayed her. "Beauty is a curse," she'd said, studying me across the table—my thick glasses, my tangled hair pulled back in a tight ponytail. "You should count your lucky stars that you're not saddled with it. Being smart will get you further, in the long run, than being popular. I was homecoming queen, you know. And just look where it got me!" She'd looked around our kitchen, and I saw it through her eyes: the ditch she'd lurched into when the train of her life had run off its tracks.

"I was engaged once," I told Anjali. "Just a couple of years ago."

"Oh, I am so sorry," she said again. "What happened? Did he die?"

"No, he didn't die." I closed my eyes, thinking of Tom, trying to find words that would make sense to her. "I just changed my mind."

I gave her a retouched version of the story, with all the sex air-brushed out—just a contest between two different men, one of whom I wanted, one of whom wanted me. "I haven't seen Tom since I gave the ring back. He must have been terribly hurt." I was on a train in the foothills of the Himalayas with my mind still coursing down the same familiar California tracks, as if suffering from some peculiar form of jet lag: *You should have married him. No, you never should have dated him in the first place.*

Anjali was looking sympathetic but confused, as if I had been speaking a language she had read but never heard spoken. "But how could you make such a choice? To reject a man who would marry you, for one who would not?"

"It didn't even feel like I had a choice. My body rejected him on its own, like an organ transplant."

She shook her head. "In India, your body does not have that choice, to reject. You accept."

"And does it work out? Are you happy?"

Anjali looked out the window. We were rattling through another village: clusters of concrete houses, none of which seemed quite finished, although they were already decaying. Beams of rusty rebar protruded in bristles from the tops of them, like badly trimmed hair. "You say you are yoga student. So you are knowing the Bhagavad Gita, yes?"

"Yes, of course." We had studied it in my yoga teacher-training program: an ancient hymn to the god Krishna, the transcendent power of love that illuminates the whole universe. I'd read it sitting on Ocean Beach, eating gingersnaps, my book balanced on thighs slick with sunscreen.

Anjali nodded out the window, where houses were being swallowed up again by a plain of yellow mustard flowers. "Just here, on these very fields, is where the Lord Krishna appeared to the warrior Arjuna in his chariot." She spoke casually, intimately, as if speaking of events that had happened only a few days ago. "In the Gita, Krishna tells Arjuna that it is his dharma—his role in life—to be a warrior. His spiritual task is to live that dharma as best he can. Just so, my dharma is to be wife to this person. Now I must find the joy within that assignment."

"But does it work?" I persisted. "Are you really happy?"

"When I was first married, I was very sad. I missed my mother and my family so much. Oh, so much! It was too hard. In my home, where I grew up, it was more like small village. And although my parents were not very educated, I went to very good school. I studied English literature. I was even editor of the school literary magazine."

In the seat next to her, her little girl shifted in her sleep and murmured something in Hindi. Anjali's hand moved to stroke her head.

"My husband's home is in the city. It is much smaller, more crowded. My husband is from family of businessmen. They are very kind people. But all they know is business. They do not know art, they do not know music, they do not know poetry."

"And what do you do all day?"

"I clean the house, I do the shopping, I cook. It is not just for me and my children, you understand. It is for whole household—grandmother, mother, cousins. Whole extended family."

"And do you still read poetry?"

She shook her head. "Only in my heart."

The landscape outside had shifted to a city; we must be getting near to Haridwar. We rattled along the banks of a mud-brown river lined with gaudily painted temples. I leaned my head against the window, suddenly weary.

Anjali and Arjuna seemed so clear about their assignments in life. Arjuna was a warrior. Anjali was a wife and mother. Case closed. But what was *my* dharma? Dog walker? Yoga teacher? Travel guide writer? Spiritual seeker?

If only I knew.

*Devotedly with the pure heart who so ever comes to Rishikesh, the Bramtheerth (Supreme Pilgrimage), and stays one night becomes godly. Rishikesh is now round the year destination. Get the best of Rishikesh as per your interest.*

—www.rishikesh.org

# CHAPTER 7

ONE WEEK AFTER I had arrived in Rishikesh, I stood on a footbridge over the Ganges River, tossing pebbles of fish food over the railing into the bottle-green, foam-flecked water fifty feet below, and trying not to cry.

From the bridge, I looked out over riverbanks frothing with ashrams and temples—peach and pale yellow and pink, turreted and domed, trimmed with crimson, emblazoned with excerpts from Hindu religious texts in scrolling script. Behind them rose the gray-green arc of Himalayan foothills, where for centuries yogis and saints had come to meditate in caves and bathe in the sacred waters of the goddess Ganga. Rishikesh was a pilgrim's paradise, the ultimate yoga fantasy; even the Beatles had found God here. But what good was it to be in a mind-blowing place if you didn't have a friend to turn to and say, "Isn't this amazing?"

A moped rattled across the bridge behind me, with an orange-robed sadhu hitching a ride on the back. A gang of tall, blond yoga students in immaculate white kurta pajamas—the collarless, knee-length shirt and drawstring pants that were the traditional outfit of Indian men—tromped after it, arguing heatedly in German. I tossed another handful of fish pellets into the water, thinking of the grubby little girl who had sold them to me: the back of her ragged dress flapping open, a trail of snot smeared across her face. A school of carp surfaced, jostling and fighting each other, mouths gobbling.

I was surrounded by thousands of spiritual seekers. And I'd never felt so alone in my entire life.

MY FIRST FEW DAYS in Rishikesh, I'd been ecstatic. The sunny cobbled alleys that lined the Ganges were blazoned with hand-lettered banners advertising yoga classes, meditation courses, ayurvedic massages. I even spotted a hotel called Enlightenment House. Incense wafted from storefronts; bhajans crooned from temple loudspeakers and CD shops. The Incredible India Yoga Festival was about to start at a riverside ashram. Sadhus sat on the ghats, the polished granite steps that led to the sparkling river, and wandered through the streets along with the free-roaming cows and ponies. At sunset, I sat by the ghats and watched a spectacular puja, or devotional ritual, in front of a thirty-foot metal Shiva statue; a chorus of ashram boys in orange robes sang bhajans in sweet, high-pitched voices while a priest swung a flaming bowl of fire over the rushing waters. *Jaya Jaya Om Jaya Jaya* . . . I was giddy with delight. At this rate, I'd find an enlightened master in a couple of days. My book was practically going to write itself.

But the Incredible India Yoga Festival turned out to be staffed almost entirely by teachers from California; I even recognized a couple of names from The Blissful Body. Enlightenment House was run by a former investment banker from Massachusetts. And the yoga ashram I checked into was a giant tourist hotel crammed with travelers from all over Europe, Australia, New Zealand, and America. The resident swami was nowhere to be found, although there was a hatha yoga class every morning, taught by a brisk young Australian woman with sunburned cheeks who barked out the asana instructions with hearty enthusiasm. My next-door neighbors were a group of Rastafarians from Germany, who stayed up late every night smoking pot, playing guitar, and singing reggae with thick German accents. I had dropped in on another ashram, but it was populated almost entirely by Japanese men in business suits.

My third morning in Rishikesh, a monkey with a raw red bottom had swung down from the bridge cables and snatched my expensive REI sunglasses off my face. And that evening, sitting by the river at the evening puja, I had watched an armed guard chase away a begging sadhu so he wouldn't disrupt the ritual for the foreign tourists.

*It's okay. No one expects you to find enlightenment the very first week. Remember how it was with the wine book, all the overpriced wine you had to swill before you found the great local vineyards that no one knew about.* At least with all this distraction, I hadn't had any time to think about Matt. Oh, damn, now I was thinking about him again.

I turned away from the railing and began walking back into town. A man in a brown lungi, bare to the waist, was turning an iron wheel to operate a sugarcane press; he ladled the spurting juice into metal cups. Through the open door of a gem store, I saw two blonde women in saris sitting across the counter from an Indian salesman in a suit and tie. All three of them cupped immense amethyst crystals in their palms. Their eyes were all closed. They were all chanting Om.

I cut across an alley and into the Ganesha Health Food Internet

Café. Inside, Bob Marley was playing, the pitch warbling slightly as the CD player speeded up and slowed down with the fluctuations in power. Travelers crowded elbow to elbow at tiny tables and sprawled on foam mattresses covered with tattered fabric. A few people hunched over computers, lost to the world. I sat down in front of one of the computers and studied the menu lying next to it, although I already knew it by heart.

"I'll have a Yogi Chai," I told Ashok, the Indian man behind the counter, who was frying potatoes on a griddle over an open flame. "And a plate of macaroni and cheese."

"No problem. And you, madame? You are well today?'

*I'm lonely and scared. I don't know what I'm doing or where I'm going. For all I know about India and enlightenment, I might as well be writing about nuclear physics. I'd give the advance back and call the whole thing quits, but the thing is, I've already spent most of it.* "Yes. I'm great, thanks."

As Ashok shook a package of macaroni into a pot of boiling water, I turned to the computer and clicked on the familiar Yahoo! logo. Perched on the top of the computer was a statue of Ganesha, the elephant-headed god who removes obstacles, next to a stick of smoldering incense. As I typed in my password, the power went out in the restaurant, and the lights went dim. But the computer had a battery backup. It kept on glowing and humming—as if the virtual world were the stable place, and India the fragile reality that could crash at any moment.

From: Maxine@bigdaybooks.com
To: Amandala@yahoo.com

Amanda, we're wondering how you're doing on this enlightenment gig. Any chance you could get it to us quicker? The Yoga World Magazine conference is in New York at the same time as the ABA and we'd like to have books at both. Also, we need pictures for our fall promo package. Please send us some jpegs right away of someone looking as enlightened as possible, preferably someone with nice teeth, exotic outfit, dark skin but not too ethnic looking.

A few spam emails from Target and Amazon; a new schedule from The Blissful Body. And nothing from anyone else. Nothing, in particular, from Matt.

I knew that this is what we had agreed on—no calls, no letters, no email—but still it made my stomach hurt. I had hoped that the silence would mean that I would stop thinking about him. Instead, I seemed to be thinking about him more and more.

I opened up a blank message and typed in his address: offthematt@gmail.com. A few keystrokes, and I could connect with someone who—for all his flaws—knew me inside and out. I could even suggest that he meet me here, a side trip on one of his many travels.

If I could be sure that he would be alone when he got the email, I would do it.

I sat on my hands. I took a few long, deep breaths. Then I logged out.

I sat down at a table to wait for my food and looked wistfully over at a mattress in the corner, where three or four travelers lounged laughing and drinking lassi. If Lori were here, she'd have marched right over and joined them for a chai and a masala dosa. She'd probably already be friends with that Swedish girl with the raucous laugh and the calves of a mountain climber. She'd already have been asked out by that German guy with the blond ponytail and the rudrashaka mala around his neck. But I had always been shy about meeting new people. Everyone here was on the move—it was like trying to sustain a conversation with someone on a train platform.

I felt tears sting at the back of my eyes. Who was it I missed?

Matt? Lori? Tom? My mother? My father? Here in India, everything that was hidden in America was out in the open: garbage tossed in the street for cows to eat, people praying and bathing in the river while tourists strolled by, no toilet paper so you couldn't even avoid your own rear end. Now India was ripping the lid off my heart as well, and everything I'd packed away was boiling to the surface.

"Your macaroni, madame." Ashok placed the steaming plate in front of me. The macaroni was piled high on a metal thali tray. The cheese sauce was a fluorescent orange.

Two gray-haired British women chatted at a table next to me. "So how are you enjoying India?" one of them asked. "Oh, I love it!" the other said. "I feel so at one with the people here. Perhaps it's because they used to be a colony."

I took a bite of my macaroni and studied the titles on the bookshelf next to me, a collection donated by previous travelers: *Le Divorce. Say It in Tibetan. Working Miracles of Love. Trekking in Bhutan. The Da Vinci Code.* "Let's get together and feel all right," sang Bob Marley. A cow wandered past the open door, a half-eaten milk carton sticking out of the corner of its mouth. *I could just go home.*

"Hi, mind if we join you?"

I looked up. Standing by my table was a skinny guy with dirty, carrot-colored hair matted into shoulder-length dreadlocks. His skin was pale, with a spray of freckles over the nose; his eyes were a watery blue; he was wearing a brown wool shawl wrapped over his cotton dhoti, the long piece of cloth knotted around his waist like a skirt. He was holding a steaming cup of chai in one hand, a giant plate of spaghetti with tomato sauce in the other.

"Sure," I said gratefully. "Want to pull up a few more chairs?"

"No, we will only need one." He sat down and bowed, his hands in prayer position at his heart. "Namaste. Our name is Devi Das. 'Servant of the Goddess,' it means, in case you were wondering."

"Amanda. As far as I know, it doesn't mean anything. In case you were wondering."

"Pleased to meet you." He began scooping the spaghetti into his mouth. "Man, this is fantastic. We've been staying in an ashram for the last six months where all we ate was rice and dal. Very sattvic. Very good for our spiritual practice. But we lost so much weight that when we sat down to meditate, we got bruises on our butt bones."

"Where was the ashram? Here in Rishikesh?"

"No. It was in Gujarat. We would have stayed there, but the guru got brought up on tax evasion charges and had to go to his center in Sweden instead."

"Sounds like he wasn't much of a guru."

"He was awesome! He taught us the most amazing practices. He changed our life." He sucked a dangling strand of spaghetti into his mouth. "Before we came to India, we had a lot of mental problems. We had to take medication every day. Now we don't take any drugs at all. We just meditate. And we are truly happy for the first time in our life. It is so wonderful to finally be living like a normal person."

I decided to let that one slide. "Can I ask you a personal question?"

Devi Das beamed. A large smear of tomato sauce decorated his cheek, like the badge of some oddball Hindu sect. "For us, nothing is personal any more."

"Why do you call yourself 'we'?"

He swallowed the last bite of his spaghetti and began wiping the sauce off the plate with a bony finger. "It is a spiritual practice our first guru assigned us. It's supposed to break down our ego attachment to the idea of a separate self." He took a sip of his chai. "To the rational mind, it appears that there is an 'I' and a 'you' sitting at this table. But in reality, there is no separation. Our 'we' includes 'you,' too." He gestured to Ashok. "Could we get some more chai, please? And a piece of apple pie?"

"Shouldn't you make it two pieces? One for each of you?"

"We tried that for a while. But we started to get love handles."

He first came to India five years ago, he told me as he ate his pie. He had been a religion major at the University of Kansas, researching his senior thesis on Hindu spiritual practices. He had lived in an ashram in Kerala, then another in Bangalore. Then he decided to become a sadhu. He changed his name and let go of his past identity and his plans for the future—but not the interest on the trust fund his grandfather left him, which was only about two hundred dollars a month, but it let him live like a raja here. Now he just wandered from ashram to ashram, teacher to teacher. "Someday we might go back to college," he said. "We made so many notes for our dissertation. But they fell off the roof of a bus in Sikkim."

"What about your family?" I asked. "Don't you miss them?"

"Our father dropped his body. Our mother dropped out of touch." He licked the sugar off his fingers. "This is why we must find spiritual parents instead."

"I'm trying to find all the best spiritual teachers in India. I'm writing a guidebook about how to find enlightenment."

He settled back in his chair and patted his belly. "A guidebook for enlightenment! What a beautiful idea. One of our teachers used to tell us, 'When you are ready to awaken, the teacher will appear.' But if you are successful, he will be able to say, 'When you are ready to awaken, the guidebook will appear!'"

"But what do you think? Are there any particular teachers you'd recommend that I visit?" I fumbled around in my daypack and pulled out my notebook.

"Have you ever heard of Swami Ramdas? He is no longer in his body. But he had a wonderful method for traveling around India. He would go to a train station and simply see what train was waiting at the platform. He would get on it and ride until a ticket collector threw him off the train. At whatever station Ramdas found himself, he would set about finding a spiritual teacher. We think that is the best method for you!"

I put my pen down. "I have a book contract. I can't leave my research up to the whim of a ticket collector."

"But you see, Ramdas believed that every person he met was Ram—God—in disguise. His whole trip was therefore in divine hands." Devi Das stood up. "We were thinking of taking a little walk along the river. Would you like to go with us and see some real yogis?"

I hesitated, gazing down at my list from that morning: *Buy laundry soap—where? Find enlightened master—where? Buy deodorant—where? Arati by Ganges, 6 o'clock—p.m.? a.m.? bring candle and camera. Where? Email Maxine—about what? Write sample chapter—about what?"*

"Don't worry," he assured me. "We practice celibacy. Soon we will be so advanced in our tantric practices that we won't even have nocturnal emissions."

"It's not that. It's just that I was supposed to email my editor this afternoon."

"Wonderful! This will give you something to tell her."

We left the restaurant and made our way back across the bridge. Then Devi Das veered off onto a path that wove through a tangle of trees and bushes along the river banks. The trail was lined with crumbling whitewashed buildings and shacks made of logs and trash bags. "Yogi huts," explained Devi Das. He pointed down at the sandy beach below us. A sadhu sat on a river-smoothed stone, his legs folded in full lotus. He was holding one of his arms straight up in the air. Next to him, another sadhu was standing on one leg, his upper body supported from a sling that hung from a tree branch.

"These yogis are performing austerities. The one hanging from a tree has taken vows not to lie down for twelve years, even if his legs turn gangrenous and rot. The other one has been holding his arm up in the air for so long that it has atrophied into a stick."

"But why?" *Dear Maxine, I've got a great theme for the fall promo package: Self-mutilation!*

"Yogis believe that suffering turns our mind to God."

I looked down at the yogis again. They were less than twenty feet away, but their world still felt as impenetrable as if I were flipping through a coffee-table book back in California. "But isn't there enough suffering in life already?" *Idiot's Tip: If you want to get enlightened, you can hold one arm up in the air until it withers. Or to save time, just get a boyfriend!*

"Yes. Life is so full of pain that is a wonder we are not all God-intoxicated all the time." Devi Das turned to me and beamed. "We have just had a beautiful idea! In the hills around here are many caves where yogis live and meditate in solitude. They live on tree leaves and Ganges water. We were planning to go up there for a few months. Why don't you come with us?"

"Wow, I . . . I totally love tree leaves and Ganges water. But unfortunately, I'm scheduled to be in Maharashtra in just a few days. I'm visiting a famous yoga teacher who has a center there. I arranged it weeks ago."

Devi Das shook his head. "In our experience, you can't chase down awakening in India. You have to sit still and wait for awakening to come to you."

I picked up a rock and tossed it into the river. "Unfortunately, I don't have time for that. I'm on a *deadline*."

"Yes. We can see that you still believe in your plans more than you believe in Ram's plan. But that is okay! That, too, is part of Ram's plan!" He smiled. "Clearly, Ram has drawn us together for a reason. So if you will not come with us, then we must come with you. Shall we take the train tomorrow morning?"

"But I thought you were going up to a cave to meditate!"

"Our plans are like the Ganges. They keep flowing."

I could hear Lori's voice: *Amanda! This is a bipolar sadhu from*

*Kansas, currently off his medication, who refers to himself in the first person plural! What are you doing? Read my letter!*

"Sure," I said. "I'll meet you at the rickshaw stand at seven o'clock."

"We don't wear a watch," he said. "But you can find us meditating by the water."

# cobra pose

# (вhujangasana)

*Lie face down, your elbows bent and your palms pressed lightly into the ground by your chest. Anchor your tailbone into the earth as you roll your spine up and open. Spread the wings of your rib cage. Slip your shoulder blades down your back to cradle your heart. Feel the electric wave of pleasure ripple from your pelvis to your skull.*

*Is the quiver you feel excitement, or terror? Coiled at the base of your spine is a sleeping serpent—the passionate goddess who seeds all life. As you arch into Cobra, feel the serpent shudder. Feel her hot pleasure, her potent joy, as she shakes off her slumber and begins to writhe.*

*If you cannot see your little toe, how can you see the Self?*

—B. K. S. Iyengar (1918– )

# CHAPTER 8

THE NEXT MORNING, Devi Das and I left on an overnight train to the vast industrial city in India's southeastern plains that was the unlikely home of the up-and-coming yoga master Mr. Vikas Kapoor.

The vendors sang out their wares as they walked up and down the aisles: "Chai, chai, chai! Chikki, chikki, chikki! Chocolate! Samosas! Idli!" "Shoeshine, shoeshine!" called a man paralyzed from the waist down, as he slid himself along the corridors with his arms. A blind musician in a white lungi played a one-stringed sitar and sang ballads. A little boy swept under our feet with a bundle of twigs, and held out his palm for change.

All my doubts about the wisdom of traveling with Devi Das melted away within an hour, as he guided me straight to the right car, bought some samosas on the platform, and firmly turned away the dozen or so men who waved tickets at us and insisted that we were in their seats. By day, he regaled me with stories about enlightened masters all over India, with some colorful tales about ex-girlfriends thrown in. At night, we slept in narrow, swaying bunks stacked one above the other, with Devi Das handing me his shawl to sleep under.

We arrived in the midafternoon and stepped off the train into a suffocating blast of heat and petrol fumes. On the platform, a skeletal man with a stump for a leg lay on a pile of jute rags. He gestured feebly toward his mouth, too weak to lift his head. I set a tangerine by his head. But when I looked back, I saw a dog carrying it away.

Our rickshaw swam through choking smog and crumbling cement buildings. Through the mob of honking trucks, I caught a glimpse of a grim, dingy bullock dragging a cart. "Hotels near yoga center all full," said the rickshaw driver. "So many yoga students! Yoga man is richest man in city. Oh, so very rich! But I find you good place, very cheap, very short walk."

"Could you get us something with an Internet connection?" I asked.

"Phone fax Internet chai, all services, very short walk, no problem."

"Remember," said Devi Das beatifically, "the rickshaw driver is God in disguise."

The hotel God was talking about turned out to be a collection of bamboo huts on stilts, mosquitoes the size of bumblebees drifting in and out of holes in the tattered walls. I hung a tent of mosquito netting from the rusty overhead light fixture, then cowered inside it. When I lifted my mattress, three large cockroaches scuttled out from under it. The floor pitched like a ship at sea whenever Devi Das turned over in his bed on the other side of a paper-thin wall. At dawn, wood smoke began seeping up through the cracks in my floor; someone was boiling chai over a fire beneath my hut. When I pulled on my yoga clothes, they smelled like smoke and were covered with a pale layer of dust.

"No! Go away!" I turned and stamped my foot at the scrawny dog that was following me down the alley through the gray dawn light. "Go!"

The dog sat down and whimpered. Seated, it barely came to my knees; its fur, coming off in patches, was the same dull tan as the dust in the road. Its left eye was swollen almost closed, with a trickle of yellow pus coming out of the corner.

"I'm sorry." I squatted and patted its head gingerly, and it went into a paroxysm of ecstasy, its whole rear end wagging with joy, its mouth stretched in a slobbery grin: love! love! love! As it leaped up to lap at my face, I stood up. "But you have to go home." I bent over, picked up a rock, and pretended to make a threatening gesture. The dog cringed and shrank away, but its eyes still shone, in a weird combination of hope and terror.

I'd been wandering through the streets for over half an hour, squinting at the map I'd picked up at the train station—a map that seemed to bear only the most tangential reality to the city itself, as if drawn by mapmakers who had only visited it in dreams. As I picked my way down a potholed alley, I remembered what I'd heard about Vikas Kapoor: a yoga master in his late fifties who had been teaching yoga for twenty years in relative obscurity in the reform school he ran for teenage boys. Three years ago he'd been discovered by a Peace Corps volunteer who'd gone to the school to lecture the boys on safe sex. Now the studio he ran in the converted basement of his home was the latest mecca for Western yoga students. In a habit apparently carried over from his juvenile hall boys, his devotees all referred to him either as "Mr. Kapoor" (pronouncing the word *mister* with reverence, as if it were a title like *pope* or *king*) or, more simply, as "Sir." *It's awesome. It's the best of Ashtanga AND Iyengar,* one of his devotees had told me, when I grilled her about him after class back in San Francisco. *Sir will sweat you into a puddle in the morning. Then in the afternoon, he'll crucify you over a metal folding chair.* She said it with a tone of hushed excitement, as if being crucified over a metal chair by Mr. Kapoor were not just a privilege, but a thrill.

I'd made my way into what seemed to be a residential neighborhood: rows of houses jammed close together, most of them painted a streaky cream, with black mold growing up the sides. The occasional cow was lying in the shadows, still asleep. The streets were littered with scraps of plastic garbage, the only things the cows wouldn't eat: a bag, a water bottle, the rings from a soft drink six-pack. I peered at the map again, and turned down a random side street; although some of the streets on the map had names, there were no street signs visible anywhere. I paused to collect my bearings. Then, from a nearby window, I heard a familiar sound: the deep, throaty hiss of *ujayii* breathing. I'd found it.

I went around to the side of the house and stepped through a screen door into a dark basement room—already getting hot, although it was only five in the morning. The room smelled of sweat and the rotten-egg smell of *hing,* an Indian spice. The breathing washed over me: a rhythmic puffing, as if from a dozen differently pitched steam trains. As my eyes adjusted to the light, I saw that the room was packed with wall-to-wall yoga students, their mats lined up touching each other, flowing at their own pace through a series of poses they all apparently knew by heart. The men were stripped to the waist; the women were in shorts and tiny tank tops. After traveling through India, it was startling to see so much bare skin, as if they were practicing in their underwear. They glistened with sweat; they erupted in an occasional grunt or groan. In the corner, a young woman with tattoos lacing her arms was balanced in a handstand. Near my feet, a man tucked his legs into full Lotus, folded forward, and snarled.

In the back was a man I knew must be Mr. Kapoor. As far as I could tell, he was the only Indian in the room. He was a stocky, barrel-chested man with a shock of salt-and-pepper hair, every muscle in his abdomen chiseled. He was holding a balding man with a gray ponytail at the hips as the man dropped over backward. The student's face was contorted with terror and ecstasy in a way that looked familiar. It took me a minute to realize where I'd just seen that expression: on the dog I had just chased away.

Without saying anything, Mr. Kapoor looked up at me and wagged his head in a gesture of invitation. I picked my way through the students and found a place where there was a tiny bit of room to spread out my mat. The woman next to me shot me a baleful glance and scooted over three inches. I stepped to the front of my mat and swept my hands overhead, folding into my first Sun Salutation. I'd gone through this sequence a thousand times back at The Blissful Body. For the first time since I'd been in India, I actually felt like I knew what I was doing.

The physical feelings were so intense that for a while, they drowned out all thoughts, leaving nothing but the burn of muscle, the whistle of breath, the metronome count of the increasingly grueling poses. I'd do a thousand Sun Salutations, if I could just sweat Matt right out of my system. After yoga class, in the old days, I used to go over to his house. We'd roll around on his futon. He'd lick the sweat off my neck. I'd bite his arm. *Upward Dog. Downward Dog. Breathe. Focus.*

A shadow fell over me, and I opened my eyes. Mr. Kapoor was getting down on his knees behind the young woman to my right, who was folded over her legs in a seated forward bend. He straddled her and sat down, thrusting his groin against the base of her spine, then draped the whole length of his body against her sweat-soaked back. She let out a low, throaty moan, a strange mingling of pain and pleasure, like someone having an orgasm while lying on a bed of red-hot nails.

•   •   •

"MINIMUM STAY IS one month," Mr. Kapoor said flatly.

Class was finished, and we were sitting in a pair of flowered armchairs in his tiny upstairs living room, where I'd come to register and explain my mission. Both of us were sipping chai, milky and sweet, from china cups. I was nibbling on a lump of butter and sugar that tasted as if it had been soaked in formaldehyde. Mr. Kapoor had changed into a traditional Indian kurta, but his barrel chest still swelled powerfully; he seemed too large for his chair. The teacup looked absurdly fragile in his immense hand. On the wall behind him was a framed picture of himself standing with his arm around— could that possibly be *Paris Hilton?*

"But Sir, I can't stay for one month. That's what I've been saying. I can only stay for a couple of weeks. I have to go to many places researching spiritual teachings. This is just one of them."

He set down his cup and glowered at me. "You are like a man looking for water in the desert. He digs one hole here, six inches deep. No water. Digs over there, six inches, no water. He digs many, many, many holes and never finds water. He dies thirsty."

I nodded, panic welling up inside me. "But . . . I am making a map so other people can find water."

"Oh! You are a mapmaker! So you will die thirsty, but your map—all done. It is for this you have traveled twelve thousand miles?" He slammed his hand against the table so hard the teacups rattled in their saucers. "Last week, I asked a yoga student why she had come to India. To know God, she told me. I asked a few more questions and she told me that her boyfriend had broken up with her. So now she is in India, with the mala beads around her neck. As soon as she has a new boyfriend, pah! The search for God will be over. I ask you—is that how it is for you, too?"

"Oh no! Not at all! Of course I'll stay for a month!"

"Pah! You can stay for three weeks, not one day more than that. This is a place for people who want to find God in their bodies! It is not for people who want to put God in their books!" He leaned back in his chair and regarded me fiercely from under his bushy white eyebrows. "But—you will pay for one month. Be grateful that I do not charge you double."

Oh well, I could stay; that was the important thing. I pulled out my daypack and handed over a wad of rupees. Maybe he really was the richest man in the city.

When I stepped out into the street, the sun hit me like a furnace. I blinked in the glare. My muscles were already starting to throb; I'd be sore this afternoon. A cow was dozing in the shade of the building with a crow on its back, pecking at bugs on its skin; another crow hopped by its face, feeding on something in its nostril. A third was roosting on its head, but every time it pecked, the cow gracefully inclined its head forward, like royalty bowing to the populace, and the bird fluttered off.

As I started down the street, I heard a whimper and looked down to see the dog, trotting after me in a cloud of dust. I turned around. It sat down and gave me an ingratiating grin, its tongue lolling out.

I thought of the dogs I used to walk back at Doggie Day Care— locked alone all day in luxury apartments, except for the brief, ecstatic hour that I'd take them out to chase balls at the park. One guilty owner had bought his dog a special DVD that he left running all day on a widescreen HDTV, featuring a rotating series of shows oriented for canine pleasure: *Let's Go Rabbit Hunting. Chasing Frisbees with Bob and Sue.*

Why did this little dog tug at my heart more than all the maimed beggars I'd tromped past, eyes averted, in the last couple of weeks? The toothless old women stretching out shriveled hands, the men with stumps of arms, the big-eyed children who banged on the windows of the taxi, pleading with me to roll down the window? Maybe it was because this was a manageable suffering—a problem I might actually be able to do something about.

I pictured myself bringing the dog back to my hut with me: washing it, treating its eye with antibiotics, fattening it up on scraps from my meals. I'd smuggle it into ashrams and temples. I'd fly it home to San Francisco, where I'd throw balls for it in Golden Gate Park.

*Remember, Amanda. You've got a job to do here.* I reached into my daypack, pulled out a packet of sugar biscuits, and emptied the whole thing onto the road. "I'm sorry," I told the dog, as it hungrily gobbled them up. "But that's the best I can do." Then I walked away fast, trying to get away before it came after me.

From: Lori647@aol.com
To: Amandala@yahoo.com

So who is this Devi Das guy? This isn't going to be one of your weird little flings, is it? He sounds like he might have serious psychological problems. I know it's hard to be all on your own but you don't want to get all entangled with someone who doesn't even have a last name, let alone a job.

From: Maxine@bigdaybooks.com
To: Amandala@yahoo.com

Amanda, Production is pressing me about art and design so I'm hoping I can get some sample chapters from you soon. If you haven't found enlightenment yet just leave that part blank, we'll dummy something in until you get it.

"ROLL YOUR FEMUR OUT!" Mr. Kapoor's voice boomed through the studio as he strode up and down the military rows of sweating students. His massive chest, covered with a pelt of gray hair, swelled over his shorts. "Now, from the head of the femur, draw the skin of the inner thigh down, down, down!"

After lunch, an exhausted nap back at my hotel room, and a brief visit to the Krishna Cyber Chai House to check my email, I'd returned to Mr. Kapoor's studio for the late afternoon session. No more sweaty, flowing practice; now we were dissecting each pose like a laboratory frog. I drove my feet hard into my mat, my arms and legs spread wide in the muscular geometry of Triangle Pose.

"Roll the right side of the navel to the right and move the left side of the navel toward the navel's center. Drive the armpit of the groin deep into the inner wall of the sacrum!"

Oh damn. Could I have heard that right? Where was the armpit of my groin? Was I the only one who didn't know? I closed my eyes and silently chanted a mantra: *Please don't let me screw up. Please don't let me screw up.* I was back in sixth-grade PE, flat-chested and scrawny-thighed, a phalanx of boys watching contemptuously as Mr. Hittle shouted at me to run faster in the fifty-yard dash. Mr. Spittle, we'd called him. No matter where you were injured—a sprained wrist, a bloody nose—he put ice on your crotch, a phenomenon we were all afraid to comment on lest he ice it again.

"Now draw back the left armpit groin toward the tailbone to rotate the legs in the other direction!" I turned my feet, hoping my armpit groin was doing the right thing. The tiny studio was sweltering, despite the two standing fans that blew a current of steamy air across it. Nausea rolled through me. *Heat is good. Back in the States, you pay extra for hot yoga.* I could smell the armpits of the man next to me, the chilies on his breath. My stomach heaved. *Oh, God. I'm going to throw up.* I lifted halfway out of the pose, willing my stomach to stay steady, praying for invisibility. But in a flash Mr. Kapoor was beside me.

"Why are you stopping the yoga pose? Did I give instructions to stop the yoga pose?"

"No. I'm sorry." I stood all the way up, nausea drowned out by sheer terror. "I was just feeling a little sick."

" 'Just' is incorrect understanding!" he roared. "If you are yogi, you understand this: Everything is karma. Every action has a consequence. You must pay attention!" He pointed at my stomach. "This nausea—this is simply your lack of attention, your ignorance, taking physical form. This is what karma is. Mind goes dull, actions go dull, bad food gets eaten, poses are practiced incorrectly, stomach gets sick. You understand?"

"Yes, Sir," I said, faintly.

He looked at me, then shook his head. "You understand nothing." He gestured to the wall of props. "Go get two wooden blocks, a sandbag, a strap, and a bolster. Healing the stomach can happen in a couple of hours. Maybe in forty or fifty years, your mind will heal, too."

## Enlightenment for Idiots: Sample Chapter Draft

If you're lucky enough to find your way to a class with Mr. Vikas Kapoor—the rising yoga star who's been turning heads from Hollywood to the Upper East Side—congratulations! Located in the heart of a charming modern city in beautiful southwestern India, the Kapoor Institute is just the place to get your quest for enlightenment off to a rousing start!

Virtually unknown in the Western yoga world until recently, Mr. Kapoor claims on his website, www.topyogamaster .com, that his years of teaching delinquent boys have uniquely prepared him for the challenges of teaching Western yoga students. ~~Although some may find his personal style over-bearing~~

~~If you're having difficulty achieving an enlightened armpit~~

~~I can't believe Matt hasn't emailed me yet. I know this is what we decided, but still I thought~~

[REST OF PAGE ILLEGIBLE DUE TO CHAI SPILLED ON NOTEBOOK.]

"I THINK MY kundalini woke up this morning in Urdhva Dhanurasana," said the slim blonde woman in the red thong bikini.

"How could you tell?" asked the guy in the Speedo who was rubbing coconut sunscreen on her back.

"I felt this throbbing, this intense throbbing, right here." She touched the base of her sacrum, just between the perfect globes of her buttocks. "And then it ran up my spine like electricity—like, oh God. And all day long, I've just been in this state of total bliss."

I was lying with five or six yoga students on the warm cement by the swimming pool in back of the Ashok Hotel, the most expensive hotel in the city, favored by international business travelers. Few of the yoga students stayed here, but it was a ritual to come here every afternoon, order Coke or lemonade, and cool off in the pool until it was time to go back for the afternoon yoga session. A green lawn surrounded the pool. Parasols shaded tables from the blazing sun. The concrete was baking hot, the water cool and blue. By the water's edge sat two Japanese men in navy-blue swim trunks, talking on cell phones. The only Indians in evidence were the waiters, waiting discreetly in the shadows in white cotton uniforms.

"Does it strike you as at all odd that we're drinking sodas and swimming in a pool, while just outside those gates people are dying because they don't have enough to eat?" I asked the woman in the red bikini. I was trying to force myself to gather material for my book, when really my whole body yearned just to lie in the shade and sleep. I wondered where Devi Das was. He left me alone most of the days—to focus on my work, he said. "Yoga class is not really our scene, anyway," he said cheerfully. "There is a yogi living under a tree a few miles away who can drag a jeep twenty feet using just a rope tied around his penis. We find that more accessible." I was beginning to worry that this wasn't my scene, either. Many of these people had been here for months, even for years. By comparison, I was a dilettante, a window shopper not worth investing time in. My bathing suit, borrowed from the yoga student in the hut next to mine, made it clear that I was bulgy in places that shouldn't bulge and not bulgy in places that should. I had forgotten to bring a razor, and curly strands of hair hung out along my bikini line. Somehow I hadn't envisioned bikini-line maintenance being part of my spiritual pilgrimage.

"Karma," the woman said. "It's all karma." She rolled over on her back, lifted a long, brown leg into the air, drew it behind her head, and rested her neck in the crook of her knee. "I spent many lifetimes serving others. This is the life where I get to focus on my own spiritual development."

The heavyset woman on the other side of me looked at her with hostility badly disguised as admiration. "Jesus, I wish I could do that. I'll never be able to do that."

She smiled reassuringly and hooked the other leg behind her neck: Supta Kurmasana, Reclining Tortoise Pose. "Not in this lifetime, maybe. But it's like Sir says. 'Keep doing your practice, and all doors will open.'"

I envied her clarity that this was the right path, that there was no other. I had never been that certain about anything in my life, and—

lying here by the swimming pool, sucking on ice cubes—I wanted to be. *Maxine, I've been in India three weeks and I've already found the true path. Please send the rest of my advance. I will be staying here at the Ashok Hotel, drinking lemon Cokes and writing my bestselling guidebook.*

I closed my eyes, feeling sick again. I didn't have the right clothes to be here. I didn't have the right attitude. I didn't even have the right yoga props. All the other yogis had given up their American latex sticky mats and were practicing on scratchy blankets woven out of jute fiber. "I've been meaning to ask." I summoned the courage to break into the conversation. "Where do you all get those wonderful yoga blankets?"

"Aren't they fabulous?" the blonde responded. "They only cost a couple of dollars. We get them at the jail downtown. The prisoners weave them."

IN. OUT. In the dim dawn practice room—already hot—the sound of my breath whistled in my ears, joining the other yogis in their sibilant chorus. I spread my legs wide and folded forward between them, hooking my legs over my shoulders. Kurmasana: Tortoise Pose. It had always been a struggle for me before. But the heat and the punishing workouts seemed to be paying off. My body was melting like butter.

I was halfway through my second week with Mr. Kapoor, and I was having the best yoga session of my life. Waves of pleasure rippled up my spine. There was nothing in my mind but the hum of the breath, the quivering animal sensation of muscles stretching and flexing. Every nerve quivered with bliss. *This is it. I'm finally getting it. The yogis are right—it's beyond words. I can't wait to write about it.*

*In, out. Breathe. Flow.* I folded one leg up on my thigh into half lotus, then crossed the other one over it. I reached around behind my back, crossing one arm over the other, straining to reach my toes. I'd never been able to do it before. But now it was almost within my grasp. *Almost there, almost there* . . . "Lower!" cracked Mr. Kapoor's voice in my ear. "Your legs must go lower. Your legs must touch the ground." He sat behind my back and leaned his chest against my spine. His hands pushed down, hard, on my knees.

*Aaaaaa.* I yelped, involuntarily, as pain sliced through my left knee, with an audible pop. Mr. Kapoor gave my arms a tug and my hands clasped around my feet. *Got it!* "Now you are master of your body," he said, triumphant. He moved on. I straightened out my leg, feeling the pain radiate through it. When I stood up, it buckled beneath me.

BACK AT THE swimming pool, the consensus was clear: "If you are injured, it's not the fault of the practice. It's your own karma from previous lives."

"You should be grateful," said the blonde woman, whose name, I had learned, was Claire. She rolled over onto her back and pulled the straps of her swimsuit down to tan her cleavage. "Your impurities are coming to the surface. That means they're on their way out."

I massaged my knee gingerly. "I can hardly walk. I don't know how I'm going to carry my backpack."

"But it's worth it!" said Jamie, the guy in the Speedo. "You got your hands to your feet in full Lotus! Did you ever do that before?" There was a note of approval in his tone that had never been there before: I was wounded. Now I was in the club.

"Never," I admitted.

"The pain is probably just your body telling you that it wants you to stay longer," said Claire. It sounded almost like an invitation.

"Maybe you're right." Despite the pain in my knee, my body still pulsed with the pleasure of the morning practice. Or was it just the feeling of belonging that was so intoxicating? Either way, it didn't matter. I lay back on my back and closed my eyes, the sun a red glare through my eyelids. I was a decorated veteran of the spiritual wars. I was happy. *And what's great about this happiness is that it's coming from the inside! It doesn't need any outside validation! I can't wait to tell Maxine.*

After I left the pool, I wove through the traffic on my bike, almost crashing into a herd of pigs making their way across the street. Each time I pressed the left pedal, pain shot through my knee. *Who needs a meniscus, when I'm almost enlightened?* I pulled up to the Krishna Cyber Chai Shop, locked my bike to a rusty railing, and ducked inside to zap off an email.

I got there just as a burly Australian woman was leaving, her face streaked with tears. I recognized her from yoga class, where she'd been struggling—her shoulders were tight and she couldn't do backbends. I wanted to ask how she was doing, but I refrained. There was an unspoken etiquette at these places, where you were dipping into your private life in such a public forum—a place where your whole past was eerily accessible yet so far away. It seemed better just to look the other way.

I sat down at the computer and began hastily composing an email.

> Dear Maxine—I just want to let you know that I'm really getting the hang of this enlightenment thing! It turns out you don't have to meditate or pray or anything like that. You just have to breathe and sweat and get your body in the right alignment. I did hurt my knee a tiny bit this morning, but it's nothing serious. Anyway, I just wanted to let you know that you don't have to worry. At this rate, I'll get the book written in a couple of months.

I hit Send. Then I checked my Inbox.
And felt enlightenment evaporate.

# Anne Cushman

From: Lori647@aol.com
To: Amandala@yahoo.com

Maybe I shouldn't tell you this, but I'm going to anyway: The other day Joe and I went to lunch at Café Gratitude and we ran into Matt. He was with a girl, no one I've seen before—long red hair, blue eyes, lots of tattoos. He told us she was a model for an ad he was shooting. She was looking at him like he was God. They were sharing an I Am Sensual smoothie with only one straw.

I'm only telling you this because knowing you, you're still hoping that he's going to miraculously turn into some other kind of person and that you'll be able to get back together and do the whole thing all over again. So I'm here to remind you: It's over.

*Do your practice, and all is coming.*

—K. Pattabhi Jois (1915– )

# CHAPTER 9

P RESS THE TIPS of your elbows toward the floor! From the roots of your arms, reach into the space between the third and fourth finger!"

I was arched backward over the seat of a metal folding chair, my feet pressed into the baseboard of the wall, squeezing a foam block between my thighs. My arms were reaching back over my head, elbows pressing toward the floor, hands straining to reach the legs of the chair. *I thought Matt hated Café Gratitude,* I was thinking. *Besides, I thought he was in Mexico.* "Now draw the skin of your left shoulder in toward the third thoracic vertebrae. Swallow the energy of your throat down to your kidney. Inflate the kidneys with breath! Inflate! Inflate!"

The edge of the metal chair dug into my back. My knee throbbed. Where exactly were my kidneys, anyway? *What kind of an ad was he shooting? Probably Victoria's Secret.* Trying not to whimper,

I sneaked a glance at the yogini on the chair next to me, a slender woman whose turquoise tank top and perfect poses I'd been envying all morning. She was thin and flexible, with mile-long legs and a jet-black ponytail. She arched in a graceful curve over the chair seat; even upside down, her chiseled features were exquisite. Her eyes were closed; her face was taut in concentration. I had no doubt that her kidneys were inflated. I felt the sudden, intense urge to yank her chair out from under her.

After class, the other students left in packs to have dinner at a restaurant down the street. I could overhear scraps of conversation: earnest debates on whether the head of the femur rotates outward, or inward, when you do Revolved Triangle Pose; debates on whether it was all right to do a Headstand on the very last day of your period. The black-haired goddess who'd been practicing next to me had slipped into a long, flowing dress; she walked off with a man who looked like a Calvin Klein underwear model. *Of course. They're probably a couple. They have this great, spiritual relationship, like Shiva and Shakti. After dinner, they're going to go back to their hotel and have excellent, precisely aligned sex involving lots of straps and blocks and a folding chair.*

The heat felt like an animal wrapped around me. The yoga seemed to have upset my stomach again; I was too nauseated to eat, too nauseated even to talk. I began limping back toward my hotel, my knee throbbing. After the precision of the yoga class, the world felt broken down into precise units of awareness, their intensity almost too much to bear: the traffic not just traffic, but rickshaws, trucks, a bicycle laden with bamboo, a donkey with a dead goat flung over its back. Garbage along the street not just generic trash, but banana peels, orange peels, discarded coconut husks, plastic bags, sanitary napkins, cigarette cartons, and a spotted dog rooting through it all, looking for dinner. The sounds not an undifferentiated din, but bird calls, rickshaw roars, the constant *tonk-tonk* of a bird pecking a tree.

Back in my bamboo hut, I lay down on my bed and sipped water from a plastic bottle, hoping my stomach would settle down. The sounds from outside were penetrating but not disturbing, as if they were happening inside my own head: the clanging of a metal bucket, the barking of dogs, voices raised in a shouted, incomprehensible argument, the roar of traffic. My body was lit up in my awareness, little muscles I didn't even know I had had proclaiming their existence. Some other body, perhaps, could be the doorway to enlightenment; surely not this one. I'd inherited my mother's thin, wiry frame, without an ounce of extra padding. But there were parts of it that were not my mother's; the delicate hands, for instance, with the long, nail-bitten fingers. "You have your father's hands," my mother had told me once, looking at them as I washed the dishes. "What do you mean?" I'd asked, grasping for scraps of information. For a moment, I hoped a door would swing open, and she would tell me everything about him: how he laughed. The sound of his voice. The way he put those long hands on her belly, feeling me kick. But a dish slipped through my soapy fingers and smashed on the floor. "Goddamn it," my mother said. "That's just like him, too. He broke everything he touched."

Another wave of nausea passed through me. It must be the water. I had been religiously drinking nothing but the ubiquitous Bisleri water in plastic bottles, but I didn't trust it. Earlier that day, one of the yoga students had told me that someone had tested the Bisleri and "the E. coli count was so through the roof, you might as well be drinking toilet water." Was this just a traveler's myth? I stared at the bottle by my bed, envisioning small bits of fecal matter swimming around in it. After all, what was to stop someone from just filling water bottles with tap water, and selling them?

For that matter, what was to stop someone from filling yoga centers with fake teachings, and selling them, too?

*Her long red hair swirling around them, her tattooed arms around his waist.* I knew I'd never make it to the bathroom in the main hotel building. Instead, I leaned out the window of my hut and threw up into the dirt.

A FEW DAYS LATER, fifteen minutes before my late afternoon interview with Mr. Kapoor, I limped into his empty yoga studio. The fans lazily stirred the hot air. The room smelled of sandalwood, mildew, and sweaty feet. I sat down on the floor and folded into a forward bend, trying to center myself before going upstairs for the interview. *Breathe. Relax.* This was an incredible opportunity. How many yoga students would kill for the chance for a one-on-one with Sir? I imagined myself back in San Francisco, mentioning my interview casually over sushi after yoga class: *When I was in India interviewing Sir—yes, he's really quite charming when you get to know him . . .* At the pool after class that morning, trying to soothe my aching knee, I'd drunk a beer and fallen asleep in the sun. Now I was so sunburned that it hurt to bend forward. My head was throbbing. I closed my eyes, trying to remember what I had wanted to ask first. Something about his own journey toward awakening. Where had he first—

"You journalists!" Kapoor's voice cracked from behind me. "You think that my yoga is not spiritual! But let me ask you this—where is the spiritual person who does not have a body? Show me that person!"

I jerked upright. "Oh, Sir, I know your yoga is very spiritual. I just have some questions about how—"

He sat down cross-legged next to me and leaned forward, thrusting his massive face toward mine. "Can you meditate without a body? Can you sing the praises of God without a body?"

"No, no, you are right." I fumbled in my pocket for my tape recorder. The interview, like everything else on this trip, seemed to have begun before I was prepared for it.

"Of course I am right!" he bellowed. "We are not here to debate who is right and who is wrong."

I pressed the record button, hoping I had put in a fresh tape. "So let's start at the beginning. In your system of yoga, how does one reach enlightenment?"

I seemed to be making him angrier and angrier. "Enlightenment? Who are you to be even using the word?" He slapped his hand against the floor. "You want to feel God. But can you feel the skin on the back of your neck? You want to know the Divine. But do you know your thighbone?"

Only the thought of Maxine gave me the courage to go forward. "But, Sir, isn't it a problem to fixate so much on your body, when it's going to grow old and die?"

"Old age! What do you know of old age? If you had really contemplated old age, you would not be talking! You would not be hesitating! You would be throwing yourself into the fires of practice. You would not be coming to the yoga shala with your sweat stinking of beer. You would not be sitting on the sidelines, asking questions: Is this the way? Is that?" He leaned forward, his chest swelling like a rooster. "I tell you this: At this age, if I let my body do what it wanted, it would fall into decay. So I tell my body this: I am the master. It will obey my commands."

"But what about when the body does not obey? For instance, my knee—"

"Your knee! Pah! That knee shows your resistance to surrendering to the teacher. If you are truly surrendered, injuries do not happen."

"So, Sir, would you say that in your system, the path to awakening involves controlling—"

"Words! Words! Only words." He stood up. "You will come to class. You will do your yoga. That is the only way to know anything."

That night, in my room, I sat trying to write by the dim light of the bare bulb dangling over my mattress. Mosquitoes whined outside my netting. My pen left inkless scratches on the page, then spurted enthusiastically, puddling blue blots on the paper. Given the failure of my interview with Mr. Kapoor, I wasn't sure what to take notes on. The women in bikinis slicing through the cool pool waters? My throbbing sunburn? My knee?

Abruptly, the power went out. The darkness was sudden and absolute.


THE NEXT MORNING, after yoga, I went out with Devi Das, looking for a store to buy a flashlight and some sunscreen. We walked down a side street that looked like a war zone—gutted buildings, dusty treeless expanses of dead grass. The buildings all seemed to be placed on the landscape haphazardly, as if spilled there from a giant toy box. All of them seeming to be crumbling at the edges, covered with a layer of powdery dust. I felt as if I were crumbling, too—the edges of my personality eroding, with nothing familiar to remind me of who I was.

Out of the smog on a street corner, a sadhu appeared, making his way through the bicycles and trucks, looking as incongruous here as if a pilgrim from *The Canterbury Tales* had appeared in the middle of modern downtown London. *Maxine, this is how India is—the past and the present appearing simultaneously, as in a dream, as if every civilization that had ever been on this land is still here, nothing ever thrown away, just built over.* The sadhu was spinning in circles, muttering to himself. His eyes were rolled back in his head.

"Is he okay?" I reached for Devi Das's hand, nervously, then dropped it, remembering that men and women must never touch each other in public.

"He's a *mast,*" said Devi Das. "That's a person who has given everything over to God—even his mind."

"He looks crazy."

"In the States, he'd be locked up for sure. But look at him, he is happy."

The man came closer. He had no teeth. His robe was in tatters. But his face was lit up in a smile, as if he'd just been given a gift he'd been waiting for his whole life.

"He is a divine lunatic," Devi Das went on. "But in India they believe an encounter with a mast is a blessing. Such beings have insight into ultimate truth, although they do not understand the workings of the material world."

The man approached, holding out his hands. Thinking he was asking for money, I began reaching for my rupees. But instead he reached his hands toward my belly, pausing with them a few inches away. His eyes came into focus on my face. He said something in a language I didn't understand.

"Excuse me?" I asked, stupidly.

He smiled again, deep folds crumpling into his cheeks. He put his hands together in namaste. "Ba-by. Your baby."

"Excuse me?" I asked again.

He bowed and held his hands toward my belly again. "Blessings on your baby," he said. His eyes rolled back in his head again, and he spiraled away into the traffic.

I looked at Devi Das. "What was he talking about? What baby?"

Devi Das didn't say anything. He just looked at my belly. Then he turned and bowed in the direction the sadhu had disappeared.

I looked down at my belly, too.

"Oh, shit," I said. "Shit. Shit. Shit."

*What greater calamity can a person suffer in this world than their own youth, which is at once the abiding-place of passion, the cause of dreadful agonies in hell, the seed of ignorance, the gathering of clouds that hide the moon of knowledge, the great friend of the God of Love, and the chain that binds together innumerable sins . . .*

—*Sringara Sataka,* AD 600

# CHAPTER 10

RAVELING ALWAYS THROWS off your cycle. I'm probably just late." I poked at the crispy masala dosa, a giant crepe stuffed with potato and spinach. When I'd ordered it, I'd been ravenous. Now the smell turned my stomach.

"Yes, that's probably it. I'm sure the holy man got it wrong." Devi Das took a huge bite of his dosa and chewed. A little sauce dribbled out the corner of his mouth. "What he meant to say was 'Blessings on your late menstrual cycle.' But his English wasn't good enough."

I closed my eyes for a moment, too anxious and exhausted to

answer. We were in a little restaurant a few blocks away from our hotel—if "blocks" could be used to describe the maze of rutted alleys jammed with randy goats and rusted bicycles. If "restaurant" could be used to describe this one room that looked like a converted garage, with a pitted cement floor and a few wooden tables and a gas stove in the back with a mustached man cooking on an iron skillet. If "we" could be used to describe this random pairing of me with Devi Das, a sadhu with dirty dreadlocks and curried potato on his chin. My vision of how things should be was so disconnected from the way things actually were that I felt seasick.

I couldn't be pregnant. I just couldn't. It would ruin everything. Bail out on my trip, go back to California and have a baby? Find an abortion clinic in Mumbai? Go back to California and terminate the pregnancy, then fly back to India and get on with my quest for enlightenment as if nothing had happened? Abortion was common in India; I knew that. I'd just read an article about it in *India Today*. The article said that women usually ended their pregnancies late, in the fourth month, after they had determined through amniocentesis that their child was a girl. I'd seen the posters on the train, trying to convince women not to abort: "Your girl, Your pearl," they said.

I picked up my metal cup of steaming chai and took a sip—a sweet, comforting jolt of sugar and caffeine. Devi Das stopped chewing. "Are you sure you want to be drinking that? Of course, it's none of our business. But isn't it supposed to be bad for the baby?"

*The baby.* I set the cup down immediately, feeling a visceral surge of maternal concern: *Must not give caffeine to the baby.* "I'm *not* pregnant." Jesus. One minute I'm figuring out how to stamp it out so it doesn't disrupt my life. The next I'm tending it like a rare plant I've been trying to grow for years. And I don't even know if it exists. It? Him? Her? I took a deep breath, picked up the cup again, set it down without drinking any.

"What I've got to do is get a pregnancy test. Where do you get a pregnancy test in India?"

Devi Das licked his fingers. "We know of a little temple just outside of town where the priest will hang a red silk thread over your belly and tell you if your child will be a merchant, a saint, a politician, or a robber."

"You know that's not what I mean. I want one of those little sticks that you pee on and they change color."

"Those you can get at the pharmacy around the corner, the one where you bought your toothpaste the other day."

"Oh, great. It was bad enough going in there to buy tampons. The guy behind the counter couldn't stop smirking at me, like we had a fabulous one-night stand that I'm pretending didn't happen. Now I have to go in and buy a pregnancy test? He'll think we're married."

"Don't worry. We'll buy it for you, as soon as we finish our dosa."

"Okay." I looked down, poked at my own dosa some more. It had gotten cold; the edges shone with oil.

He looked at me. "On second thought, we're not that hungry. We'll go get it right away."

"Thanks." I almost burst into tears, I was so grateful. Watching him head out into the street, I wondered how often sadhus walked into Indian pharmacies to buy pregnancy tests. Would this be a first for this country? Probably not.


MATT HAD ALWAYS been very clear that he didn't want to have children. "I don't get how anyone could even consider it, with the planet in the state it's in," he used to say. Americans already gobbled up the lion's share of the world's resources. How could I even consider adding another person who in the course of a lifetime would consume acres of trees and rivers of fossil fuel, add clouds of greenhouse gases to the already toxic atmosphere? "Look at that," he whispered in my ear one evening as we were pushing a cart through the produce aisle at Whole Foods. He pointed to a mom maneuvering a double stroller past a huge heap of bananas. "What do you see?"

I looked: two red-haired toddlers in corduroy overalls. One of them was gnawing a bagel. The other sucked a purple smoothie through a plastic straw. The mom was talking on her cell phone. "They don't have the wild salmon, just the farm raised," she was saying. "Do you still want it, or should we go with the sea bass instead?"

"I see a pretty normal family," I said. We were planning a stir-fry for dinner; I put a handful of shiitake mushrooms in a plastic bag. "A lot like the ones I used to nanny for, in fact."

"I don't. I see three big fat mindless consumption units. How many cell phones do you think she's already put in landfills? Not to mention that she probably spent a fortune on fertility drugs." He put on a falsetto voice, held an imaginary phone to his ear. " 'Honey, we can't have any wild children, because while I was busy kissing my boss's ass at a multinational finance company, all my eggs went bad. Shall we just farm-raise them instead?' "

"You have a cell phone, too." I picked up a Japanese eggplant, put it in our basket. "I suppose if it were up to you, you'd adopt."

"Yeah, adopt, there's an idea. You *forget* to have kids until you're in your forties, then you go off to Ukraine and *buy* one for forty thousand dollars." He put on the falsetto again. " 'Honey, let's get a Chinese one, that's where the smartest kids are coming from these days.' "

I looked into the shopping cart. Suddenly, none of the food looked appetizing any more. "Why are you being so nasty about this? It's not like anyone's asking *you* to have a baby."

"And why are you so touchy all of a sudden? It's not like anyone's asking you to, either."

I let go of the cart and began walking away from him. "You know what? I don't know if I feel like cooking dinner with you after all. Maybe I'll just head over to Joe and Lori's house."

He caught up with me in front of the vitamin counter, pushing the cart with one hand. "Hey Amanda—look. I'm sorry if I got a little edgy. It's just—sometimes when you talk about kids in the abstract, I get the feeling that you're actually talking about *your* kids. Yours and mine." The woman behind the counter looked up at us then down at her fingernails; clearly, this wasn't a situation where nutritional supplements would be helpful. "And you really, really have to get this about me. I don't want kids. I feel like I barely survived my own childhood. I don't want to be responsible for screwing up someone else's."

I nodded. I looked at our basket. Shiitakes, red peppers, spinach, tofu. We'd make a nice stir-fry together. We'd have great sex. Maybe he'd spend the night; maybe he'd even stay for breakfast. But by lunch, he'd be gone. "Don't worry. I understand."

MY DOSA STILL sat in front of me, cold and greasy. Devi Das sat down across the table from me and handed me a flimsy plastic bag.

"What did the guy say when you bought it?" I asked.

"He asked, 'She is American? Or German?'" Devi Das eyed my dosa. "Would you like us to finish that for you?"

"Go ahead." I stood up. "I'm going to go pee."

The bathroom was tiny and reeked of urine. The toilet was Indian-style, a stained porcelain hole in the floor. Maybe I should wait until I got back to my hotel. But I couldn't bear the thought. I had to know what was going on. Maybe everything would be fine, and I could go back out and order another lunch.

The pregnancy test came in a pink box with a radiant Indian woman on it, holding a giggling baby. *Her girl, her pearl.* I tore off the plastic wrapper and stared at the contents: a flat stick shaped like a thermometer, with a blank square on one end like a window into my future.

I squatted over the toilet and peed messily onto the stick. Then I pulled up my pants and waited, holding the stick behind my back.

Three minutes, the instructions said. I had no watch. Most songs, I'd read once, are somewhere between two and four minutes long. So I tried to do the chant we did at the start of yoga class—*Vande gurunam, charanara vinde*—but the familiar words had slithered out of my mind. Instead, I shut my eyes tight and began to sing the first song that popped into my head: *Well, shake it up, baby, now (shake it up, baby) / Twist and shout (twist and shout . . . )*. My mother had been a big Beatles fan when I was a kid. I'd ride in the backseat of the car on the way to preschool, sucking juice from a sippy cup and eating graham crackers, listening to *The White Album,* feeling the car awash in music and my mother's vast, unexplainable sorrow.

The door rattled and someone outside shouted something in Hindi. "In a minute," I called. "I'll be out in just a minute."

I took a long, deep breath. I pulled my hand out from behind my back and looked at the stick.


"Just remember, Amanda," said Devi Das. "You do have options."

We were walking back to our hut hotel, down a crowded back alley jammed with tiny shops, their wares heaped on carts and tables protruding into the road: batteries, bananas, fabrics, mangoes, magazines, cookies, small unidentifiable electronic parts, a partially disassembled ham radio set.

"Yeah, I know. I have great options." I stepped sideways to skirt a pig that was rooting around in the gutter, eating a wadded up athletic sock. "I can bail out on my book and go home and have a baby. Go back to waitressing, since I'll never get another assignment again. Or I can stay in India, get an abortion, and write my book on finding enlightenment and the perfection of every waking moment. Fabulous choices." The word *abortion* was jagged in my mouth. I wondered how often *abortion* and *enlightenment* got said in the same sentence.

Devi Das stopped by a fruit stand and began turning over the papayas, lightly squeezing each one. "Or you could stay in India, finish your research, and have your baby here."

"What, have a *baby* in India?" I reflexively picked up a papaya, too, although I didn't want one. It was firm and orange, streaked with green; the end gave slightly when I pressed it, a sign of perfect ripeness.

"Well, clearly some people do manage to do it." Devi Das handed a few rupees to the girl behind the fruit stand; she took them, eyeing me curiously. She couldn't have been more than fifteen. But her forehead was already marked with the turmeric powder that indicated she was married.

Another wave of nausea washed through me. I was sick of Devi Das, sick of India, sick of never being clean. My knee throbbed. "I've got to go lie down," I said. "I'll talk to you later." I set the papaya down and turned away. Our hotel was just a block away. I hoped I could make it without throwing up.

"Amanda," he said as I started to step into the street. "Just know that whatever you decide, we will be there for you."

I looked back at him, holding a papaya in each hand, his face grimy and damp, his red dreadlocks hanging past his shoulders. "Great," I said bitterly. "I'm sure you'll be a huge help."


INSIDE THE HUT, I lay on my back on the mattress on the floor. The ceiling fan hummed and buzzed, swirling the dust motes through the shafts of light from the window, but creating no discernible coolness. My breasts felt swollen and sore. Now that I knew what was going on with my body, I was astonished that I hadn't suspected before.

This was just a careless error, like a bounced check. If I had been a little more careful, it never would have happened. This was just a slip of the pencil drawing the picture of my life. It could easily be erased. One little side tour on my journey to enlightenment. No one would ever know.

*Just a clump of cells.*

Had my mother felt this way when she first found out she was pregnant with me? It was something I had never discussed with her. It was my father whom I had wondered about as I lay awake at night, watching the bars of light pass over the ceiling. But my mother—she must have had moments like this, lying in her bed, thinking, *I could erase it like it never happened.*

My mother, who never finished what she started, whose life had gone off the tracks and stayed there. I had always sworn that I would never end up like her. It was part of why I had come to India to write this book—to prove to the world, and to myself, that I was not a failure. That I was someone who could not only dream about great projects, but actually complete them.

My thoughts were becoming fuzzy. I remembered the pleading eyes of the stray dog, the desperate joy with which it had gobbled the cookies from the dirt. The heat pulled me down into a deep pool of sleep, and the room dissolved into dreams.

*I AM DOING poses I have never done before: dropping into effortless splits; balancing on my hands as my toes drop back to the crown of my head. The energy in my body is getting more and more intense; the yoga room is glowing with a brilliant light. I am on the verge of breaking through to something big, I can tell. But there is a baby crying in the next room, louder and louder. I try to focus on my breath, but the baby is crying so hard I can't concentrate. Finally, I get off my mat and go looking for it, anxious and annoyed—why is its mother not taking care of it? The baby is lying in a crib in a smelly diaper. I pull off the diaper but the child is still filthy—a baby girl, covered in poop.*

*I begin giving her a bath in a sink. She is giggling, waving pink arms and legs. But she begins shrinking, growing smaller, smaller, smaller. She is slipping through my fingers, the size of a bug. I try to pick her up without squishing her, but she slips through my fingers and disappears down the drain. I am weeping.*

*Mr. Kapoor is in the room with me. He pushes his face close to mine. "You understand nothing," he roars. "Without a body, how can you touch God?"*

WHEN I woke up, smoke was drifting up through the floor again. I reached for the belt that held my passport and money, fumbled around inside, and drew out the business card the Indian man on the plane had given me. It was already a little tattered around the edges. A. J. Rao, 159 Mahatma Marg, Bangalore.

His wife was a doctor, he'd said. She ran a women's health clinic. *"If you get into any trouble . . ."*

When I pushed open the door to Devi Das's room, he was meditating in the corner. He opened his eyes to look at me and smiled a beatific, gap-toothed smile.

"Guess what," I said. "I think I'm having a baby."

"Cool! We always wanted to be a daddy. Are we going back to California?"

"I don't think so," I said. "Not yet, anyway. Tomorrow we're going to Bangalore."

Anne Cushman

# Headstand
## (sirsasana)

*Interlace your fingers and place your forearms on the floor, touching the crown of your head to the ground as you cup your skull in your palms. Walk your feet toward your face, stacking hips over shoulders. Then float your feet to the sky, entrusting the weight of your body to the fragile stem of your neck.*

*Headstand stimulates the production of amrita, the drink of the gods—the nectar of immortality that drips from your third eye. In ancient times, the gods teamed up with the dark demons they most feared to churn this ambrosial beverage from the oceans. To drink it yourself, you too must be willing to befriend your demons, churn your soul, and turn your world upside down.*

*Be good, see good, do good.*

—Sathya Sai Baba (1926–    )

# CHAPTER 11

O F   C O U R S E , it's entirely your decision whether you want to go home or not," said Devi Das, swaying next to me on the hard wooden seat as our train rattled toward Bangalore. "But honestly, we don't see what the big deal is. We'll just take the baby with us to all the ashrams. We'll paint stripes on its forehead. It will be our little sadhu baby."

We were rattling through countryside straight from a Kipling story: banana plantations with thatched A-frame huts scattered amid the trees, the delicate green of rice paddies broken with red earth and silver pools of water. Occasional giant rocky hills loomed up, craggy and red, like irregular teeth. The motion of the train was making me queasy. I looked out the window, then down at the floor, trying to find a place to rest my eyes so I wouldn't throw up. "Devi Das? Have you actually ever *seen* a newborn baby?"

"Not up close," he admitted. "But we've seen some cute pictures of them."

"They cry," I said. "They pee. They poop a lot. Then they cry some more. They can't even hold their necks up. They're actually a whole lot of trouble."

"Taking care of ourselves is also a whole lot of trouble," he said cheerfully. "But we have gotten used to it over the years."

The train pulled into a tiny station and paused, huffing, as if it were just catching its breath before heading on. "Just a minute," said Devi Das, and jumped out onto the platform. My stomach tightened in a moment of primal fear: *Don't leave me! I'm pregnant!* But two minutes later he was back, holding two masala dosas wrapped in a large banana leaf.

"Look," he said as we pulled out of the station. He handed me a dosa. "There he is again." On a wall by the tracks was a life-sized poster of a dark, immensely fat man in an orange robe, his bald head gleaming, his hand raised in benediction.

"I know. He's stalking us." I took a bite of hot crispy crepe wrapped around spicy coconut chutney. "If this were a dream, I'd be thinking that it meant something." The ticket seller in the train station had been wearing that man's picture on a locket around his neck. His image had been painted on the side of a bus that had careened down the road next to the tracks. His name was Hari Baba, Devi Das had told me; he had millions of devotees around the world, who came by the tens of thousands to visit his ashram in a village about a two-hour train ride from Bangalore. He cured the lame, gave sight to the blind, and manifested objects from thin air with a wave of his hand: pens, statues of Hindu deities, *Star Wars* action figures, showers of flower petals. He appeared in visions to his devotees and told them what to do with their lives, their careers, their savings accounts.

"His followers believe that Hari Baba is an avatar," Devi Das said now.

I licked my fingers. "Isn't that something in a computer game?" In college, I'd briefly dated a guy who was fanatically involved in an online game called Lord of the Dance—a scrawny engineering major with dandruff flakes on his shoulders. His avatar, he'd told me, was a superhero with the ability to melt iron with his gaze.

"In Hindu mythology, avatars are human incarnations of the Divine. According to his devotees, Hari Baba can look into your heart and see your destiny. And then, if he chooses, he can change it."

"Do you really believe that?" I looked out the window at a group of women in jewel-colored saris, walking along a path by the train tracks, rag-wrapped bundles piled high on the tops of their heads.

"When we are in the United States, we don't believe anything. But in India, we believe everything. Things seem to work out better that way." He pulled out his Swiss Army knife from his cloth bag and pried the top off a virulently orange soda in a dirty glass bottle. He wiped the top on his shirt, then handed it to me. "So. How do *you* know so much about kids?"

"I used to work as a nanny."

"Wow. Was that before you worked as a dog walker? Or after?"

"During." I took a swig of the soda, shockingly sweet, and tried not to think about what kind of dye was in it. My mom once told me that when she was pregnant with me she survived on Slurpees and nachos. That would be a comforting thought, if only I felt like I basically came out all right. "That's how I got into it, in fact. The same people who didn't have time to take care of their dogs also didn't have time to take care of their kids, as it turned out. One thing led to another and pretty soon there I was, taking care of everyone."

"We don't understand that at all. Why have dogs and kids, if you don't want to take care of them?"

"For some people, kids are just an accessory. Dot-com orphans, the nannies at the park used to call them."

"So how long did you do it for?"

"Just for six months or so. I couldn't handle it. Both parents were lawyers downtown. They had a five-year-old boy and a two-year-old girl." The carbonated bubbles tickled my nose as I drank; my eyes started to water. "I'd get to their house in Pacific Heights at six thirty in the morning to help make the kids breakfast. I wouldn't leave until the parents got home in the evening—around seven thirty, on a good night."

"What did you do with them all day?"

"Sam was in kindergarten all morning, so I'd just take Tamara to the park. Then, in the afternoon, we'd all go on adventures together. You know, the beach. The zoo. Sometimes, when it rained, we'd just stay in and bake."

"It sounds idyllic."

"It was actually unbelievably tedious. I remember one afternoon I read *If You Give a Mouse a Cookie* aloud twenty-seven times. I could probably still recite it to you."

Truth be told, I'd been a marginally competent nanny, scrambling through my days in a sea of lost socks, spilled juice, forgotten lunch boxes, missed playdates. I routinely sent Sam to school in his pajama top. Often I was so bored and irritated I'd wanted to flush them both down the toilet. One afternoon I'd played hide and seek for about two hours, "finding" Sam and Tamara over and over again in the same obvious hiding place under the comforter on their parents' bed. I'd wanted to shout, "I see you, you morons! Your feet are sticking out! And there's a big lump on the bed, besides! What kind of a fool do you think I am?" I'd wanted to run screaming out of the house and into my future, that exotic continent of romance and adventure. So why now—riding a train through India, inhabiting the future that had been my fantasy then—was I suddenly filled with nostalgia? For a moment, it seemed that I would give anything to be safely back there, flattening peanut butter cookie dough with a fork.

"So why did you quit?"

"The kids were getting so attached to me. It was like I was their mother." We flashed past a yellow billboard with red letters proclaiming *Om Hari Ram. Help ever, hurt never. Hari Baba.* "When their actual parents came home, it was like they didn't even know them. Usually, Tamara was already in bed, anyway. But one day, they came home early, so I left when she was still awake. She started screaming and throwing her arms around me, saying, 'Manda don't go.' I was always there when she went to bed, there when she got up in the morning. Turns out she hadn't even known that I didn't live there." Outside the window, a white buffalo pulled a cart down a dusty road. "So the next day, I called in sick. And the next. At the end of the week I quit."

"You quit?" Devi Das looked at me, his dosa halfway to his mouth. "What about the kids? Didn't you miss them?"

"My days were numbered. I saw the look in the mom's eyes." *She stood there in her gray wool jacket, clutching her leather handbag, looking at her little girl weeping and clinging to another woman's leg. In the next room, her husband had already turned on CNN.* "If I hadn't quit, I'd have been fired. I'd rather be the one to walk away."

Devi Das didn't say anything. He had finished his dosa and was just sitting there, a stranger with whom I happened to be sharing a train seat, a spiritual journey, a pregnancy.

"Don't look at me like that. I was just the babysitter." Tamara must be six or seven by now; Sam must be eight or nine. I wondered what nanny took my place in their life. I wondered if either of them ever woke up in the night, crying, and wondered where I went. Or maybe they didn't even remember me. Perhaps my only legacy was a persistent feeling of insecurity, the nagging sense that it wasn't safe to count on anyone at all.

I'd told myself that I was getting out before I was thrown out. But in truth, I had been afraid that if I didn't leave then, I never would. I'd been afraid I would be sucked down into the quicksand of domesticity. The mother would sail away into her world of power lunches and power suits, and through some mysterious alchemy I would in fact become the children's mother, trapped forever in a world of spilled flour and leaky diapers and infinite hours spent pretending to look for what was hidden in plain view.

I put my hands on my belly and closed my eyes. Maybe what I needed was a nanny of my own. Someone just like me, only more competent, to raise my child and do my laundry while I got enlightened.

"Excuse me," lilted a fluty voice with a refined British accent. I opened my eyes to see a willowy woman standing in the aisle next to me, with pale skin, immense blue eyes, and a cloud of red ringlets around her face. She was dressed in a peach-colored sari, swirling around her, which made her look like Glinda the Good Witch. "I'm Ginger. Are you on your way to see Hari Baba?"

"No, we're not, actually," I told her in what I hoped was a polite but unencouraging voice.

"Then why are you on the train to Bangalore?" She said it as if the entire city of seven million people existed for the sole purpose of ferrying devotees to the Hari Baba ashram.

"Um . . ." I couldn't think quickly enough to lie. I glanced at Devi Das, hoping he would bail me out, but he was tipped against the window, his mouth slightly open, his eyes shut. He looked like a wilted dandelion. "Medical reasons, actually. We're going to see a doctor." Perhaps she would think I had a communicable disease and flee.

"Oh, are you sick?" She sat down on the edge of the bench next to me. "Baba can heal you. He is the ultimate doctor. My best friend went to him with thyroid cancer. She spent two days there and"—she snapped her fingers—"it was gone immediately. When she went back to the hospital, they said she didn't even *have* a thyroid anymore. If you stay with Baba long enough, all your internal organs turn to pure light anyway."

"Well, as soon as I go see the real doctor, I'll probably head up there."

"Oh, no, you must go right away." She seemed to feel that my hesitation was a personal affront. "Baba will only be there for a few days, then he is leaving to go into seclusion for three months."

"I'm sorry, but I really need to go to—"

"Here, take this." She shoved a pamphlet at me. She reminded me of the Jehovah's Witnesses who used to come by my house in San Francisco—earnest young men with short-cropped hair and wide eyes, dressed in suits. One of them had buttoned his shirt wrong, so it bunched up around his neck in an endearing way, like a toddler's. *You have a God-shaped hole inside you that only God can fill,* he told me. I looked down at Baba's bald head, his chubby, snub-nosed face. He reminded me of the pig in *Alice in Wonderland*.

"Okay. I'll think about it."

I began flipping through the pamphlet: "Sri Hari Baba is a spiritual master who inspires millions of people throughout the world to lead more kind and moral lives." Nothing to object to, there. "Sri Hari Baba communicates with all people heart to heart. There are no go-betweens between Himself and those pilgrims who yearn to taste God."

Maybe Hari Baba was the key to my whole book. I could go see Hari Baba, experience God, and then go home before I'd even hit the second trimester. I could get the rest of my advance to pay for the midwife. I'd be a fully awakened yogini with a bestselling guidebook and a baby. I'd bring my baby with me on my book tour, signing autographs with her slumbering in one of those denim frontpacks. *Yes,* I'd say modestly, *I had a little bit of morning sickness, but it all went away as soon as I got enlightened.*

The train was pulling into the Bangalore station. My knee throbbing again, I limped out of the train with Devi Das into a cavernous waiting room with dark mold creeping down the cinderblock walls. Off to one side I saw a restaurant with a dirty linoleum floor and wooden tables lit by the glare of fluorescent lights. I felt as if I would pass out if I didn't eat. I'd never known hunger like I'd felt since I got pregnant—fierce and urgent, as if the creature inside me were saying, *Get me food or I will kill you.*

"Just get some food into me and then we can take a rickshaw to the clinic." We walked into the restaurant and I sat down at a table. Weird how I had started to order Devi Das around as if he were my husband. He was probably more amenable to it than Matt would have been, actually. Matt hated the casual familiarity with which longtime couples treated each other: the way they'd sit across from each other in the corner café, reading different sections of the same paper, hair unbrushed, not even talking. Whereas I had always envied it. What must it be like to be so sure that someone wouldn't leave that you could stop entertaining them for a while?

Devi Das fetched me a metal plate of *idlis*—steamed rice cakes in a soupy orange sauce—and some lumpy, sour yogurt in a metal bowl. I ate it it greedily. High on the wall, above the door, hung yet another picture of Hari Baba, draped with a garland of plastic flowers. Blinking neon lights ran in circles around it. On the opposite wall was a neon Pepsi sign, also blinking. Were these twin emblems a sign I was supposed to go see Hari Baba? Or just a sign I was supposed to drink a Pepsi?

I swallowed the last bite of food, wishing there were more. Then a wave of nausea hit, and I wished I hadn't eaten anything at all. How could I trust my decisions about something as important as having a baby? I couldn't even decide what to eat. I could see the appeal of having a guru tell you what to do. It was permission to take your hands off the wheel for a little while. Eat nothing but bananas, they tell you, and you do. Don't have sex, and you don't. Stand on your head for ten minutes a day. Breathe through your left nostril before you eat. The path to liberation clear and simple ahead of you, the burden of doubt and responsibility lifted from your shoulders.

"Excuse me?!" Ginger was standing next to me, Tinker Bell in a sari. "You're about to miss it!" She handed me two slips of paper. "Here. I tuned into Baba. He wanted me to buy you tickets."

Suddenly, I was too weary to argue. Hari Baba. Sure; why not? Maybe he would shed some light on my situation. I looked at Devi Das. "Should we?"

Devi Das smiled. "Ram's disguises are infinite."

"HARI RAM, MADAME, but Hari Baba does not care about your book," snapped the Indian woman behind the scuffed wooden counter at the ashram's Public Relations–Foreigner Registration Office. She was a short woman in a white sari, with a birthmark on one cheek shaped like the palm of a hand. Her office was in a tiny lean-to just outside the massive iron ashram gates, where the three of us had gone as soon as we got off the train, at Ginger's direction, to register our passports and request a room for the night. I had made the mistake of telling the registrar about my book in the hopes of getting some sort of journalist's pass, perhaps even access to an interview with Baba himself. But far from endearing me, the information seemed to have enraged her. "Hari Baba does not need your publicity," she spat. "He knows that I am telling you this at this moment. He knows that you are here. If I expel you from the ashram for trying to compare him to other teachers, when he is in an uncomparable category shared only by the gods, that is his wish as well."

As I start to protest, Devi Das stepped forward. "Hari Ram, auntie. We know we are here only at his bidding. We expect no special treatment."

She looked at him hostilely. "Hari Ram. Ladies and gents must not associate together, unless they are family. You will be required to stay in separate buildings. You may not stand together or talk together or sit together."

"Oh, but we are indeed family. These are our sisters. They have come all the way from the United States for no other purpose than to be in the presence of Baba himself."

She grudgingly stamped our visitor's passes and handed them to us. "Hari Baba has come to help people realize they are divine. And to teach them to lead the good life. The joyful life. That is all." She spat the words out. "The miracles are not important. He doesn't care about the miracles at all. He only performs the miracles to attract people to God. Hari Ram!"

We walked out of the office. The street outside was jammed with beggars, holding out deformed limbs, lifting blinded faces at us, and crying out, "Hari Ram! Hari Ram!"—a phrase that I was beginning to realize could be used, at this ashram, to mean anything from "excuse me" to "glory to God" to "please give me money" to "screw you." "Hari Ram," I muttered, apologetically, filled with the usual mixture of guilt and repulsion, and we pushed our way through the ashram gates, flashing our pass at the uniformed gatekeeper.

The ashram, it turned out, was like a small city in itself—an enormous complex of temples and cafeterias and dormitories and apartment buildings, the whole thing painted in pastels of peach and baby blue and pale yellow, sweet as an Indian dessert. Towering over it all was a fairy-tale temple, with rosy-tipped minarets rising like giant nipples from buxom domes. The pathways were swarming with visitors, mainly Indians, although I caught a glimpse of the occasional Westerner as well.

"Should we worry about being kicked out?" I'd come a long way out of my way to meet Baba. I didn't want to be denied a divine visitation on a technicality.

Devi Das shook his head. "She doesn't care if we stay together or not. She only wants us to admit she has the power to say if we stay together or not. She is a junior devotee. This is the only power she has, and it is important to her that we acknowledge it."

"We must have compassion for her," Ginger said, flitting along beside us. "It's well known that all of the people who work in the for-eigner's relations office are incarnations of evil demons from the time of Rama. In return for their services, Baba has promised them libera-tion from their karma in this lifetime."

We made our way through the throngs of people to the lodgings we'd been assigned, a four-story brick building painted the fleshy pink of calamine lotion. We climbed the stairs to our fourth-floor room, a bare cinder-block box. There were no beds, just a few thin cotton mats piled in the corner. Through a doorway with no door, I could see a small bathroom with a squat toilet and a sink.

"Where's the shower?" I demanded, as if I expected Hari Baba to manifest a Japanese sunken tub with a wave of his hand. *If he's every-where and knows everything, doesn't he know that I'm pregnant? Doesn't he know that I need a hot bath?*

"Once you get to the ashram, it's not about what you want. It's about what Baba wants." Ginger pulled a mat off the pile, laid it on the ground, and began spreading her pale green shawl prettily on top of it. "Actually, that's how it is all the time. But when you're here, you realize that fact."

From: customerservice@HeyBaby.com
To: Amandala@yahoo.com

Thank you for registering with HeyBaby.com, your number one site for pregnancy information and products! We'll be holding your hand throughout this miraculous journey, offering you week-by-week updates on your health, your baby's development, and products that can make your journey into motherhood easier!

As the hormones increase in your system, you may be feeling queasy, exhausted, and all-around icky these days! Take a few days off work to lower your stress level, pamper yourself with a nice mas-sage, and ask your husband to handle the housecleaning (with a new baby on the way, he'd better learn how now!). If smells have you gag-ging, carry a small pump bottle of air freshener in your purse! Click below for special deals on scented candles, shampoos, lotions, and air-freshening spray.

From: Maxine@bigdaybooks.com
To: Amandala@yahoo.com

Hi Amanda, just checking in to see what sort of progress you're making on this enlightenment thing. I'm wondering if there's any way you could link it in to any kind of fashion or beauty statement. Like, what are enlightened people wearing this year? That way we could get some good promo coverage in Vogue and Vanity Fair.

## Enlightenment for Idiots: Sample Chapter Draft

Be sure to get to bed early, because you'll have to get up bright and early—well before 4:00 a.m.—if you want a chance to see Hari Baba! The mere sight of a being on this level is supposed to bring great spiritual blessings. Line up outside the gates to the temple courtyard, men and women sep-arately. At 4:30 a.m., the gates to the temple courtyard will open and you'll be let inside. Don't be tempted to sleep by the temple in the hopes of getting into the courtyard in the front row; the rows are selected to go inside in a random order to prevent precisely that sort of scheming. Ashram officials say it's all based on your karma from a previous life!

* * *

MY KARMA MUST have been neither good nor bad, because when Ginger and I filed through an airport-style metal detector into the packed courtyard the next morning, we were right smack in the middle of the crowd. I scanned the men's side of the courtyard, looking for Devi Das, but I couldn't see him. It was chilly; I pulled my wool shawl tight around my shoulders. Ginger and I sat cross-legged on the cobblestones, squeezed knee to knee with the people around us: a plump Indian woman; a couple of older women dressed all in white, talking to each other in German; a doe-eyed Indian girl, hardly more than a teenager, who was too shy even to meet our eyes.

Ginger handed me a scrap of paper and a pen. "You can write Baba a note with a question on it. If you are lucky, he will take it from you."

I looked skeptically across the sea of people at the stage in the front, where Baba would appear. "He'll never get it."

"But that doesn't matter. If you tune in, he will answer the question in your heart." She began to write. I looked down at my paper. I could think of nothing to say. *Dear Baba, Having a wonderful time, wish you were here. Dear Baba, Any chance you would consider putting a bathtub in every room?* Ginger nudged me again. "Just write," she hissed.

I start writing: "Dear Baba: Should I go back to California to have my baby? Or stay in India and seek enlightenment?"

A hum of excitement moved through the crowd, although nothing appeared to be happening. The people in front of us stood up. Ginger remained seated, but I stood, straining my neck to see: Was Baba coming? But no—the people in front of me were sitting down again. I tried to sit down, too, but one of the German women behind me had moved into my spot.

"Excuse me," I said, "but that's my seat."

"You stood up," she accused. "You gave up your seat. You must go to the back."

133

"I'm sorry," I said, meekly. "It's my first day. I didn't know what was happening."

"Yes, it's hard at first." She didn't move. "But you have to learn."

I shot her a dirty glance and crouched down anyway, squatting just above her sandaled foot. My knee twinged in protest. Music started to play from big speakers on the side of the courtyard—a lilting flute melody, Baba's theme song. A side gate opened and two devotees walked in, pushing Baba in a wheelchair. In person, he looked even larger than his photos: he must have weighed close to three hundred pounds. His neck bulged in folds of fat from the bald dome of his head. "It looks like he's gained weight," I whispered to Ginger. "No, he hasn't," she whispered back. "It's an illusion. He's always changing form. Sometimes he's large, sometimes he's small. Sometimes his skin is light, sometimes dark, sometimes blue. It's all just a game to him."

A buzz of excitement moved through the crowd. Everyone swiveled toward Baba as he rolled across the stage, occasionally tossing out handfuls of flower petals. Hundreds of arms reached toward him, holding out scraps of paper. "The marigolds come from nowhere," said Ginger. "See? No baskets. He just materializes them. See the sparkles in his hands? He's manifesting jewelry for people."

The whole thing felt curiously anticlimactic. I couldn't understand what all the fuss was about. "Feel the energy?" asked Ginger. Her eyes were closed. She was swaying from side to side. "Feel the divine power?" I closed my eyes and tried to feel it, but I wasn't getting a thing. "Mmm," I said, not wanting to disappoint her. "I do think I feel a little something."

But in any case, the event appeared to be over. Baba was exiting through a gate on the other side of the courtyard. Everyone was leaving. "Breakfast," said Ginger, and stood up. "Do you want scrambled eggs at the Western kitchen? Or idlis and dosa at the Indian one?" I crumpled up my letter in my hand and stuck it into my pocket, and we made our way out the door. "You see," said Ginger triumphantly, and pointed to the ground, as if presenting incontrovertible evidence of Baba's divinity. "Do you get it now?" Here and there, on the dirt, were the trampled petals of marigolds.

LATER THAT AFTERNOON, I stood in my bathroom, washing my face in the sink. I'd just thrown up again. Ginger had gone out to wait for Hari Baba's afternoon appearance. I had told her I needed to stay back and meditate. But instead I lay down on my bed. I was so tired of being filthy: lines of grime around my neck, clothes stained and unwashed, fingertips dry and papery, the soles of my feet cracking and brown. I pulled out my notebook and tried to write, but all facts seemed to swim in a sea of rumor. Hari Baba had founded schools—how many? Hari Baba had founded orphanages—where? There was a planetarium nearby—why? He occasionally rode on an elephant—where was it kept? There were five thousand people at the ashram today—or were there two thousand? Or ten thousand? Over Christmas, Ginger said earnestly, there were half a million—"and Baba fed them all." Where could I check any of these facts? Where could I go for answers?

I closed my eyes. Maybe I should go into town and buy a silk scarf, or a sandalwood Ganesha. I had seen some beautiful ones in a shop by the main gate. I pictured myself back at home, my room hung with embroidered silk tapestries, my Ganesha on my altar. *I picked them up at the Hari Baba ashram,* I am telling an admiring visitor. *He's a manifestation of God himself, you know.*

From a distance, I heard the tinkling flute music again: Baba must be making his appearance. I shut my eyes and tried to empty my mind and wait for Baba to answer my questions. But all I got was the sound of a whisk broom down the hall.

*The span of human life is a hundred years. Half of this is wasted by a person lacking self-control, because he sleeps stuporously in the dark of night. Twenty years go by in childhood, when one is bewildered, and in youth, when one is preoccupied with playing; another twenty years go by in old age, when one is physically impaired and lacking in determination. The remaining years are wasted by that person who, out of great confusion and insatiable desire, is madly attached to family life. How can a person who is attached to family life, with his senses uncontrolled and bound by strong ties of affection, liberate himself?*

—*Bhagavata Purana*, ca. AD 900

# CHAPTER 12

WE'LL HAVE TO get the blood work back to be certain. But judging by the size of your cervix, I'd say you are about nine weeks pregnant."

Dr. Gita Rao sat down in the chair across from me, looking down at the folder of paperwork in her hands. She was a young woman—in her midthirties, I guessed—with her hair cut short in a sleek, jaw-length style; her slim figure was concealed in white medical scrubs. Between the twin plucked arcs of her dark eyebrows was a red bindi: the cosmetic symbol of the third eye, the seat of the soul, the center of intuition.

I was perched on her examining table, still dressed in a paper robe tied together at the back; my skin was goose-bumped in the blast of the too-cold air-conditioning. A poster on the wall depicted a diagram of the female reproductive apparatus, with labels in Hindi, Kannada, and English. On a wicker bookshelf sat a pink plastic pelvis with a plastic baby curled in a fetal position inside it.

Dr. Rao's office was in a high-tech ob-gyn clinic and birthing center—next door to a six-story medical complex—that primarily catered to upper-class, educated Indian women and Western women living and working in Bangalore. Dr. Rao worked here three days a week, she'd told me. The other two, she volunteered for a charitable organization in the Bangalore slums, educating women on reproductive health and offering free medical care.

I'd poured out my whole story to her in a torrent as I lay on her table: the pregnancy, my book, Matt, Devi Das, enlightenment, Mr. Kapoor, Hari Baba . . . I hadn't realized how desperate I'd been to confide in someone, anyone. I didn't know what I'd expected—sympathy? Scolding? Advice? Cookies? But so far, her only response had been calm and clinical, as she drew blood and conducted my exam with cool efficiency.

"Are you feeling any nausea?" she asked.

I nodded. "A lot. And not just in the morning. It's pretty much all day long. I thought it was just the food."

"That will go away in a few weeks. Until then, just eat whatever you can keep down." She handed me a small bottle. "Here are some good prenatal vitamins. I wouldn't trust the ones from the pharmacy. Any food cravings?"

"Oh . . . buttered toast. Spaghetti." Actually, my memory was spewing up visions of all the food I myself had eaten as a child, as if accepting take-out orders from a younger version of myself: macaroni and cheese with hot dogs cut up on top of it. Grilled cheese sandwiches and Campbell's tomato soup. A casserole my mother used to make out of canned chili poured on a bed of Fritos, topped with bag of pregrated Kraft cheese. "Cheeseburgers, even though I don't eat meat any more."

"Well, treat yourself to anything you want. You can drop by one of the big hotels and get Western food. They have an excellent brunch at the Oberoi; I go there myself sometimes when I get a sudden craving for pancakes and eggs."

She plucked the plastic baby out of the plastic pelvis and began running her hands over its smooth, shiny head. "It is good to eat familiar food when you are carrying a child, at least once in a while. I remember when I was pregnant with my son. I was in the United States, in Boston, in my last year of my medical residency at Harvard. It was cold, so very cold! I'd never imagined that any place could be that cold. I was so nauseous and the only thing I could imagine eating were masala dosas, the way my mother used to make them, stuffed with potato and spinach . . . or idli with sambar. I'd go to the Indian restaurants and try to find them, but the spices were all wrong. I remember sitting in the cafeteria after my shift at the hospital, weeping, thinking, *I should just go home to India. Give up my dream of being a doctor. How can I have a baby in this strange land, so far from all of my family?*"

"So what did you do?"

"I finished my residency and had my baby there one month later." She gestured at a framed picture on the bookshelf, a smiling boy about three years old. He was wearing a crimson sweatshirt emblazoned with the slogan "Harvard Class of 2025." "It was very lonely and hard. But now I have realized both dreams: I am a doctor *and* a mother." She picked up a white wand, attached by what looked like a telephone cord to a small box with a speaker. "So now, would you like to try to hear the baby's heartbeat?"

"Can I really hear it this soon?" I lay back on her table.

"It's early, but it's possible, with luck and a little help from the Doppler." She smeared my belly with a cold jelly, placed the wand on it, and began moving it slowly across the surface. "You're very slender, which makes it easier. Listen—there it is. You can tell it's the baby's, not yours, because of how fast it is." From the speaker came a rapid patter. *My baby's heart!* My hand flew to my belly. I saw tiny fingers curled around mine; cheeks soft as flower petals; big eyes looking up at me trustingly. I looked at the picture of Dr. Rao's son. "So . . . do you think that I could stay in India for my pregnancy, just the way you stayed in America? Try to finish my book? Or is that crazy?"

She shook her head. "That decision I cannot make for you. It is yours alone. I can tell you what I know is important: good nutrition. Lots of rest. Regular medical checkups and good medical care. Reduced stress. A calm life. These are things you can get in America or in India, or not get in America or India."

Involuntarily, I glanced at the window. We were on the third floor of an office building; I couldn't see into the streets below. But I remembered the rickshaw drive over here, careening in and out of traffic with my hand clapped over my nose and mouth in a futile attempt to screen out the fumes. At our hotel last night, a blocked drain in the shower had flooded the floor of our room—when we complained to the manager, he'd sent an eleven-year-old boy to fix it, who had climbed out the fourth-floor window and dangled there, banging at a pipe with a hammer.

The heartbeat galloped on. Dr. Rao smiled at me, as if reading my mind. "Correct me if I am wrong," she said gently. "But I have heard that ashrams are often very tranquil places."

An ashram. Not a giant Hari Baba institute: a small, intimate ashram, just a handful of devotees and an enlightened master who personally guided their every movement. I closed my eyes, imagining myself in a nun's cell, white robes draping my enormous belly.

"For the birth itself, of course, you would want to be at a Westernized hospital," Dr. Rao said, as if reading my mind. "I can recommend several good ones in Delhi, or Mumbai, or right here in Bangalore. Or you could go back to the U.S. as the time gets near."

I nodded, but I couldn't envision it. Instead, I saw myself leaning against a tree, like the Buddha's mother. An oxcart waits nearby. A thunderclap splits the sky. My baby pops out of my side, takes three steps, lifts his chubby hand, and announces: *I am the world-honored one.*

From: Lori647@aol.com
To: Amandala@yahoo.com

I only have three things to say to you: (1) You're insane. (2) You're insane. (3) You're insane. I know how much this book contract means to you. I know how much your spiritual practice means to you, too. But we're talking about your BABY, for God's sake! Are you really willing to risk your baby's life—and yours, too, I might add—by having it in some second-rate third-world hospital? Not to mention, what if you get sick during your pregnancy? What if you get hepatitis, or parasites, or malaria, or dengue fever, or one of those nasty worms that starts in your stomach and ends up crawling out your nose? Did you know that a thousand people get killed EVERY SECOND in Indian traffic accidents??? You can't just think about yourself, any more. You've got someone else you have to take care of.

"So TELL ME again how this works," I said to Devi Das. "This guy is a kind of fortune-teller?"

The day after my appointment with Dr. Rao, Devi Das and I were seated in the backseat of a small taxi, making our way through traffic-clogged streets on our way to visit a swami who Devi Das informed me was a "palm leaf reader." Attached to the dashboard by rubber suction cups were three plastic figures with clownlike faces, which bobbed and flailed as we careened around corners: a trident-wielding Shiva, a blue-faced Krishna, and a beatific Jesus with a scarlet heart emblazoned like a bull's-eye on his chest. *Covering his bases,* I thought, as we swerved around a bus and through an intersection, horn blaring, narrowly avoiding knocking over a wooden fruit cart as one of our wheels lurched up onto a sidewalk. *On roads like this, it's probably a good idea.*

"He's not really a fortune-teller. More of an interpreter. Four thousand years ago, the story goes, God dictated predictions to a group of sages, who wrote down everything he said on palm tree leaves. The leaves have now been turned into a library full of books that are kept for safekeeping at this temple in Bangalore. You tell the interpreter the exact date, time, and place of your birth, and he will look you up in the palm leaf manuscripts and tell you what God said about you."

"A bunch of Indian sages took dictation about *me?* Four thousand years ago? That must have been entertaining for them. I thought Bangalore was supposed to be the Silicon Valley of India. Haven't the palm leaf interpreters all been replaced by websites? Predict your future at palmleafbook.com?"

"It sounds far-fetched, we know. But it's amazingly accurate. We went there ourselves, a couple of years ago. The interpreter told us that we were on a spiritual path that would lead us either to enlightenment or to insanity."

I looked at Devi Das. That morning, he had gathered all of his dreadlocks into a kind of topknot, which sprouted from the top of his head in an untidy fountain. "Gee, I wonder how he figured that out."

"But he said all kinds of other things that he couldn't possibly have known. For instance, the palm leaves mentioned our identical twin brother."

"You have a twin? You never told me that!" One Devi Das seemed improbable enough; I couldn't imagine a second one. "Where is he? Meditating in a cave somewhere?"

"He died when we were a teenager. We don't talk about him much."

"Oh, I'm so sorry." I didn't know what to say. It struck me that I really hadn't tried to get to know Devi Das very well, although we'd spent almost a month and a half together. I'd been so absorbed in my own drama that I hadn't even bothered; he was just the backdrop to my own adventure. "Were you very close to him?"

"We were inseparable. Even our own mother had a hard time telling us apart." We were paused at an intersection; an old man hammered against the window of our car, holding out his hand, one eye a red and oozing hole. "We had our own private language that nobody else understood."

*We.* Suddenly Devi Das's plural resonated with a new meaning. *Two red-haired babies, nestled back to back in the same crib. Two red-haired boys, flying model planes in a meadow.* "How did he die?"

"There are sometimes inaccuracies when translating from the ancient Sanskrit. According to the palm leaves, it was a chariot accident." He looked out the window. "Look, we are here." The cab had pulled up in front of a small, squat temple built out of brick and painted white. On the roof was a giant, crimson-painted statue of Shiva dancing in a ring of fire.

We got out of the car and Devi Das handed the driver a handful of rupees. I got out too, still fumbling for words. "I'm so sorry," I said again.

He looked at me the way my mother used to look at me when I asked about my father, a look I had learned to respect. It was a look that said, *If I begin talking, I will break into a thousand little pieces, and you will spend the rest of your life trying to put me back together again.*

"We don't think about it much. For us, it is as if it happened in another lifetime."

"ACCORDING TO THE palm leaf manuscripts, this prophecy is to be given to you on the day that your age is twenty-nine years, eight months, and twenty-seven days," pronounced the palm leaf interpreter. He was a white-haired man, dressed in the orange robes of a swami, as small and thin-boned as a bird. He perched on the other side of a rickety wooden desk. "So I see from your birth date that you have come to me on exactly the correct day."

"It's nice to be on time for once." I was starting to feel a little light-headed; I wished I had eaten in the car. There was a paper cone of peanuts in my backpack, but I was pretty sure it would be rude to pull it out and start munching while receiving a prophecy.

He nodded. "Indeed." He bent over a small bound book, crumbling at the edges. "You were born in a distant country, far from India. Correct?"

"Yes."

"According to the leaves, you have been born in India many, many times before. You have lived many past lives devoted to yogic disciplines."

Well, okay. Maybe this guy was worth listening to, after all.

"For most of those lifetimes, you were a man. And so you have had the opportunity to study with many of the greatest gurus of India. But in your last incarnation you would not follow your teacher's instructions. You ran away from the temple and became a merchant and householder. Because of that disobedience, you have been incarnated as a woman."

*Oh great. So this is my first time in a female body. No wonder I'm having a hard time figuring out how to do it.* "You mean, being a woman is supposed to be some kind of punishment?"

"Not a punishment," he said. "Just—a consequence." He peered at his book again. "Your romantic life has been . . . troubled. You have had difficulty forming lasting attachments. By the age of thirty, you will not yet be married."

I glanced at my ringless finger. "Um—how about by the age of thirty-five?"

"The leaves indicate that you are on the verge of a great change in your life. At the age of thirty, you will meet a great spiritual teacher. This teacher will be a reincarnation of the master you ran away from last time. This is why you have come to India. This will be another opportunity for you to recommit to the teacher you studied with last time around. But in this case, you must surrender completely. If you do not, you will miss your opportunity for enlightenment."

He leaned back in his chair, pulled out a handkerchief, and blew his nose so forcefully that I was afraid he would blow himself out of his chair. "Do you have any questions?"

"Do the leaves say where I will find this guru?"

"Unfortunately, the leaves are not specific on this point. But they do indicate that at the present moment, you are in India, and the guru is definitely residing in India as well."

"Um . . . Do the palm leaves say anything about . . . children? A family? A partner?"

He shook his head. "On the subject of marriage, the palm leaves are silent. But do not be discouraged. Although rare for a woman, the life of a renunciate is a noble one."

*Renunciate.* I looked down at my hand again. Ridiculously, I felt like I was about to cry. Outside, a rickshaw horn repeatedly warbled the first notes of the "Hallelujah Chorus." "Just leaving the palm leaves out of it for a minute. Do you *personally* have any idea where I might find my teacher?"

He frowned, then slid open the rickety drawer of his desk and pulled out a Palm Pilot. "There is one teacher I have heard good reports of. He has a small ashram in West Bengal, not far from Calcutta. For those on the path of purification, he is said to be unsurpassed." He clicked on his Palm Pilot and began scrolling through names. "His name is Sri Satyaji. I will give you the information, and you can do the needful."

## Lotus pose

# (padmasana)

*Sit on the ground and cross your right foot high on your left thigh. Now place the left foot over it, tucking it high on the right thigh. Greet the ache of your hips, the twinge of your knees, the knot of muscles that snares your breath in its trap. Let the stalk of the spine grow long from its roots in your pelvis to the floating blossom of your head. Close your eyes and melt the ice encasing your heart. Feel the wind of your breath blowing through your forest of muscles and bones. Notice how stillness is always filled with movement.*

*Celibacy is to a Yogi what electricity is to an electric bulb.*
*Without celibacy no spiritual progress is possible . . . Do not*
*think of the opposite sex. Do not look at the opposite sex. Look-*
*ing at the opposite sex will create desire to talk to them. Talking*
*will create a desire to touch them. Eventually you will have an*
*impure mind and will fall a victim.*

—Swami Sivananda (1887–1963)

# CHAPTER 13

A FEW DAYS LATER, after a sixteen-hour train ride, Devi Das and I arrived in Calcutta—a city so thick with smog that whenever I blew my nose, the tissue turned black. Plateglass office buildings loomed over festering slums. On a roadside billboard, an Indian woman in a Western yoga leotard leaned on a giant tub of "India's first probiotic ice cream." At an ancient Kali temple, we watched a Brahman priest jerk back the head of a baby goat and slit its throat with a knife; as the blood spilled on the stone floor, throngs of pilgrims tossed hibiscus flowers at the altar where the black-faced goddess towered with her red tongue hanging out. "Kali destroys our egos," Devi Das explained, as I backed away, shaking and sick. "She slaughters the obstacles to our spiritual awakening." Back in my hotel room, a generator throbbed outside my window. I lay down on my bed and pulled the blankets over my head, dizzy and nauseated and scared. *What am I doing here? I'm out of my mind.* It wasn't until later that night that I looked at the date in my plan book and realized that it was Thanksgiving Day.

"Sri Satyaji has decreed that we all wear white at his ashram, as a manifestation of the divine purity to which we all aspire." The white-saried, gray-haired British woman sitting at the desk in the ashram reception office eyed my bedraggled blue *salwar kameez* and Devi Das's brown robes as if we had showed up wearing nothing but thongs and nipple pasties. "Suitable white clothing is available at the ashram store for a minimal fee."

I nodded, too queasy to answer. Devi Das and I had taken an overnight bus from Calcutta, the roads growing more potholed the farther we got from the city. For the previous two hours, we'd lurched and swayed down a winding country road that was more dirt than pavement. The outside of the bus was streaked with vomit. Inside, it was crawling with cockroaches. Devi Das had slept, oblivious, letting the bugs crawl over him. But I had stayed on guard, flicking them off my bare skin with a shudder, stamping at them futilely in the dark. Just after sunrise, the bus had stopped outside the gates of the Satyanam Ashram to let us off; then it had rumbled away toward the nearest village, fifteen miles away. Now all I wanted was to get in bed.

"Men and women must stay in separate accommodations, even if they are married. Conversation between men and women must be avoided whenever possible, and any physical contact is strictly forbidden. It is best to avoid eye contact, as well, to minimize the potential for distraction. In the temple and the eating hall, men and women will sit on opposite sides of the room. Liberated from allurement, the mind is freed to concentrate upon the Divine."

I nodded again. Who was I to argue? If Matt and I had been practicing yoga on opposite sides of the room, maybe I wouldn't be in the mess I was in.

"After you have settled into your rooms, you will be assigned a job to assist in the functioning of the ashram, such as washing dishes, sweeping the meditation hall, cleaning the bathrooms, etcetera. When performing these practices, please remember that women are forbidden to touch Sri Satyaji's meditation cushion, his robes, his eating bowls, his laundry basket, his sheets, or any other of his personal items, which are all labeled with an om sign and may only be handled by his personal attendant. Sri Satyaji is very sensitive to energy, and a female touch on his personal items will cause him severe psychic distress, in addition to causing him to break out in a rash all over his body."

"That is exactly what happens to us when we eat cashews!" said Devi Das delightedly. "Sometimes our tongue swells up so we can barely talk." I jabbed him in the side with my elbow, willing him to shut up. The next bus wouldn't pass until tomorrow morning. If we got thrown out of here, we'd be sleeping under a tree.

"And please remember this: Women are strictly forbidden to enter the meditation hall when they are on their menstrual cycle." The woman looked at me accusingly, as if expecting me to demand tampons on the spot.

*Oh, that won't be a problem. I'm ten weeks pregnant.* I opened my mouth, then closed it again. Something told me that this was a fact I should keep to myself for now.


THE SATYANAM ASHRAM was a tumble of small brick buildings, nestled in a crook of a sluggish river that wound through a green valley lined with rice fields. After buying a white *salwar kameez* and a white wool shawl at the ashram shop—really just a walk-in closet in the back of the reception office—I made my way down a winding dirt path to a tiny building marked with the wooden sign WOMEN'S RESIDENCE HALL. A few chickens clucked and pecked in the dirt by the steps.

My room was a clean cubicle with whitewashed walls and two side-by-side cots with barely a foot between them. Bright sun streamed through a curtainless window. I would have a roommate, I'd been told, a German woman whose Sanskrit name was Darshana. But she wasn't there when I arrived, and I couldn't hold my eyes open. I peeled off my filthy clothes and crawled into bed between rough, clean sheets that smelled of basil. Wood doves cooed outside. I was asleep seconds after my head hit the pillow.

*IN MY DREAM, I've just given birth to a litter of kittens. I chase them around the hospital room, frantic, praying no one will notice they aren't human. Perhaps if I nurse them and diaper them they will morph into babies? But they won't stay still on the diaper table, and I can't find a litter box anywhere. Maybe Matt will know what to do. But where is Matt?*

WHEN I OPENED my eyes, the pooled sunlight was gone, and the ashram room was in shadows. I couldn't remember, for a few moments, where I was, or even who I was.

"You have been asleep for hours. It is almost dinnertime." The voice was crisp and curiously formal, with just the barest hint of a German accent. I rubbed my eyes and sat up, dizzy and disoriented. Cross-legged on the opposite bed sat a woman who looked about fifteen years older than me—and about twenty times more beautiful—plaiting a waist-length mane of golden hair.

"I didn't want to wake you." Her face was severe, with sculpted features and pencil-thin eyebrows arched over steely gray eyes. "But you were talking in your sleep. Who is Matt?"

"Just a guy I used to know." I pulled the covers tighter around my bare shoulders, looking at the white clothes I had hung on a hook in a corner. I felt at a disadvantage being undressed while she was clothed.

"We all have people from our past who haunt our dreams. But as we do the meditation, our mind purifies our ancient karma, and they trouble us less and less." She stood up, tall and slim as a model, in a white linen sari with bits of silver thread flecked through it. She must have had it specially made; I'd seen nothing so fine in the ashram shop. "The shower is down the hall, on your left. I will meet you outside after you are clean and escort you to dinner."

Darshana had been at the Satyanam Ashram for almost three years, she told me as we walked toward what she referred to as the "dining temple." Before coming to India, she had been the art director at a lingerie mail-order catalog in Berlin. But now she returned to Germany only once a year, to visit her mother and renew her visa.

"Don't you miss your friends? Your family? Your job?" I pictured her in a business suit and stiletto heels, a fashion dominatrix presiding over layouts of anorexic blondes in push-up bras.

"No. My former identity has been burned away in the fires of practice." We stepped into a small stone building that looked like a remodeled stable. "I have no interest in reclaiming it."

Inside, we took our places cross-legged on a brown clay floor, our backs to the wall, along with about ten or twelve other women—about half of them Western, half Indian. About the same number of men were lined up facing us along the opposite wall. I sneaked a peek at Devi Das, outfitted in what looked like a pair of white pajamas, but he kept his eyes dutifully downcast as the devotees put their hands in prayer position and began to chant.

When the chanting was over, servers began moving down the lines of devotees, laying out a banana leaf and a metal cup in front of each person. I copied Darshana, keeping my hands in prayer position at my heart as women with metal buckets began walking down the line, ladling out food onto our leaves: sticky white rice, runny lentil dal, a pile of spinach, a scoop of yogurt. Another woman ladled water into our cups. "Don't worry," said Darshana, reading my mind. "All the water at the ashram is purified. Just as we will be, if we do the practices correctly!"

There were no utensils—I scooped the food into my mouth with my fingers, clumsily, trying to remember not to touch it with my left hand. (The left hand, Devi Das had told me, was for wiping after you used the toilet; to touch your food with it—or anyone else, for that matter—was viewed by Indians as not just rude, but disgusting.) "We follow a sattvic diet here at the ashram," Darshana explained, deftly flicking a ball of rice into her mouth. "No onions, garlic, or spices of any kind—nothing that will inflame the passions or agitate the nervous system."

*So that's how I got pregnant! Too much garlic!* I licked my fingers. I would become purified, and I would do it quickly, before anyone noticed that my belly was starting to get bigger.

The sun was setting as we walked back to our room. White egrets flapped over the rice fields. Somewhere nearby, a cow lowed. I could feel my whole body start to relax. This was a place where I could really make some spiritual progress. The next morning, I would start my meditation training. I would find inner peace, like Darshana. How hard could purification be, anyway?


"ENERGY CAN LEAK from any of the holes of the body—eyes, ears, mouth, sexual organs." Sri Satyaji sat at the front of the meditation hall on a stack of white cushions, his white robes draping over his folded legs. He was a stocky man with a black beard and bushy black eyebrows that met in a straight line over the bridge of his nose and leaped up and down as he talked. "It leaks through our inattention, our craving, our habits of distraction. The more it leaks, the less we have available for God realization. So we must control our habits to restrain our energy."

Sitting cross-legged on a cushion in the back row, I swallowed a yawn. Darshana had woken me up before dawn to come to the hall for morning meditation. Walking through the pale predawn light, my new white shawl draped around me, I'd felt uplifted and exotic, like someone playing a leading role in a film about spiritual practice. I could hear the sound track playing in my head: an Indian raga, or maybe something by Philip Glass. But now I was sleepy and hungry, and I desperately needed to pee. My knee hurt. Was there anywhere I *wasn't* leaking energy? A summer camp song began singing in my head: *There's a hole in the bucket, dear Liza, dear Liza* . . . Next to me, Darshana sat still as a statue, her eyes downcast, her thumb and forefinger lightly pressed into a perfect mudra, and her mouth curved in a slight, blissful smile.

"Gather your energy into one point, behind your third eye," intoned Sri Satyaji. "Now concentrate on the sound of *hum* . . . *sah*. *Hum* on the inhale, *sah* on the exhale."

*Huuum* . . . *saaahh. Huuum* . . . *sahhh. With what shall I fix it, dear Liza, dear Liza, / With what shall I fix it* . . . *Huuum* . . . *saaahh.* My favorite camp treat had been s'mores, toasted marshmallows and chocolate melting between graham crackers. My stomach rumbled. Darshana had told me that we were only allowed sweets at the ashram on special Hindu feast days. Maybe one was coming soon? *Huum* . . . *sah. Huumm* . . . *sah.* "Let the sound of the mantra quiet the waves of the mind, so it becomes like a clear lake reflecting the sun of the true Self." Sri Satyaji's voice was hypnotic; I could feel my head sagging forward. At least my morning sickness had subsided. I could hear birds chirping. I pictured my baby floating inside me, her tiny fingers forming a mudra just like Darshana's. Or *his* tiny fingers? *Hey. Suppose my baby is a boy? Is he sitting on the wrong side of the meditation hall?*

• • •

"YOU MUST LOAD the dung into this wheelbarrow, like this." Darshana lifted the pitchfork full of cow manure and with one deft gesture slid it into a rusty red wheelbarrow—a feat she managed without getting even a speck of it on her white sari. "When the wheelbarrow is full, take it out behind the cowshed and spread the patties in the sun to dry."

"To dry? Why?"

"We burn it as fuel in the kitchen stove. Here, you try."

I picked up the pitchfork and scooped up a steaming pile. *For our special today, we're offering a manure-grilled eggplant* . . . As I was lifting it, the fork tipped. Cow manure cascaded down my leg, leaving a green streak on my white pants.

We had finished our silent breakfast—sweet, sticky porridge drowning in boiled milk. Now Darshana was introducing me to what she called my "yogi job": cleaning the cowshed. The cowshed was a brick building with a packed earth floor covered with a thick layer of wood shavings and sawdust. Ten or fifteen cows wandered in and out at will, through wide doors opening onto a grassy field with a clump of cottonwood trees at one end.

I looked around the shed, strewn with patties of cow dung. It smelled of manure and wood chips. "Will you be working here with me?"

"No. My yogi job is vegetable chopping."

Perfect. I saw her in a clean sunny kitchen, French-cutting carrots into crinkly slices. "Any chance I can help you with that instead?"

"Cleaning the cowshed is actually a very sacred duty," reproved Darshana. She pointed to the wall, where a Vedic inscription was painted in red letters on the battered wood:

*The Cow is Heaven, the Cow is Earth, the Cow is Vishnu, Lord of Life.*
*The heavenly beings have drunk the outpourings of the Cow.*

*When these heavenly beings have drunk the outpourings of the Cow,*
*They in the Bright One's dwelling place pay adoration to her milk.*

I nodded. I had come here for secret teachings about enlightenment. Instead, I was going to be shoveling shit.

From: Lori647@aol.com
To: Amandala@yahoo.com

Please make sure you are eating lots of vegetables, especially leafy green ones (but cooked, never raw, because of the microorganisms). And lots of dairy products; make sure they're pasteurized. I've been looking into home-birth midwives for you; you can deliver the baby at our house. You need to stay as far away as possible from the medical establishment. Did you know that the rate of C-section in the U.S. is higher than any other country in the world, except South Africa and Iran? Oh wait, no, maybe that's the incarceration rate I'm thinking of.

From: Maxine@bigdaybooks.com
To: Amandala@yahoo.com

Interesting story in the *Times* today about yoga teachers trademarking the names of certain yoga postures. Very foresightful of them. I suppose "yoga" was taken centuries ago, but any way we can lock up the word "enlightenment"? Please look into it.

"PRAKRITI—MATTER—IS inherently unsatisfying," pronounced Sri Satyaji. "Only by discovering our identity with *purusha*, eternal spirit, can we find bliss. Confusion of *purusha* with *prakriti* is the soul's bondage; disassociation of *purusha* from *prakriti* is the soul's liberation."

It was almost noon, and the meditation hall was stuffy; I felt a thin trickle of sweat traveling down my spine. I was always hot these days, as if my whole body were an oven that had been turned on high to cook the baby. "*Purusha* = spirit = good," I scribbled in my notebook. "*Prakriti* = matter = bad."

"Disentangling spirit from matter is the path through which the soul can come to know itself. Meditation is the path by which this can be accomplished," Sri Satyaji droned. I pictured spirit and matter all tangled up in a wadded ball—like my hair, dirty and perpetually snarled, a matted frizz of *prakriti*. Whereas the goal of practice was to have hair like Darshana's—an untangled, shimmering waterfall of pure *purusha*. "Meditation = conditioner," I wrote.

By the end of my first week at the ashram, my days had begun to fall into a rhythm as steady as a well-ordered kindergarten. Up at dawn, for morning meditation. Breakfast of porridge, fresh boiled milk, and tiny, sweet bananas. Then off to clean the cowshed—a task that, to my surprise, had become my favorite time of the day. The shed smelled like hay, earth, and milk. The cows were small and dish-faced, with velvety noses and luminous, intelligent eyes, like deer. Sometimes I'd bring them scraps from breakfast—pineapple rinds, banana peels—and let them eat them out of the palm of my hand. Two of the cows had baby calves, still spindly legged and wobbly on their feet. Leaning over the edge of the fence, watching them suck, I felt a strange tugging deep in my own belly. What would it be like, to have a baby feeding off my body? I'd always been small-breasted. But now they were starting to swell and get tender, the nipples chafing against my bra.

Sometimes, as I wheeled the wheelbarrow out to dry the cow dung in the sun, I'd catch a glimpse of Devi Das on his way to his yogi job—weeding the vegetable garden just past the cowshed. We never spoke. But once, as I spread the patties in the sun, I caught his eye, and he lifted his hand in a silent greeting.

I wanted to stay with the cows all day. But, of course, I couldn't. After work meditation was done, I'd walk to the meditation hall for another lecture and meditation session with Sri Satyaji. These sessions were perpetually bewildering to me. I felt as if I had stumbled into a graduate course in quantum mechanics when I hadn't even taken basic arithmetic yet. Not only that, but I was expected to write a dissertation.

It wasn't that the teachings were terribly complicated. Day after day, they were variations on the same theme: restrain the senses from chasing after tastes, sensations, sounds, smells. Renounce the transient pleasures of the body; rest in the eternal joy of pure spirit. How could I argue with that? My life in the world had brought me nothing but trouble.

But the more I struggled to be peaceful, the more chaotic my inner life became. No one else at the ashram, I was sure, was secretly pregnant. No one else lay awake at midnight fantasizing about a lover who had left her and worrying about getting through labor without an epidural. No one else spent her meditation sessions imagining what she'd tell Oprah about enlightenment. No one else burst into tears when her wheelbarrow full of cow dung hit a rock and tipped over. Each afternoon, we'd gather with candles and oil lamps for puja, or worship. We'd stand in front of a white-draped altar, chanting prayers in Sanskrit, while the room filled with sweet sandalwood smoke and the music of a harmonium played by a Danish man with the face of an angel. And I'd feel as if I were locked outside in a snowstorm, looking in through an impenetrable glass window at a hearth by a blazing fire.

"When you meditate, does your mind wander?" I asked Darshana one morning. We were standing side by side in the bathroom, performing our morning kriya: a ritual cleansing of the sinuses that Sri Satyaji said helped prepare the body for meditation.

She shook her head. "Meditation brings me immeasurable bliss," she said. She scooped a cupful of warm, salty water from a metal bucket and poured it into her neti pot, a small spouted cup that looked like a miniature watering can. Then she leaned over the sink, tilted her head to one side, and poured the water into one nostril, letting it flow out the other.

*Well, goody for you.* I grabbed my own neti pot, leaned over the sink, and poured. The water tickled the back of my nose, and I gagged, coughed, and sneezed a spray of snotty water all over the sink.

Darshana was just too perfect: Her sari always clean, her face always calm, her movements always graceful and precise. Everything about her grated on me: the way she stood next to me at the sink every morning, cleaning her tongue with a metal tongue scraper. The way she sat next to me in the meditation hall, her straight spine a silent reproof to my own slumping and squirming. Every night, she changed into a lacy white nightgown, while I put on an old sweatshirt of Matt's, with his karate dojo's name stamped on it in Chinese characters. It was comforting to have it wrapped around me—the only piece of Matt it was safe to get close to. I'd drift off to sleep in its fuzzy embrace, listening to the soft snuffle of Darshana's snores—a small imperfection that I found somehow reassuring.

"I think I'm defective. I don't think I even *have* any *purusha,*" I whispered to Devi Das one afternoon, when I ran into him behind the cowshed. I was spreading the patties of dung in the sun to dry. He had come there to pick up a load of them to take down to the garden. "I try to concentrate on *hum sah* and instead my mind keeps playing that music from *Survivor* that means you're about to get voted off the island."

"We have the same problem," he whispered back. "But we keep playing cat food commercials." Both of us were trying not to move our lips and mouths, pretending to focus on the cow dung, in case we were being observed.

"So is this normal?" I patted the tops of the cow patties down with the shovel.

"We are perhaps not the best person to ask about what is normal. But we have heard it said many times that when you begin to purify the mind, all that comes up at first is the obstacles to purification."

"But that's what I'm saying." I looked down at the piles of manure, flecked with bits of undigested hay and corn. "I'm starting to think that all I *am* is obstacles. I mean, if you take away my thoughts and opinions and body and feelings, what's left?"

"Maybe that's what Sri Satyaji wants us to find out."

I was silent. My favorite cow meandered up, a brown heifer with glowing golden eyes and a sickle-shaped white spot on her forehead. I'd christened her Crescent, and secretly saved the juiciest scraps of papaya and pineapple for her. She butted her head against my hand like a cat, and I scratched between her eyes. Was this the *prakriti* I was supposed to be disentangling myself from? This world of cow, and manure, and pineapple? What about the child growing inside me, with its tiny beating heart? Earlier that week, checking my email in the ashram, I'd skipped over to HeyBaby.com. "Your baby has grown to roughly the size of a jumbo shrimp and weighs just an ounce," I'd read, while the British receptionist glowered at me suspiciously from her desk. "Despite the small proportions, there's a fully formed baby inside your womb now! His head is a third of the size of his body. His tiny, unique fingerprints are already in place."

"Devi Das?" The question came out of nowhere, fully formed, as if I'd been waiting all week to speak it. "Can you tell me more about how your brother died?"

Devi Das leaned on his pitchfork. He was silent for a long time. "We had both just gotten our driver's licenses," he finally said. He wasn't whispering any more. "We tossed a coin to see who got to drive to the swimming pool. I won." Outside the meditation hall, the bell had begun to ring, calling us to afternoon puja; a sonorous clang carrying over the green fields. The cows flapped their ears at its sound, but kept on eating.

"We were following a car that a friend of ours was driving—this girl named Ellen that we both had a crush on. We looked alike, of course, but for some reason the girls always went for him first. I was saying that this time, he should let me have a chance to ask her out. Her car made a left turn on a yellow light. I pulled out after her without even seeing that it had turned red. The car coming from the right slammed into us."

I could hear the chanting beginning, the singsong Sanskrit already getting more familiar to me after a week in the ashram: *Om thryambakam yajaamahe sugandhim pushti-vardhanam urvaarukamiva bandhanaan mruthyor muksheeya maamruthath . . .* I'd memorized the translation at the bottom of the blurrily xeroxed chant sheets: *We worship the three-eyed One who is fragrant and who nourishes all beings. May he liberate us from death for the sake of immortality, even as the cucumber is severed from its bondage of the creeper.*

"Oh, Devi Das. I'm so sorry." I wanted to give him a hug. But what if someone saw me? We could both be expelled from the ashram.

He leaned his pitchfork against the cowshed wall. "We should go," he said. "We're late for puja."


"HAVE YOU EVER been in love?" I asked Darshana that night.

I was lying on my bed, watching Darshana brush her hair. She brushed it exactly the same way every night: a hundred strokes with a boar-bristle hairbrush with a silver handle she told me used to belong to her grandmother. The hair crackled with static electricity, lifting and floating in threads of spun gold. Freed from its severe braids, it looked like it had a life of its own—as if it might walk out the ashram gates and set out down the road, carefree and passionate, leaving Darshana behind to meditate without it.

"Sri Satyaji says that human love is but a pale mirror of the divine love that awaits us in meditation." The brush beat with a steady rhythm: twenty-eight, twenty-nine, thirty . . .

"I know what Sri Satyaji says." I wished that Lori were here, lying on the bed opposite me. I missed our all-night conversations, giggling about men and sex and chocolate. For that matter, I missed men and sex and chocolate. "But I'm talking about before. Before you were Darshana."

Thirty-eight, thirty-nine, forty. *Oh well. What was I thinking, trying to be girlfriends with an enlightened German lingerie stylist?* I rolled over on my side, pulling my blanket around me. I wondered where Matt was right now. I put my hand on my belly, just slightly swelling. I could feel the lump of my uterus, hard as an apple. I wondered what my baby would look like. Would it have my wild curls? Matt's mismatched eyes?

"Before I was Darshana, I was Angelika." Darshana's voice startled me. I had already started to drift into sleep. "And yes, I was in love. In fact, I was married."

"Really? *Married?*" I saw Darshana walking down an aisle in a cloud of white lace, a handsome German man slipping a ring on her finger. "For how long?"

"Five years. I was thirty-six when I met him. We were married within six months."

"So what happened?" I kept my eyes fixed on the ceiling, afraid that if I looked at her the conversation would stop.

"Children were very important to him." The steady beat of her brushing went on. "And as it turned out, I was not able to have children. After my third miscarriage, he left me for another woman. They now have two little boys."

*Darshana—Angelika—rolling in fetal position in the corner of the bed, her arms crossed over her empty belly, sobbing.* "I'm so sorry," I said, for the second time that day. Who would have thought that Devi Das and Darshana both were carrying so much pain? No wonder yogis wanted to dwell in pure *purusha*. *Prakriti* was nothing but trouble.

Ninety-nine, one hundred. She lay down the brush and began dividing her hair, preparing to bind it in braids again. "It has all turned out for the best. Without that sorrow, I would not have come to spiritual practice and opened to divine love."

*But does divine love wrap its arms around you when you are crying? Does divine love tell you funny stories until you laugh so hard you beg it to stop? Does it run on tiny feet through your apartment, spill juice on your carpet, snuggle in your lap?* "I was in love once, too," I said. "In fact, I think I still am." I waited for her to ask for my story. We'd swap advice, commiserate about how men are from Mars and women are from Venus. We'd raise my baby together here at the ashram. It would be the child she'd never had. She'd be the sister I never had.

But she got up and turned away, sliding the hairbrush back into her top drawer. "It is almost time for the lights to go out," she said. "We should not be talking this way. We should be fixing our minds on God."

From: HeyBaby.com
To: Amandala@yahoo.com

Welcome to Week 13! Congratulations, you're almost in the second trimester! Your uterus is now the size of a small grapefruit, and with any luck, your morning sickness is just about over. You can blame those wild mood swings on your raging hormones!

Now that you're out of the risky first trimester, your thoughts are probably turning toward creative ways to share the exciting news with your loved ones. You might try gathering them together for a group picture—then just before you snap, instead of saying "cheese," say, "We're pregnant!" Then click, and you'll have their reaction preserved forever!

From: Lori647@aol.com
To: Amandala@yahoo.com

Just wanted to let you know that I ran into Tom yesterday at the Green Expo, looking at solar panels. He asked how you were doing. He was trying to act casual, like it didn't really matter, but he couldn't pull it off. He's obviously still obsessed with you. Of course I didn't tell him you were pregnant. But some day you're going to have to.

And speaking of making announcements—have you said anything to your mother yet?

"Is THE MIND beginning to rest in pure spirit?" Sri Satyaji asked me.

Three weeks after I'd come to the ashram, I was sitting across from him in his chamber, both of us cross-legged on cushions, for my first private interview on the progress of my spiritual practice. He sat slightly above me, on a raised dais, so my face was about at the level of his belly. I had to crane my head to look up at him.

"Um, yes. I think so," I said. "A little bit."

"Are there distractions clouding the mind?" A small, brightly painted clock on the wall clicked, whirred, and began playing "It's a Small World After All," about twice as fast as I'd ever heard it.

"Yes, a few." The song wound down and the clock struck three times, also too fast, although as far as I knew it was late morning.

"What are these distractions?"

"Um . . ." *I'm pregnant? I want to strangle my roommate with her mala beads? I'm worried that my book on enlightenment won't ever get written, and I'll have to pay back the advance by answering calls for my roommate's phone sex line?* "Things here are very simple," I finally said. "But my life—outside—is complicated. My relationships are complicated. And I don't know how to bring the simplicity and purity that I find here into the world outside."

He nodded and stroked his beard. "It is common to be distracted by sexual thoughts, especially for someone of your age," he said, as if that had been what I was talking about. "The practice of celibacy is an essential tool in disentangling the spirit from the bondage of the flesh. By practicing celibacy, you harness the mighty river of sexual energy and use it to turn the wheel of liberation."

"Yes, I can feel how powerful celibacy is." I felt like I was presenting a make-believe version of myself for my spiritual teacher, like the false set of accounting books Ernie had helped me concoct just for the IRS. It was like washing your hair before going to get it cut, or shaving before getting your legs waxed: I didn't want the person whose job it was to clean me up to see just how far I had let things go. I tried to shift the conversation onto less volatile ground. "I've been told that doing yoga poses, too, is a useful way to channel physical energy into spiritual form."

He looked as if I had suggested that disemboweling small children would be helpful as well. "Yoga postures must be avoided at all costs. They are a corruption of the path. They pull you deeper into the trap of sensual entrapment. I hope that you have not been tempted to experiment with this very dangerous technique?"

I'd actually been doing Downward Dog that very morning between our beds, while Darshana was in the shower, trying to loosen the knot between my shoulder blades that got so tight during meditation. I wondered what would happen if I told him that. Would he break out in a head-to-foot rash? "No, of course not. It was just something I heard about." Who would have thought the path to enlightenment would involve so much *pretending*?

The clock chimed again, six times. Sri Satyaji looked over at it solemnly, as if its timekeeping had some direct correlation with reality.

"Our time together is finished," he said. "But before you go, I will give you your dharma name. You may kneel before me."

I knelt and bowed my head down to the ground, as I had seen Darshana do in the meditation hall. His feet were bare; his toes were an inch or so before my face, their nails beautifully manicured, thick black hair sprouting around the knuckles. I wondered if he clipped his nails himself or if his assistant did it. "Your name is Santosha," he said, extending his hands in the air about six inches over my head. "This is a Sanskrit word that means contentment. When you are feeling unhappy or distracted, focus on this, your true name, and you will feel better."

FOR THE NEXT week, I tried as hard as I could to be Santosha. And it definitely beat being Amanda.

Amanda, frankly, was kind of a drag to be around—constantly worrying about whether she was eating enough B vitamins and iron, about whether she'd get her book written before her money ran out, about whether anyone would ever want to make love with her after she was all stretched out from having a baby. She was given to bouts of uncontrollable weeping or giggling during morning puja, and she had developed an anxious habit of gnawing on the skin next to her thumbnail.

But Santosha—Santosha was serene. Her mind settled on her mantra and didn't waver. She ate her meals slowly, savoring each bland bite of rice and dal and overcooked vegetables. She sang along at the pujas with the Sanskrit chants, whose words she was gradually starting to learn. She tried not to let herself feel the gradual tightening of her waistband over her slight but expanding potbelly. Because if she felt it, she would snap back into being Amanda again.

As Santosha, I began to fall in love with the ashram: the clanging of the bells that woke me at dawn; the whispering of the trees as I fell asleep; the white-robed figures gliding in silence from kitchen to garden to temple; the sonorous sound track of the Sanskrit chanting. Sri Satyaji was the wise and beneficent father I had never had, presiding over an island of peace and purity in a messy, crazy world. And all I had to do, to belong to this family, was become peaceful and pure myself.

As Santosha, I walked slowly toward the meditation hall one morning. The sky was a brilliant blue; I imagined drawing its color into me with every breath, until my whole soul was a cloudless sky. The hibiscus bush outside the meditation hall was a blaze of crimson. I had never felt so happy. I had finally found somewhere that I really belonged. I could stay at this ashram forever.

"Pssst." Devi Das was walking next to me, his eyes downcast. It had been almost ten days since we'd spoken; I was astonished at the way my heart leaped when I heard his voice. After all, this was just Devi Das. It wasn't as if Matt had materialized next to me.

He walked close, his shoulder brushing against mine, then slipped a small, hard square into my hand, like a drug dealer making a handoff. I glanced down: A Cadbury dark chocolate bar. Santosha disintegrated, and Amanda sprang to life. *Chocolate!* On the list of forbidden substances at the ashram, chocolate was right up there with crack cocaine. "Where did you get that?" I hissed.

"We took the bus into town yesterday to buy a new hoe for the garden. We bought this at the fruit stand next to the pharmacy."

From across the path, Darshana shot us a reproving look and shook her head: *No talking to men.* I slipped the chocolate deep into my pocket and went into the meditation hall. I was Santosha again, contentment incarnate.

After meditation, I walked slowly to my room, peeked out the window to make sure Darshana wasn't anywhere around, and slipped the chocolate bar under my pillow. I would eat it that evening after dinner, while Darshana was slicing bananas and mangoes for tomorrow morning's breakfast. I would eat it slowly, appreciating every bite. It would be a religious experience.

All day, the chocolate bar shimmered in my mind, a dark, sweet promise of happiness to come. Technically, we were not supposed to eat chocolate at the ashram—or sweets of any kind, for that matter. But surely, now that I was Santosha, now that I was practically enlightened, I was beyond such strictures. Besides, I was pregnant. It was important to indulge my cravings, even the doctor had said so. Probably the chocolate had some nutrients in it that the baby really needed: antioxidants or something like that.

After dinner, I walked down the path to my room as fast as I could while still appearing peaceful. I had about half an hour before Darshana came back. I could eat the candy bar and burn the wrapper in our meditation candle. No one would know.

I slipped into my room, looked out the window to make sure the coast was clear, and picked up the pillow.

The chocolate bar was gone.


TWENTY-EIGHT, twenty-nine. Darshana's boar-bristle brush whipped through her hair. I lay on my bed, seething with rage and suspicion.

It must be Darshana who had taken it. Who else could it have been? No one else had been in our room. I opened my mouth to ask her, then closed it again. I couldn't ask her about a chocolate bar I wasn't even supposed to have in the first place. She'd deny all knowledge of it and then go straight to Sri Satyaji, and I'd be thrown out of the ashram.

Fifty-two, fifty-three. That chocolate bar had been mine. She had no right to take it away, even if it was forbidden. I closed my eyes and imagined getting up in the night and cutting off her hair while she slept. *Ha-ha-ha,* I'd say when she awoke shorn. *That's what you get, chocolate thief.* I started to roll onto my belly, my favorite sleeping position, then rolled back; it was supposed to be better for the baby if I slept on my side.

Eighty-five. Eighty-six. *Okay. Be calm. It's just a candy bar.* I took a deep breath and tried to summon Santosha. But I was stuck with Amanda, wallowing in self-pity. I was pregnant and without a partner in a foreign country. I couldn't even sleep on my belly. Couldn't I at least have a piece of chocolate?

Darshana leaned over and blew out the candle. I lay in the dark and let the tears dribble down my cheeks, trying not to sniffle.

*I AM TRYING to put an enormous contact lens into my eye. It is as large as a school bus but I keep trying to make it fit. My eyes are watering, but I lean closer and closer to the mirror, pushing the lens into my eye, saying, "I want to see clearly." But as I force the lens into my eye, my eyeball itself pops out of the socket and rolls across the floor. When I bend over to chase it, the other one falls out, too. I get down on my hands and knees, blinded and terrified, scrabbling around in the dark for my lost eyes.*

I JERKED OUT of the dream and sat bolt upright, hugging my blanket tight around my shoulders. My heart was thudding. Pale moonlight streamed into the room, illuminating the sleeping figure of Darshana, curled under her covers with the blankets pulled up over her head.

I closed my eyes and put my fingers gently on the lids: both eyes still there. But the horror of the dream still hung around me. I listened for the reassuring whistle of Darshana's snore, but it wasn't there. In fact, I couldn't hear her breathe at all. *What if she's dead. What if I'm lying here alone in the dark with a dead body.* I leaned over and peered at the sleeping bundle of blankets: no movement at all. *Oh God.* I leaned over and put my hand on top of it. It was soft and squishy. I yanked back the blankets—nothing but a pillow and a heaped-up bundle of white clothes.

Where was Darshana?

I looked out the uncurtained window. A full moon hung over the fields. *She's gone somewhere to eat my chocolate.* Not even bothering to change out of my sweatshirt, I pulled my white clothes on over it, wrapped my white shawl around my shoulders, and headed out into the night.

Wind whipped at my hair; a storm must be coming in. Thick clouds scudded past the moon. Trees, buildings, and gardens leaped into moonlight, then vanished in shadows. I walked down the path to the cowshed and peered inside at the shadowy shapes of the sleeping cows. "Darshana?" The cows shifted slightly; one of them gave a grumbling snort.

I walked on, shivering, past the vegetable gardens. I felt driven by an urgency I didn't understand. It felt as if the key to all life's mysteries—my missing chocolate, my lifelong sadness, enlightenment itself—would be handed to me when I found Darshana. I headed past the meditation hall, then up the winding path—forbidden to all devotees except his personal assistant—that led to the guru's hut.

The windows glowed with candlelight; Sri Satyaji must be meditating. Darshana had explained to me that he needed only about half an hour of sleep a night, and spent the rest of the time meditating on world peace. "Last night," she'd told me at breakfast that morning, "he stayed up all night sending healing energy to the Middle East."

Women were not supposed to go within a hundred yards of the house. But I moved closer until I stood in the shadow of a bush, less than ten feet from the steps.

The door opened. I shrank back into the shadows, preparing my excuses: *I wasn't feeling well. I needed some fresh air. I was sleepwalking. Please forgive me.*

But it wasn't Sri Satyaji who came out of the door. It was Darshana. Her loose hair cascaded around her bare shoulders. Her white sari was half undone. She closed the door behind her, pulled her shawl tight around her, and began walking down the path. I stepped out of the shadows and cut her off.

We stood still, looking at each other in the silver light. I'd never seen her look so beautiful. Her hair tumbled in a wild river; her eyes glowed; her lips were parted and swollen.

We looked at each other in silence. Then she shrugged and began to walk past me.

"Wait," I said. She turned back.

"It was you who ate my chocolate," I said.

She shrugged again. "And if I did? How would that change your practice, Santosha?"

*In Varanasi, whatever is sacrificed, chanted, given in charity, or suffered in penance, even in the smallest amount, yields endless fruit because of the power of that place. Whatever fruit is said to accrue from many thousands of lifetimes of asceticism, even more than that is obtainable from but three nights of fasting in this place.*

*—Tristhalisetu,* ca. AD 1618

# CHAPTER 14

"WELL, STRICTLY SPEAKING, maybe she wasn't lying," Devi Das told me, as our train rattled through the night. "Many devotees view a sexual relationship with a spiritual teacher as just another form of darshan, or transmission of wisdom. They don't look at it as sex at all."

I was crammed into the dark, narrow top berth of a sleeper car—just a padded shelf about a foot and a half wide—with Devi Das on the berth opposite me, about an arm's length away. An icy wind leaked around the edges of the windows. Even wearing every layer I had—long johns, two pairs of baggy pants, fleece jacket, wool shawl—I was shivering.

"But then why didn't she just come out and say that she was his lover? Why all the talk about celibacy and purity?" In the berths below us, an Indian family was sleeping—a mother and father with four young boys piled on top of each other like puppies. They didn't speak any English, but they'd shared their dinner with us—foil-wrapped chapatis, eye-wateringly spicy vegetable curry, sticky sweets oozing ghee. I could still taste the food every time I burped, which was every few minutes: My swelling uterus was beginning to press my intestines up into my stomach, which was refusing to yield without a fight.

"I'm sure she believed it while she was saying it." Devi Das rolled over, his bony knees and elbows poking off the edge of his berth. "We have noticed, in our own life, that it's possible to tell ourselves two contradictory stories and believe them both at the same time."

My hand slid down to cup the hard little lump that swelled between my pubic bone and my navel. *Right.* But somehow I'd expected more from a spiritual teacher. I'd wanted to escape from my own grubby life into a sweet-scented heaven of candles and incense and chanting. It was so disappointing to discover that that luminous world was as screwed up as my own. Probably Darshana was just the tip of the iceberg. Probably the gimlet-eyed British receptionist was running an S and M dungeon with the angel-faced Danish boy. Heck, even the cows were probably up to something naughty.

"Here, take this." Devi Das tossed his heavy woolen shawl across the aisle. "The last thing you need is to get sick."

"You can't give me that. It's the only warm thing you've got. You'll freeze." I pushed it back at him.

"Oh, we have been colder than this before. It is a good opportunity for us to work on our yogic powers. There are yogis in Tibet who can dry wet clothes in subzero temperatures just through raising their body heat. We've always wanted to learn how to do that ourselves."

"Let's share it, at least. Come on over here. It will be warmer if we're squeezed together. And I'm so cold that I'd snuggle up to a goat if I had to." I paused, embarrassed. "I mean—I don't mean that you're—"

"Don't worry. We like goats, too." He scrambled across the gap between our berths and we wedged ourselves together, both of us turned on our sides facing the wall. He pulled his heavy shawl around us, its rough wool scratching my neck. He wrapped his top arm around my waist. I could feel his breath on the back of my neck, the knobs of his hips prodding at my kidneys, his ribs colliding with mine. "Plenty of room, as long as we don't both inhale at the same time."

My awkwardness dissolved as I relaxed into the warmth of his body. When Matt and I first became lovers, we used to sleep like this: twined together, holding on tight, as if we were each afraid the other would slip away in the night. It was one of the surprising pleasures of our connection—how well we literally *slept* together. We'd drop into sleep at the same moment and turn from side to side together all night, as if in some intricately synchronized dance. We'd share complementary dreams: He'd awaken from harvest celebrations after I'd been planting all night; he'd dream of flying with owls, and I'd spend the night picking feathers from my roof.

But gradually, as things got more complicated between us, our sleep patterns had changed. Drifting off, we'd squabble wordlessly over pillows, over blankets, over whether the comforter should be pulled up tight around our necks (me) or down around our armpits (him). Our silent arguments would churn on long after we'd fallen asleep. Once, I'd awoken to find that he'd pulled all the covers to his side of the bed and was rolled up in a woolly cocoon, snoring. When I yanked at the edge of his blanket, he turned away in his sleep and murmured, "Give me a break, Trish." *Trish?* I let the blanket drop and lay there in the dark, shivering, trying not to cry, gazing up at the fading constellations of glow-in-the-dark stars he'd arranged on his ceiling in the exact configuration of the sky on the night of his birth.

Devi Das began making a low, chuffing noise, like a steam train starting up, and I felt his breath coming in short blasts against my neck.

"What on earth are you doing?" I asked sleepily.

"*Kapalabhati*. Breath of fire. It will raise our body temperature even higher. You'll feel like you're curled up to a hot-water bottle."

"Stop it. They'll think we're having some sort of kinky American sex."

"Fortunately, the train is so loud they can't even hear us."

I'd been so disappointed in the way things had turned out with Matt—so hurt and let down. Maybe that was part of why I was so upset with Darshana and Sri Satyaji. I'd wanted there to be someone whose purity I could trust. I'd wanted to believe in something.

I thought of the hasty email I'd fired off to Maxine before I bolted from the ashram, trying to sell her on my next destination: *I'm off to Varanasi, the city of death! It's the ancestral home of Shiva, the lord of the yogis, the god of destruction, who lives in the charnel grounds and feeds on the bodies of the dead. So I'm sure to get lots of good enlightenment tips there.* With so many of my illusions dead, a crematory city seemed an appropriate destination.

Devi Das's huffing quieted into a long *ujayii,* a rhythmic, soothing hiss. My mind crumbled into disjointed images: *Darshana's hair crackling with electricity under her brush. Matt's lopsided grin. The swinging plate of fire at the ashram's evening pujas.* Then Devi Das's voice whispered in my ear, so soft I wasn't sure it wasn't part of a dream: "Amanda. Even if the teacher is a fraud, the teachings can still be real."


THE TRAIN PULLED into Varanasi early in the morning. I hobbled off the train, my knee aching again after the long, cramped trip. The platform was dingy and dim; the light of an occasional vending machine cast flickering shadows over families sleeping on the floor, wrapped in shawls and blankets. Some of them were cooking breakfast over small camp stoves. Peddlers carried baskets on their heads piled high with oranges and finger-sized bananas.

Outside the station, the air smelled of rotting garbage, feces, and smoke. A mob of rickshaw drivers descended upon us like flies on roadkill. The driver we chose stopped before leaving the station to buy a packet of reddish powder that Devi Das told me was *paan,* a stimulant made from ground betel nut: "It will give him the courage he needs to drive on these roads."

The driver spewed a stream of crimson spit into the road, floored the accelerator, and began to sing—*"Shiva Ram, Jaya Ram!"* I wrapped my shawl around my face and eyes to keep out the choking fumes. We swerved around a bicycle rickshaw, dodged the craggy black behind of a water buffalo. My lungs were burning. *Am I poisoning the baby?* I grabbed onto Devi Das. "Make him turn around! I've changed my mind. I want to go home."

"Don't worry." He leaned forward and said something to the driver in Hindi. The driver shouted something back; spat again; then turned off the main road and began to jolt through rutted stone streets so narrow I could reach out my hands and touch the buildings on either side. Along the edges, families were getting up out of low-slung hammocks where they'd apparently spent the night: cooking breakfast over small fires, brushing their teeth and spitting into the street, washing their hair under hand pumps that drained into sludge-filled gutters.

"Where are we going?" I asked Devi Das.

"We're going to a wonderful bed-and-breakfast where they serve an American-style brunch." We swerved around a mother sitting on a set of crumbling stone steps, picking lice from the head of her little girl. "It's pricier than we've been paying, but you look like you could use a vacation."

*Pancakes. Maple syrup. Sausage.* Maybe everything was going to be okay after all. But the rickshaw had stopped in the middle of an intersection to let three camels pass, huge bundles of wood swaying on their humped backs.

"Wood for the funeral pyres," Devi Das said. "People come here from all over India to die, because if you die in Varanasi, your soul is guaranteed a favorable rebirth."

I nodded. I'd imagined Varanasi as a solemn place, a cross between a funeral home and a Gothic cathedral. But this city was seething with life, so raw and unfiltered that San Francisco seemed wrapped in plastic by comparison.

As if on cue, the rickshaw lurched forward, then stopped again. Pushing through the crowd in front of us were five or six men carrying a bamboo platform on their shoulders with a long bundle on top of it, wrapped in gold silk. Two more men beat on small hand drums. They were all chanting: "Ram Nam Satya He, Ram Nam Satya He, Ram Nam Satya He . . ."

"The name of God is truth," Devi Das translated.

The men were just a few feet away from me. It took me a moment to understand that what I was seeing was a shrouded dead body.

"Ram Nam Satya He. Ram Nam Satya He." The chanting was swallowed up in the noise of the crowd, and our rickshaw began moving forward again. I closed my eyes, stunned.

"This happens hundreds of times a day in Varanasi," Devi Das said. "You'll get used to it."

From: Maxine@bigdaybooks.com
To: Amandala@yahoo.com
Re: Progress!

Amanda, Satyanam Ashram's getting raves from editorial, especially the pics. Such a handsome guru, especially if we do something in Photoshop about those eyebrows. City of DEATH? Tell me I didn't get that right.

From: Lori647@aol.com
To: Amandala@yahoo.com
Subject: Don't touch the water!

I just read that the E. coli level in the Ganges at Varanasi is 150 times the legal limit. They dump EVERYTHING in the river there: dead bodies, raw sewage, nuclear waste, you name it. And you aren't even supposed to be changing kitty litter! Will you please come to your senses?


From: HeyBaby.com
To: Amandala@yahoo.com

Week 14, and clothes starting to get a bit tight? Your husband's clothes may fit you in the waist, but what about those hips and that belly? Well, don't worry—today's maternity fashions are as cute as your baby's going to be! Check out the links below for bargains on maternity styles for the office, the gym, the beach, and the boudoir!


OUR HOTEL TURNED out to be a New England–themed bed-and-breakfast with a view of the Ganges. I sat at a table with a checked, waxy tablecloth, pulled a cloth napkin out of a carved maple leaf ring, and ate French toast slathered with maple syrup. Just outside the window, I could see the silver curve of the river and an intermittent stream of traffic: a herd of water buffalo lumbering to the banks to drink; pilgrims with six-foot staffs on their shoulders, weighted at both ends with bundles of clothes and cookwear; sadhus with pitchfork-sized tridents.

"Merry Christmas!" said the waiter, cheerfully, as he poured us coffee. *Oh, right.* I had forgotten. Tomorrow was Christmas Eve. I turned to Devi Das. "Remind me to call my mother."

"Are you going to tell her your big news?"

"Not yet. I can't face her reaction. Besides, I don't want to wreck her holiday." I pushed the thought away and looked out the window again. A beggar sat on the steps below next to a shiny motorcycle. A goat nibbled the marigold garlands off a Shiva shrine under a tree. "How old is this place, anyway?"

"Varanasi is one of the oldest continuously inhabited cities on earth." Devi Das stirred a packet of creamer into his coffee. "It was already ancient when the Buddha visited here, twenty-five hundred years ago. It's even older than Athens or Rome."

"Yeah, but in Athens there aren't Greek warriors walking by in loincloths with olive leaves in their hair. There aren't priests at the Parthenon still sacrificing goats to Athena and Zeus."

"Too bad. We'd go there immediately."

Upstairs, the shower in our room was astonishingly hot; on the inside of the bathroom door hung matching robes in red plaid flannel. Devi Das and I flopped down side by side on a queen-sized bed covered with a flannel comforter printed with snowmen and sleds. *Don't worry about me, Mom; I'm spending Christmas in an L.L. Bean catalog!* I picked up a hardcover book from the bedside table: *Banaras, City of Light,* by Diana Eck. Perfect. The real city of light was too intense, too overwhelming. All I wanted was to pull the curtains, get under the covers, and pretend I was in Vermont on a snowy day, reading about India. I skimmed the first page.

> *Long flights of stone steps called ghats, reaching like roots into the river, bring thousands of worshippers down to the river to bathe at dawn. In the narrow lanes at the top of these steps moves the unceasing earthly drama of life and death, which Hindus call samsara. But here, from the perspective of the river, there is a vision of transcendence and liberation, which Hindus call moksha.*

I slid deeper under the covers and closed my eyes. This was Shiva's hometown; I could feel its wild, primal energy. What was I doing, pregnant so far away from everything safe and familiar? I saw myself scurrying through the crowded, narrow lanes of my life, buildings pressing in on all sides. I was lost in the alleys of samsara. People waved at me from overhanging balconies: Mom. Maxine. Lori. Tom. Did a vision of liberation really wait for me in the river? How could I find my way down there?

*I AM PART of a funeral procession. I am beating on a drum. My belly is swollen huge: shouldn't I be going to the hospital to give birth? Why am I marching to the burning grounds instead? In front of me sways the bamboo platform bearing the corpse. Everyone around me is weeping. "Ram Nam Satya He," I chant. "The name of God is truth." But who has died? Suddenly, the corpse sits up, peeling back its yellow shroud, and looks at me. Its face is pale, its head is shaved. "Hey, Amanda," the corpse says. "Did you say something about truth?" It is Matt.*

I OPENED MY EYES, drenched in sweat. How long had I been asleep? Dim light filtered through the curtains—was it afternoon, or the next morning? Next to me, Devi Das was snoring—a low bubble with a whistle in the middle, like a malfunctioning teakettle. I got out of bed, pulled on my clothes, and headed to the guest computer I'd spotted just off the dining room. I logged on with a curious sense of inevitability, as if living out a dream whose conclusion I already knew.

From: offthematt@gmail.com
To: Amandala@yahoo.com
Subject: Don't delete me

Amanda, I know it hasn't been a year yet. But this is too good a chance to pass up. I'm going to be in India this week, in Bodh Gaya.

Just passing through for a few days on my way to Thailand. Are you going to be anywhere near there? If so maybe we could meet up. I miss you. Matt.

"So what do you think I should do?" I asked Devi Das. "Should I see him?"

It was dawn the next morning. Devi Das and I were sitting in the back of a wooden rowboat, being paddled up the Ganges by a white-bearded boatman wrapped in a brown woolen shawl. He looked like a boatman in a children's storybook, the kind who would grant you three wishes if you answered his riddles correctly. But I was the one who was asking the riddles.

"Whatever you want to do, we will support," said Devi Das. "But you should know that we're just a few hours by train from Bodh Gaya. We could go there tomorrow, if that's what you want."

"I don't know what I want." I dropped my hand over the edge of the boat, trailing it in the water, then jerked it back. *Raw sewage, dead bodies, nuclear waste.* I watched a clump of marigolds and coconut husks float by on the scummy surface, an offering to Shiva. "He's the father of my baby. Maybe I should at least let him know that the baby exists."

"That is true."

"On the other hand, whenever I see him, my whole life falls apart."

"That is true, too."

The river was wide and gently curved. Along the banks, a jumble of buildings brooded in the pale dawn light, a muddle of past and present: decaying temples to Shiva and Kali, glass-fronted luxury hotels, an abandoned maharaja's palace with a tree growing out of its roof. Temple bells clanged. Naked sadhus bent over glowing fires in riverside tents. "They're naga babas, who never wear clothes. They're burning the ash to smear on their bodies to keep them warm," Devi Das told me.

As the sun hit the water, the buildings lit up pale gold. We floated past three sadhus chanting mantras, in up to their necks, their eyes rolled back in ecstasy; then past two fat-bellied men perched on rocks, lathering their armpits with bars of soap.

"Bathing in Mother Ganges at Varanasi washes away seven generations of bad karma," Devi Das said.

I peered at the scummy water again. "Suppose I just dip my fingers in? Will that buy me one generation?"

"Don't get caught in appearances. Think holy, not E. coli."

We floated past a man sitting on the prow of a fishing boat, mending his nets. Women beat wet laundry on rocks. A sadhu in an orange loincloth standing outside his tent answered a ringing cell phone. A group of girls squatted on the banks, brushing their teeth with twigs and swishing palmfuls of river water into their mouths.

"I can't believe they're brushing their teeth in that water."

Devi Das nodded. "In America, we are used to maintaining the illusion that drinking is entirely separate from pissing, that life is entirely separate from death. It's hard to get used to seeing them so close together."

Our boatman paddled downstream, toward a ghat where fires glowed red and plumes of smoke billowed. The acrid smell of smoke hit my nose, along with a darker, thicker stench that turned my stomach. As we drew closer, I saw that bamboo racks were stacked casually along the steps, each one bearing a silk-wrapped corpse. I closed my eyes for a moment, dizzy and disoriented. We were rowing back a thousand years, and into the underworld. I'd booked a hotel room with a balcony overlooking the portal to Hades.

"In most places in India, the burning grounds are viewed as unclean, so they are outside the city limits," Devi Das explained. "But here in Varanasi, death is sacred. It's invited right into the heart of the city like an honored guest." I opened my eyes, expecting our boatman to row on past. But instead he pulled in closer. Other boats jostled near us, crammed with tourists: German, Japanese, Italian, British, French. Five or six fires blazed, some roaring, some dying out. On the pyre closest to us, not yet lit, lay a body draped in silk and garlanded with red hibiscus flowers. A family circled it: an old man in a dhoti, a little boy in a red sweatshirt, two middle-aged men in Western suits. A couple of scrawny dogs sprawled casually in the dirt nearby. A goat nosed by the water, eating discarded hibiscus garlands. One of the men was carrying a flaming bundle of twigs. He bent and lit the pyre, and a cloud of sharp-smelling smoke billowed up.

"They light the fire from a flame that's been burning for three thousand years," Devi Das said. "After the body burns, they throw the ashes in the river, along with some of the big bones that don't burn all the way. You know, the pelvis. The rib cage."

The smoke stank of burning hair. Devi Das's words seemed to be coming from a long way away.

"They don't burn children, though. Or pregnant women. They just tie stones around their bodies and sink them in the middle of the river."

I put my hands on my belly. I felt as if I were about to faint. The veil between dream and waking, unconscious and conscious, was dissolving. Gods and demons were everywhere. How many hundreds of thousands of bodies had burned in this spot?

The men piled more wood on the fire. I stared at the burning body. Some mother had carried that dead man inside her as a baby. Did he have children? A woman who loved him more than life itself? What was I doing, watching someone else's heartbreak as if it were a tourist attraction?

"Our brother wanted to be cremated." Devi Das didn't look at me. "We're sure of it. But our parents wanted him buried in the family plot. So when we first came here, five years ago, we brought a picture of him, and his old teddy bear. We burned them on the banks of the Ganges and scattered the ashes in the river."

I put my arm around him, not sure if I was comforting him or begging for comfort myself. His body felt brittle as kindling. But it was something to hold onto. "I'm so sorry."

"Amanda. We don't want to tell you how to live your life. But when we hear you talk about Matt, we remember something we once heard the Zen teacher Thich Nhat Hanh say. 'When you quarrel with your beloved, stop and look in his or her eyes. And then picture yourself and your beloved, one hundred years from now. Then I think you will know what to do.'"

I didn't say anything. The fire had engulfed the body. I could hear fat sizzle, joints pop. Two sadhus sat on the steps above, playing cards. Next to them, a teenage girl in a flowered sari sang bhajans to the syncopated beat of her silver handbells.

I looked down at the river lapping at my feet. A blob of feces floated past in a swirl of marigold petals and cigarette butts. Was this holy water? A cesspool? Both? If there was anything I was learning from India, it was this: *Nothing is the way it appears on the surface.*

In the pit of my belly, just below my belly button, I felt a flutter. It was slight but unmistakable, like the flapping of butterfly wings. It felt as if I were being caressed from the inside.

"Hey, Devi Das," I whispered. "Guess who I just felt?"

# Dancer pose
## (Natarajasana)

*Stand on your right leg. Bend your left knee, reach your left hand behind you, and clasp your left foot. Draw the foot out behind you as you arch in a deep backbend. Stretch your right arm out in front of you, graceful as a ballerina on the lid of a child's jewelry box. Feel how balance demands that you waver and catch yourself, over and over again.*

*Nataraja is the dancing Shiva, the god of destruction. He dances in a ring of fire with a serpent twining around his waist, trampling your ego under his feet. He rips away everything you ever dreamed you could count on. If you let go of your foot and tumbled, what new life might be born among your scattered bones?*

*Your worst enemy cannot harm you as much as your own thoughts, unguarded. But once mastered, no one can help you as much, not even your father or your mother.*

—The Buddha, *Dhammapada*, ca. 500 BC

# CHAPTER 15

THE MORNING AFTER Devi Das and I arrived in Bodh Gaya, I stood in the courtyard of the Mahabodhi Temple, just footsteps away from the spot where the Buddha attained supreme enlightenment while meditating under a tree, and pondered an ancient Zen koan: What is the best way to tell your cheating ex-boyfriend, who doesn't want kids, that you're pregnant with his baby?

It was a brilliant, chilly December morning. The temple loomed in front of us, a sandstone pyramid with spires reaching toward a cloudless sky. The courtyard was swirling with Buddhist monks and nuns, the wind whipping their robes around them: black-robed Japanese, maroon-robed Tibetans, saffron-robed Sri Lankans and Thais, gray-robed Vietnamese and Koreans.

"So what time are you meeting him?" Devi Das asked.

"Not until noon." I watched two Tibetan monks pass in front of me. Every few steps they threw themselves on the ground in prostration, their elbows protected with pads against the force of their devotion.

"More than two hours! So we have plenty of time to meditate under the Bodhi Tree."

"Or to change our minds and run for the train."

"So much transformation can take place in a couple of hours! Look at what happened to the Buddha."

"Yeah, well, the Buddha didn't have a lover to distract him."

"Didn't Mara, the Lord of Delusion, send fleets of beautiful women to tempt him?"

"Were any of them pregnant with his babies? That might have helped." My feet were throbbing and swollen. I sat down on a stone bench facing the temple and began to massage them through my sandals. *Wonderful. Even my feet are getting fat. What's next? My nose?* Under a nearby tree, a Tibetan monk was doing prostrations on a polished board, with a plastic water bottle next to him. I pulled my notebook out of my daypack and flipped through my scribbled entry from that morning.

## Enlightenment for Idiots: Sample Chapter Draft

If there's one place a seeker should visit in India, it's got to be Bodh Gaya, the site of the Buddha's enlightenment! 2500 years ago, a few years after leaving his wife, his family, and his princedom to study with the greatest yogis of India, the wandering ascetic Siddhartha Gautama moved into a cave in the hills on the outskirt of this little town, and spent a few years torturing and starving himself in an attempt to beat his body into submission (for a taste of something similar, you might drop in on certain yoga studios in Manhattan). Finally, on the verge of death, he decided that self-mortification was not the way to enlightenment. He left his cave, and disgusted his fellow ascetic yogis by accepting a bowl of rice from a village girl. Then he sat down under a pipal tree on a cushion made of grass, vowing not to get up until he broke free of the chains of delusion and attachment that bound his mind. The next morning at dawn, he succeeded, and became the Buddha, or "Awakened One."

Today, pilgrims come from all over the world to visit the site of the Buddha's triumph, where an ancient pipal—now known as the Bodhi Tree, or tree of awakening—still marks the spot where he sat. ~~Some come seeking relief from their own personal suffering~~

~~2,500 years later, the human condition is still~~

~~Matt, I have some wonderful news~~

~~Matt, I know this isn't exactly what you want, but I hope you'll~~

[Whole sheet torn out, crumpled up, then smoothed out and stuck back in notebook with dab of chewing gum.]

I CLOSED MY notebook with a snap. Two Tibetan boys in maroon robes ran by, holding plastic airplanes and making motor noises with their mouths. "Look at those kids. They can't be more than eight years old. How can they be monks already?"

"For Tibetan families, it's common to send one child to the monastery to pray for the whole family." Devi Das sat down on the bench next to me. "Sometimes a child is even recognized at birth as an incarnation of a high lama."

"Wow. I wonder how they can tell?" I pictured a posse of lamas arriving at my door in San Francisco: *Amanda, we have good news! Your child is the next Dalai Lama!* I could pack him off to a monastery and get back to hooking up with guys in yoga class. I wouldn't have to worry about getting him into preschool. He'd visit me on vacations and I'd take him to the park. He'd be the only kid on the monkey bars in robes. I looked at the young monks again. Did they ever cry for their mothers at night? Did their mothers ever cry for them?

We walked toward the temple, pausing outside its massive walls. I looked up at a frieze of Buddhas and saints, garlanded with marigolds, butter lamps flickering on a ledge below them. Their serene faces gazed back at me. I could practically see them shaking their heads in despair. The temple, I'd read, had been abandoned for centuries when Buddhism died out in India—swallowed in forest, buried in silt. When British archaelogists had stumbled on it in the nineteenth century, local farmers were using it as a place to keep pigs.

We walked around the end of the temple and there—suddenly, unmistakably—was the Bodhi Tree. I had been wanting to come here ever since Matt showed me one of its leaves, the night we first slept together. Its massive, papery white trunk was surrounded by a stone fence with a locked iron gate. Over the fence spread a canopy of delicate, heart-shaped green leaves. Seated in the courtyard below, several dozen Tibetan monks chanted in a sonorous rumble, punctuated by the clang of cymbals and the steady beat of a drum. A pack of Sri Lankan women recited devotional texts in a high, nasal singsong.

"So this is it. This is where it happened." Devi Das put his palms together and bowed. "Right under this very tree, the Buddha liberated himself from all desires."

"It can't be this very same tree."

"Well, no. But pipal trees do live for hundreds of years. New ones spring up in the same place from their roots."

We peered through the stone fence at the tree trunk, swathed in yards of bright orange silk, its branches strung with white plastic flowers. Next to us, a Thai monk was pressing pieces of gold leaf on the stone fence as a Japanese monk took his picture with a digital camera.

Devi Das sat down on a stone ledge and folded his legs. I sat down next to him, closing my eyes. The chanting surged around me. This tree had died and been reborn over and over. The temple had been buried for centuries. Strangely, it gave me hope. If a temple could be resurrected from a pigsty, maybe I wasn't crazy to be getting together with Matt again. Maybe our relationship could sprout again from its dead stump. Freedom from suffering was possible for everyone, the Buddha had said. But his life hadn't been a wreck like mine. Surely no one as screwed up as me had ever sat under this tree.

*Hummm . . . sahhh.* Was it okay to use a Hindu mantra to meditate at a Buddhist temple? Or was it sacrilegious, maybe even dangerous, like mixing Clorox with Ajax when you cleaned the toilet? I sneaked a peek at my watch. Only fifty-five minutes until Matt was supposed to meet me right under this tree. There was still time to get out of here. I could walk back to our hostel, pick up my backpack, and head to the train station. Not see Matt until the baby was, say, in college. Or married with kids of her own. *Great to see you again after all these years, Matt! You look good. Oh, and by the way . . . you're a grandpa.*

*Hum . . . sah.* Maybe things would be different this time. Maybe I'd changed. Maybe *he'd* changed. He might even be excited to hear that I was pregnant. That *we* were pregnant. Maybe we'd find a lama to marry us right here under the Bodhi Tree. I'd wear a crimson silk wedding sari. We'd honeymoon in Varanasi, watching corpses float down the Ganges and making love for hours under our snowman-print flannel comforter.

*Hum . . . sah.* Unless . . . What if he was seeing someone else already? Maybe he'd hooked up with that red-haired girl Lori had seen him with. Maybe he was even traveling with her. "I'll be right back," he was telling her tenderly, right at this very moment, as he zipped up his jeans. "Just a quick lunch with my ex."

A flock of magpies began to squabble in the branches. I opened my eyes. Opposite us, on the other side of the tree, a dozen Tibetan nuns were assembling. Nunhood! That was the way to go. No more shaving your legs, no more agonizing about whether some guy had left a message on your voice mail. Although maroon wasn't really my color. I should go with the Thai tradition, that nice rich ocher.

But maybe each of these monks and nuns had their own inner torment, their own tangled dramas? Maybe that was why they were chanting with such fervor?

I closed my eyes again. The chanting throbbed into my belly, vibrated my spine. I felt the baby quiver. Maybe the door to joy was open. Maybe all I had to do was walk through it.

"Amanda."

My eyes flew open, and Matt was standing in front of me.

He looked thinner and browner than I remembered him. His hair had grown back and fell in shaggy locks across his forehead, flecked with gray. Were those gray hairs new? Or had I just airbrushed them out in my mind? Maybe this wasn't really Matt. Maybe he was just a demon sent by Mara. "You're not supposed to be here yet!"

"I thought I'd get here a bit early and try to get enlightened before I saw you. But it looks like you had that idea first." He sat down facing me and looked at Devi Das. "Hi. I'm Matt."

"Oh—I'm sorry. Matt, this is my friend Devi Das. We've been traveling together." The monks were still chanting, undisturbed by any of the human dramas unfolding around them.

Devi Das unfurled his legs. "We are delighted to meet you. But unfortunately, we were just leaving to catch lunch at the Thai temple. We have been dreaming about their tofu curry for the last twenty minutes."

Matt looked at me as Devi Das walked away. "We? How many invisible friends does he have with him?"

"It's a long story." Somewhere along the long journey of our relationship, Matt and I had dispensed with hellos and good-byes. We prided ourselves on picking up conversations right where we had left off, as if we'd seen each other just the other day instead of five or six months ago. It was a way of pretending to each other—and ourselves—that we didn't spend most of our time apart.

"You look great, Amanda." He studied my face. "I'd say radiant, if it weren't such a cliché. Is it the force of your spiritual practice? Or just some new kind of makeup?"

*I'm pregnant.* "Oh, just a little eau de Ganges. It does wonders for the complexion." I wanted to throw myself in his arms. But I knew if I did, he'd immediately feel the new little bulge of my belly, hidden under my baggy tunic and shawl. Instead, I picked up my notebook and began to flip through the pages, as if I'd already written a script for how to handle this meeting, and I just had to find it.

He nodded at my notebook. "So how's the book going?"

"Really fantastic!" I'd never been good at faking it with Matt. "Well—okay. Honestly, Matt, it's a lot harder than I thought it would be. This is nothing like visiting vineyards in the wine country. I'm in way over my head. I might as well be trying to write a guide to designing interstellar space stations."

"That's how it always feels when you're working on anything worthwhile. It's the same with my photos. The ones where I feel like I know what I'm doing—they're boring. Predictable. It's when I take risks that things come alive."

"Well, then, this manuscript is so alive that Maxine will have to chop its head off so it doesn't crawl off her desk." I wanted to bite his neck. I wanted to reach out and run my hands down the muscled curve of his arm. "How about you? What are you doing here?"

"The Dalai Lama was here last week. A friend of mine did a story on it for *Slate,* so I came along to shoot some pictures." He looked at my face, which was freezing into a grimace of a smile. "My friend *Peter.* He's a very fat, hairy male."

"Right." For a moment, everything that we weren't saying heaved up between us. "Well, I'm glad I happened to be in the area!" I said brightly.

"Oh, I knew you were headed this way. Otherwise I'd have gone straight to Thailand."

"How'd you know that? Lori?"

"Are you kidding? I think she's set her spam filter to delete me. Not just my emails—me, personally. No, I called your editor. She was practically hysterical, saying you were filing dispatches from a crematorium, and would I please talk some sense into you."

He stood up. "It's too crowded to talk here. Are you up for taking a hike?"

"A hike? Where?" I'd been envisioning a cup of chai at the Om Restaurant. Or sitting on a bench under a tree. It was something I always forgot about Matt when I wasn't with him—the way some part of him was perpetually in motion, always leaning toward the next adventure. I used to find it exciting. But now—my feet sore, my body bloated—it was exhausting. He was the galloping horse, and I was the bucked-off rider with my foot stuck in the stirrup, being dragged along behind him. "Weren't we going to have lunch?"

"I picked up some fruit and some samosas. We can have a picnic." He reached out a hand to pull me to my feet, but I scrambled up without taking it. I was afraid that if I started touching him, I wouldn't be able to stop.

TEN MINUTES LATER, we were on the outskirts of town, wading ankle deep across an icy river. Soft sand sucked at my bare feet.

"This is where the Buddha himself used to cross the river. You can tell by the electrical lines." Matt gestured at the cables slung overhead.

"So that's where his power came from." The current tugged hard at my legs. I scrambled up the bank. "At some point, are you going to tell me where we're going?" My uterus was pressing down hard on my bladder. I was trying not to pee in my pants. My knee hurt. Less than half an hour with Matt, and I was already chasing after him, destination unknown. And I still hadn't told him about the baby. I had a feeling that this was not what my therapist would call healthy boundaries.

"Just over there is the cave where the Buddha spent years doing ascetic practices." Matt pointed toward an arc of dusty hills. "Well, I guess he wasn't the Buddha yet. He was just a young yogi still trying to get enlightened."

"Wow—I've heard about that place. You mean the actual cave is still there?" We began to make our way across a patchwork of fields—lentils, mustard, wheat, chickpeas—walking on the raised dirt ledges that separated them. The air was filled with the coos and trills of wood doves, the twitters of sparrows, the caws of crows. Haystacks dotted the landscape like golden stupas.

Matt snapped a picture. "Mmm-hmmm. There's a little Tibetan temple up there. Peter took me up there last week. But my camera battery died after just two shots."

"Oh. So this is actually a photo shoot?" I felt a familiar feeling wash over me: that I was circling around Matt as if he were a locked refrigerator, looking for an emotional meal that I knew was in there, if I could just get the door open.

"It's for both of us. You can even have one for your book."

"Well, thanks. Just think, this whole day can be a tax write-off."

"Come on. Don't pick a fight. Tell me about some of the other places you've been visiting."

"Oh, Matt. It's been insane. If I'd had any idea what these places were like, I'd never have agreed to take this book on." As we tramped along the edges of the fields, I told him about my adventures: Hari Baba, Mr. Kapoor, Sri Satyaji. I hadn't realize how eager I'd been to talk to someone—how eager I'd been, specifically, to talk to him. I'd missed that feeling I'd always had that his mind locked into mine like intersecting LEGO pieces; that thoughts that had existed half formed within me sprang to life under the light of his attention.

"And then I had this roommate, Darshana, this fashion model, who was so into purity and celibacy—"

"And let me guess. She was screwing the guru."

"How did you know?" We had entered a village and were winding through a dirt alley between mud huts. Chickens clucked and pecked. A woman in a sari walked in front of us carrying a heaped basket of grain on her head.

"The ones who seem the purest have the biggest shadows. Be wary if someone says they don't have a toilet. Because what are they doing with all their shit?"

"And what about the ones who *don't* seem pure?"

He grinned at me. "They're slightly less dangerous. That's why I don't even try to pretend."

We dodged sideways to avoid a rooting pig. In front of a mud hut, two women squatted shelling peas into a clay bowl. Having this conversation with Matt in this place reminded me of sleepwalking when I was a child. I would walk through the familiar landscape of my house, but superimposed on it would be the dream landscape: trees sprouting up between the armchairs, dragons perched on the lamps. Although in this case, was Matt the dream? Or was it India?

"And then there are people like you," Matt said. "That's what I like about you. You're not pretending anything. You are exactly as neurotic as you appear to be."

"I'm going to try to take that as a compliment."

"It *is* a compliment." He reached over and tapped my nose. "Like, for instance, most women would have put makeup on that zit."

"What zit?" My hand flew to my face.

"Amanda. I'm kidding. Do you think I'd point out a zit if you actually had one? I only point out your *imaginary* flaws."

*Now. Tell him now.* "Matt? I'm—"

He looked at me inquiringly. My nerve failed me. "I'm thirsty."

He pulled a water bottle out of his daypack and handed it to me. I took a long swig. "And hungry."

"Don't worry, we're almost there. We just have to hike up that hill." He gestured at a rugged slope with a whitewashed temple clinging to the jagged red cliffs at the top. Grinding up a winding road toward it was a tour bus.

I stopped. "Wait a minute. You mean we could have taken a *bus* here?"

"Well, sure. But that would have spoiled the adventure."

By the time we reached the top, the busload of Sri Lankan tourists was already leaving. "Another sacred site checked off their list," said Matt. Strings of red and yellow and green prayer flags were looped from tree to tree, fluttering in the wind. A Tibetan monk came out to greet us with a bow. His face was grooved with wrinkles; his smile was toothless and radiant. He wordlessly offered us clay cups of chai, and we sat on a low white wall to sip them, overlooking the valley below, a patchwork of green and brown fields.

Matt snapped a shot of the monk, then turned the camera on me. "Hey, gorgeous. Give us one for the collection."

I stuck my tongue out at him, and he clicked. "There's your photo for your book jacket."

"For God's sake, Matt. Put that thing away and get out the food. I'm ravenous."

Matt pulled out the food from his daypack: samosas and chapatis wrapped in aluminum foil, tins of rice and dal. I began eating greedily, too hungry to be polite. Since I got pregnant, meals had felt like feeding time at the lion cage.

"Peter said that while he was living here, Siddhartha starved himself until his backbone was poking out through the skin on his belly," Matt said with his mouth full. "Of course, Peter may have been exaggerating. Peter's idea of asceticism is not eating a second dessert."

"I heard that toward the end, the yogis ate just one grain of rice a day." I reached for another samosa, stuffed with spicy potatoes and onions.

"Frankly, I don't really get it." Matt dipped his chapati into the dal. "Why deliberately torture yourself? Isn't life hard enough already?"

"Maybe that's why they did it. *Because* it was so hard." My sudden vehemence surprised me. "They just didn't want to be at the mercy of it any more. They didn't want all their important decisions to be made by their stomachs and their dicks. They wanted to know that they could let go of anything, even their own bodies, and survive."

"See, I have the opposite philosophy. Since it's all going to be taken away from us eventually, anyway, why not enjoy it to the max while it's here?" He scooped up the last of the dal. "Speaking of which, I was thinking . . . After you're done in India, maybe you should come to Thailand and visit me for a while. Relax on the beach after all this work."

"You know I can't do that." *He's finally come to his senses! I'll have the baby in Thailand on the beach. It will be a water birth, with dolphins swimming all around.* "I have to write my book."

"So write it in Thailand. You could get a little hut right up the beach from me. Send in everything by email. When you're done, we'll celebrate with a scuba-diving trip."

*Me and Matt and the baby sprawled in a bed together, napping under a palm frond roof. Me and Matt walking on the white sand, the baby in a sling on Matt's chest.*

"Matt. There's something I have to tell you."

"What? You're staying in India and becoming a guru yourself? You're on the right career path for it."

I couldn't summon the words. Instead, I stood up. I turned sideways. I flattened my billowing tunic down over the slight but distinct bulge of my potbelly.

There was a long, long silence.

*Somewhere in a parallel universe, Matt is throwing his arms around me. "Amanda, that's wonderful! What great news!" he is saying.*

"Please tell me that's not what I think it is," Matt said.

Apparently, our spaceship was not going to be traveling anywhere near that universe. I sat down again. "Actually, it is."

"And—are you telling me that it's mine?"

"It's definitely yours."

*"I'm so happy! When is it due?" asks the parallel-universe Matt.*

"When is it due?" asked Matt. I knew that look on his face—opaque and preternaturally calm, as if a veil had been drawn across the back of his eyes so I couldn't look in. It was the look he got when he was so angry he could barely speak.

"The middle of June."

"So you're almost four months along. What if I hadn't come to India? When, exactly, were you planning on telling me?"

"Well, you did come to India. I'm telling you now."

"Now that it's too late to do anything about it. This affects my life, too, Amanda. Didn't I deserve to be part of this decision?"

"You and I aren't together any more. You were screwing some other girl." My voice was shaking. "I was supposed to ask your permission to have a baby?"

"So is this your way of punishing me?"

"A punishment? Is that what our baby is to you?" I felt like I was about to throw up. What had I been thinking, getting together with him? I'd been doing fine. Now my heart had bitten down on the bait on his fishing hook, and he was reeling it out of my body.

"You know how I feel about having kids. The planet is falling apart. Bringing a child into this fucked-up world is one of the most irresponsible and selfish things you can do."

"*You're* calling *me* irresponsible and selfish? All you do is hide behind a camera! Take pictures so you don't have to deal with anything!"

Matt stood up. "Look, Amanda. I came here to see you because I've missed you like crazy. But I've seen what happens when people have kids. They disappear. Their life gets narrowed down to this tiny little world of diapers and spit-up and LEGOs and conversations about who's driving carpool on the fucking field trip to the fucking sticker factory. I can't do it. It's the end of creativity. It feels like death."

"That's funny. To me, it feels like life."

Matt shoved his hands deep in the pockets of his jacket. "If you wanted to make a life with me, there were other ways you could have gone about it. Like not tricking me into being a father, for starters."

"You know what, Matt? This isn't about you."

"Apparently not," he said. "So in that case, I might as well be going."

I wanted to throw myself weeping to the ground and grind my face in the dirt. I wanted to scrape up handfuls of earth and eat them. *Don't leave. Don't leave. Please, please, don't leave.* "Don't let me stop you," I said.


So many times, at moments like this, I'd said that I wanted to crawl into a cave. This time, I could really do it.

The yogis' cave was tiny, only about ten feet across, just high enough to sit up in. Butter lamps flickered on a low altar, painted red and gold. The walls were black with centuries of smoke. I squatted on a meditation cushion and hugged my legs into a ball at my chest, wrapping my arms around my shins. I felt as if a nuclear bomb had detonated inside my chest.

Maybe it wasn't too late. Maybe I should run down the hill after Matt, fling my arms around him while the pigs and the chickens rooted and pecked at our feet. *Please don't leave; please come back and torture me some more.* I fumbled through my daypack looking for a chocolate bar. I pulled it out and ripped the wrapper off. As I stuffed it into my mouth, I began to cry in jagged, hiccupping sobs. I didn't have any tissues. I wiped my sleeve across my face, smearing snot and tears and chocolate all together.

How many times had I cried like this over Matt? Why had I thought it would be any different this time? If I could escape this pain by starving myself, I would. If I could bully my heart into numbness, I would. I looked at the gaunt Buddha on the altar, the bony rack of his ribs. Is this the kind of heartache Siddhartha and his friends were trying to escape? Funny—the Buddhist sutras didn't say anything about Siddhartha's own suffering. Sure, the Buddha-to-be sneaked out of the palace and saw old age, sickness, death, and loss. But they were all happening to *other* people. Did he ever go mad with grief and longing himself? Did he ever feel so alone in his own skin he couldn't bear it? Was he ever shipwrecked on the rocks of love, sick with desire for a palace dancing girl, insane with rage because his wife didn't love him the way he wanted to be loved?

I blew my nose on the sleeve of my shirt. Well, if he did, he dealt with it the way most guys do: He bolted. What about his wife? Was she devastated when he sneaked away in the middle of the night without even leaving a note? She probably just sat back at the palace, sobbing and thumbing through the Pali equivalent of *Women Who Love Too Much*.

I put my hand on my belly. *I'm sorry,* I whispered, and started to cry again. *I'm sorry I've screwed up your life before it's even started.* Funny how it was mainly men who felt compelled to go off and torture themselves in caves. If men could feel this life moving inside them—if they could feel a new human being incarnating in their bellies—would they still need to do all these tortuous practices just to wake themselves up?

The air was thick with incense, sweet and spicy. The walls curved in all around. Being here was like crawling back into the womb. No wonder the yogis wanted to hide out here. Siddhartha was in his late twenties when he first sat down here, in his early thirties when he finally left—just the age Matt was now, come to think of it. A young man whipping himself toward some kind of luminous perfection, a mind state impervious to sorrow, to loss, to longing, to despair. To chase it, he'd walked away from everything he'd held most dear.

*The Buddha: Awakened master? Or just another guy who was afraid to commit?*

# tortoise pose

# (kurmasana)

*Sit on the floor and spread your legs wide. Bend both knees and slide your arms under them. Then gradually straighten your legs, pressing out through the heels, and using your legs to tug your shoulders down to the floor.*

*Withdraw the head and legs of your senses into your bony carapace. Don't smell. Don't taste. Don't hear. Don't see. Don't feel.*

*Turtles live long and move slowly. They have all the time in the world to get where they're going. Once a turtle is in its shell, nothing can disturb it.*

*Vipassana is observing the truth. With the breath I am observ-*
*ing the truth at the surface level, at the crust level. This takes*
*me to the subtler, subtler, subtler levels. Within three days the*
*mind becomes so sharp, because you are observing the truth.*

—S. N. Goenka (1924– )

# CHAPTER 16

THROUGH YEARS OF breakups—and observing the breakups
of those around me—I had learned a few things not to do afterward.

Do not go to bed with the guy instead of going home, hoping that
if you pretend you didn't just break up, he'll forget that it happened.

Do not call his voice mail at three in the morning to persuade
him of what a terrible mistake he has made by leaving you.

Do not become best friends with the woman for whom he left
you, so you can commiserate with her about his chronic inability to
commit while secretly waiting for them to break up so you can get
back together with him.

Two days after my fight with Matt, I had a new rule: Do not—repeat, *do not*—sign up for a ten-day vipassana meditation retreat.

I was ten hours into the first day of my New Year retreat, which was held at the Bodh Gaya Vipassana Meditation Headquarters, a brick building that squatted off a crowded alley a few blocks from the Mahabodhi Temple. I was sitting cross-legged on an under-stuffed black cushion, trying to concentrate on the sensations of my breath moving at the tip of my nose. My underwear had crawled up my crotch, and I couldn't figure out an inconspicuous way to pull it out. Someone seemed to be prying my kneecaps off with a crowbar. My neck itched. Through the open windows, I could hear the din of bus engines, truck horns, pony hooves, rickshaw motors, crows cawing, cows lowing, a rooster crowing, and a distant, intermittent hammering.

I'd signed up for the retreat a couple of days ago, the evening after Matt bolted. Devi Das and I had gone to the German Bakery so I could smother my grief with chai and cinnamon rolls. We'd sat down at the only empty seats, which were at a table already occupied by a ponytailed guy from UC–Santa Cruz whose girlfriend had just left for the market to shop for a brass Tara statue.

"If you really want to learn to meditate, vipassana is the only way to go," he'd lectured us, digging his fork into a slab of apple pie heaped high with whipped cream. "It's the exact same method the Buddha used. It's been passed down for thousands of years without changing a thing."

I dipped the end of my cinnamon roll into my chai, watching the sugar dissolve and float on the surface. "Does your girlfriend do vipassana, too?"

"No. She's into the Tibetan thing. She says the guys are hotter." He crammed another bite of pie into his mouth. "She's not really my girlfriend, actually. It's more of a friends-with-benefits kind of thing.

But the amazing thing is, I've developed so much equanimity through my vipassana practice, I don't give a shit any more."

That had sounded good to me.

But now it was only Day 1, and already things weren't looking so good.

I stared down at a scuffed linoleum floor and waited for the meditation teacher to strike the bowl-shaped bell that sat on a massive cushion at the other end of the room. I felt like one of the dogs I used to walk at Doggie Day Care, whining, staring at the leash, its whole body one quivering knot of longing: *Now . . . now . . . oh, please, now . . . now? Oh for God's sake, what are you waiting for?* Not that anything particularly exciting would happen when the bell rang: I'd just get to stretch out my aching legs, get up, and stalk back and forth in the garden at a pace of about two steps per minute, trying to concentrate on each sandaled foot touching the ground. Within ten minutes of doing that, I'd be looking forward to the bell ringing again, so I could sit back down on the cushion and resume concentration on the tip of my nose.

I'd been plodding along like this since five o'clock this morning, in a forced march through a sensory desert: Sit for forty-five minutes. Walk for thirty minutes. Sit. Walk. Sit. Walk. The afternoon stretched forbiddingly in front of me. Lunch—the big excitement for the day—was far behind, though the aftertaste of curried eggplant and yogurt still burped into my mouth. In the distance shimmered the oasis of afternoon tea.

When the teacher's voice cracked through the silence, I nearly jumped out of my skin. "If your mind has wandered," he suggested in a thick Australian drawl, "simply draw it back to the physical sensations of your breath."

*Drore it back. Sen-sie-shuns.* I'd been expecting the retreat to be led by an Indian monk in saffron robes, like the one who glared from the cover of the pamphlet I'd flipped through in the registration office. Instead it was team-taught by Karen, a beak-nosed New Yorker in her sixties with iron-gray hair and a dancer's posture; and Harold, a boyish Australian with brown curls, a disarming grin, and a Buddha tattooed on his right bicep. The room was packed with about fifty meditators—all of them also Westerners, as far as I could tell—sitting knee to knee, castaways in little islands of cushions, benches, shawls, used tissues, and water bottles.

*I'll tell them I have a heart condition.* I tried to wiggle my nose in a way that relieved the itch on my left cheek. *I'll tell them my mother is dying.* The itch crept around to my hairline. *I'll tell them I'm having contractions.* The itch burrowed into my ear canal. *Oh God. It's an earwig.* My hand flew to my ear, unbidden, and my finger poked around inside. Empty. I opened my eyes and peeked around to make sure no one had seen me. The woman on my left was shooting me a sidelong glare of withering contempt. *You loser,* said her eyes. *You just ruined my entire meditation.*

I closed my eyes again. How hard could it be, really? The instructions couldn't be simpler: I was to sit in silence, without moving, and anchor my attention in the present moment—"The only moment there is, mates," Harold had drawled. "The only moment in which enlightenment is possible."

He must be talking about some *other* present moment. My shirt was glued to my back with sweat. My pubic bone ached. My armpits smelled like a skunk. Every few minutes the man on my right released the sulfurous smell of rotten eggs. Rickshaws rumbled by, their horns warbling. My left leg had fallen asleep.

I remembered the Satyanam Ashram with nostalgia. Just a half hour or so of meditation, and then you got to chant! Light incense! Sing bhajans! From the perspective of a vipassana retreat, these activities seemed wildly decadent, like going clubbing.

Three more hours until tea.

## DAY 2

MY YOGI JOB was to wash the breakfast dishes—in silence, with concentration and awareness, as a kind of meditation in itself. I stood at the sink scrubbing clumps of burned apple crisp off Pyrex pans, rinsing sticky stewed-prune juice off stainless steel serving bowls.

Yesterday, I had liked this job. I had liked having a task laid out in front of me, with my progress so steady and clear, unlike my progress in meditation: first the dishes are dirty; then I apply effort; then they are clean. Maybe meditation retreats weren't so bad after all. Maybe I'd go on another one someday—in Hawaii this time, where I'd wash dishes again, mindfully, happily, looking out the window at banana trees and blue surf.

But today, another yogi showed up to help me: a surly young man who looked like Johnny Depp. I became nervous immediately. I splashed hot water down the front of my apron. I dropped my steel wool in the sink; fumbling for it under the suds, I nicked the tip of my finger on a chopping knife. I sensed his unspoken scorn. He dried the dishes so efficiently that I couldn't keep up; he stood twirling his dish-cloth, radiating impatience. I handed him a pan, and he handed it back to me with a grimace, pointing at a smear of blood on the handle. My face flamed with self-loathing. I lost my steel wool again.

## DAY 3

MY MEDITATION CUSHION had been compacted into a solid brick. When I closed my eyes, I felt as if I had been locked into a closet with a lunatic with a megaphone. With every breath, my bra dug into my ribcage. Why couldn't we take off our bras at the door along with our shoes? I pictured neat rows of hooks over the shoe racks, dozens of bras dangling, cups empty.

By midafternoon, I had developed a stabbing pain between my shoulder blades. On a bathroom break between meditation sessions, I did Downward Dog in a corner of the garden, trying to relieve it. But Karen swooped down on me. "No yoga," she hissed. "Be with your experience as it is. Do not attempt to manipulate it." Her expression implied that a yoga mat was a slippery slope: *One minute, you're in Downward Dog. The next minute, you're sitting in a gutter with a needle in your arm.*

## DAY 4

WE WERE NOT allowed to read or write, and I was starved for words. As I made my tea, I read and reread the milk carton: *Total fat, 15 grams. Saturated fat, 3 grams.* As I washed dishes, I read and reread the labels on the kitchen shelves: "Mixing Bowls." "Serving Bowls." "Please do not pile paper towel rolls more than three deep." I read and reread the sign in the bathroom: "Please do not put any item other than toilet paper in this or any other toilet."

But doing walking meditation in the garden, it hit me how blissful it was to be without words, to be in direct contact with experience instead: the sun on my face. The brilliant crimson of the hibiscus. The stench of the sewer in the street. The twitching of my baby inside me. The glimpse of wordless bliss was so powerful that I was seized with the compulsion to sneak back into my room and find my journal. *You want to capture the butterflies of experience in the net of words,* I told myself sternly. *But all you'll have left is dead bugs.* Then I sat on my cushion and recited this insight over and over, so I would remember to write it down.

## DAY 5

TIME HAD SLOWED to a crawl. Colors, sounds, and scents were stunningly vivid. At lunch, I chewed each bite for several minutes, marveling at the web of flavors and textures: onion, garlic, turmeric, salt, the silky crumble of potato, the snap of string bean. It was so delicious that it was almost painful.

After lunch, I sat on a bench in the small, enclosed back yard staring for twenty minutes at a branch: its veined, intricate leaves; the small buds of dormant flowers. Everything was intense: the touch of the wind on my skin; the smell of jasmine and exhaust, the cooing of the wood doves, the faces of the other yogis, who moved around the courtyard slowly, as if underwater. Even the roar of the traffic sounded like music. I felt my baby floating inside me.

So this was what they mean by "being present"! Well, no wonder people bothered to meditate. From now on, this was how I'd be all the time. I saw myself back in California, beaming at Ishtar and Ernie, washing their greasy two-day-old pasta-with-pesto dishes without a hint of resentment. At the park, children would flock to me, drawn by the peace I emanated. I would sit at The Bookends Café and write my guide to enlightenment, and guys would come to my table and ask if they could sit across from me while I wrote. *Just being around you makes me feel happy,* they'd say. *Want to go out for a drink sometime and tell me your secret? No secret,* I'd say. *I'm just savoring every passing moment, no matter how small.* And then, when I did hook up with one of them, the sex would be fabulous, because *I would be so present.*

The bell rang. I realized I had been gone for the last fifteen minutes.

## DAY 6

ALL MORNING, I felt the baby fluttering inside me: the faintest of butterfly wings deep in my pelvis. Sometimes I was sure I could feel the beating of its tiny heart.

I worried that my silence would frighten it. During walking meditation, I ducked into a bathroom and closed the door. "I'm still here," I said out loud, my voice husky from the long silence. "Don't worry." There was something else I want to say, but it took me a minute to figure out what it was. Then, "I love you," I whispered. As I said it, I knew for the first time that it was true. It was a feeling completely unlike the yearning I felt for Matt, or the affection for Lori. It was fierce, and protective, and as impossible to remove as my own skeleton.

## DAY 7

*IN. OUT. IN.* I was peace, I was light, I was infinite consciousness, vast as the sky. In. I was ambushed in the space between breaths by a memory of the time Matt took me rock climbing on the cliffs by Stinson Beach. Partway up the cliff, I'd missed a handhold and slipped, and suddenly I was spinning out into space, dangling on the end of his belay rope. *It's okay*, he'd called, holding the other end of the line. *I've got you.* For a moment I just hung there, relishing the fact that he had been there to keep me from plummeting to earth. Then I had reached out and grabbed onto the rocks again.

He'd always been the one opening the doors into the unknown so I could follow him through. It was one of the things I'd loved about him. But sitting alone on my meditation cushion, it hit me that the adventure of pregnancy and motherhood was as wild as any of the ones that Matt had invited me on. And he wasn't coming along.

*Out.* Tears began to trickle down my face. I was not supposed to wipe them away. I was not even supposed to wipe my nose. Maybe enlightenment was just the booby prize, the thing you went after when what you really wanted didn't work out. *We're so sorry,* says the game show host. *It looks like you won't be getting the perfect relationship, after all. But you do have a chance to win total inner peace! Okay,* you say, trying not to look disappointed. *I'll give it a shot.*

## DAY 8

WE SPENT THE morning sending *metta*—the Pali word for "loving-kindness"—to ourselves. To people we loved. To people we found difficult. To the whole universe. "May I be happy," I recited doggedly, hour after hour. "May I be peaceful. May I be free. May you be happy. May you be happy. May you be free."

The more I did it, the more annoyed I got. Half the people in the room were weeping. Others were beaming, as if they just couldn't contain their love, as if they were popcorn poppers exploding little emotional kernels into a fluffy white cascade of good feelings. I seemed to be the only one who wasn't getting it.

Then, in the middle of the afternoon, it hit me—a golden river of emotion breaking through a dam. I loved my baby, wriggling inside me. I loved the woman with irritatingly perfect hair on the cushion in front of me; the acned guy in the corner with the T-shirt proclaiming, "Darling, I Suffer, Please Help." I opened my eyes and beamed at Harold. *Thank you! Thank you for showing me my own inner radiance! I don't need Matt. In fact, I don't need any man to open the door to my heart.*

And then, bang! I was in love with Harold.

He was perfect for me! He was so evolved spiritually that he wouldn't mind the fact that I was having someone else's baby, because ordinary life is the best spiritual teacher there was, he said so himself in the dharma talk last night. We would travel around the world leading meditation retreats together. I would teach yoga, he would give dharma talks. Students would babysit for us as their yogi jobs.

I floated through the next few hours on a cloud of bliss. Late that afternoon, I looked out the window during walking meditation and saw Harold in the garden, talking to a young woman with a pink streak in her black hair. Rage and suspicion flooded me. *Talking! How can he be talking? Here I am struggling away hour after hour, trying to become enlightened—for our sake! For our survival as a couple!—and he is talking to a woman??*

It was all over between us.

## DAY 9

ONE BREATH, I longed for the retreat to be over. The next, I wished it would never end. It was hard to believe that what I wanted made no difference.

That evening, the wind picked up. It rattled around the building, whipped through the screens, blew a thin layer of reddish brown dust over the floor, the cushions, the bell. Karen closed the windows and lit candles on the altar. The room was a dark cocoon of peace. I didn't need anything, didn't want anything. If I could just stay there forever, I would be happy.

I remembered a rainy winter night at Tom's apartment, not long after we'd started seeing each other. Candles flickered on a low table in front of a fire in the fireplace. He'd picked up take-out Thai food, and we'd eaten in front of the fire: soup with coconut and lemongrass, red curry tofu. Then we'd watched a DVD of *My Big Fat Greek Wedding*.

The whole night had been so ordinary, so domestic; so unlike anything I had ever experienced with Matt. I'd called it dull, at the time; added it to the secret arsenal I was accumulating of Reasons Not to Be with Tom. But looking back, I now understood that Tom had picked out every detail with me in mind: ordering tofu instead of chicken because I was a yoga student, selecting a chick flick he'd never have watched on his own. With Matt, I was along for the ride on his wild adventure. With Tom, it was always all about me. And that in itself had been enough to make me dismiss him.

### DAY 10

THE RETREAT WAS OVER. A river of words flooded the meditation hall.

Out in the street, bicycle rickshaws pedaled down a street jammed with shops selling shawls, CDs, sandals, luggage, Buddha statues. A pony trotted past pulling a cart emblazoned with an Airtel slogan. A cow rooted through garbage by a crumbling wall painted with an underwear ad: MACHO INNERWEAR. NOTHING FITS BETTER. I stared at everything with incredulity and awe. I couldn't tell what was ordinary, what was extraordinary.

Devi Das and I picked our way through the traffic, heading back to our room at the Japanese temple guesthouse, pursued by a pack of boys selling malas made from seeds from the Bodhi Tree: "You buy! Good karma!" I bought one for a hundred rupees, even though Devi Das told me I shouldn't pay more than ten. I ran the rough, speckled seeds through my fingers, marveling. Who would think that something so huge could grow from something so small?

*In the pleasure-room, decorated with flowers, and fragrant*
*with perfumes, attended by his friends and servants, the citizen*
*should receive the woman, who will come bathed and dressed,*
*and will invite her to take refreshment and to drink freely. . . .*
*At last when the woman is overcome with love and desire, the*
*citizen should dismiss the people that may be with him, giving*
*them flowers, ointments, and betel leaves, and then when the*
*two are left alone, they should proceed . . .*

—*The Kama Sutra*, ca. AD 400

# CHAPTER 17

THE MAN AND the woman were naked, locked in an embrace.
The man was balanced on one foot, with the other leg twined around
the woman's waist; the woman was also on one foot, with a leg twined
around the man. Naked servants supported them on either side,
hands tucked coyly between their own legs.

"This position is impossible without yoga!" Our tour guide,
Rajesh, flashed light from a handheld mirror toward the sculpture.

The noon sun beat down on the sandstone lovers and the temple walls they were carved on. Sweat beaded on Rajesh's mustache and soaked the armpits of his pressed linen kurta. "At the time these temples were built, many people were becoming Buddhist. These temples showed people that it was much more fun to be Hindu. All the carvings represent the union of the human being with God. Now move along, please."

"The *rudest* sculptures I ever saw," sniffed a British man to his wife, as our clump of a dozen or so tourists trailed after Rajesh, snapping pictures and marveling in Japanese, French, English, and Hindi. "Personally, I can't comprehend why they can't become one with God with their clothes on."

THE THOUSAND-YEAR-OLD temples of Khajuraho were in the central plains of India, a three-day trip by train and car from Bodh Gaya. So that had given me plenty of time to think about sex on the way there.

Not just ordinary sex, of course. *Tantric* sex. Sex that could lead directly to enlightenment, without breaking your back over metal chairs or sweating on a cushion trying not to scratch the heat rash in your armpits. Sex that I could write about for Maxine, who had sent me a blistering email warning that the notes I'd sent her about my vipassana retreat were about as inspiring as the instruction manual for repairing a vacuum cleaner.

Now I pushed my sweaty hair back from my forehead and followed Rajesh. My underwear was getting too tight; I yanked the waistband down to accommodate my belly. Rajesh paused before another carving. "In tantra philosophy, God energy is not separate from sex energy!" He pulled out a bandanna and wiped the sweat from his forehead. "This one is also known as Monica Lewinsky pose." He waited for the obligatory titter, then flashed his mirror at another frieze. "And this group of sculptures shows the wedding night of

Shiva and Parvati. All the women in village are preparing for the celebration—bathing, putting on makeup, things like that."

Devi Das and I stepped closer. I examined a woman bathing, her filmy undergarments clinging wet to her skin, one arm reaching back to soap her spine. Another woman studied her face in a mirror, her lips pursed in an expression I recognized from watching girls put on makeup in the high school bathroom. Simultaneously complacent and critical, absorbed in making herself beautiful. Convinced that her beauty, once achieved, would make her happy forever.

"The marriage of Shiva and Parvati equals union of world with God," Rajesh said. "Shiva and Parvati are divine lovers." He gestured at the wall again. "Energy, matter. Form, formlessness. Spirit, flesh. They make love and make the whole universe. Without Shiva and Parvati—there is nothing. Am I clear?"

*Clear as Ganges water.* I looked up at what I presumed was a statue of Shiva and Parvati. Their regal faces were pressed close together, their arms laced around each other's waists. Let's see . . . Shiva's first wife was Sati, but in a fit of rage because her disapproving father didn't invite Shiva to a sacrificial feast, she immolated herself. Insane with grief, Shiva scattered her ashes all over India and went back to his lonely ascetic life, thereby threatening the existence of the entire cosmos. So Sati was reincarnated as Parvati (also known as Shakti), and—with the help of Kama, the god of love—was able to seduce Shiva from his yogic meditations.

But then Mr. Big showed up again and . . . wait, no, I was confusing it with the plot of *Sex and the City*. *Sex and the Siddhis?* The sun glared off the sandstone; I squinted, wishing I hadn't left my sunglasses on the train. I pulled my sweat-soaked shirt away from my belly, fanned myself with my bundle of postcards. Black spots danced in front of my eyes. The sculptured walls began to swim.

"Hey, are you okay?" Devi Das grabbed my elbow as I swayed against him.

"I think I just need to sit down for a minute."

Devi Das steered me down the temple steps and over to the shade of a fig tree. We sat down on the clipped grass, and I took a long swig from my water bottle. My hands were shaking. "Sorry. I should have brought a hat."

"It's not just the sun." Devi Das pulled a chocolate bar from his bag and handed it to me. "Here, have a bite of this. The energy in a place like this is powerful. Remember, it's a *thirtha*."

"A what?" I unwrapped the chocolate and took a bite.

"A *thirtha*. It literally means a ford in a river, a place where you cross over to the other side. But on the spiritual level, it means a place where the divine and the human worlds intersect. The veil between humans and the gods is thin in a place like this."

I reached out and picked up a soft, ripe fig that had fallen from the tree. I rolled it over and over in my hand. "Devi Das. You've been celibate a long time. Don't you ever miss having sex?"

He shrugged. "Oh . . . we miss it sometimes. But we don't miss all the drama that goes along with it. We don't miss the pain. We find that it's simpler just to skip the whole thing."

"But don't you get lonely?"

"Having a girlfriend is no guarantee we won't be lonely. Some of the loneliest people we know are in relationships." He took the fig out of my hand and bit into it. "And anyway, statistically, most relationships don't work out. Even most *marriages* don't work out. Not to mention the fact that there's a hundred percent chance that eventually one of you is going to die and leave the other person alone."

"But, when you look at it that way—isn't everything doomed, eventually? Sex, love, marriage, family, career, home—why do any of it, when it's all just going to end in death?"

Devi Das beamed at me. "Now you're talking like a good sadhu!"

"What I mean is—does the fact that something is going to end mean it's not worth doing? Shouldn't we throw ourselves into things, while they're here? While *we're* here?"

"And now you're talking like a good tantrika!" He lay back on the grass. "We're going to take a little nap. We recommend that you do the same thing."

I lay down next to him, turning onto my left side; according to HeyBaby.com, I wasn't supposed to lie on my back anymore, for fear of cutting off blood supply to the uterus. I propped myself up on my elbow, reached for my notebook, and scribbled the first few lines of a chapter for Maxine.

*If meditation, yoga, and celibacy aren't your thing, don't worry! Enlightenment has something for everyone. In the ancient tantric rituals, all that was forbidden in traditional yogic practice became a sacred act. The tantric yogis and yoginis ate meat, drank wine, and had ritualistic intercourse on the sacred altar. Through sexual activity, the tantrikas believed, they could awaken and unite the cosmic energies of masculine and feminine deities that flow within everyone. Then they could draw these energies up the spine to bring the mind to enlightenment.*

I put down my notebook and gazed at the temples, their peach-colored sandstone reflecting white in the sun. Parvati had managed to seduce Shiva, an ascetic god—the ultimate unavailable guy. Now their love for each other kept the whole universe alive. Why couldn't any of my relationships look like that?

"Excuse me," said a voice by my ear. "But I was just wondering— are you a huffer?"

I opened my eyes and sat up. Squatting next to me was a guy with brown hair cascading loose over his shoulders, a beard, and soulful brown eyes. He was dressed in white kurta pajamas. He looked like Jesus at a slumber party.

"A *what?*"

"I'm sorry—I thought you might be from Huff. A lot of us here this week are huff people." I stared at him blankly. *Huff the Magic Dragon? I huff and I puff and I blow the house . . .* "You know—the Human Un-foldment Foundation," he clarified. "HUF. They're based in Ojai, California. They've been holding a tantra workshop in the Taj Hotel."

"Oh. No. No, I—don't huff."

"HUF is open to anyone. All they need to have is a genuine open-ness to exploring their own sacred sexuality." He held out his hand. "My name's Om."

I put my hand in his. "Amanda."

He held my hand for a moment in both of his, then gave it a gen-tle squeeze before setting it down. "I'm really happy to meet you." He continued to gaze in my eyes, a little too intently. I recognized the look of someone who'd been overdosing on personal-growth work-shops; overpumped emotions, like the biceps of a guy who'd been working out too much. Sensitivity on steroids, Matt used to call it.

"So what do you do at a HUF workshop?" I asked.

He nodded in the direction of the temples. "Exactly what they used to practice right here. We learn to free up our sexual energy so that we can come together in the primal dance of Shiva and Shakti, without shame or inhibition."

He looked at Devi Das, sprawled out asleep next to me. His skinny legs stuck out below the fringe of his lungi. A fly buzzed around his face, landing on his upper lip, then darting away each time he breathed out. "So, is that your consort?"

"Oh—no! No. He's a sadhu. He's celibate. We're just traveling together."

"Ah—celibacy." Om shook his head in disbelief, as if I'd just told him that Devi Das had squandered an inheritance in a night of gam-bling at Las Vegas. "What a misguided concept." He reached into his pocket, pulled out a folded piece of pink paper, and handed it to me.

"HUF is hosting a party tonight in our suite at the Taj. I'd love it if you and your sadhu friend could make it."

I opened the flyer. On the top was a blurry photocopy of a detail from a Khajuraho sculpture: a woman and man seated naked with their legs wrapped around each other's waists. Beneath it, in ornate calligraphy, the text read: "An evening of music, dancing, ritual, and sensual exploration for gods and goddesses of all ages and sexual orientation. Invitation only."

"Bring your yoga mat," said Om. "It's always good to have a non-skid surface."

From: HeyBaby.com
To: Amandala@yahoo.com

With all the focus on decorating the nursery and planning the baby shower, don't forget about romance! You're in Week 18, well into the second trimester, and with morning sickness well behind you, you may notice that you're feeling frisky again. Pick out some sexy maternity lingerie and plan that candlelit dinner with your husband. Substitute a nice sparkling grape juice for champagne. And don't worry—you can't hurt the baby by making love!

SIX HOURS LATER—after a nap, a shower, and a falafel dinner at the Mediterranean restaurant near our guest house—Devi Das and I were walking into the marble-floored lobby of the Taj Hotel. A doorman in a red uniform with silver buttons held the door for us, averting his eyes from Devi Das's bare feet. Crystal chandeliers sparkled. A fountain bubbled behind a goddess statue holding out a bowl with an oil lamp burning in it. A flute player sat cross-legged by the elevator, playing a raga.

"I wish I had stopped in town to buy some nicer clothes," I said as we stepped into the elevator and pushed the button to the top floor. I'd put on the white *salwar kameez* I used to wear at the Satyanam Ashram, just because it was the cleanest thing I owned; but even after repeated scrubbings, there was still a faint green stain of cow manure on one leg. Not to mention that it radiated celibacy. Still, it seemed more appropriate than my yoga pants or my vipassana shawl. I hadn't realized that the road to enlightenment would require so many different outfits.

"Don't worry. Isn't the whole idea that you'll be taking your clothes off, anyway?"

We walked down a carpeted corridor and knocked at the door of the Royal Suite. It was opened by a chubby man in a white T-shirt, which was riding up to expose a pale roll of flesh hanging over the top of his jeans. He scrutinized our invitation, then greeted us each with a long, intimate hug, as if we were best friends with whom he shared a history so private that even we didn't know about it yet. "Make yourselves at home. Drinks are on the table under the window. You'll find dance cards next to them, if you want to start making plans for later in the evening."

He gave us each a friendly pat on the rear, then headed back into the room. I looked at Devi Das. *"Dance cards?"*

He pirouetted.

Inside, a couple of dozen guests drifted through the suite of rooms, which were illuminated by candles and the bluish glow of a large-screen television. The brocade curtains were drawn shut. The beds and sofas had been pushed to the sides to make room for futon-like pads scattered here and there on the floor, piled with silk pillows. Most of the women were wearing filmy dresses belted loosely at the waist, like togas. The men were wearing loose cotton pants and T-shirts, except for one mammoth man in an Indian lungi with metal-studded leather straps around his biceps. On one wall a slide show of images from the Khajuraho temples was being projected, one image dissolving dreamlike into the next. Flute music crooned reassuringly from speakers nested in a grove of potted palms.

"Wait here. I'll get us some juice." Devi Das headed toward the table under the window, where bottles stood sweating next to a stack of paper cups.

The air-conditioning was set too cold; goose bumps stood out on my bare arms. Trying to look nonchalant, I edged deeper into the room to look at the enormous television. On screen, an erect penis waved back and forth, with a mouth in violet lipstick a few inches away. Red-nailed fingers kneaded a mass of curly black pubic hair. I looked away quickly.

"Nice, isn't it?" Om had materialized next to me, holding a plastic cup in one hand and a paper plate full of pretzels in the other.

"Um, sure. I guess so."

"It's mine."

I couldn't think of a socially appropriate response. My skin suddenly felt too tight, like a badly fitting wet suit. In my peripheral vision billowed a pair of giant testicles.

"It's sixty inches," he informed me.

*"Sixty?"*

"HD. Sony. LCD. I had it flown in from Mumbai just for the weekend."

"Oh! You mean the TV." To cover my embarrassment, I reached out and grabbed a foil-wrapped after-dinner mint from a basket on the table next to me, and began to tear it open.

A young woman with olive skin and catlike eyes walked up behind Om and put her hand on his shoulder. She was wearing a purple silk sari, but she had left out the blouse that was supposed to go under it; the sari flowed gracefully over naked shoulders. Jasmine flowers were twined in her dark hair. If I had attempted that look, I'd look like I had gotten my hair snagged while crawling through underbrush wearing a bedsheet.

"Hi. I'm Natasha." She had a faint accent that I couldn't place: Russian? Czech? "I'm here with Om."

"We're together, but we're not exclusive," Om clarified. "We're into polyfidelity."

"Sounds like a new feature on your HDTV." I tugged at the foil wrapping of my mint and looked around for Devi Das. He was standing in the corner, a plastic cup in each hand, talking to a pink-haired girl wearing lavender yoga pants and a lacy bra with no shirt. She was laughing. She ran her hand down his freckled arm. Although I'd never felt the tiniest bit of romantic interest in Devi Das, I felt a flash of possessiveness. *Get your hands off my sadhu!*

"Polyfidelity has nothing to do with electronics," Natasha corrected me. *You even think of hitting on my man and you'll be in the gulag for life,* said her eyes. "Polyfidelity is when you have committed relationships with more than one person at a time."

"I know. I was kidding." Matt used to talk about polyfidelity as the way of the future, along with solar-powered cars and Green Party control of the Senate. But the idea always made me exhausted, like having call-waiting on your entire relationship. And I could tell that Natasha was not entirely on board either. *Don't worry,* I felt like telling her. *I don't want him. I'm just trying to salvage my manuscript.*

Natasha nodded at my belly. "So. When are you due?"

I'd been outed. I took a deep breath. "June."

I waited for Om to kick me out of the party. But instead his eyes lit up. "Wow! You're just doing it on your own?"

At a HUF party, unwed pregnancy was apparently an accessory as hot as a labia ring. "That's right." I'd finally gotten the wrapper off the mint. But something didn't feel right. I looked down and realized that I had actually been unwrapping a condom.

Om looked down and laughed. "Eager to get started?"

I opened my mouth to explain and a gong clanged; for an awful millisecond, I imagined I had emitted the sound myself. I looked around. In the center of the room, an immense woman swathed in purple silk with a wreath of leaves in her hair was banging with a spoon on a metal tray. "Time for the opening circle," she called. "All avatars and dakinis, please gather round!"

"That's Honeysuckle," Om informed me. "She's our workshop leader, along with her consort, Reuben. On the first day of the HUF workshop, we all looked at her cervix with a speculum."

I grabbed a meditation cushion from a pile by the wall and sat down next to Devi Das. On the other side of him sat the pink-haired girl in the lacy bra, with one proprietary hand on his knee. Om sat down next to me, with Natasha on the other side of him. The woman with the wreath in her hair was sitting in the center. Next to her, holding her hand, was the chubby man who met us at the door.

"I want to get out of here," I hissed to Devi Das. "I'm afraid Om's girlfriend is going to slit my throat with the cheese knife."

"Remember, it's research," he whispered back.

Honeysuckle clapped her hands to call for silence. "Welcome," she proclaimed, distributing smiles to right and left. Her purple sari billowed over miles of jiggling flesh. "Welcome to our sacred sensual space. Welcome to a place where flesh can embody spirit, as the goddess intended."

*Please don't show me your cervix.*

"Some of you have been journeying with us a long time; others have just joined," Honeyflower continued. "But we have all been drawn here through ancient karma. Maybe this is your first time to the temples of Khajuraho in this lifetime. But we have all incarnated here before. Tonight, we will reenact the sacred union of Shiva and Shakti as we meet in the dance of yoni and lingam." She held up a wicker basket. "Just remember that safe sex is the house rule. You'll find baskets of condoms at convenient locations."

"Don't worry. I get tested every month," Om whispered in my ear.

"We've also provided mango-vanilla massage oil, which, you'll
be happy to know, *is* edible"—she displayed a small vial—"and a va-
riety of lubricants, in case of an emergency."

*Terrorist attack? Earthquake? Not to worry—we've got Astroglide!*
To ward off a giggle, I stared hard at Honeysuckle's hands, which fluttered like plump white pigeons. The hands swooped down, pounced
on another item, and held it up: a box of plastic wrap. "And, of course,
a sheet of this is indispensable. Believe me, you'll never even know it's
there."

I found it difficult to manage plastic wrap even when I was just
wrapping chicken drumsticks: the way it clung to the edges of its box,
stuck to itself in wads. The giggle erupted through my nose. To cover
it, I began coughing, and fumbled in my backpack for a nonexistent
Kleenex. Honeysuckle flashed her teeth in my direction. "Any questions, before we get started? No? Then let's all get up and form two
concentric circles for the invocation."

We all scrambled to our feet and gathered in two sloppy circles,
facing each other. Sitar music whined. "Open the heart; look in the
eyes; kiss the hand; and step to the left," Honeysuckle intoned. "Open
the heart; look in the eyes . . ."

I picked up the damp, fleshy hand of the man across from me and
gazed into his worried eyes. "Kiss the hand . . ." As he lifted my hand
toward his lips, I tried to picture the yogis and yoginis of Khajuraho
doing this dance: robed monks, bejeweled princes, dancing girls. Did
what we were doing here have even the slightest bit in common with
what they were up to? For that matter, did what we were doing on
our yoga mats have anything to do with what the ancient yogis were
doing in their Himalayan caves? "Step to the left . . . Open the
heart . . ." I picked up the bone-dry hand of an older woman, which
lay in my mine delicate as a leaf. Her blue eyes were filmy and sad as I
brought the back of her hand to my mouth.

I remembered how Tamara used to spend hours chatting on her

toy cell phone, ordering items from catalogs spread out all over the al-
phabet rug on her playroom floor. She even had a fake credit card that
she'd whip out of her plastic purse. When the tea party set that she'd
ordered from Pottery Barn Kids never arrived, she was inconsolable.
It turned out she hadn't realized that her props weren't the real thing.

The music stopped. I stood opposite a man with a long beard and
gray eyes. The silence went on and on. Was I supposed to look at just
one eye, then the other? Both at the same time? My contact lenses
were drying out; I was afraid if I blinked, one would pop out of my
eye. I studied a quivering vein at the tip of his nose.

Honeysuckle rang the gong. We all bowed, our hands in prayer
position at our hearts. Then everyone started looking for someone to
hook up with.

Om grabbed my right arm and drew me to my feet. Panicked, I
looped my left forefinger through Devi Das's sash. The pink-haired
girl wrapped her arm around Devi Das's waist. Natasha latched on to
Om's right hand. As if playing Crack the Whip on a crowded playground, the five of us wobbled through the room and collapsed on a
futon.

"It's good to grab a spot right away, before they all get taken,"
Om told me. He ignored Devi Das, as if he were an accessory that
could be removed later, like a bra.

"Good job," said Devi Das's escort happily. She had the most perfect breasts I had ever seen, displayed like twin peaches in their lacy
black cups. No wonder she didn't want to wear a shirt. Her breasts
looked like they should be on display in a museum exhibit called
"What You are Supposed to Look Like." I stared at my toenails, splitting and crusted with dirt. All around us, people were starting to slip
out of their clothes.

"I know," said the pink-haired girl. "Let's give each other massages to break the ice. We can take turns—one person receives while
all the rest give. We'll draw straws to see who goes first." She reached

into a nearby basket and sorted through a handful of condoms. "Okay—I've got four Trojans and one MAXX Plus. The one who draws the MAXX gets lucky. Everyone close your eyes!"

There was a flurry of colliding hands. When I opened my eyes, I was holding the MAXX Plus condom.

"Lucky you!" The pink-haired girl seemed to have assumed the role of camp activities director. "Take off your clothes and lie down. Five minutes each, then we'll switch."

Reluctantly, I began to pull off my *salwar kameez*. The party was starting to feel like one of those nightmares where I found myself standing naked on a spotlighted stage, running for president. At what point did I call the research off? I lay down on the futon, leaving on my bra and underwear, which stretched like a rubber band over my swelling belly. This way I could at least pretend I was in a bathing suit.

"Genitals or no genitals?" The pink-haired girl was as matter-of-fact as a waitress offering fresh-ground pepper.

"None!" I said, too quickly.

"Wow." Om cupped his hand over my belly. "Your belly is beautiful. Is it okay to touch it?"

I felt like crying. How many times had I longed for Matt to feel the baby kick? I rolled on my side. "Actually, why don't I lie this way and you can do my back."

Om and Devi Das and Natasha and Pink-Hair-Girl began pouring Kama Sutra oil into their hands and rubbing it on my skin. It was thick and sticky and smelled like cotton candy. I shut my eyes. Hands coast and glided over my body, with varying degrees of pressure and expertise: kneading my shoulders, rubbing my head, massaging up and down the length of my spine. "Your heart is like the sun . . . ," crooned the CD player. "You are the light of the Universe . . ." I'd been longing to be touched for months. But this was even less satisfying than the ten-minute promotional massages they sometimes offered at Whole

Foods, where you sat in a massage chair next to the meat department and someone squeezed your shoulders while other customers ordered free-range beef.

"Tell us what you like," murmured Om.

"Oh—it all feels good." I'd always hated that question. That question presumed that my body was a map with fixed landmarks. But instead it felt like a mysterious, ever-changing estuary where waters were constantly flowing in and out, and what was a sand dune yesterday was a tide pool today. That used to drive Tom crazy; he wanted to know that the button he pushed yesterday would yield the same result today. "Making love with you is as complicated as a moon launch," he'd told me once. But Matt had loved it. "You're an entirely new woman every time I'm in bed with you," he'd said. "It's like having multiple relationships with one woman."

*Must not think about Matt.* Someone began to knead my sacrum. Someone else began to run their fingers in and out of the spaces between my toes. I flinched away; my feet had always been ticklish. I opened my eyes and noticed that the sofa next to our futon had been occupied by a pair of colossal buttocks, glowing blue in the tinted light. Squinting, I saw that they belonged to Honeysuckle, who was kneeling with her dress hitched up around her waist. From between her billowing thighs protruded two flailing, spider-thin legs, naked except for a pair of Nikes.

I sat up. "I'm sorry," I said. "I need to leave."

BACK AT THE Kama Sutra Lodge, I lay on my side on my thin mattress, exhausted. My skin smelled like a candy stand at the county fair. Devi Das flopped across the end of my bed.

"You could go back there if you want," I told him. "I feel bad about wrecking your evening."

"Will you stop apologizing? You probably saved us another fifteen incarnations, at least. That girl had 'samsara' written all over her. She's exactly what we became a sadhu to get away from."

"The sad thing is, I really could use a good massage. I just couldn't do it with Honeysuckle frolicking three feet away."

"You've been needing a massage? Why didn't you say so?" Devi Das sat up, scooted down the bed, and put his hands on my back. "That we can definitely handle." His bony fingers kneaded expertly up and down my spine. I felt my muscles soften under his touch.

"Hey. You're pretty good at that."

"We actually studied shiatsu in a previous life. We were planning to be a bodyworker."

Yet another thing I hadn't known about Devi Das. Who would he be—who could he be—if he'd just take off his sadhu suit for a while? But maybe that was as futile as asking me to stop pretending to be Amanda. I closed my eyes, let out a deep breath I hadn't realized I'd been holding. I felt my brain melting, as if it could run in a gelatinous shampoo out of my ears and into the pillow.

"Did you notice, when we were at the temples this morning, that the sculptures were all on the outside walls?" Devi Das's hands moved down to my sacrum. "When we got inside, the walls were bare."

I nodded, too tired to answer. The temple we went into had been cool and dark, a respite from the sun. An immense stone lingam, the phallic symbol of the god Shiva's power, nested in the inner sanctum. I'd leaned my cheek against a stone wall. I could have stayed there all day.

"Our guru once told us that that's how it is in our life, too. All the things we're so busy with—sex, work, travel—they're just beautiful decorations on the outside walls. But when we close our eyes and really go inside, there's nothing but space and silence."

I was starting to drift off. I pictured my life as a sandstone temple standing in the blazing sun. Sculptures snaked around the walls: Matt. Tom. My mother. Lori. Sam and Tamara. My baby. There were carvings of computers, yoga mats, dogs, wine bottles, boogie boards, pacifiers. Ishtar was there, and Ernie, and Darshana, and Om. There were spiritual teachers: Harold, and Mr. Kapoor, and Hari Baba, and Sri Satyaji. Every surface was boiling with life, every detail lovingly rendered. *Look,* the sculptures proclaimed. *Look. Isn't life crazy? Isn't life wonderful?*

What would it be like, to open the doors of that temple and walk inside, where the walls were bare? Would I be lonely? Or would I just rest in the quiet darkness, finally at peace?

Anne Cushman

# Reclining Bound Angle Pose
# (supta baddha konasana)

*Lie on your back, your spine draped over the length of a bolster. Put the soles of your feet together and let your knees fall out to the sides. Spread your arms out to the sides, palms open to the sky. Spelunk your awareness down into the dark cave of your belly.*

*Here in the liquid darkness of your own womb lives Devi, the great Mother Goddess of fertility, rain, and earth. Go into the temple of your own pelvis and bow down before her altar. But don't be surprised if what appears is your own mother instead. You may meet her rage, or passion, or terror, or tenderness. You may meet her longing or broken dreams. Her life is lodged in your cells. Her story quivers below the surface of your own. And everything she couldn't allow herself to feel you have swallowed whole. It rests like a stone inside your belly, waiting for you to digest it.*

*The Divine Mother is to be meditated upon as shining in a vermilion-red body, with three eyes, sporting a crown of rubies studded with the crescent moon, a face all smiles, a splendid bust, one hand holding a jewel-cup brimming with mead, and the other twirling a red lotus . . .*

—*Lalita Sahasranama*, ca. AD 1000

# CHAPTER 18

RIGHT HERE'S THE baby's head," said Dr. Rao. "It's got its nose pressed right up against the placenta. See?"

I was lying on an examining table in Dr. Rao's office in Bangalore with Devi Das standing beside me. Dr. Rao had smeared a cold jelly all over the taut dome of my belly and was moving the ultrasound wand slowly across it, studying a monitor next to the table. I peered at the screen: pulsating blobs of white on a black background, swirling like a satellite photo of an incoming storm.

"Sure," I lied.

"We don't see it at all." Devi Das studied the image. "But that's okay. Once we spent three weeks in a Tibetan monastery trying to visualize a green Tara. Instead, we kept visualizing the lady on the Green Goddess salad dressing bottle. We worried that that would slow down our spiritual progress. But it actually seemed to accelerate it."

So far, Dr. Rao had told me, everything at my nineteen-week checkup looked like a textbook pregnancy: perfect weight gain, perfect blood pressure, perfect numbers on my blood work. But part of me was still waiting for the other shoe to drop: for Dr. Rao to tell me that I needed to go back to California immediately, doctor's orders. I wasn't sure whether these orders were something I dreaded, or longed for.

"Here's the spine, running right along here. The baby's lying on its back." That I saw: a delicate, almost reptilian curve. "And look, there's the heart." I stared at the throbbing blob, then looked away. The truth is, I didn't really want to see inside my uterus. It felt like opening the oven door while the soufflé was rising. Instead, I studied Devi Das's hands resting on the edge of the table: the knuckles raw and chapped, dirt ground into the grooves around the fingernails.

"And here's the pelvis . . . and the bladder. Everything's looking good. Do you want to know if it's a boy or a girl?"

"You mean you can already tell?"

"Well, it's not a hundred percent accurate unless we do an amnio, which there's no reason to do in your case. But we can usually be about ninety-nine percent sure."

This was all happening too fast. I looked at Devi Das. "We're the wrong person to ask," he said. "We peek at hidden Christmas presents. We read books from back to front."

"Um . . ." I studied the image on the screen, which now resembled a poodle: ultrasound as Rorschach test. "Sure, go ahead and tell me." And then, changing my mind, I said, "Actually, don't!" while, at the same time, Dr. Rao said, "It looks like he's a little boy."

A boy. A boy? "Wow," I said. Dr. Rao was looking at me

expectantly, so I repeated myself, with more enthusiasm this time: "Wow! A boy!"

"A boy!" echoed Devi Das. "You can name him after us!"

The truth is, I was going to need some time to get used to the idea. I hadn't even realized it till this moment, but all along I'd been assuming I was carrying a smaller version of myself, tucked inside me like one of those Russian nesting dolls. Instead, I was incubating a little creature who would someday forget to return some girl's phone calls; who would say "That was fun" instead of "I love you" while getting out of bed with her; who would surf the Internet while she was on the phone trying to talk about their relationship, then try to make her feel better by driving her up the coast to a bed-and-breakfast, ruining the effect by listening to his iPod through headphones the whole way.

"And here are his feet . . . see the little toes?" Dr. Rao had moved on, but I was still stuck. A boy. What did I know about boys? Cacophonous drum and bass blaring from a bedroom, pizza crusts on the kitchen floor. I would try to talk to my teenage son, but I wouldn't know what to say, and he and his friends would roll their eyes and ignore me, and it would be exactly like being back in high school.

The ultrasound was over. I wiped the jelly off, sat up, and pulled down my shirt. Dr. Rao was still talking—nutrition, kick counts, Braxton Hicks contractions, epidurals—but I could barely focus. She handed me a stack of pamphlets. "If you have any questions about what we've been discussing, these should help. I recommend that you come back for another checkup in about a month. Where are you going after this?"

"To an ashram by the ocean in the south." I flipped through the pamphlet on the top: *What You Should Know About Circumcision.* Yikes. "There's a woman guru there named Prana Ma who's supposed to be an incarnation of the Divine Mother. You know, the goddess who made the whole universe."

Dr. Rao raised her dark eyebrows. "I see mothers all day long. To me, they are all divine. What could be more powerful than bringing another human being into the world through your own body?" She turned to the printer in the corner. "But many of them are just coming to the clinic for the 'sex test.' If they discover that they are carrying a little girl, they abort her rather than bringing another woman into the world. Last week at the free clinic, I saw a pregnant woman with burn scars all over her face and body. Her husband had doused her with kerosene and set her on fire because her family failed to provide a sufficient dowry. And this is not unusual. What is unusual is that she lived." The printer started up with a whine. "If half of the people who are so thrilled about visiting a Divine Mother were to turn their attention instead to taking care of some actual mother right in their own village—maybe right in their own house—India would be a better place."

She turned back to me, holding out a small stack of pictures. "Here you go. These are a few of the images from your ultrasound."

I took one and looked at it: a space alien with immense eyes, a bulging forehead, a tiny mouth budded with teeth. He was looking straight at me, one hand lifted, as if he were greeting me from across a galaxy.

From: Lori647@aol.com
To: Amandala@yahoo.com

That's fantastic! Boys aren't all hopeless: look at Joe. You just have to make sure you housebreak him properly. I read somewhere that if little boys challenge your authority, you have to do this thing called the "alpha takedown," where you throw them to the ground on their backs and stick your face up close and yell in their face. Oh, wait, no, maybe that's dog training I'm thinking of.

THE FERRY RIDE from the train station to the ashram took all day, a dreamlike glide through lush backwaters. Our boat was a small barge with no chairs, just a few patched blankets tossed on the rough deck. It churned through coconut groves and rice paddies, along banks dotted with huts thatched with bamboo. Outhouses woven out of palm fronds hung over the water.

Around us glided dugout canoes and fishing boats with hooked prows—carved from jackfruit wood, Devi Das told me, and tarred black to make them waterproof. They were poled by wiry, stern men in white lunghis. Women in saris blazing with color—vermilion, turquoise, lemon—waved at us as we glided by. Naked children dove in and out of the water like otters.

Half of the deck was covered with a tattered awning, but for now I just lolled in the sun, my wide-brimmed straw hat shading my face. The passengers were mainly Indians, with a few Westerners I suspected were also ashram bound: a woman in Birkenstocks and a turquoise sari whose dirty-blonde hair fountained from a topknot; a shirtless guy in a ponytail and khaki shorts with a blue-faced Krishna tattooed on his hairy chest. Devi Das sat beside me, eating mango after mango that we'd bought from a fruit seller at the dock. At twenty weeks pregnant, my body felt swollen all of a sudden—nipples puffy, breasts blue-veined and tender. That morning, I had noticed that a dark line had appeared down my belly from my navel to my pubic bone. The baby danced inside me. I felt lazy and ripe—a banana tree laden with fruit, an ocean bursting with fish.

"I can't believe I'm going to have a *son,*" I said to Devi Das. Now that I'd gotten used to it, the idea enchanted me: A toddler in overalls, digging for worms. A boy with a mop of curly hair shooting baskets in my driveway.

"Well, technically speaking, you *already* have a son."

"I guess so. Wow. So does that mean I'm already a *mother?*"

He patted me on the back. "Congratulations, Mom."

*Mom.* I rolled the word around in my mind, trying to make it apply to me. *Mom.* A person who could be counted on to carry

Band-Aids in her purse, frost and decorate cupcakes, construct toy airplanes out of paste and popsicle sticks. Not that my mother was ever like that. If the Divine Mother were anything like my mother, the world would be half finished—mountain ranges partially dusted with trees, then abandoned; oceans boiling away untended until all the water evaporated and the ocean floor was burned black, like a forgotten teakettle. Come to think of it, maybe that *was* what was wrong with the world these days. The Divine Mother had gotten distracted, wandered on to some more compelling project in some other universe. *Sorry, darling,* she was saying, looking down at Earth tugging at her robes. *I lost track of time.*

"Were you close to your mom?" I asked Devi Das.

He shrugged. "Our mom wasn't what you'd call close to anyone, except maybe her shrink. I think she had some kind of obsessive-compulsive disorder. She had a C-section just so she wouldn't have to deal with the sloppiness of giving birth. The main thing she noticed about us and our brother was how messy we made things."

"Do you keep in touch at all?"

"We send her a postcard every once in a while. And every Christmas she sends us a check for $457.43. I think it's some formula her tax accountant figured out." He pulled another mango from his shoulder bag and sliced into it with his knife, tossing the peels over the edge of the boat. They bobbed on the waves, gently falling away behind us. Silver fish broke the surface, snapping at them. "How about you? Have you told your mother you're pregnant yet?"

"Not yet. I'm still getting up the nerve."

"What are you afraid of?" He offered me a slice of mango, slick with juice.

"I guess I'm afraid she'll make it all about her, somehow." I popped the fruit into my mouth, slippery and luscious. A boat glided past: an older man in the prow poling it along, a young boy in the back casting a rope net into the water. "There was only room for one drama queen in our house, when I was growing up. And my mother always made clear that that was her."

The couple of times I'd brought home boyfriends to meet my mother, she'd alternated between manic charm and outright hostility, as if she couldn't decide whether she wanted to seduce them or obliterate them. I remembered one year, shortly after Matt and I began seeing each other, when he'd come home for Christmas with me. It was not a home I'd ever been to before: a studio apartment in Santa Barbara, overlooking a parking lot, where my mother was trying to start a new career as a real estate agent.

"The market is booming," she'd told us. "One big sale, and I've got the down payment on my own place." My mother had ordered Christmas dinner from a gourmet deli up the street. Matt and I sat at the table with her, opening white take-out boxes and dumping their contents into pottery bowls and platters she'd fired herself the week before, while she drank glass after glass of Gallo chardonnay and told us about her latest boyfriend's experiments with Viagra. "When he turned fifty, he went out and bought himself a motorcycle," she had told us, pouring another glass of wine. "As if I wouldn't notice his little problem if he rode up on a Harley." I heaped mashed potatoes into a white serving bowl with a nude, winged goddess painted on it, carefully burying a triangle of purple pubic hair.

When Matt excused himself to go to the bathroom, I screwed up my nerve to tell my mother that I'd prefer she not discuss her intimate life in front of my boyfriend. She flew into a rage and stormed out of the apartment. After waiting for an hour, Matt and I started to heat up the food in the microwave, but of course my mother's bowls weren't microwave proof. The naked goddess shattered, spewing mashed potatoes and gravy mixed with particles of ceramic. My mother didn't come back until morning.

Still, when things didn't work out with Matt and me, my mother was upset, as if our breakup was a personal rejection of her. *You should have fixed yourself up a little more,* she told me on the phone; *you should have been more tolerant. Men need a long leash.* She called back an hour later. *No, you should have been firmer, laid down the law right from the beginning, let him know how things were going to be. Your road or the high road.* My failure to keep Matt was just another way that I had fallen short—and another way that men had let her down, yet again.

"It's as if every drama in my life had to become her drama," I said now. "I don't want this to happen with my pregnancy. Whenever I tell her about something, it becomes hers. And then she retells it and reshapes it until I don't even recognize it any more."

"Well, this is your baby, not hers. How could her knowing about it make that any different?"

"It's hard to explain. I'm so different from her. But still sometimes I don't know where she ends and I begin. It's like she's inside me, commenting on everything I do. And it's hard enough for me to tell what I think about this pregnancy. I don't want it to get all mixed up with her feelings about it."

After the incident with Matt, I'd erected a kind of firewall between me and my mother: going home as little as possible, and when I did, telling her as little as possible about my life. Now I put my hands on my belly. *A mother. I'm a mother.* The thought was terrifying.

I wasn't just afraid of becoming a mother. I was afraid of becoming *my* mother.

## Enlightenment for Idiots: Sample Chapter Draft

In Hindu mythology, the great goddess manifests in countless forms: the bloodthirsty destroyer Kali, with her long red tongue and the garland of skulls around her neck; the toothsome Parvati, the consort of Shiva; the mighty Durga, who annihilates the demons of ignorance with her own ferocity.

Now hundreds of thousands of people around the world believe that the Divine Mother has incarnated as Prana Ma, a plump, radiant Indian woman whose ashram in southern India hosts thousands of devotees every year. In her "darshans," or face-to-face blessings, Prana Ma blows on the forehead of each one of her followers—a "breath of life" that is believed to lift the devotee to a whole new level of spiritual existence. To date, according to the ashram brochure, she has blown on over 20 million people around the world.

~~Prana Ma is a fountain of divine maternal love, which may be particularly healing to those whose own mothers lacked~~

~~If the image of mother love isn't a particularly soothing one to you~~

~~Dear Mom—I know you'll be as excited as I am to hear my wonderful news~~

"WHEN I MET Prana Ma, I was nineteen years old." The woman on the sleeping mat next to mine peered at me through the veil of mosquito nets that separated us—a waif with stringy hair and worried eyes, dressed in a white *salwar kameez*. She was clutching a stuffed doll to her chest. Her name was Kalyani, which she had informed me was a Sanskrit word meaning "blissful." "I was working in a diner in Albuquerque, cracking eggs into a bowl, when a friend of mine walked in and said, 'I just heard about an avatar in South India.' And all the hair on my body stood on end."

"Mmm." I tried to communicate as little interest as possible without actually telling her to shut up. My head pounded; my lower back ached; my eyes were swollen and itchy from dust. I could hardly hear Kalyani over the wail of the bhajans playing from the speakers in the courtyard outside, endless hymns to the Divine Mother that made my head throb even harder. *Kali Ma, Durga Ma, Kali Kali Durga Ma...*

"That afternoon my boyfriend left me," Kalyani continued. "Two days later, my puppy died. Next week, my cat ran away. Then the restaurant folded. Within a month, I was in India."

"Mmm." I closed my eyes. Was there anywhere in this ashram I could find a Motrin?

"When I first met Ma, I put my head in her lap and cried. Three days later, I saw her heal a leper, and that was it."

Kalyani and I were in the women's dormitory of the massive Prana Ma Ashram—really just an huge, unfurnished room on the tenth floor of an apartment building, jammed with devotees, where you could roll out a cotton mat from a stack in the corner. I'd tried for a private room, or even a double, but the ashram was packed with thousands of pilgrims in anticipation of an upcoming festival, an annual extravaganza in which Prana Ma was apparently going to appear as the Divine Mother in all her glory. So I'd tried to carve out the illusion of personal space by attaching one end of my mosquito net to the corner window ledge behind me, the other end to the straps of my backpack, which I'd laid at the end of my mat. But a few mosquitoes had still managed to get in—they zoomed around my head, fat and bloodthirsty, whining death threats.

"I'm sorry, but I need to be quiet for a little while," I told Kalyani. "I'm really not feeling that great."

"Oh, I'm so sorry." She thrust out her rag doll toward me: a squat little figure whose face I recognized from the flyers lying all around the ashram. Its red mouth was pursed in a whistle. "Would you like to hold my Prana Ma doll?"

"Uh—no thanks." I pulled out a yellow leaflet and studied the schedule printed on it. *Bhajans . . . meditation . . . work . . . darshan . . . more work . . . scriptural study . . . more bhajans . . .* I rolled over onto my side. "I'll just take a little nap until dinnertime."

"If you're feeling tired, the best thing to do is go to darshan and get blown on. It will give you all the energy you need."

I was going to strangle her. I truly was. "I'm sure I'll appreciate it more after a little sleep."

"Prana Ma never sleeps. She's plugged into universal energy. I went on tour with her last year as one of her personal assistants, and it just about killed me. She was up until four in the morning blowing on people, every night, and all of her assistants had to stay up with her. Then she would sleep for two hours and get up and do it again. After the tour was done, I had to check into a hospital for a week. *That's* how powerful her love is."

*Maybe if I just lie here, she'll go away.*

"When Westerners come here, our heads are so full. We are so dry. That's why Mother doesn't talk much. There's this aching wound in us, this longing for love. That's what she gives us."

*Then again, maybe she won't.*

Kalyani sat up and looked at her watch. "Oh, look at the time. We better go or we'll miss darshan. Besides, in just a few minutes the work practice crew will be coming through here to mop the floors."

*I give up.* I sat up. Okay, I'd go get blown on. Who knew? Maybe Prana Ma would blow me all the way to enlightenment, and I could go home to California and have my baby.

# Anne Cushman

•  •  •

DARSHAN TOOK PLACE in an auditorium with doors and windows open to let in the humid breeze. Kalyani and I joined a queue of hundreds and began inching toward Prana Ma, who sat in a padded armchair on a stage at the front of the room. I did the math in my head: *Let's see . . . roughly three hundred people ahead of me . . . Let's say each blow takes ten to fifteen seconds . . . that means I'll get mine in about . . . an hour and a half?* My feet ached, my shoulders ached, my pubic bone ached. But as I flipped through the pamphlet I picked up at the door, I began to get excited. Prana Ma's breath on your face was like diving into a pool of infinite love and compassion, her devotees claimed. Your mind went still. Your heart bloomed open. You fell into infinite darkness; you lit up with infinite light. Maybe there was no need to do endless hours of yoga, to sit for hours in meditation, to purify *prakriti* from *purusha* or get massaged by strangers in frilly bras. Maybe all it took was getting breathed on by the right person.

Two hours later, I was within ten feet of Prana Ma. The line was feverish with anticipation. Devotees jostled together, riveted on the tiny woman on the stage, who was leaning forward, blowing on one person after another. Kalyani had forgotten all about me; I was just another body competing in the crush. My nose was jammed between the shoulder blades of the sweaty man in front of me. Pulling back, I stepped on the foot of the woman behind me. Before I could stammer my apology, she drove her elbow hard into my kidneys.

A white-robed Indian woman pushed a laminated card into my hands. I looked down at it: "Remove glasses," it warned. "Wipe off perspiration. Blow nose. Don't blow on Prana Ma, just let her blow on you." Then I was down on my knees, wiggling toward Prana Ma in a crush of people. In front of me, a middle-aged Western man was kneeling before Prana Ma. Her hands were cupping his face; she was alternately blowing on his forehead and murmering something in his ear. He was sobbing. His bald spot glistened with sweat.

Now it was my turn. I knelt in front of Prana Ma. She smelled like jasmine perfume, sickeningly sweet. Her hands cupped my face. She was crooning something in my ear in Malayalam, singsongy as a nursery rhyme. Her breath was a warm blast on my forehead. It smelled like breath mints.

Prana Ma spoke again, and the slender Indian woman next to her leaned forward to translate. "Mother says, blessings on your baby girl," she told me.

"Oh—thanks," I said. I must really be showing now. "But actually, it's a boy."

Prana Ma gave a peal of laughter and shook her head. "Not boy," she said in English, patting my back indulgently. "Girl." She said something else to the translator, who leaned forward again. "Prana Ma says: You are having a little girl. You will have some troubles with the pregnancy, but do not worry—all will be well. And you will name her Aradhana, which means 'worship.'"

*The mother's thoughts during her pregnancy play an important part in the child's character. That is why in olden times a mother would always chant the Divine Name during pregnancy. If this is done, the child also will be one who remembers God.*

—Mata Amritanandamayi (1953– )

# CHAPTER 19

I CAN'T BELIEVE IT." Kalyani sat down across from me at a long table in the cafeteria. "What an incredible blessing. Your very first time seeing Prana Ma, and she gives you a name for your baby." She eyed me with a mixture of envy and hostility, as if she couldn't decide whether she wanted to kill me or *become* me. "I was with her for a whole *year* before she even told me that my dog that died had been reborn as a little boy in India who would one day be her devotee."

"The only problem is, Aradhana is a girl's name. My baby is a boy." I scooped the runny rice and dal off my metal tray with my fingers. The line at the Western café was too long, so we had come to the Indian canteen instead. I was having a hard time letting go of my fantasies about mashed potatoes and steamed vegetables, but I just couldn't face standing in another line.

"What's the diference? It's Sanskrit," said Devi Das. "No one will even know. You can call him Ari. Or Dan."

"Oh, it will be a girl," said Kalyani. "Prana Ma's never wrong about these things."

"The doctor saw the ultrasound." Across from us, a Western guy in a brown ponytail was shaking spirulina from a ziplock bag onto his dal. I watched in repulsed fascination as he stirred it with his fingers, turning it into a viscous green slime. "The baby had a penis."

"Well, those machines aren't a hundred percent accurate, are they?" Kalyani licked yogurt off her fingers. "Besides, Prana Ma can remove a penis, no problem."

"Please," said Devi Das. "Can we not talk about removing penises? It makes us uncomfortable."


MAKING CHAPATIS, it turned out, was harder than it looked. The next morning, I stood at a long wooden counter in the industrial-sized kitchen with a row of other women, mainly Indian, all wearing white saris. Their hands flew here and there, coated with flour: scooping up apple-sized blobs of dough, flattening them with their palms, then rolling them into neat circles with wooden rolling pins. In the time it took mc to roll out one lumpy, misshapen chapati, the woman next to me produced ten, dusting them with flour and piling them high.

She probably learned this from her mother, I thought, watching her hands. But in my mother's world, the closest we ever came to baking was the time we bought a roll of Sara Lee chocolate chip cookie dough, planning to slice it up and make cookies for an after-school treat. I must have been in second or third grade at the time; my mother was between jobs, so she was actually home in the afternoon, a rare occurrence at that time of my life. As we started to slice, my mother remembered that we didn't own a cookie sheet. So we ended up sitting at the kitchen table, eating the dough raw straight out of the package.

My mother put on a jazz CD and poured a glass of wine for herself and a wineglass of apple juice for me. She sat down next to me and gave me a hug. "You see, darling," she said, sounding surprised herself. "Sometimes what actually happens is even more fun than what you had planned."

I tried to peel my chapati off the countertop, but it shredded to pieces. The woman next to me took pity on me. "Need more flour." She sprinkled her own spot with a handful to demonstrate. "No sticking."

"Thanks." I scraped the dough off the counter, shook more flour on. "I'm sorry—I've never done this before."

A wide smile lit up her whole face. "Every time, getting better. Soon—very good." Her hands never stopped moving. "You baby—coming when?"

Funny how women could tell immediately that I was pregnant, even with my baggy clothes. Whereas so far, not a single man had guessed. "June."

"I have three childs. One girl, two boy."

"That must keep you busy."

"Happy—yes. Always very happy." She rolled out another chapati in four neat strokes. "You husband—where?"

"Um . . ." I gestured vaguely out the window in a gesture I hoped encompassed the entire universe. "Coming soon."

"You mother—where?"

I gestured again. "In America."

She ticked her tongue against the inside of her teeth. "You mother—missing you. You go—you mother house. Have baby in you mother house. You understand?"

"I understand." I peeled up my chapati carefully, trying not to tear it. "But my mother's house is a long way away."

She shook her head. "You mother—missing you. You having baby, first you go to her."

I set the chapati on top of my pile. What was my mother doing right now? It must be ten or eleven at night in California. I pictured my mother alone, watching a DVD. Drinking a glass of wine. Flipping through catalogs from Nordstrom and J. Jill, circling dresses she liked but would never get around to ordering.

THAT NIGHT, after darshan and dinner, I headed for the International Phone Centre, which was located across from the Krishna Shrine Room and right between the Internet Café and the Doll Shop.

I'd seen people all over the ashram cuddling and talking to dolls, presumably for a source of comfort when Prana Ma wasn't around to blow on them. I stepped into the shop and looked at them heaped in their wicker baskets: blue-necked Krishna dolls, elephant-headed Ganesha dolls, ferocious Kali dolls with their red flannel tongues hanging out. Maybe I should buy one of those for the baby. *Here you go, sweetie! This is Kali. She likes to drink blood. Shall we sacrifice the kitty to her?* At least it wasn't a Bratz.

I picked up a Prana Ma doll and gazed at its smug face, its black button eyes, its perpetually puckered mouth. "I never do anything without consulting Prana Ma," Kalyani had told me this morning, hugging her doll to her chest. "But it's just a rag doll," I'd protested. "I know," she'd said. "But she reminds me to turn my heart in the direction of the real Prana Ma." Now I tried out a prayer: *Prana Ma, help me know what to say to my mother.* The doll looked back at me, inscrutable. A small tag protruded from her neck: "Made in India. Hand wash only."

I knew I was procrastinating. I continued on to the phone room, where three phones were separated by flimsy barriers to give the illusion of privacy. *I hope you're as excited about this as I am* . . . I picked up the phone. "I don't need you to take care of me. I just need to know that you *want* to take care of me," wailed the woman on my left. "Can you connect me to your supervisor?" demanded the woman on my right. I dialed the long-distance code, country code, area code. The phone rang, then clicked into the screech of a fax: Like everything else in my mother's life, her answering machine seemed to be operating according to its own laws. It might take my mother weeks to figure out why no one was leaving her messages.

The ashram fax machine was across the hall in the Lakshmi International Business Centre. I sat down on a stool and began to write.


A WEEK AND a half later, I still hadn't heard anything back from my mother.

I checked the fax room compulsively, every couple of hours, in between darshans and kirtans and work meditations and meals. I even emailed Lori to see if she'd heard anything from my mom. Maybe my fax hadn't even gone through. Maybe my mom was out of town. Or maybe the fax was just sitting in her machine along with some ads for 900 numbers in Las Vegas.

In the meantime, life with the Divine Mother was settling into a lulling rhythm. I went to kirtans and sang hymns to Kali and Durga, rocking out with the crowd as Prana Ma rattled her tambourine. I waited in line for a couple of hours each day for another minty breath on the forehead. I visited one of Prana Ma's orphanages, where a couple of hundred girls sat at sewing machines, making rounds of rose-scented soap that they wrapped in rice paper for sale at the ashram store. Maybe it was just a coincidence, but ever since Prana Ma had blown on me, the lingering pain in my knee seemed to have disappeared.

Maybe this was what I'd been looking for. Maybe I'd stay here and have my baby. Maybe Prana Ma herself would attend at the birth. By dwelling in the energy field of the Divine Mother, I'd finally learn how to be a mother myself.

One afternoon toward the end of my second week at the ashram, I took a walk on the black sand beach. The sand was punctuated with land mines of human feces. The burnished gold coin of the sun was dropping toward the ocean. I sat down on a rock and watched a boy toss a net into the water and haul it out full of writhing fish.

I remembered coming home one day in fifth grade to show my mother a math test I'd gotten a 99 percent on. She took the paper from me and studied the gold star at the top, then the red X halfway down the page. "Why did you miss that one, honey?" she asked. "It's so simple."

Why should I even care whether she answered my fax? I had Prana Ma to kiss my boo-boos.

"Amanda?" said a voice as familiar as my own. I spun around and saw her coming toward me—a whirl of blonde hair, a gray silk pants suit, a gold necklace, a red-lipsticked mouth.

"Your bizarre young friend with the unusual hairdo told me you were out here." My mother studied my outfit. "Amanda, honey, you need to come home so we can buy you some decent maternity clothes."


"I HAVE TO SAY, white is not really your color," my mother said, sipping her chai at the Jaya Jaya Chai Shop. "And darling, when was the last time you got your hair cut? You're nothing but split ends."

"Mom, this is an ashram, not a beauty pageant. And anyway, hair has not exactly been at the top of my list of things to worry about."

"Being pregnant doesn't have to mean you let yourself go." She bit into a cinnamon bun. "Especially under your circumstances, it's important to keep yourself looking attractive. When I was pregnant with you, I got my nails done every two weeks. A man at the bar where I was a waitress asked me out on a date when I was already a centimeter dilated."

"Mom? I think that's more than I need to know." I took a gulp of chai. Running into my mom at an Indian ashram was like spotting the Dalai Lama at a Las Vegas strip club. "You must be exhausted. Why don't I take you to your room, and we can talk more tomorrow."

"Don't be silly. I had a lovely night at the nicest hotel in Trivandrum, and a comfortable limo trip here this morning, although I must say the roads leave something to be desired. I think all this fuss about how difficult India is is a bit overrated."

"Well, sure, if you're traveling first class. I still can't figure out how you pulled this trip off. It must have cost a fortune."

"Not at all. I've been dating a lovely man for the last month or so who happens to be the events coordinator for Hyatt International. He has enough frequent-flier miles to fly me around the world three times." She wiped her mouth. "In fact, after you and I leave here, he's offered to put us up at a resort in Thailand for a week before we fly back home."

"Wow—that's great." I'd been through this so many times with my mother that I couldn't get too enthusiastic. "But—what exactly do you mean by 'when you and I leave'?"

"Well, sweetie, that's what I've come to talk to you about." She licked the sugar off her fingers and settled back in her chair. "Obviously, you can't stay in India in your condition."

"Why not? Millions of Indian women do."

"Yes, well, millions of stray cats birth their litters under Dumpsters in alleys. That doesn't mean that my daughter has to do it."

"Are you comparing Indian women to alley cats? That's the most racist thing I've ever heard."

"Don't you dare call me a racist, young lady. When I met your father, I had my eye on a handsome young Mexican man who worked with me. If things had been a little different, you might be speaking

Spanish right now. And I can tell you one thing for sure: If José had been your father, he'd be telling you the same thing I am—get yourself home to a good American hospital."

"And I'd be telling him it was none of his goddamn business."

"And I'd be saying, don't you dare speak to your father that way! Of course it's his business. He's your father. He changed your diaper. He stayed up with you all night long when you had the croup, holding you in his arms with the shower on so you could breathe the wet air."

"Well, even if he is my father . . . I mean, if he were my father . . ." I leaned my head in my hands, confused. What were we talking about? I had the feeling that I so often got with my mother—that she had deliberately led me into territory so tangled and overgrown that only she had the map to it. "Mom—I'm a big girl now. I can figure this out for myself."

"Well, now, that's just the point, Amanda. Obviously, you can't. I mean, just look at you. Look at . . . this." She gestured around the café. At the table across from us, a woman sat alone, singing to a Prana Ma doll as she spread jam on its croissant.

THE NEXT MORNING, Kalyani and I stood at the counter in the kitchen, where—just as I was getting competent at the chapati making—they had switched my assignment to grinding spices. I was smashing cardamom seeds in a granite mortar with a matching pestle. The smell rose spicy-sweet and intoxicating.

"Prana Ma called her here," said Kalyani. "It's obvious. It's all part of her plan."

"Well, I wish Prana Ma would tell her to go home. She's going to drive me crazy."

Kalyani looked at me as if I were threatening to turn down a date with Brad Pitt. "If my mother would come, I would be so happy."

"Where is your mother?" It was only eleven o'clock, and already my legs were hurting. I glanced around the room, but I didn't see a stool anywhere.

"She remarried a few years ago, and she doesn't want me around. She's afraid if her husband finds out that I'm with Prana Ma, it will break up their relationship."

The kitchen door opened and my mother sailed in, wrapped in a white sari, with a splash of hibiscus flowers in her hair. "Good morning! I had a fabulous sleep, and I just went and got breathed on. Very sweet. But someone should tell that woman to cut down on the carbs; she's getting a belly."

Apparently, my mother had launched into ashram life with the enthusiasm with which she approached anything new. Beginnings, my mother had always been good at. Whenever we moved, we'd have a massive garage sale in which we'd sell off all her abandoned identities: barely used tennis rackets, a series of wind and stringed instruments, a Pilates Universal Reformer. I was always astonished by the ease with which she sloughed off her previous versions of herself, like a snake shedding a skin.

Now she kissed me on the cheek. "You shouldn't be standing, sweetie, it's not good for your circulation. Be sure you put your legs up for an hour a day or you'll get varicose veins." She spotted a stool behind a stack of burlap bags full of rice and pushed it toward me. "Here, sit down right here."

"No thanks. I'd rather stand." Suddenly, I was thirteen years old again, a sulky teenager.

She sat down. "Suit yourself." She watched me pound the cardamom seeds. "Oh, no, honey, you're doing it all wrong. You don't hammer down on them like that. Look, let me show you." She took the mortar and pestle. "You just set the pestle in the middle and kind of rooooolll it—like so—you see?" Her hands rolled in deft circles. "Then it goes so much faster."

I had to admit, her way was working better. "Since when do you know how to grind spices?"

"It's not that different from mixing paint pigment. And for a while, when you were little, I had that job in the Indian restaurant, re-member? That's also where I learned how to wrap a sari." She poured the powdered cardamom into a big ceramic bowl, added a handful of cloves. Kalyani was hanging on her every move, awestruck, as if my mother were a visiting expert brought in to give a professional demonstration of motherhood. "So, sweetie. We need to talk seriously about what you're going to do. You can't have the baby in India, that's obvious."

"Why not? Maybe I'll have even have it right here. There's a good hospital." I reached for the mortar and pestle. "Want to give that back to me?"

"Yes, what a blessing to have the baby here!" breathed Kalyani. "She will be a child of the Divine Mother."

My mother kept on grinding without even glancing in Kalyani's direction. "And then afterward? What would you do then? You can't take care of a baby all by yourself."

"Why not? You did."

"That's right. That's how I know you shouldn't do it."

"You always said it was easy."

"Well—it wasn't."

"What do you mean?"

My mother stopped grinding and looked up at me. "You want to know what it was like? I was there all alone in that little studio apart-ment, nothing in there but one big mattress for both you and me, and a couple of towels I'd spread out instead of a changing table. My pri-vates were all torn up—I had to have stitches—so it hurt to walk, hurt to sit down. And you screamed and screamed and screamed—your body stiff, your face purple, like you had a hot iron up your behind. That second night home alone, I actually called the emergency room.

'It's probably just gas,' they told me. By the third night, I was afraid I would throw you out the window.

"One night, I just walked out the door and went down to the bar. I left you lying in the middle of the futon, screaming your little head off. It didn't seem to make much difference to you if I were there or not. I sat there and drank a Pepsi and looked at the men playing pool and thought, 'I could just walk away, just like her father did. Get on a bus and never come back.' It seemed plausible, for a moment, like I really could do it. But, of course, I didn't. I turned around and came back home. You'd given up crying by then and gone to sleep, all alone in the middle of the futon with your little thumb in your mouth."

The smell of cardamom and cloves hung around us. "Why didn't you go home to your family?"

"Pride, I suppose. I had finally gotten out of there. I didn't want to go back and hear all of them saying, 'I told you so.' I didn't want to want them to know how bad it had gotten." She put the pestle down. "Amanda. I don't want that sort of stupid pride to prevent you from coming home. Just think about it, that's all I ask. You could stay with me. You wouldn't have to work. You could just focus on the baby. Let me take care of you."

"*You* take care of *me?*" I tried to wash the incredulity out of my voice. "I'm sure your new boyfriend would love that."

"I know I've made some mistakes. But I tried my best. You'll find out what it's like soon enough. As a mother, all you can do is just bumble along doing the best you can. Maybe, when you get desperate, you read a parenting book, but none of them tell you anything worth knowing, really. And meanwhile, it feels like your life is racing away from you, and you keep on trying to chase it down, but it's always just a few steps in front of you. Like you're a greyhound chasing a mechanical rabbit around and around a track.

"It took me years to realize that my life hadn't run off somewhere else. It was actually happening, right there, with you, all that time I was trying to find it. And by the time I started to realize that, you were gone."

Kalyani had pulled her Prana Ma doll from her backpack and was clutching it as she watched us, spellbound. I couldn't believe it myself: My mother was actually talking to me about her feelings. Maybe Prana Ma's breath had done some good after all. I couldn't have been more surprised if I'd seen a leper cured, a cripple walk.

"I don't want you to make the same mistake," my mother said.


FOR THE REST of the week, the whole ashram went into a frenzy of activity preparing for the descent of the Divine Mother, as if we were expecting a visit from Oprah. In the kitchen, we stepped up the preparation of chapatis, rice, dal, and spices. My arms ached from rolling dough, and the smell of turmeric clung to my hair. Every day, more devotees streamed into the ashram, including hundreds of local Indians, dressed for a festival in brilliantly colored saris and suits, their faces lit with an eagerness that reflected thousands of years of devotion to the Divine Mother. The Westerners milled about, all seeming slightly anxious, like children lost at the mall.

By the time the bhajans began, in the early evening, the hall was packed knee to knee with people, pressing thigh to sweaty thigh. The chanting was wild, ecstatic, accompanied by drums and tambourines and a harmonium: a wave of communal ecstasy, the energy soaring higher and higher. The faces of the Indians were bright with faith; the faces of the Westerners were bright with the longing for faith. On my left, Kalyani was weeping. On the other side of her, Devi Das rocked back and forth, his eyes closed. On my right, even my mother was singing and clapping her hands. Why did something in me always hold back?

I felt a pressure against my knee. I opened my eyes. Just in front of me, a white-haired Indian woman in a mauve sari was slipping sideways onto the ground. Her face was wet with sweat; her eyes were rolled up in her head. In the frenzy of Mother worship, no one else seemed to notice that an actual mother had collapsed. I pulled out my water bottle and dabbed water on her face, but she didn't respond.

"Should we carry her outside?" I shook Kalyani.

"No!" she hissed. "Prana Ma is about to appear as the Divine Mother. We can't disturb the ceremony."

The bhajans stopped. Horns blared, a bell rang, and the curtains rolled back to reveal an empty throne on the stage, with a crown on it. The singing began again, and the curtain closed. I looked down at the fainted woman; her face was clammy. I caught the eye of an ashram official standing a few feet away. I pointed to the woman lying on the floor. The ashram official shook her head sternly, lay a finger on her lip, pointed at the stage, then at her watch: *Later,* she pantomimed. *Later.* The crowd kept on singing: *"Kali Ma! Durga Ma! Lalita Ma!"*

The curtains pulled back once more, and the crowd roared: Prana Ma was on the throne in a silver crown and a gold dress. A priest bowed in front of her, offering a flame from a ghee-soaked wick blazing in a silver bowl, as the crowd sang: *"Om Jaya Jagadeesha hare . . . Swami Jaya Jagadeesha hare . . . "* What if this lady died in my lap? I turned to my mother. "Mom? What should we do?"

My mother stood up. "Well, who cares if we disrupt the ceremony?" She bent and scooped up the woman in her arms. "She doesn't weigh more than a feather pillow. Let's get her out of here."

We pushed our way through the crowd to the door, as people began lining up for darshan, still singing. Out in the courtyard, we set her down on the dusty bricks. My mother took my water bottle and began sprinkling water on her face, pressing it to her lips. Her eyes blinked open.

"It was just the heat and the crowds," said my mother to both of us. "And the excitement. That used to happen a lot at the football games at A&M. I once had to carry a cheerleader out of there just like this." The woman watched her face as she talked, then pushed herself up to a sitting position and leaned against the wall. My mother and I sat next to her.

"This is what being a mother is all about," my mother said to me smugly. "You just take care of what's right in front of you."

In one corner of the courtyard, a man sat on the ground saying mantras. Children darted here and there, kicking an empty water bottle. The line for darshan wound out the door of the temple and around the courtyard. I looked at my mother.

"I can't go home with you this week, Mom," I said. "But I'll come back to California in time to have the baby. I promise."

# upward-facing bow pose (urdhva dhanurasana)

*Lie on your back. Bend your legs and plant your feet by your buttocks and your hands by your shoulders, fingers pointing back toward your heels. Press into your hands and feet and roll your spine to the sky as your heart arches open. Imagine roots tethering your hands and feet to the earth. Feel the strength of your muscles lashing together the steel girders of your bones.*

*Below your surfaces, rivers of prana course through an intricate network of subtle channels—creative and unpredictable. Now open your inner floodgates and set the rivers free. Let your body ripple and ride on their currents. Let it blow in the wind of your breath.*

*Without structure, the pose collapses. But without prana, it is as useless as a polished brass jug with no water inside.*

*The thought "Who am I?" will destroy all other thoughts, and like the stick used for stirring the burning pyre, it will itself in the end get destroyed. Then, there will arise Self-realization.*

—Ramana Maharshi (1879–1950)

# CHAPTER 20

a WEEK LATER, my mother left—blowing a last kiss to me out the window of her hired car, her hair wrapped in a silk scarf against the wind as she headed to the airport. For about thirty minutes, I was giddy with relief. Then I began to worry that I should have gone with her.

My worry rode along with me as Devi Das and I took the bus inland a few days later, heading for an ashram at the base of a mountain that Kalyani had told us was one of the most famous pilgrimage sites in India. "Mount Arunachala is sacred to the Lord Shiva," she'd told us. "All you have to do is walk around it and you'll get enlightened—if not in this lifetime, then definitely in the next. It's guaranteed." Our bus lurched along potholed roads; my window was jammed halfway open, so dust and fumes billowed in. We alternated between hurtling down the road at a sickening speed and stopping for long periods for mysterious reasons. Rumors flew up and down the aisle: There was a strike blocking the road a mile ahead; a truck had overturned, spilling coal across the road. The woman in front of me was carrying a bucket of live fish flopping in a little water; as the day went on, they died one at a time.

I was five and a half months pregnant, and in the last week my belly had mushroomed. The baby somersaulted inside me. My uterus pressed up into my rib cage so I couldn't take a deep breath and pressed down on my bladder so I desperately needed to pee. When the bus finally pulled over to the side of the road for a pit stop, I squatted by the side of the road and pulled down my pants under my tunic, holding my nose against the stench of excrement. I felt a flood of animal relief as the urine trickled down into the dirt, then tried not to step in it as I stood up and pulled my trousers back up. Back in the U.S., the other moms on the HeyBaby.com bulletin board were taking their swim aerobics classes, picking out curtains that matched their crib bumpers, buying baby-wipe warmers and diaper tables, practicing their Lamaze breathing with their husbands as coaches. What was I doing here?

Our bus pulled into town after midnight, too late to go to the ashram. So we checked into a run-down hotel down the street from the bus station, directly across the street from the thousand-year-old temple to Shiva. Our room was hot and whining with mosquitoes; I discovered I'd left my mosquito net at the Prana Ma Ashram. So Devi Das and I pulled our twin beds close together—avoiding looking too closely at the stained, lumpy mattresses—so they'd both fit under his netting, which we rigged from the bare-bulb light fixture. It seemed to me that most of my trip had consisted of rigging and dismantling mosquito netting.

As soon as we turned out the light, Devi Das began to snore. I was exhausted, too, but I couldn't sleep. My mother had lit a worry fuse inside me, leading straight to a dynamite keg of terror. Her voice hammered out questions in my head: *How are you going to make money, Amanda? Who's going to watch the baby while you finish your book? Can you afford a babysitter? Will your roommates let you have a baby in the house? Are children even allowed under your lease? And even if they are, where will the baby sleep?*

How had I avoided these questions for so long? The money I'd been paid by Maxine would last me two or three months, tops; I'd have to finish the book to get the rest of the advance, and how would I finish it while I was taking care of a baby? I still had the basic health insurance Tom had insisted I get while I was living with him; that would cover the cost of the birth. I could buy all the baby gear used. But the lease on the apartment was in Ernie's name, and it was a big deal for Ernie when Ishtar got a *parakeet*. How would I afford a deposit on a new place? I'd have to live with my mother, and we'd drive each other to nervous breakdowns.

Something was biting my thighs and inner arms—I hoped it was fleas and not bedbugs. Just before dawn, as I started to doze off, raucous chanting began to blare from the temple across the street. The speakers were turned up so loud that all the high notes screeched, all the low notes buzzed. When I couldn't stand it any more, I reached over and shook Devi Das's shoulder.

"Mmpph?"

"Devi Das. What am I going to do?"

"Use earplugs."

"The birth is only three months away, and I'm nowhere near done with my book. If I don't find an enlightened master soon, I'll have to give back the advance, and I've already spent most of it. And then how am I going to support a baby all alone?"

He sat up, pulling the blanket around his bony shoulders. "We wish we could be more help. But we don't know anything about supporting babies. We don't even know much about supporting ourselves. We do know this, though: People come here from all over the country to bring their troubles to Shiva. Maybe you could try that."

"Isn't that a bit risky?" I thought of the corpses on the pyres in

Varanasi; Shiva covered in ashes, meditating and watching them burn. "Shiva is the god of destruction."

Devi Das put his arm around me, enveloping me in the smell of unwashed armpits and camphor incense. "Are you saying you have a problem with that?"

A COUPLE OF hours later, Devi Das and I emerged into the roar of the streets. I was exhausted and covered with fleabites, including a row down the inner crack of my buttocks. Bikes and bullock carts fought for space with autorickshaws and cars. The street in front of the temple was mobbed with pilgrims and barefoot sadhus leaning on staffs. We stopped at a stall and bought green coconuts; the coconut seller split off their tops with a single *thwack* of a machete. I sucked the cool milk thirstily through a plastic straw.

We paid a rupee to leave our shoes at the sandal stand and walked barefoot up the street to pay our respects at the Shiva temple, at Devi Das's insistence. We passed shops selling garlands of jasmine, and heaps of perfumed powder, and steel plates and tiffin canisters, and bangles, and plastic buckets, and pictures of Shiva and Parvati and Krishna and Ganesha. Then we passed through the arched stone gateway into the courtyard of the ancient temple, where a morose, dull-eyed elephant stood caparisoned in crimson and gold silk. At the gesture of the elephant keeper, I offered him a handful of rupees. He reached out his trunk and took them delicately from my hand. Then, with his curled trunk, he caressed the top of my head as if in blessing.

Devi Das and I walked through another arch into the inner sanctum: a dank cave with intricately carved stone walls, where a Brahman priest in a dhoti, naked to the waist, beckoned us past two stone bulls glistening with ghee to a smooth pillar of a Shiva lingam, wet with water. Devotees pressed close, waving their hands over the puja flame and fanning their faces with the blessings from the fire. I was walking into a chamber of the collective unconscious, peering into a primal soup of archetypal visions. But there was no time to sit in silence, soaking it up; the priest performed a hasty puja, then pressed a packet of ash into our hands. "Donations," he said, gesturing with his head toward a collection plate.

From: HeyBaby.com
To: Amandala@yahoo.com

As you sail into your third trimester, the good old "nesting instinct" is kicking in strong! If you haven't already, now's the ideal time to start picking out a crib and a car seat, choosing a theme for baby's room, and stocking up on receiving blankets, booties, mobiles, rattles, and other goodies. Click below for a special deal on Shrek-themed bedding.

Symptoms you may be feeling include drowsiness, heartburn, indigestion, flatulence, bloating, headaches, bleeding gums, nosebleeds, varicose veins, hemorrhoids, itchy abdomen, clumsiness, leaky breasts, absentmindedness, increased fantasizing about the baby, anxiety, boredom, clumsiness, backache, leg cramps, constipation, and thick white vaginal discharge.

Be sure to savor every minute of this special time!

From: Lori647@aol.com
To: Amandala@yahoo.com

I wanted to let you know that I just got a call from Tom. He wants me and Joe to do the landscaping this weekend on the new house he just bought in Half Moon Bay. I just wanted to clear it with you first. There are a million people he could have called for this job more locally; I know he's just using this as an excuse to get news about you. But I could really use the money. Is it all right if I tell him yes?

## Enlightenment for Idiots: Sample Chapter Draft

If you're looking to increase your odds of spiritual awakening, you can't do better than head for Mount Arunachala, a solitary rocky red hill thrust up in the middle of the arid plains! Devout Hindus believe that this 3,000-foot outcropping of igneous rock is a piece of Shiva himself—not just his dwelling place, but his upthrust "lingam," the actual god himself in phallic, physical form. The sight of this mountain—in fact, even the mere thought of it—is believed to neutralize all your negative karma and lead to the state of ultimate knowledge of your true nature. If you walk all the way around the mountain, it's said that all your deepest wishes will come true.

"YOU ARE LUCKY," said the receptionist in the ashram office, a sweet-faced Indian man. "Normally, ashram is booked many months in advance. But last night only, one married couple is canceling. You are married couple, yes?" He glanced at Devi Das's sadhu garb and my swollen belly.

"Yes, we are," said Devi Das firmly. "Thank you for finding us a room. My wife is expecting, as you can see."

*My wife.* It was the first time I'd ever been referred to that way, and it was amazingly comforting, even though it was coming from a dreadlocked sadhu who was sworn to celibacy.

The ashram was an oasis of green lawns and stone buildings nestled in the snarl of roads at the base of Mount Arunachala. Nothing was required at this ashram—no meditation, no chanting, no work practice, no yoga. The guru had died many years before. And so for the first week and a half there, that's exactly what I did—nothing. I just lay on my bed for hours at a stretch, looking out my screen door at the mountain poking up its craggy peak behind the ashram buildings. It was curiously peaceful, lying there, watching the clouds drift by it in a blue sky. I could hear the sweet, high-pitched croon of the Brahman boys chanting in the ashram temple. Giant monkeys rattled the bars that shielded my open windows, leering in at my stash of bananas and tangerines. I left my room only for meals in the ashram dining room, where we scooped our food off banana leaves with our bare hands: rice cooked with mustard seeds and coriander; spicy coconut chutney; sweet sticky balls of cardamom, sugar, and ghee.

Occasionally, I picked up some of the ashram pamphlets to leaf through the teachings of the deceased master. "Waking is long and a dream short; other than this there is no difference. Just as waking happenings seem real while awake, so do those in a dream while dreaming." A house. How had Tom managed to buy a house? I couldn't even afford a crib. But it shouldn't surprise me—Tom always had been a real grown-up. Whereas Matt and I had always felt like kids, gleefully ducking out of all the trappings of adulthood, like mortgages and business suits and savings accounts and matching eight-place flatware settings. Now I was having a baby, the ultimate grown-up gesture. But part of me still believed I was just the nanny, snooping through the closet to try on the real mom's clothes.

Midmorning on our tenth day at the ashram, Devi Das sat down on the side of my bed. "It's time to get up and get going. You can't just lie here forever."

"Give me one good reason why not."

"Well, for one thing, we've been hearing about a teacher you probably should check out. She holds satsang for her devotees in a house just down the road. She's supposed to be a fully awakened being. Several people have told us that just being in her presence can destroy the I-thought for the rest of the day."

"Or the We-thought, in your case."

"Her name is Saraswati. She's from Santa Barbara."

I'll give her a call when I get back to California. Maybe we can go rollerblading together." But I heaved myself up to sitting, yanked my shirt down over my belly. "Okay. Where's my notebook?"

After over a week in the ashram, it was a shock to be out in the streets again. Buses roared past, sending chickens and pigs scrambling. Bicycle rickshaws painted with bright flowers zipped past bullock carts laden with burlap bags of grain. When we finally made our way into the small house where Saraswati held her satsang, it had already started. Twenty or thirty devotees were sitting around the living room on puffy silk meditation cushions. At the front of the room, reclining in an armchair draped in royal-blue silk, was a petite woman with short platinum hair and turquoise eyes, dressed in a white sari. On a table to her left was a vase of jasmine, a crystal bowl half full of scraps of paper, and a tall glass of water. She flashed a smile at us as we entered. Her teeth were so white they were practically translucent.

We sat down on cushions in the back of the room. Saraswati reached into the crystal bowl, drew out a slip of paper, and read it aloud. "Beloved Saraswati. Your presence in my life has opened my heart to a vastness that I never dreamed I would touch." She nodded and smiled. "But when I am away from you, my spiritual practice feels dry and arid. I do yoga and meditate and pray, but I cannot find my way back to the waters of bliss I feel in your presence."

Saraswati looked around the room. "Beloveds, this is a common complaint. Who wrote this letter?" She spoke with a slight Indian accent overlaid over a Valley-girl drawl.

A wiry woman in yoga pants came forward and sat before

Saraswati, her body rigid with hope and anxiety. Saraswati looked at her and shook her head. "You are trying so hard, running so fast. And yet you get nowhere, is that correct?"

The woman nodded. Tears began trickling down her face.

"The bliss you feel in my presence does not come from me. It is you. You are able to feel it simply because you have stopped striving, for a moment, to be somewhere else." Saraswati looked around the room, stern. "I say this to all of you—do not do yoga. Do not meditate. Do not fast and pray. Do not chase around India looking for one guru after another to show you the door to enlightenment. Simply be who you are."

Oh great. My book was doomed.

"But I don't like who I am!" wailed the woman in yoga pants, as if reading my mind.

Saraswati leaned forward. "Who is the I who does not like you? And who is the you she does not like? Ask yourself that! Then you will be free."

The yogini walked back to her seat, sniffing. Saraswati pulled another slip of paper from the bowl. "Beloved Saraswati-ji. Thank you for the blessings with which you have showered me. Since coming to you and seeing my true nature more deeply, I rest in bliss on a daily basis. But I still cannot stop thinking about women."

A stout, middle-aged German man came forward, looking simultaneously proud and embarrassed. "Who is it who can't stop thinking? Not you!" said Saraswati. "Thoughts come and go, and there is no thinker. Freedom from thoughts is an illusion. So is bondage to them. Let go of thoughts, let go of no-thoughts. Let go of women, let go of no-women."

"Thank you." The man looked as if he were longing to ask her out on a date. "You have helped me so much."

"I have not helped you, because I and you are both constructs of your mind. You have the illusion that you are this person, Gustav, in this place, India, on this day, March 10. But those concepts have nothing to do with who you really are."

Wait a minute . . . March 10? Was it really March 10? I'd lost track of the date. My birthday was March 14. In four more days, I would be thirty years old. No wonder I was depressed. I was three decades years old, I was broke, I was pregnant, and I was nowhere near enlightenment. By the time my next birthday rolled around, I would have a nine-month-old baby.

Gustav was walking back to his seat. I remembered my last birthday, when I turned twenty-nine. I had broken things off with Tom and gotten back together with Matt just a couple of months earlier, and I was still swimming in the blissful delusion that things were going to be different this time than they had always been before. For my birthday, Matt had taken me to a hot-springs resort in the mountains north of the wine country. We had plunged naked into the steaming sulfur bath, so hot that it hurt to move, hurt to even breathe; then dipped into the icy spring-fed tub next to it, so cold it knocked the air out of me. Hot, cold, hot, cold—by the time we lay side by side on the wooden deck, I was dizzy and stoned.

The stars were glittering chips in the dark velvet sky. Matt had reached out and took my hand. "I love you," he had said. "But sometimes I feel like I should warn you to keep away from me. I'm not the kind of guy you make a life with. Being with me is like falling in love with a forest fire." I'd rolled toward him. "So go ahead," I'd said. "I dare you. Burn me up."

So here I was, a year later, sitting in the ashes. Would he even remember that this was my birthday? And if he did, wherever he was, would he care?

Devi Das dug his elbow into my side. Everyone in the room was looking at me expectantly. Saraswati's turquoise eyes drilled into me.

"I'm sorry," I stammered. "I didn't quite catch that."

"I asked, and what about you? What is the question that has brought you here? And what is the story playing in your mind that is so compelling that it takes you away from this unfolding moment?"

"Oh. Well." Was I supposed to go up and kneel in front of her? I stood up, then sat down again. "I don't know if you really want to hear my story."

"Go ahead, beloved. Do not be afraid."

*If she calls me beloved again, I'm going to clock her.* I stood up again. "Okay, here's the deal. My life is a mess. I'm pregnant and I don't have a partner. I'm trying to write a book, and it isn't going very well, but if I don't finish it I won't have any money to support me and my baby." To my horror, my voice was starting to quaver. "And frankly, all this talk about 'I am not my thoughts' isn't helping very much. I mean, give me a break. If 'I' is just a concept, who's going to write my book? Who's going to pay the rent? Who's going to take care of the baby?"

Saraswati shook her head. "Do you think it is *you* who is growing this baby inside you? Are you designing eyebrows, making bones, crafting intestines and eyes and brain? You do nothing—but a baby grows.

"It is the same with your book. It will be written. But no one will write it. The baby will be born, and mothering will happen. But let go of the idea that you are the mother, that you are the writer. Then you will be free."

From: Ernie@northwesternmutual.com
To: Amandala@yahoo.com

Amanda, congratulations on your exciting news. After talking it over, Ishtar and I have decided that it will be fine for you to have the baby here at our house, although naturally it will increase your rent. We'll have to figure out by how much. The baby won't really count as a whole new person since it won't have its own room. We could calculate it by weight, in which case a baby would be about a twentieth of an average adult; or we could do it by noise level, in which case it will probably be about six times a normal adult, unless we're comparing it to the African drum teacher who lived there before you. I'll think about it some more and let you know. P.S. Now that you're a mother, will you be wanting life insurance?

"SARASWATI GOT enlightened just waiting for a bus," a middle-aged German woman named Maya informed me and Devi Das that evening, at the potluck dinner she and her husband were hosting for Saraswati devotees. She was a tiny woman, with a perpetually startled face and blue eyes opened so wide that there was a little ring of white around the iris. She was on a six-week vacation from her job as a home health nurse specializing in rehabilitation after head and spinal cord injuries.

"Which bus was that?" I asked, hopefully. Holding my plate of rice salad in one hand, I looked around the room, which was full of people, most of whom I recognized from Saraswati's satsang that morning: two Swedish girls with dreadlocks; a couple of surfers from L.A., who told me they'd first met Saraswati at a satsang at a yoga studio in Hollywood.

"The bus was late, and Saraswati was getting more and more stressed and impatient," Maya's husband chimed in, ignoring my question. He was a philosophy professor on sabbatical from a university in Berlin, with a mane of reddish-blond hair, a bushy beard, and a booming voice. He had introduced himself as Siddhartha, but Maya sometimes slipped and called him Hans. "Her impatience was like a vice, clamping down on her. Then, suddenly, she heard a voice saying in her head, 'Where is it you think you are going? You are always right here.' And the world dissolved into light and joy, which has never abated."

Across the room, a few people had pulled out guitars and were beginning to strum Sanskrit chants and Beatles songs. A few more chimed in on tablas and shakers. "Arunachala Shiva," they sang, passing a joint from hand to hand. "Blackbird singing in the dead of night . . ."

"Actually, it wasn't an ordinary bus," Maya corrected Siddhartha. "It was a limo. She usually says 'bus,' though. It makes the experience more accessible for ordinary people."

For the next hour, Maya and Siddhartha regaled me and Devi Das with enlightenment stories: the Zen master who got enlightened by hearing a grain of rice drop to the bottom of a pot. The Indian schoolboy who realized his true Self while contemplating his own death.

During all my time researching a book on enlightenment, this was the first time I'd heard anyone use the word so casually. The yoga students were more comfortable talking about the nuts and bolts of the body: the state of their psoas muscles, the alignment of their lumbar vertebrae, the precise muscles that gripped in their pelvises when they tipped into a forward bend. The Buddhists had droned on about sensations, emotions, and thoughts, putting each present moment, no matter how tedious, under the microscope until it fractured into an explosion of microscopic details. Sri Satyaji had mainly been obsessed with controlling the impulse to experience anything pleasurable. Sure, enlightenment was supposed to be the brass ring that everyone was grabbing at. But it had always seemed kind of tacky to talk about it too much, like admitting you fast-forwarded through an artsy French film just get to the sex scenes.

But the Saraswati devotees weren't afraid of trotting their spiritual ambitions right out in the open for everyone to look at. In their view, enlightenment was highly contagious, like Ebola, and they could get it just by being in the presence of someone who had it. I started to feel my spirits lifting. *Maybe they're right. Maybe it's possible.*

*I just have to find the right teacher. Maybe my book won't be such a disaster, after all. And maybe with an enlightened mother, my baby won't even miss having a father.*

"So you really think enlightenment is possible for anyone?" I asked. "Even for someone like me?"

"You already are enlightened!" Siddhartha assured me. "You just have to realize that fact."

He leaned back and put the tips of his fingertips together. In the corner, an elderly Italian man stuck two pieces of lit incense into his tangle of gray hair, flung off his orange robes, and began to dance in his boxer shorts.

*Fax from: Mom*

*To: Amanda*

*Darling, I am just remembering this day 30 years ago, when you arrived and destroyed my life as I knew it. Happy birthday!*

THE MORNING OF my thirtieth birthday, I walked up the mountain, up a red stone-cobbled path, to sit in the cave where the ashram guru had lived for seventeen years in God-intoxicated solitude. He'd eaten one meal a day, I'd read; he had sat for hours staring unblinking into the sun and into his own Self. The sadhu who lived there before him had meditated so deeply that he had spontaneously combusted into a pile of ashes.

It was hot, and I'd forgotten my hat; I could feel my cheeks scorching. Great, now I had a sunburn on top of a pimple so big a sadhu could live inside it. From outside the cave, I could see the town sprawled out below me, with the spires of the ancient Shiva temple rising out of a haze of smog. Inside, it was hot and airless. The cave was about fourteen feet in diameter, with a smooth black marble floor. No one else was there. On the altar, candles flickered next to a sculpted red replica of Mount Arunachala. I sat down and closed my eyes to meditate. The baby rolled inside me.

"Erase the thought of me, of mine," Saraswati's voice admonished me in my head. I was sure that if I'd mentioned my birthday to Devi Das, he would have celebrated with me. But for some perverse reason, I'd avoided telling him. It was as if I'd wanted to guarantee I would feel as miserably alone as I truly was. Sweat dripped down my ribs. I wished *I* could combust into a pile of ashes; surely it would be better than remaining as I was. *I am not my thoughts. I am not the stories I tell about myself. Then who am I?* If this was what "already enlightened" looked like, I was in trouble.

"Amanda?" said a voice at the entrance to the cave. I opened my eyes and looked up.

Tom was standing silhouetted in the sunlight. He was wearing khaki shorts, a yellow polo shirt, and sunglasses; he was carrying a daypack. He looked like the cover of a J.Crew catalog.

"Lori told me what was going on with you. I got on a plane a week later." He stepped closer and held out his arms. "Happy birthday. Can I take you out to dinner?"

*Who you are is already on the other shore, already free, already the source of all wisdom, clarity, and beauty. Who you are is what all is, stillness itself.*

—Gangaji (1942–    )

## CHAPTER 21

To ENLIGHTENMENT." Tom raised his wineglass.

"I'll drink to that." I clicked it with my tumbler of apple juice.

I was sitting across from Tom at a little vegetarian restaurant in the fanciest hotel in town. I'd spent the afternoon in the ayurvedic spa downstairs, getting a haircut, a pedicure, and a massage with warm sesame oil—the birthday treat he'd insisted on. I'd taken a long nap in the room he'd booked for me, right next door to his, then put on the maternity outfit he'd brought—a silk pant suit that was the cleanest thing that had touched my skin in months. My blow-dried hair flew around my face in a soft cloud.

"You look fabulous," said Tom. The weird thing was, I could tell that he meant it. I smiled back at him happily. "So do you." It was such a relief to see a guy who wasn't wearing ripped jeans or a lungi. I felt like there was solid ground under my feet for the first time in months. I was remembering what I found so appealing about being with Tom: When I was with him, I could relax a certain vigilance that I carried with me almost all the time, a sense of being braced against some unknown threat that might appear from any direction. Tom had kept me safe in a fortress of kitchen appliances and digital media systems and matching towel sets. It had felt like a trap, back then. But now it felt as if an apartment with a coffee table and matching end tables might just keep me from slipping into the void.

I studied the menu, which looked like it had been lifted from a California café. Pasta with pesto, corn chowder, fettuccine with mushrooms—I tried not to drool too obviously. I told Tom what I wanted, and he ordered for both of us when the waiter came—a habit that had always annoyed me before. But now it was a soothing buffer between me and the rest of the world.

"So I hear you bought a house!" I reached for a crust of baguette and dipped it into olive oil. "Things must be going well."

He nodded. "Apple picked up the last piece of software I designed and is using it as a training module for all their new salespeople. Want to see the house that Mac built?"

He pulled out his Treo and showed me pictures: a wraparound redwood deck overlooking the ocean. A master suite with floor to ceiling windows. A kitchen with acres of granite counters, miles of stainless steel appliances. The refrigerator alone looked big enough to house an Indian family.

"It's gorgeous." Our entrées had arrived; I took a bite of "mushroom stroganoff," canned mushrooms swimming in a creamy sauce that tasted, unexpectedly, of chilies. "Huge, too. You must be planning some big parties."

"It is big." He twirled his fork in his fettuccine. "Way too big for just me. I didn't understand why I wanted it until I talked to Lori."

"What, are you going to hire Joe and Lori as groundskeepers?" I honestly didn't grasp what he was hinting at. Then I looked up and saw his face. He had put down his fork.

"Amanda. I know we haven't seen each other in a long time. And I know your life has gotten . . . complicated. It always has been, I suppose. But I've never stopped thinking about you."

I studied my mashed potatoes. Part of me wanted him to stop talking so I could devour them in peace. "Tom. In case you haven't noticed: I'm six months pregnant. With someone else's baby."

"There's a little baby room right off the master suite. We could put an au pair in the in-law unit. There's even a room for a yoga studio downstairs." He leaned on the table. His eyes were wide and blue, his cheeks pink. He was as light as Matt was dark. "I'm not trying to put any kind of pressure on you. You could have your own bedroom. We wouldn't have to decide anything about us, right away. This is about you, and what's best for you and the baby."

I stared at the butter melting on my green beans. "Why would you even consider doing something like this?"

"Because—you bring me to life. You wake up parts of me that have been sleeping for years." He reached across the table and picked up my hands. "I like who I am, when I'm with you."

*That's how I feel when I'm with Matt.* His hands were dry and cool on mine. I didn't say anything.

"And I'm worried about you. You shouldn't be here in your condition. You should be back in your own home, with someone who loves you taking care of you."

"Have you been talking to my mother? I'm taking care of myself just fine." But my words sounded unconvincing even to me. He shook his head.

"You have no idea how crazy your life has gotten. You're like one of those frogs in a pot of water that's getting hotter and hotter, and you're just sitting there waiting for it to come to a boil and cook you.

Maybe at two or three months pregnant, sure, you could travel in India. But at six months—you don't know what you're doing. You're taking a terrible risk for yourself and your baby."

I started to defend myself, but I just didn't have the energy. What he was saying was too much like what I'd been feeling myself for the past couple of weeks. "I know it's crazy. But I just feel like . . . I'm so close. It's not that I think I'm going to get enlightened. But I just want to have at least a *taste* of what all these teachers are talking about. I want to get at least a glimpse of something beyond—all this." I gestured around at *all this,* not sure myself what I meant: Me? The baby? Tom? The restaurant, with its brass candleholders in the shape of Hindu gods?

He shook his head. "So what's wrong with 'all this'?"

*I'm with the wrong person. I* am *the wrong person.* My life felt like my mushroom stroganoff—an improvised imitation of the real thing. I didn't say anything.

"Amanda. You're sitting across the table from someone who loves you more than anyone else in the world, and who's willing to love your baby as if it were his own. Can't you let that be enough?"


LATER THAT NIGHT, I lay awake in the room he'd booked for me. The air conditioner wheezed, drowning out the traffic. My skin still carried the scent of the spicy oil from my massage. I still tasted the creamy sweetness of the crème brûlée we had shared for dessert, still felt the aftershock of Tom's lips on mine as he kissed me good night: a chaste but affectionate kiss on the lips, hovering somewhere between the sensual kiss of lovers and the cheek peck of friends. I was lying on my side, my belly heavy, acutely aware, as I had been for several weeks now, that there were two people sharing this bed.

It was soothing knowing that Tom was asleep just on the other side of the wall; it gave me the primal sense that I could go to sleep and know that I wouldn't be eaten by lions. It was so delicious being taken care of like this. Why not let it continue? As I drifted off to sleep, I imagined myself dissolving into a new identity. Or rather, picking up an old one, right up off the floor where I had dropped it like a discarded pair of yoga pants. Tom's fiancée.

*I AM AT Tom's old apartment, doing laundry in the efficient little laundry room off the kitchen. I am stuffing my India clothes into the gleaming German-made washing machine:* my *salwar kameez,* my *white ashram clothes, even my sandals are going in. The clothes are filthy with dust and sweat and grass stains and blood and spilled food; I dump in bleach and stain removers. But as I start the machine, dark gray soapsuds begin boiling up, spilling out onto the floor. I look for a mop, but I can't find one. I begin frantically mopping up the spill with some of Tom's monogrammed towels, turning them gray as well. As I bend over to the floor easily—too easily—it hits me: Where is my baby? I look down at my flat belly. Did I give birth and forget about it? I look in the washer and dryer. I run around the apartment looking under couches, in closets—looking for a baby, a crib, a changing table, any sign that a child has ever been here. I must have left the baby at Mount Arunachala; that's the last time I remember being pregnant. I race out of the house and down to the garage; I'll drive Tom's car to the airport. But when I unlock the car, someone else is already sitting in the driver's seat. I look over and it is Saraswati. She says, "Ask yourself. Who is it who is having a baby?"*

I JERKED AWAKE. The air conditioner rumbled; it was cold in the room, but I was burning up under my comforter. My hands flew to my belly and, as if in answer to an unspoken question, the baby rolled inside me. Relief flooded me.

I pushed the comforter down and rolled to my other side. But I didn't go back to sleep for a long time. I just lay there, staring into the darkness, thinking about Tom dreaming on the other side of the wall.

THREE DAYS AFTER my birthday, Devi Das and I set out from the ashram after breakfast to walk around the base of Mount Arunachala.

We started at dawn to avoid the heat—and also to avoid the thousands of other pilgrims who would also be walking around the mountain on this auspicious full-moon day. But hundreds of people were already surging down the road. The crowd was so thick I couldn't even see the pavement—a shouting, laughing, chanting mass of young women in brilliant saris, their faces painted yellow with turmeric powder; men in jeans, suits, lungis, or dhotis, their foreheads streaked with stripes of ash from the temples they'd visited; teenage boys shouting and pushing each other off the road; bent old women with withered breasts swinging loose, holding little children by the hand. The road was not barricaded against traffic; the crowd itself was the barricade. Trucks and buses periodically rumbled through, horns blaring, sending pedestrians scampering.

"This is a madhouse," I said. "Are you sure this is the best day to do this?"

"Better today than on a day when it's not a full moon. I've heard that out on the main highway, the trucks hit a couple of pilgrims a day. One sadhu was crippled last month. At least where there are this many people, we can slow down the buses and trucks just through our sheer numbers."

As we stepped into the river of people, Devi Das frowned at my Birkenstocks. "You realize, of course, that you're supposed to do this barefoot? Some of the local people have complained that the monsoons have been late the last few years because of Westerners going around the mountain with their shoes on."

I looked down at the rutted pavement, thick with rotting

garbage, oil spills, gobs of spit stained red with betel leaf. "Can't we just tell Shiva I'm pregnant and that I'll get varicose veins if I don't wear shoes with proper arch support?"

"Oh sure," said Devi Das darkly. "I'm sure Shiva's never heard *that* excuse before. But go ahead. Ruin the crops. Cause a famine. Don't let us stop you."

We made our way down the street, which was lined with makeshift stalls selling snack foods: pakoras, samosas, fried bananas, paper cones of roasted nuts. Devi Das stopped to buy a paper cone full of chole, chopped chickpeas fried with chilies and ginger. He offered me a handful, but they were so spicy that just the smell made my eyes burn. A rickshaw pushed past us, horn blaring; we jumped aside and toppled into a line of people waiting to get a blessing at a roadside temple.

I grabbed Devi Das's elbow. "I thought pilgrims were supposed to go around the mountain in silence, with our eyes and heart fixed on its sacred peak. Isn't that what I read in the ashram guidebook?"

"As long as our hearts are quiet, the gods will smile upon us. But if you'd prefer, we can take the inner path." Devi Das steered me off the main road and through a wrought-iron ashram gate. We cut across a weedy courtyard and up the hill behind the temple to a dirt footpath, marked with occasional splashes of white paint on the red rocks.

"This will be quieter. And be sure not to walk too fast. The gurus say that circumambulation of the sacred mountain should be done slowly, as if you were a woman in the ninth month of pregnancy."

"That, I think I can manage."

We hiked along in silence for almost an hour, the roar of the crowd fading. The crown of the mountain was shrouded in silvery mist, turning peach-colored as the sun rose higher. The red earth path was lined with scrubby bushes with long, sharp thorns, which caught at my clothes when I walked too close to the edge. Within ten minutes, my legs were aching; the weight of my belly tugged at my sacrum, making my lower back throb. I tried to focus my mind on the mountain. For hundreds, maybe thousands of years people had been paying homage to this hill. I wanted to tap into the force field of their faith. But doubt hammered away at me with a sledgehammer. What was I doing, setting out on a seven-mile hike around a mountain when I was over six months pregnant? Plodding around this particular mountain on this particular day was supposed to be auspicious. But what if Tom was right, and with every step I was walking closer not to enlightenment, but to disaster?

We stopped in front of a burned and gutted temple, with a tank full of scummy rainwater in front of it. A giant lizard perched on a rock. Wood doves cooed. The sun was barely up, but it was already hot. I sat down on a rock in the shade of a scrubby tree, wondering if it was too late to turn back.

"So. He's gone?" Devi Das reached into his bag and pulled out a water bottle.

I didn't need to ask who he's talking about. "He left last night."

"Did he take it hard?" He handed the water to me, and I took a long drink.

"Not as hard as I expected. He told me that if I changed my mind, the offer still stood." I handed the water back to Devi Das. "I think on some level he was actually relieved. His intentions were sincere. But the reality of seeing me pregnant with another guy's baby must have been a lot to deal with."

Devi Das pulled a lemon PowerBar from his sadhu bag and ripped off the wrapper. He tore it in half and handed part to me. "And you? Are *you* relieved?"

I bit into the bar, sweet and chemical tasting. "I don't know. Half the time I'm beating myself up for making a terrible mistake. The other half of the time I think it was the only honest thing I could do." I could see Tom's face as he hugged me good-bye at the hotel. My belly had pressed against him, a pulsating globe, as big as everything we weren't talking about: *my clothes on hangers in his closet. A gold ring with a diamond sparkling on it, sitting on a kitchen counter. My arms wrapped around another man's neck, my breath hot in another man's ears.* I had told him to go home. So why did I feel, as I watched him get into the rickshaw with his duffel bag, as if I were the one being tossed off the life raft to the sharks? "What do you think? Did I make a mistake?"

He shrugged. "In our opinion, we generally have less choice in these matters than we imagine we do."

He picked up the daypack, and we plodded up another ridge. In the distance, we could see other mountains jutting up out of the plains.

"What makes this mountain sacred, and not those?" I asked.

Devi Das shrugged again. "Why is one person born a saint, and another a pickpocket? This one is Shiva's lingam; those are not." We headed down the slope. "And speaking of saints . . . We didn't want to say anything before, because we didn't want to influence your decision. But the other day at satsang with Saraswati, while you were with Tom, everyone was talking about a woman saint named Maitri Ma who's been living alone in a cave in the Himalayas for the past ten years. A couple of backpackers stumbled upon her last summer when they got lost in a rainstorm north of Gangotri and she let them stay in her cave. Apparently, it was a mind-blowing experience. They were just a couple of guys from Sprint visiting Delhi for a cell-phone conference, who took a week afterward to do a little trekking. Now they're both Maitri Ma devotees."

"Hmm. So what are her teachings?" The question was automatic; I didn't really want to hear the answer. My back was aching. My feet were aching. Tom was on the train to Madras to catch a plane home tomorrow. If I got the last train out this afternoon, I could still catch up with him.

"Well, she doesn't talk at all—just writes on a chalkboard. But her English is excellent. Apparently, she spent forty years teaching English lit in a private girls' school in Delhi. She's in her sixties or seventies—raised three children and a pack of grandchildren. But after her husband died, she began seeing visions of Shiva and ran away to the mountains."

"It's amazing she even survived." Reluctantly, I was intrigued. "I wonder if she's packing a gun."

"Well, she must be packing something pretty powerful, because apparently all you have to do is sit in her presence and your mind just stops and your heart gets blasted open. So far only a few Westerners have been to see her, because the roads to Gangotri are closed all winter. But there were a couple of people at satsang who had made the trek in. They looked totally high. Just hearing them talk about it was enough to put us into an altered state for the rest of the day."

I didn't say anything for a long time. We made our way around the side of the mountain, heading back into town again. Open sewers crisscrossed the path, assaulting us with the stench of raw sewage. A sadhu overtook us, walking briskly: a young, bespectacled man with a keen businesslike face, like a computer engineer who had inadvertently become covered with ashes on his way to work. He was walking fast, swinging his arms, and gabbling a mantra with extreme efficiency.

"I don't know," I finally said. "I've gotten my hopes up so many times, thinking I was about to find the ultimate teacher. How do I know this one will be worth the trip?"

"We're telling you, we saw the look in those people's eyes. It looked like they'd stared into the sun for an hour." We could hear the din of the main road drawing nearer. Beggars were starting to line the path—eyes missing, faces paralyzed by strokes, deformed limbs reaching out to us. A man with a white, pigmentless face and raccoon-black eyes reached out his hands, crying "Ma? Ma?"

"This could be the real thing," said Devi Das. "It could be what you've been looking for all this time."

Horns blared as we step onto the main road again. The crowd was surging. How could I meditate on the mountain in the middle of this din? I looked at the chaos around me. It seemed like the harder I chased enlightenment, the more of a mess my life became.

But what if this woman really *was* the real thing? It sounded like the best lead I'd had so far. Maybe I could go to the mountains and get my personality blasted away. I'd get a taste of who I truly was when my thoughts stopped and my heart opened. And then I could go home and have my baby in peace.

A truck roared by, and Devi Das and I stumbled to the side of the road. I narrowly missed stepping in a pile of cow manure.

"Sure," I told him. "Let's go."

# mountain pose
## (Tadasana)

*Stand with your feet hip width apart, your arms relaxed by your side. Let thunder clouds gather around your head. Ground into the bedrock of lava that pushed up through the crust of the earth to form you.*

*Let cheetahs hunt your slopes. Let winds blow through your grasses. Let saints meditate in your caves, and let villagers burn your trees for fuel and use your fields for toilets. Let trucks blare around the highway at your base and pilgrims circumambulate the path around you, praying for sons, and miraculous cures, and to know who they truly are.*

*In the midst of them all, stand silent and unshakeable, watching them from the vast perspective of geologic time.*

*"Not seeing things as they are" is the field where the other causes of suffering germinate.*

—*The Yoga Sutra of Patanjali*, ca. 200 BC

# CHAPTER 22

JUST OVER A week later, Devi Das and I and my bulging belly were crammed into the back seat of a rented Jeep Cherokee, winding too fast up a narrow mountain road, listening to Siddhartha and Maya argue about enlightenment.

The squabble had been going on since our plane landed in Dehra Dun that morning, when Siddhartha told Maya as the wheels jolted down onto the tarmac that if he got enlightened while meditating with Maitri Ma, he probably wouldn't love her anymore. Five hours later, she was still furious.

"It's not a personal thing," he told her for the thousandth time. "It's just that there won't be any 'I' left to love 'you.'" I could hear the quotation marks hovering around the pronouns, as if *I* and *you* were words so absurd he could hardly say them with a straight face. "My sense of a separate self will have totally disappeared."

"I thought that enlightenment was supposed to make you *more* loving, not less," snapped Maya.

"Well, of course I'll still 'love' you, in the universal sense." More quotation marks. "But it won't be possessive. My heart will be equally open to, say, Amanda. Or even Mr. Desai." He gestured at our driver, who was chain-smoking Lucky Strikes, filling the car with smoke, although I'd asked him several times to put them out.

"And suppose I *don't* get enlightened and you do?" Maya pulled out her Swiss Army knife, popped it open, and began cleaning her nails. "Am I supposed to keep on loving you?"

"I don't know why you wouldn't. I'll still be the same person. Enlightenment doesn't change your personality."

"Wonderful. I'm *so* relieved that you won't suddenly stop being a total jerk." She turned to Devi Das. "Do you have any more sodas? I forgot to tell you, I get carsick."

Like us, Siddhartha and Maya had reasons for wanting to go see Maitri Ma now, at the tail end of March, rather than waiting more sensibly until May, when the mountain roads would be clear of snow. Maya was due back at her nursing job, and Siddhartha had to complete his paper on dialectical hermeneutics in the work of Hegel and Wittgenstein for a peer-reviewed journal. Together, the four of us had taken the train to Bangalore, where I'd gotten in a visit with Dr. Rao to make sure that everything was still going well. From there, we'd caught a plane to Dehra Dun, in the foothills of the Himalayas.

Siddhartha had assumed the role of commander in chief of our expedition, choosing everything from our route to our choice of snacks. Normally, that would have irritated me. But at this point in my pregnancy, my brain seemed to have turned to pudding, and my decision-making capacity had shrunk in proportion to the growth of my belly. I was happy to waddle along in his wake, letting someone else be the grown-up.

Our driver, Mr. Desai, had one glass eye that was permanently rolled to the far right, creating the reassuring delusion that he was constantly monitoring traffic approaching from the other side of the car, when in fact he couldn't see anything at all in that direction. We roared along narrow mountain roads with crumbling edges overlooking precipitous drops. Mr. Desai's strategy around the hairpin curves seemed to be to accelerate into them to get through the danger zone as quickly as possible. Warning signs flashed by: LIFE'S A JOURNEY— PLEASE FINISH IT. CORNER CUTTERS OFTEN LAND INTO GUTTERS.

"Do you know the story of how the Ganges River descended from heaven?" Siddhartha asked us, as we passed around sodas and fruit and cookies and chikki, a peanut candy sticky with sugar and ghee. His tone made it clear that he was going to illuminate us, whether we thought we knew or not.

"What do I care?" Maya gulped at the soda that Devi Das handed her. "Apparently, *I'm* not the one who's getting enlightened this week."

Siddhartha interpreted this as an enthusiastic assent. "Well, apparently the goddess Ganga was so annoyed at being compelled to leave heaven that she descended in a great torrent, strong enough to wipe out the entire earth." I could see him smoking a pipe, lecturing Berlin undergraduates on Kant. "But Shiva, seated in meditation at Gangotri, blocked her descent with his hair, and she became entangled there for thousands of years." He turned to our driver. "Isn't that right, Desai-ji?"

"Yes, yes, all that you are saying is most correct." Mr. Desai threw his cigarette butt out the half-opened window and began fumbling around for another one. "But finally, Parvati, Shiva's wife, she was getting so jealous. 'Who is this lady playing so long, around and around, in my husband's hair?' she was asking. 'This I cannot tolerate!'"

"Totally understandable," sniffed Maya.

I loved this about Indian mythology—that even the deities were wracked with petty human emotions. It made it seem more likely that they would sympathize with my situation. I pictured Parvati stomping around her apartment in a snit, maybe even calling up one of the other goddesses on the phone to bitch about Shiva. "Get a load of this, Lakshmi. How am I supposed to deal with this one?" And Lakshmi would remind her of the Rules, urge her to act like a Creature Unlike Any Other. *If he's got another goddess playing in his hair—he's just not that into you.*

"So then Parvati demanded that Shiva wring out his dreadlocks like a wet dishrag, releasing Ganga, who then flowed down from the mountains into the plains. You can see her there below." Siddhartha gestured out the window at the river, a band of silver hundreds of feet below. "That is why Gangotri is such an optimum place to get enlightened. It marks the very spot where the goddess Ganga first touched the earth."

"Stop the car." Maya cupped her hand over her mouth. "I'm going to throw up."

Half an hour later, we were back in the car again. Siddhartha, chastened, was sitting with his arms around a wan Maya, pressing acupressure spots on her wrists and assuring her that he'd always care about her, even if the worst happened and he attained total enlightenment by the end of this week. "After all, enlightenment, per se, does not preclude the possibility of intimate personal relationships."

"Saraswati has a husband," Maya said. "I don't think she sees him much any more, though."

"Saraswati has a husband?" I asked. "Where is he?"

"He's a divorce lawyer back in Santa Barbara. A lot of Saraswati's students go to see him, once they start evolving beyond the confines of their relationships." Maya looked at Siddhartha, and I could practically hear her thoughts: *I might be evolving any minute.*

By the time we finally pulled into Uttarkashi, a freezing rain was falling, and it was almost dusk. The city roads were mired in mud, with an occasional patch of dirty, icy snow. But the fact that Uttarkashi was deserted only increased everyone's sense of excitement: We were getting to Maitri Ma ahead of the crowds. We were approaching the Las Vegas of enlightenment with a winning tip. We checked into one of the few open hotels and ate dal and rice and sour yogurt; then went to our rooms, which were cold and smelled of mildew, with mattresses we didn't want to look at too closely. I was longing for a hot shower, so Devi Das went into our bathroom and turned on the water heater, which squealed, hissed, then exploded with a bang, filling the room with scalding steam. Devi Das slammed the bathroom door shut and went to fetch the hotel manager, who turned it off for us, shooting me a reproving look: "This is not tourist season, madam." Once we crawled into our beds, Devi Das fell asleep immediately. But I lay there awake for a while, staring into the darkness, shivering.

When I was nannying for Sam and Tamara, one of their favorite games was "treasure hunt." I'd save it for those long weekend afternoons when their parents were out playing golf (him) or getting facials (her), and the kids' usual packed schedules—preschool, ballet, Mandarin, karate—gave way to the endless whine of "what can I do now?" I'd hide my clues all over the house and garden—just scribbled crayon drawings on folded scraps of construction paper, since neither of the kids could read yet. They'd climb the lower branches of the backyard oak, peer inside the chamber of the grand piano, peel the jackets off their favorite books. They'd find clues in the arches of their mom's high-heeled shoes, in the neckband of a stuffed bear, inside their dad's guitar.

My trip around India was starting to feel just like that game. I was dashing here, dashing there, following illegible clues tucked in obscure places. But who was leaving the clues? And what if he or she were truly as clueless as I was?

I rolled onto my side. When Sam and Tamara did finally find the treasure, it was never anything very big—just a bag of chocolate chip cookies, or a pair of plastic water pistols. Nothing they couldn't have gotten without all that searching, simply by asking for it. But, of course, it wasn't the treasure itself that was the point. It was the looking for it.

THE NEXT MORNING, Siddhartha headed out to the Nehru Institute of Mountaineering to find a trail guide to accompany us to Maitri Ma. The rest of us sat in the hotel restaurant, sipping chai, our backpacks piled around us. Devi Das had offered to carry one for both of us; it loomed bigger than all the rest, with two sleeping bags lashed to the bottom.

The plan was to drive up the road to Gangotri as far as we could go before snow and mudslides blocked the road. We'd heard contradictory reports: You could get within three miles of Gangotri. No, the road was blocked ten miles away. In the absence of any hard data, we'd decided arbitrarily to average them and assume that we'd have about a six- or seven-mile walk. Then we'd spend the night in Gangotri before hiking in to see Maitri Ma—a two-mile hike up a snowy trail.

It was a *good* thing that Maitri Ma was so hard to reach, I told myself. In a few years, Maitri Ma's cave would have an email address and a website; the guru would still be in silence, but she would have an assistant with an iPhone. This was my chance to experience the real thing.

But I was getting nervous that I wouldn't be able to haul my belly that far, even without a backpack. And this was the first time I wouldn't be in range of a hospital if something went wrong. I fell back on the mantra I'd used all along: *Nothing is unusual about this pregnancy. People have babies in India all the time.* Besides, Maya was a nurse. I'd be more at risk back at home driving on the freeway at rush hour. I was two and a half months away from my due date. I'd be fine.

From: HeyBaby.com
To: Amandala@yahoo.com

At 28 weeks, even though you may not feel like shaking your bootie, your need for exercise hasn't stopped! A few gentle laps in a pool or a walk around the block may be just what you need to ward off the third-trimester blahs. But don't overdo it! Heavy physical labor is one of the risk factors for premature labor. If your job or household duties require you to stand for several hours a day, cut back. Don't worry, those tightening sensations you feel are just your uterus "practicing" its contractions.

For more information, take our Pregnancy Fitness IQ Quiz now and receive a free HeyBaby bib, a package of Pampers Sensitive Wipes, and a chance to win a new Mercury Mariner!

From: Maxine@bigdaybooks.com
To: Amandala@yahoo.com
Subject: Hooray!

Amanda, this is the best news I've gotten all day. A female guru in a forest? Not discovered yet? A two-day hike in? In other words, this is our exclusive scoop? You've made my day. Be sure you get one of our friends to get a picture of you sitting with her, and do something with your hair, first; it's OK if you look a little windblown but lose the ponytail, please, and it wouldn't hurt you to put on a little bit of lipstick first. See if you can spruce her up a little, too. I imagine it's been a while since she's plucked her eyebrows. Congratulations. This might save your manuscript from the dustbin.

Two hours later, we were all in the car again, winding up the road to Gangotri.

Sitting in the front seat with Siddhartha and Maya was Vikram Singh, a taciturn mountain guide from the Nehru Institute. In a few weeks, he told us, the road would be roaring with buses and jeeps delivering pilgrims to Gangotri. But now it was almost deserted. As we climbed higher and higher, I pressed my face against the glass. Snowy peaks soared ahead of us, twenty thousand feet high. I was driving straight into every fantasy I'd ever had about finding a guru in India.

*Heavy physical labor is one of the risk factors for premature labor.* Our car maneuvered around a sadhu walking by the side of the road—an early pilgrim making the journey on foot.

I pressed my nose against the glass. It wasn't just for myself that I was doing this. It wasn't just for Maxine. It was for my baby.

I didn't have any money. I didn't have a career. I didn't have a partner. I couldn't give my baby a dresser that matched his crib or a college education fund. I couldn't give him a father, or even a grandfather. But maybe if I could offer him inner peace, then everything would be all right. I wouldn't just be a screwed-up single mom who got pregnant at the wrong time.

I couldn't turn back now.

Devi Das put his arm around me and gave me a squeeze. "Don't worry," he whispered. "Everything's going to be all right."

I closed my eyes and tried to believe him.

A FEW HOURS later, Mr. Desai pulled to the side of the road. "No more driving. Road is closed." He gestured to a three-foot-wide slide of mud and rock tumbled across the pavement.

"How much further is it to Gangotri?" asked Siddhartha.

"Three kilometers. Five, maximum."

"That means it's probably about ten." Devi Das looked at me. "Five miles, give or take. Can you do it?"

*A few gentle laps. A walk around the block.* "I can do it," I said.

We clambered over the pile of dirt and headed up the road. I plodded along, my back aching, a shooting pain traveling from my sacrum down the outside of my hip with every step. Siddhartha and Maya disappeared in the distance ahead of us. Our guide stayed with me and Devi Das, a sheepdog making sure the stragglers stayed with the flock. I was grateful Devi Das was carrying the backpack. Having my swollen belly slung out in front seemed a bad choice, from an ergonomic point of view. Why weren't babies gestated on our backs?

The mountain slopes around us were thick with trees, which Mr. Singh named for us: blue pine. Oak. Walnut. Horse chestnuts. Deodar. Rhododendron, flowering early with huge crimson blossoms. We passed an occasional sadhu; an old man leading a donkey with a pile of sticks on its back.

The Bhagirathi River snaked along in the deep gorge below us. "It's named for King Bhagirathi, who is the one who persuaded the Ganga to descend from heaven," Devi Das told me. "He sat in Gangotri and prayed for ten thousand years, begging the goddess to come down to Earth to purify the sins of his ancestors."

I looked at the river rushing below. "Do you believe in sin?"

"We believe the true nature of the soul is pure and spotless. But sometimes it gets covered over with a thick layer of grime that needs to be wiped off."

I didn't say anything for a while. We were moving too slowly even for our guide—he had walked ahead to check up on Siddhartha and Maya. "Devi Das. Do you think I'm crazy, doing this?"

"We are probably not the right person to talk about craziness. But we can tell you this: You never know where a path is leading you." He stopped to pick a pebble out of his sandal. "When our brother died, we just kept thinking, 'If only we'd made pancakes that morning, instead of oatmeal.' We almost did. We'd had fresh blueberries from the farmer's market, and some buckwheat flour, and we could have made buckwheat blueberry pancakes with maple syrup. But we decided on hot cereal instead, and just sprinkled the blueberries on the top. Afterward, we kept thinking that if we'd made the pancakes, they would have taken longer than the oatmeal. We would have gotten to that intersection ten minutes later. That guy would have slammed into somebody else, instead."

"Oh, Devi Das. You can't think like that." I didn't tell him how often I thought the same way: that if I'd just pulled a different condom out of the box, I wouldn't be pregnant right now. Or that if I'd been in a different position when it broke, this baby would be an entirely different person.

"But that's exactly our point. Who is to say what is risky, and what is not? Are pancakes safe and oatmeal dangerous? Who can say which road leads to enlightenment, and which to disaster? All you can do is trust your instincts, moment to moment."

I plodded on in silence for a few minutes. "When your brother was in the car accident. Did he die right away? Or was he in the hospital for a while?

"He was in the ICU for a week."

"And were you with him? Did you get to see him at all?"

"We were with him round the clock." He didn't look at me. "But he didn't regain consciousness. We just wanted to talk to him, just wanted to tell him we loved him. But he never woke up."

It was almost dark when Devi Das and I finally tramped into the town of Gangotri. It was a ghost town: a jumble of water-sculpted, caramel-colored granite, with the pale green river foaming and splashing around it, surrounded by abandoned buildings and boarded up tourist hotels. Snow was heaped on the tops of buildings, squeaked underfoot whenever we left the rutted, trampled roads. The peaks loomed above us, although we were already at ten thousand feet. I stopped to look up at them. Just a couple of miles up the trail was the cave where Maitri Ma was spending the winter.

We walked around the temple, closed up and barricaded with an iron gate. "Next month, the goddess Ganga will be coming back here," our guide told us. "There will be big puja and festival to welcome her home. But now, she is still living downriver, in her winter temple."

We caught up with Siddhartha and Maya in a mud lean-to where a couple of men in camouflage army jackets were brewing chai over a wood fire. I collapsed on the rickety wooden chair and gratefully gulped the hot brew, too exhausted to try to figure out who these guys were—off-duty soldiers? Deserters? Locals who picked up the jackets secondhand? The chai was achingly sweet and tasted of smoke, ginger, and black pepper. The baby wriggled in enthusiastic appreciation. Maya sat down next to me.

"How are you doing?" she asked.

I shook my head. "Not that great. My back is killing me and I've got a splitting headache."

"Any contractions?"

"No."

"Then you're fine. The headache is probably just the altitude. The caffeine should help."

A swami approached and bowed to us, wearing—in addition to the usual orange robes—a not-so-usual pair of orange bedroom slippers. Our guide spoke with him in Hindi, then turned to us. "Hotels—all closed. But Swami Nityananda will be letting us stay in his temple, fixing us dinner, breakfast, tea, all that. No money— donation only." So we followed the swami up the road to a shack made of sheets of corrugated metal attached to crumbling brick walls with what appeared to be bundles of twine. He served us piles of rice and dal on metal plates, then showed us to a warren of tiny back rooms to sleep. I stepped outside to the snowbank that served as the toilet, and squatted in the icy wind to pee. Then I lay down across from Devi Das on a thin mattress draped across a sling of rope, like a hammock, and pulled a pile of musty blankets around me. The wind whistled through the plastic bags that covered the window.

I closed my eyes, rested my hands protectively on my belly, and tried to talk myself into believing that I wasn't insane. I couldn't get comfortable. My back throbbed. My pubic bone hurt. Trying not to wake up Devi Das, I rolled up a blanket and stuck it between my knees to ease the pressure on my sacrum.

Even my *hair* was exhausted. I closed my eyes and waited for sleep to swallow me.

*MY CHILD has fallen into a dark well in a snowstorm. He is at the bottom, screaming. "Mommy!" He cries. "Mommy! Help!" I am leaning over the edge, frantic, looking for a rope to throw him. Then I realize that the only thing to do is to jump in after him. But when I get to the bottom, the well is empty. I stand there sobbing in a whirl of snowflakes.*

WITH A SHARP inhale, I jolted awake. In a panic, I reached down and gave my belly a shake. The baby kicked back, an irritated thump.

*Mommy! Help!* It was dawn. I looked around the room in the pale light. Siddhartha and Maya had their blankets pulled over their heads. Devi Das was snoring. Back in California, it was about five in the afternoon. Tom was probably sitting in traffic, listening to NPR, heading back alone to his empty palace. My mom was probably fixing dinner for her new man—attempting some elaborate meal from a cookbook she'd never tried before, then giving up halfway through and sending out for gourmet takeout from Dine-One-One. Lori and Joe must be getting in a last bit of gardening before the sun goes down. And Matt? I didn't even know what country he was in.

*Help!* For the first time in months, I remembered the letter that Lori gave me before I left, with instructions to read it when I was about to do something stupid. I sat up and fumbled through the backpack I shared with Devi Das, pulling out the pouch that held my passport and traveler's checks. The sound of the backpack zipper was

loud in the silent room, but no one moved. I pulled out Lori's envelope, gray and ragged around the edges. I grabbed a pencil-sized
flashlight, tore open the envelope, and sat up in bed.

*Dear Amanda,*

*I'm writing this thinking you probably won't ever read it. By
the time you need it, you'll probably have lost it—stuck it into some
book as a bookmark and then left it on a table in a restaurant somewhere, or written your phone number on the back and handed it to
someone. And even if you do still have it, it's the last thing you're
going to want to read. You're afraid that I'm going to tell you not to
do whatever harebrained probably lovesick thing you're about to
do—and the problem is, you want to do that thing. You really do.
And the last thing you want is me ruining your fun.*

*As I'm writing this, you're in your bedroom, zipping your
backpack, getting ready to head off on the greatest adventure you've
ever had. As you're reading this—who knows where you are?
Maybe you're on a beach by the Arabian Sea, wondering if you
should take Ecstasy with some guy you just met in a chai shop.
Maybe you're in some Tibetan monastery, wondering if you should
shave your head and ordain.*

*But—surprise. I'm not going to tell you not to do that thing,
whatever it is. I'm not going to tell you not to sleep with that guy.
I'm not going to tell you not to get on that train. I'm not going to
tell you not to raft down that river, or smoke that chillum, or drink
that cup of tea with the stranger in the next seat on the train, or head
off for that country where there's just been a revolution.*

*All I'm going to say is this—remember how special you are. It's
something you miss noticing, a lot of the time. Sometimes I think you
chase after all these adventures—Matt, enlightenment, Tom, backbends, hang gliding, whatever it is—because you think they'll give
you something you don't have. It's like you're looking for the missing*

*ingredient in the soup of your life. But the thing is—nothing's missing. You've got it all. And I don't mean that in some airy-fairy kind of way, like "the secret to life is inside you," and all that crap. I just mean it in a really ordinary way: You're fine. You really are.*

*So do whatever you want. You will anyway, I know. Just remember, I'll love you whether or not you get enlightened. It's just that if you do, it will probably be a little bit harder.*

Enclosed was a picture of the two of us taken on the first day of college. I'd never seen it before, although I did have a vague memory of Lori's mother snapping one last shot before she drove away. We were sitting together on her bed in the freshman dorm room we've just moved into. We looked absurdly young. My hair was pulled back in the tight ponytail I'd worn it in since second grade; I was peering through the lenses of my big glasses as if regarding the world from inside an aquarium. I was grinning the big, fake grin of someone who doesn't want anyone to know how terrified she is.

Lori was sitting next to me in a red sweater, chubby and confident, like a robin who knew where all the worms were hidden. Her arm was around my shoulder, although we had only met about an hour ago. But looking at her picture, I saw something that I hadn't seen then: She was scared, too. She was lonely. She needed someone to adopt as badly as I needed someone to adopt me.

"How do you know Joe's right for you?" I'd asked Lori once. "Is it a kind of electricity?"

"It's the opposite of electricity," she'd said. "Electricity is hot and bright, like lightning, or the inside of a toaster. This is more like a hot-water bottle. When I'm with him, I feel . . . calm. As if some wind inside me that I hadn't even known was blowing had stopped, and I can hear the birds singing outside the window."

This was so far from the way I felt with Matt that I hadn't known what to say. Matt caused an electrical storm all through my body. That was how I knew I loved him—all those painful lightning bolts of unquenched desire.

But it was the way I felt about Lori, I realized now. It was how I had always felt in her presence: safe.

Exactly the opposite of how I felt now.

I lay down on the bed, clutching the letter, and began to cry.


THE NARROW TRAIL to Maitri Ma's cave wound up the side of the river gorge. Jagged white mountains sliced into the ice-blue sky. My breath was shallow. I could hear the snow squeaking under my shoes. The cold, thin air stung my nostrils and burned my lungs, but still left me breathless. We paused for snacks in a snowy meadow: roasted peanuts, chocolate cookies, spicy chole mix, dried mango and papaya. Then we plodded on. My knee had started aching again. I could feel a blister starting on the back of my left heel.

The hike took longer than we had expected; it was early afternoon by the time we got within sight of Maitri Ma's cave. I was sweating and shivering at the same time, and my fingers were numb inside my gloves. Her cave was halfway up the side of a steep hill, almost a cliff, with stone steps leading up to it. As we approached, a tiny woman stepped out, bundled in orange robes and a thick brown wool shawl. Her forehead was painted with the stripes of a sadhu. A scarf was wrapped around her white hair.

We hadn't sent word we were coming, but she seemed unsurprised. We bowed, our hands in prayer position in front of our hearts. Siddhartha held out the oranges we had brought as a gift—"Namaste, Maitri Ma, we have come for teachings"—but she cut him off with a shake of her head and beckoned for us to come into her cave.

It didn't have a door, just blankets and plastic bags and burlap sacks hung over the opening. Inside, it was lit by candles and an oil lamp. A wood fire burned in a little stove in the back, next to an altar with a clay statue of Shiva on it. Five cups of tea were already set out around a tablecloth spread on the ground.

We bowed, sat down, and drank the hot chai in silence. The cup was deliciously warm under my aching fingers. My whole body hurt. I was dizzy from exhaustion and altitude. But I also felt strangely calm, in way that I hadn't felt since my travels began so many months ago. Maitri Ma looked like an ordinary Indian grandmother in sadhu's garb. But already I felt the palpable field of peace she was emanating.

My journey was complete: I had finally arrived at my guru's cave. For the first time in my travels, I felt sure that I had come to the right place. There was nothing more to do. All I had to do was sit at her feet, and see what unfolded. *I've arrived.* I closed my eyes. *I've finally arrived.*

Maitri Ma studied our faces. When we had finished, she pulled out a small black chalkboard and began to write on it.

"You are welcome to stay and pursue the path of liberation," she wrote, and I felt relief course through me.

Then she erased it.

"All except you, my daughter," she wrote, and looked me in the eyes. Her eyes were immense and so black that I couldn't tell where the pupil ended and the iris began. It was like looking into the night sky. "This is not your path. You must go home immediately."

*In stone houses and stately halls, He is not. In splendid parlors and massive temples, He is not. In holy garbs, He is not. But He is in the thoughts of those who have overcome their desires. Even though they have bodies of flesh, He grants them liberation.*

—*Tiru-Mandiram*, ca. AD 700

# CHAPTER 23

W E DIDN'T EXPECT you back for another few weeks, so Hank is still in your room." Ernie maneuvered his Toyota around a FedEx truck and up the on-ramp onto the freeway. "But you're welcome to sleep on the couch for a couple of days, until he gets his stuff out of there."

The couch. I hadn't thought about it since I left: lumpy and off-white, with springs poking up through the upholstery. For a while, we kept finding cat kibble hidden under the armrest; Ishtar finally figured out that a couple of mice were pilfering it from the cat bowl and stashing it there while they built a nest in the cushions. I felt the pieces of the life I'd left behind waiting for me to pick them up and go on, like props for a play that was resuming after a brief intermission.

"That's okay. You can just take me straight to Lori's. She said I could stay there as long as I needed to." Lori couldn't come to the airport to pick me up; she and Joe were teaching an all-day permaculture workshop at a vineyard in Napa. But she'd told me to make myself at home until they got back that evening. I stared out Ernie's car window at a manicured ribbon of freeway, so smooth and clean you could eat off it. Huge, shiny cars purred down it in an orderly line, most of them carrying only one person. Slanting afternoon sunlight glinted off the windows of the pastel houses dotting the burnt-gold hillsides. Compared to India, San Francisco looked like a city that had just been taken out of its box.

Ernie looked at me sideways. "To be honest, Amanda, you don't look so good. You look like you're about to keel over."

"What do you expect? I just got off a thirty-hour plane ride." It was 5:30 in the afternoon, and we were hitting the rush-hour traffic: a jam of commuters inching their way home, their faces all slightly worried, as if they were each watching their own private disaster movie on their windshield. In the driver's seat of the Prius stopped next to me, a woman with short blonde hair in a hooded black sweatshirt was pulling a piece of paper out of a fax machine plugged into her cigarette lighter. We crawled past her and paused next to a red Jaguar driven by a bald man talking on a cell phone. Both of their faces wore a tight, anxious look I'd forgotten while I was in India. *I have everything, but it's not enough,* their faces said. *And I'm scared it's going to be taken away.*

Ernie shook his head. "It's not just that. You look like you need a doctor. I hope you haven't let your health insurance lapse." As a Zen insurance agent, talking about health coverage was Ernie's idea of an intimate conversation, right up there with a nice discussion of the Prajnaparamita Sutra.

"No, I'm still covered. Remember? You helped me set up an auto-payment." I tilted my seat back and closed my eyes. I shouldn't be here at all. In India, it was just after dawn. In the mountains past Gangotri, Siddhartha and Devi Das and Maya were just getting up to meditate with Maitri Ma. They were sitting on the floor of a candlelit cave, wool blankets wrapped around their shoulders. They were stepping out to pee in the snow under the deodar trees, their breath fogging in the cold air. Why wasn't I with them? Why had I alone been turned away?

LORI'S KEY WAS where it always was, under the pot of geraniums to the left of her front door. I unlocked the door, hauled my backpack into her tiny living room, and sat down on the boot bench to take off my shoes. Reaching my feet had become an extreme sport; I'd been putting off clipping my toenails for a couple of weeks because it was just too challenging. I crossed my leg clumsily over my thigh to peel off the sweat-crusted socks I'd been wearing since Delhi.

I had tried to argue with Maitri Ma, then to plead. But Maitri Ma had put away her chalkboard and shaken her head. In the end, I had given up. I had trekked back down the mountain with the guide—Devi Das had offered to come with us, but I'd insisted that he stay behind. We'd spent the night with the Gangotri swami again, then hitchhiked a ride on the back of an army truck to the place where the road was open and we could catch a bus back to Uttarkashi. A bus to Dehra Dun, a train to Delhi, a plane home . . . No wonder I felt so awful. I'd been on the road for over a week.

Lori's house was as familiar to me as my own. Everything looked exactly the same as the last time I was here: the potted fern in the corner, a birthday present to me that she'd reclaimed after I kept forgetting to water it. The wall hanging she'd woven from dried persimmon branches, arching over the dark red chenille couch. The lampstands carved in the shape of dancing goddesses holding their bulbs solicitously over Joe's favorite overstuffed armchair. A pair of Joe's hiking boots leaned against Lori's sneakers in the shoe rack. Pumpkin, their elderly orange cat, curled on her corduroy cushion in front of the wood stove, where a few embers still glowed behind the glass door. The house even smelled exactly the same—a comforting collision of vanilla and cloves and sautéed garlic and the yeasty, toasty scent of fresh-baked bread.

All I wanted to do was wash my face, brush my teeth, and collapse on Lori and Joe's queen-sized bed. I heaved myself up, trudged toward the bathroom, then froze. From the full-length mirror on the back of the bathroom door, a stranger was staring back at me. She was gaunt, with enormous eyes ringed with shadows in a dirt-smudged face. Her hair frizzed wildly on one side of her head, pressed greasily flat against her skull on the other. She was wearing grubby, baggy pants and a stained lime-green shirt as shapeless as a tent. Her belly jutted in front of her, completely preposterous, as if she were a skinny child with a pillow under her shirt pretending to be pregnant.

I couldn't remember the last time I looked in a full-length mirror. How could I be so different, when everything else here was exactly the same? If this was a play, my part had been totally rewritten since the last act. When would the director give me my new lines?

"I'VE MADE YOU an appointment with my gynecologist this afternoon. She's at the UCSF Medical Center." Lori stood at her kitchen counter the next morning, cracking eggs into a bowl. "You've got to get some decent medical care."

I had awoken just before dawn in Lori's bed, groggy and disoriented, to find that I'd been asleep for almost thirteen hours. Joe and Lori were asleep on the sofa bed in their living room; I hadn't even heard them come home. Now I was sitting at Lori's kitchen table, showered and dressed in one of Lori's scoop-necked blouses and

peasant skirts, my hands wrapped around a steaming mug of pepper-
mint tea. Her tiny kitchen was separated from her living room only
by a low counter, lined with clear canisters filled with grains and
beans. Morning fog hung outside the windows; we'd lit the wood-
stove, but the house hadn't warmed up yet.

"I told you, I've been seeing a doctor in India. Less than a couple
of weeks ago she said everything was going fine."

"Right." From Lori's tone, I might as well have told her that my
positive prognosis came from a fortune cookie. She shook salt and
pepper into the eggs, added a splash of milk, and began scrambling
them with a fork. She dropped a pat of butter in a cast-iron pan and
began stirring it around with a spatula, watching it melt. "Are you
taking prenatals, at least?"

"Every day." *Almost.*

Lori poured the eggs into the pan, then pulled a bottle down from
on top of her refrigerator and handed it to me. "Well, I got you these
just in case. They're all-natural food-based supplements." She sliced a
loaf of whole wheat bread with a long, serrated knife and popped two
pieces into the toaster. "And you're doing your kick counts?"

"The baby kicks all the time." Come to think of it, I *had* read
something somewhere about counting them. I put my hand on my
belly and felt a reassuring *whomp.*

"And are you doing your Kegels every morning?" She stirred the
eggs in the pan.

"My *what?*"

"You should be contracting and releasing your vaginal muscles at
least a hundred times a day to prepare for delivery."

Yeah, right. My *vaginal muscles.* I knew there was something else I
was supposed to be doing while I was hiking up that mountain in the
Himalayas. The toast popped up. I watched Lori spread it with butter,
plop it onto a sunshine-yellow plate, slide the eggs onto the plate next to
it. My jet-lagged body didn't know what time it was: Did I want

breakfast or dinner? What I really wanted was chai: not one of Lori's caffeine-free herbal brews, but real Indian tea, boiled over a wood fire, tasting of smoke, with too much sugar in it. I wanted puffy white idli with spicy sambar sauce. I wanted sour yogurt, a little bubbly from overfermentation, and I wanted someone to call it *curd*. "You know what? I'm not really hungry. Why don't you eat those yourself?"

"You need something with protein in it." Lori set the plate down in front of me and sat down across from me. "Stop arguing. Just eat."

THE WAITING ROOM at the UCSF Women's Health Center was sunny and cheerful. Three or four other women were waiting, most of them older than me, all of them visibly in various stages of pregnancy. I sat in an upholstered chair and filled out the new-patient paperwork on a legal-sized clipboard. I hesitated over the blank marked "Baby's Father" before writing in Matt's name. Then I tried to cross it out, but his name still showed through. I crumpled up the page and asked for a new one. This time I just left that part blank.

When I was finished, I handed the paperwork and my medical records from Dr. Rao's office to the receptionist, a slim young Asian woman with a tiny gold stud in her left nostril and a nametag that said AMBER. My medical records were creased from being carried around in my backpack, stained around the edges with ayurvedic oil and spilled chai. They smelled faintly of India, a mixture of cow dung and cardamom. Amber glanced through them as she smoothed them out.

"India, huh?" She slipped them into a folder and pressed a computer-printed tag on it. "Were you doing yoga there?"

What *was* I doing there? I hesitated, then nodded. "Yeah."

"I do hot yoga," she said. "Bikram. But you'd never get me to India. I just do it at the JCC."

I stepped into a cubicle and changed into a paper gown; a nurse took my blood pressure, weighed me, and disappeared. I picked up a copy of *Parenting Now* off a side table and glanced through an article called "Ten Ways to Make Your Unborn Baby Smarter." "Play Mozart with headphones resting on your belly. Eat flax seed oil every day—it contains omega-3 oils, vital for proper brain development." Okay, well, brains weren't everything. I put the article down and began flipping through a copy of *People*. Tom and Katie, Jen and Vince, Brad and Angelina . . . It took me a while to remember who these people were and why I should care about them. But it was reassuring that their lives seemed to be as much of a mess as mine.

The doctor finally arrived, a stern, gray-haired woman who told me I could call her Dr. Pat. "You've been very lucky," she said, frowning, when I told her about my travels. She grilled me about my diet and told me she'd like to see me weigh a few more pounds. She palpated the baby through my abdomen and told me that its head was already facing downward.

"Do you want to know whether it's a boy or a girl?" she asked as she slid the ultrasound wand over my jellied belly.

"I already know."

"Mmm. Then all I need to tell you is that your baby looks perfectly healthy." She peered at the screen, frowning. "I do want to take a closer look at your cervix, though."

I lay down on my back for the internal exam, slipping my feet into the metal stirrups. Dr. Pat pulled on her rubber gloves, slipped the cold plastic speculum into me, and slid her fingers up inside, while I stared up at the white squares of the ceiling, pretending I was somewhere else. Then she drew her hand back out and pulled her glove off.

"When you leave here," she told me, "you need to go straight home and go to bed. And don't get up until the baby's born."

*Day after day, let the Yogi practice the harmony of soul; in a se-cret place, in deep solitude, master of his mind, hoping for noth-ing, desiring nothing. Let him find a place that is pure and a seat that is restful, neither too high or too low, with sacred grass and a skin and a cloth thereon. On that seat let him rest and practice Yoga for the purification of the soul.*

—Bhagavad Gita, ca. 300 BC

# CHAPTER 24

"EFFACED?" ISHTAR SAT DOWN cross-legged at the end of my bed, gold necklaces jangling. "What the hell does *that* mean?"

"It means that my cervix is starting to thin out and spread from the weight of the baby pressing down on it. It usually happens right before the baby is born." I was lying on my bed with all my clothes still on, my blue flannel comforter wrapped around me. My subletter, Hank, had been using my bedding; he assured me he'd washed all the sheets, but the comforter still held the faint, skunky smell of the marijuana plants he'd been growing in the corner. The smell made me feel like an intruder in my own room, as if he'd marked his territory like a cat before moving on. "Except that in my case, the baby isn't due for another two months."

"Whoa, back up a couple of steps." Ernie was standing just inside my bedroom door, a legal-sized folder of papers in his hands. "What exactly is a cervix, again?"

"The cervix is the opening to the uterus. It's—" I stopped. Explaining the female reproductive apparatus to a retired monk was not something I was up for right now.

"If you step into our office, I'd be happy to show you mine," said Ishtar obligingly.

"No thanks." Ernie was used to Ishtar; the offer barely registered. He waved his folder. "I've got a client coming in fifteen minutes."

"Uh-oh, I've got one coming in an hour." While I was in India, Ishtar and Ernie had begun to share the same tiny home office, a converted cubby under the stairs that used to be a walk-in coat closet; he used it for insurance consultations, she used it for tantra sessions. "Be sure to get your papers out of there when you're done. It's very distracting for my clients to see insurance brochures lying around."

"Not as distracting as it is for my clients to see thongs."

"Oh, come on. There are worse ways to sell life insurance." Ishtar turned back to me. "But seriously. How big a problem is this?"

"Apparently, it only just started to efface. The doctor said that as long as I stay lying down most of the time, I should be fine. She just doesn't want the weight of the baby to efface things any more or it could cause a premature delivery." I hadn't told anyone, yet, the term Dr. Pat had used: *incompetent cervix*. The word stung: yet another way I was failing. I hadn't gotten enlightened. My book was a disaster. My relationship was in shambles. And now even my cervix couldn't get it together.

"It's a good thing you came home, then," said Ernie.

*Home.* I looked around the room. Most of my possessions were still in boxes in the closet; the room was bare except for the bed, the empty bookcase, the door laid over two filing cabinets that served as a makeshift desk. Although I'd lived here for five years, I'd never put any energy into painting or decorating. My room had always felt temporary, a place to pause and refuel while I prepared to launch into my glorious future. But five years later, I was still trapped in the not-so-glorious present. And looking at my room with travel-fresh eyes, I saw that walls were dingy and pitted with spackling; that the shabby blinds wouldn't open all the way; that the comforter cover was stained with coffee and ink. It was the room of a person who had been afraid to put down roots for fear that they'd just be yanked back up again.

I shut my eyes, swamped by a tidal wave of fear and guilt. What if Maitri Ma hadn't sent me home? What disaster had I risked for my baby, chasing enlightenment in the Himalayas? I'd looked up *effaced* in an online dictionary just after I got home from Dr. Pat's office. "To eliminate or make indistinct by or as if by wearing away a surface," the definition had read. "Also: to cause to vanish." That was exactly how I felt: My surfaces worn away to almost nothing; my mind, like my cervix, stretched thin to the point of breaking.

I opened my eyes and looked at Ernie. Through the window behind him, I could see a patch of gray sky and the rooftop of the house opposite. A pigeon landed on the window sill, then flapped away again. *"Am* I home?" I asked.

FOR MY FIRST week on bed rest, I slept most of the time—as if I'd been waiting for months for permission to stop moving.

I curled under the covers in fetal position on my left side, because the doctor had told me that that gave me the best blood supply to the baby. I drifted in and out of tangled dreams.

*I'M BACK in India, trying to catch a train to an ashram. But when I try to read the train schedule, the letters dissolve and the paper crumbles to ashes in my hand. I look up to find all the trains have left, and I'm standing alone on the platform in the dark.*

*Instead of a baby, I've given birth to a litter of German shepherds, all of which I've named Matt. They escape from the house and I run out looking for them, running up and down the block shouting, "Matt, Matt, Matt." "You've got to change their names," Lori tells me, "or they'll never come home."*

*I am at my mother's funeral, but she isn't really dead. As they lower her coffin into the ground, she calls me on her cell phone. "Let me out. I want to be a grandma," she says.*

I GOT UP only to shower, use the bathroom, or microwave leftovers from other people's meals, which I ate whenever I happened to wake up: Lori's curried squash stew at midnight; Ernie's take-out spring rolls and Szechuan eggplant at dawn; Ishtar's complicated salad of seaweed and sunflower sprouts for a midafternoon snack. I felt as if I were floating under water, looking at the rest of the busy world—distorted, almost unrecognizable—through the shimmering blur of its surface.

My quest for enlightenment was over. I had given up all hope of spiritual awakening. And lying there in my bed—with nothing to do and no one to become—I was surprised to discover what a relief that was.

"THE FIRST THING we have to do is paint." Lori looked around my room with her hands on her hips. "A nice pale yellow or something like that. And then I'll bring over some pictures. We can't have you lying here looking at these horrible walls 24-7."

"I don't know. The walls look okay to me." Sometimes Lori's certainty had the opposite effect on me than it was intended to; I wanted to argue, even when I actually agreed with her. I suspected she was actually glad I was on bedrest; it gave her a chance to remodel my whole life without me getting in the way.

"Some cheerful curtains would help, too." She pulled open my closet door and looked at the stack of cardboard boxes. "And we've got to get these unpacked."

"I don't even remember what's in them." All my possessions had felt so important as I'd packed them up; I couldn't choose anything I wanted to discard. Now I could throw the whole lot into the bay, unopened, and not miss a thing.

"Well, fortunately, I labeled everything." Lori pulled a Swiss Army knife out of her jeans pocket, popped it open, and began slicing the tape on the first box. "This one has all your yoga props in it. You'll need these for doing restorative poses in your bed. We've got to keep your circulation going and your muscle tone up."

"Right."

"And we've also got to find you lots of good activities to keep you from getting bored. Here's a list of ideas I printed out from Mommiesonbedrest.com." She handed me a piece of paper. "Make lists of baby things, including baby names and things you will need for the baby like clothes, furniture, nursery supplies, and all the other baby equipment!" I read aloud. "Organize photos into albums, rearrange sock drawers or junk drawers, write letters, read books!"

"I could also teach you to knit and you can knit a baby blanket," said Lori.

"Lori. My cervix has effaced. That doesn't mean that I've had a total personality transplant."

"And, of course, now you can really focus on getting your book written." She was piling my yoga props neatly by my bed: a bolster, a yoga mat, a strap with a metal buckle, a couple of eyebags. "There, now you can get at them without getting up." She turned back to the closet, frowning. "Now we just have to find you something to wear. None of your old clothes will fit you, obviously. I think they have a decent maternity section at the thrift store over on Geary."

"I'll be in bed all day. What does it matter what I wear? I can just hang out in a T-shirt and a pair of old sweatpants with the waistband snipped."

"No, no, *no*!" Lori slit the top of another cardboard box. "That's the kind of thinking that makes women on bed rest go crazy. You're supposed to get dressed in a cute outfit every morning and put on your makeup, just as if you were going to work."

"I'm a writer," I said, crossly. "A T-shirt and old sweatpants *is* what I wear to work."

A week and a half into my bed rest, my confinement was starting to get old. My muscles were stiff and aching, my bones sore from pressing against the compressed cotton of my ancient futon. My room smelled like cheese puffs and dirty socks. I was afraid to check my email for fear of a barrage of messages from Maxine, who still thought I was in Gangotri, getting my picture taken with a yogini in a cave. I looked at the Mommiesonbedrest list again. "Design your own baby announcements! Host a bedrest potluck!" I crumpled up the paper and tossed it on the floor. *Clearly, you're mistaking me for someone with a competent cervix.*

"Hey, look at this!" Lori was holding up a paperback copy of *Travels in Secret India*. "This box has all your spiritual books in it. We can put them right by your bed to inspire you." She began pulling them out of the box, reading the names aloud: "*Awakening the Buddha Within. Being Peace. Living Your Yoga. Yoga Body, Buddha Mind. Relax and Renew.*"

With every title I got more depressed, as the mountain of ideals I hadn't lived up to got higher and higher. "Why don't you take them down to Bookends and trade them in for something really useful. You know—*Dating on Bed Rest. How to Make a Fortune Without Standing Up.*"

"And look! Tucked in here is a catalog for a whole clothing line based on the Bhagavad Gita." She flipped through it. "Should we order you some of these adorable Karma Capris?"

A voice came from the hall. "Karma Capris! We knew there was a reason we came back to America!" A familiar figure was standing in the doorway. He was still barefoot, still in dreadlocks, still wrapped in a brown shawl over his lungi. In his arms, he was carrying a giant purple stuffed tyrannosaurus, which he held toward me. "Here. We got it at the airport for the baby."

"Devi Das!" I started to scramble up, then caught myself and collapsed back on my bed, giddy with delight. "What are you doing here? Did Maitri Ma kick *you* out, too?"

"We kicked ourselves out." He dropped the dinosaur on the bed and wrapped me in a bony hug. He smelled like a cross between a locker room and an Indian restaurant.

"But why? Wasn't she the real thing?"

"Oh, she was the real thing, all right." He sat down on the bed next to me, tucking his bare, grimy feet into full Lotus. "She was everything everyone said about her, and more. We wished so much you could have stayed there with us."

"Well, it's a good thing she didn't," snapped Lori. She held out her hand. "Hi, I'm Lori. And for your information, Amanda's on bed rest and in danger of going into premature labor. Sleeping on the floor of a cave at ten thousand feet isn't exactly what the doctor ordered. What on earth were you thinking, dragging her up there?"

"He didn't drag me. I wanted to go. I *still* want to go." I picked up the dinosaur, clutching it to my chest as if it were an emissary from Maitri Ma herself. "Devi Das, what was it *like*? What did you *do*?"

"We didn't really do *anything*. I mean, sure, we meditated a little bit. We slept in the cave while she chanted all night. We made breakfast and lunch and dinner—lentils, rice, some of Siddhartha's freeze-dried chili. We helped her gather firewood from the forest. But mainly—it's hard to describe—we didn't really *do* anything. We just rested in this incredible . . . *not doing*. Like some knot deep inside us was being untied. We felt like we'd come home. We felt like we could have stayed there forever."

"So why didn't you?" asked Lori pointedly.

Devi Das shrugged. "We woke up one morning and knew we weren't supposed to stay there anymore. And we knew we were supposed to be here instead. It was like knowing that the sun is warm, or the snow is cold. It wasn't just a thought. Our whole body knew. Even our *toes* knew." He wiggled his hairy toes, crusted with black calluses. "We wished we didn't. We wished we'd been sure that we were supposed to stay, instead. But you can't choose what you're sure of."

He beamed at me. "We finally decided—enlightenment? Hey, we can do that anytime. They say it's always right there. But Amanda? She's something special."

He reached into his pocket and handed me a crumpled piece of paper. "Before we left, we asked Maitri Ma if she had any teachings for you. She gave us this."

I looked at the scrap of paper. On it was typed in blue letters: "Add salt to two cups water and bring to a boil."

"The other side. Sorry. All we had to write on were the instructions for Siddhartha's ramen."

I turned it over. The message was written in a neat penciled cursive, the o's fat and round, each letter precisely slanted, every "i" dotted, every "t" crossed—the handwriting of a teacher at a girl's school in Delhi.

> *I left home and family to climb the mountain path*
> *In this snowy cave the fires burn all night long*
> *Let whatever swells inside you rip you to pieces*
> *Then you will dare to surrender your heart.*

"We hope it makes sense to you," said Devi Das.

I looked at him, not sure whether to laugh or cry. "As much sense as anything else in my life, I guess."

From: Maxine@bigdaybooks.com

To: Amandala@yahoo.com

Subject: Labor and delivery

Well, I personally am delighted to hear that you're on bed rest—at least I know how to reach you now. But really, Amanda, I have to say that with your deadline in less than four months, this isn't the best time to turn up pregnant. I must stress that delivering a baby will not excuse you from delivering your manuscript.

"I THINK I'VE finally figured out the key to a successful relationship." My mother was doing tai chi in my bedroom. As soon as I'd worked up the nerve to tell her I was home, she had flown into San Francisco from Hawaii, where she had moved with her new boyfriend shortly after she returned from visiting me in India. She had come to spend a couple of weeks with me—ostensibly to help out, although so far the only helpful thing she had done was order takeout sushi, which my pregnancy books warned me direly not to eat. "Always make sure the man likes you a little bit more than you like him. And never, ever let him see you without your makeup on."

She floated her outstretched arms gracefully from side to side. In Hawaii, my mother had started eating nothing but fruit until 2:00 p.m. She looked radiantly beautiful and was about sixty pounds lighter than I was.

"I wish I could do tai chi right now." Heaving myself onto my left side, I deliberately ignore the relationship advice and steered the conversation toward neutral territory. "My back is killing me."

"So just do it! One young woman came to my tai chi class up until the day before she delivered. Twins, no less. She had a water birth with a dolphin as a midwife."

"Mom. Remember? Incompetent cervix? Bed rest? Premature labor?"

"Oh, phooey. Doctors come from such a fear-based mentality. All they care about is not getting sued. If you had the right attitude, you could be walking to Japantown for sashimi right now. But don't take *my* word for it. I'm just your mother."

On the other hand, maybe relationships were the safer topic, after all. "So don't you get bored, being with someone you aren't totally crazy about?"

"Who said I wasn't crazy about Pete? I adore him. I just don't *think* about him that much. It's very restful. He goes off to work, and I can go get a facial." She stood on one leg, the other delicately suspended in the air. "You're just the way I used to be, honey. You make things too complicated for yourself. I suppose it's inevitable at your age. But it's hard to watch." Typically of my mother, she was already flowing through the tai chi series with a dilettante's ease. I watched her with a complex, familiar combination of exasperation and envy, as if she were a younger sister I had to take care of even as she threatened to upstage me. But from where I was lying, I could see her neck beginning to crumple, the delicate network of wrinkles under her eyes: my baby's grandmother.

"Mom. Didn't you ever wish you had gotten in touch with my father?" Now that I was single and pregnant, perhaps I was finally eligible to hear the lore of her club of abandoned women.

My mother swooped her torso low to the ground in a long curve. "But I did," she said.

"You *did?*"

"Not for a long time, of course. I was too proud and too hurt and too angry. But finally, when you were four years old, I tracked him down. I left you with the neighbors for three days—remember, they had a little girl you used to play with?—and flew up to Seattle to see him. I told everyone I had a job interview."

"I remember that trip." What I mainly remembered was the smell of the neighbors' house: a combination of dirty cat litter and Pillsbury biscuits. Their daughter was a year older than me and obsessed with Barbies, which I loathed. She had told me as we were going to sleep that my mother was not going to come back, and that I was going to have to live with her for the rest of my life and play Barbies with her every day. I had believed her and cried myself to sleep in the pink glow of her nightlight. "So what happened?"

My mother kept moving, slowly, as if underwater. She didn't look at me. "I waited on a bench outside his office building and stopped him when he came out for lunch. He hustled me into a cab and we went to lunch in another part of town, somewhere where no one he knew would see us. I had brought a picture of you in your yellow overalls, climbing a tree. But he wouldn't even look at it. By that time, he was in a new relationship with someone he was very much in love with. He was terrified that I would ruin it."

"So—did you?"

"No. It turns out he had already prepared legal papers saying we had never had sex and therefore you couldn't be his child. He offered me a large amount of money to sign them and go away. Enough that I could get out of debt and get a new start in life. Move to a different town and put you in preschool. Even go back to school myself, if I wanted."

She dropped her arms and looked at me, finally. "I could have pushed for a paternity suit. But what would that have accomplished? It would have wrecked his life and not helped ours. It was better that you should have no father at all, than a father who resented you for destroying his dreams."

"Why didn't you ever tell me this before?"

She shrugged. "I don't know. Somehow I thought that the less you knew about my story, the better. Maybe that way you wouldn't have to relive it yourself." She pulled the hair-tie out of her platinum hair, shook it loose, then pulled it back in a knot and retied it. She looked at my belly. "So much for that theory, huh?"

"IF IT WERE up to us, we'd definitely go for the gold." Devi Das studied the splashes of yellow paint that Ishtar had painted on the wall opposite my bed, whose names all hinted that they had the power to transform not just my room, but my whole life: Whipped Cream Fantasy. Melted Buttercup. Peaches 'n' Brandy. Dragon's Gold.

"I totally agree. And for the curtains, something like this?" Ishtar held up a swatch of burgundy silk.

"Hmmm . . . the color is perfect. But we'd use a different fabric, something more textured, maybe a nice velvet or a chenille."

After two weeks on our lumpy living room couch, Devi Das had moved into Ishtar's bedroom. Their relationship was strictly platonic, he had insisted when I'd pumped him for details. I had my doubts about how long that would last; Ishtar was capable of coaxing lust out of a potato. But for now, they seemed to be having a fabulous time just staying up talking past midnight.

One night, long after I'd gone to sleep, I'd woken up to hear tablas rattling through the wall that separated my room from Ishtar's. "Now your hips," came Ishtar's voice. "One, two, one, two—round and round. There you go!" Ishtar was teaching Devi Das to belly dance. I started to laugh as I pictured his skinny hips gyrating, his carrot-colored dreadlocks flapping. But then I stopped with a pang of envy. It's not that I was jealous of Ishtar, exactly—I had never wanted a romantic relationship with Devi Das. But it had been so long since I'd felt that giddy rush of delight that comes with getting to know somebody new—sharing the things you love most with them, staying up all night trying something crazy you never would have tried on your own.

The days of bed rest were ticking by, as excruciatingly slow as a vipassana retreat. Every day I pulled out my India journal to try to work on my book. But my journal read like illegible notes from a dream that I had already forgotten: *White calf eating coconut husk. Beggar woman with* paan-*stained mouth. Dung fire. Stainless steel cup. Haze of dust.* Sometimes I tried to pick up one of my meditation books. But more often I read junky paperback romances supplied by Ishtar: *The Naughty Debutante. Bridesmaid of Desire. A Strictly Business Affair. The Red-Haired Geisha.*

When I got tired of reading, I shopped. In store after online store, I piled items I couldn't afford into my shopping cart, then signed out without buying them: Breast pump. Receiving blankets. Mobile. Bouncy chair. Electric wipe warmer. I pondered collapsible strollers that converted into backpacks, jogging strollers with fat tires and names that implied they'd be suitable for invading a small country. A faux fur diaper bag that I could carry to the opera; a camouflage one for those cross-country jungle crawls with my baby through enemy territory.

In quest of used gear, I logged onto Craigslist, where I bopped back and forth between "baby and kids" and "men seeking women." *Sexy Italian Man for Friday Fling. Animal Safari Crib Bedding. Angsty Intellectual Seeks PhD Model to Discuss Penguins. Kelty Convertible Backpack Stroller.* What would happen if all those guys looking for hot sex and romance were to click a few inches to the right instead, and find themselves browsing amid the long-term result—diaper genies and breast pumps? And what was *I* looking for, anyway? *Loving, sexy, spiritual yogi with spare bedroom and independent income seeks penniless yogini, eight months pregnant. Ongoing obsession with ex-boyfriend welcome. Total bed rest a plus.* I sighed and snapped back over to the baby section. I typed "diaper table" into the search box.

AFTER THE PAINT dried on my room, Ishtar and Devi Das decorated it. They slung Indian tapestries along the walls, unfurled a faded faux Persian carpet on the floor. They hung burgundy velveteen curtains from thrift-store rods with elaborate brass finials shaped like dragon heads. They draped a silk shawl over my lampshade so it cast a dim golden glow. When Lori brought over a bassinet and a diaper table she picked up at a garage sale, Ishtar and Devi Das swathed them both in shawls and tapestries, too.

"This doesn't look like a baby's nursery," Lori told them when they had finished. "It looks like a bordello."

"Language, please." My mother looked up from her seat in the corner, where she was painting her toenails peach. "Remember, there's an infant in the room."

"Wait, we're not done." Devi Das stood on my bookcase and attached one end of a string of Tibetan prayer flags to the curtain rod, the other end to the light fixture in the ceiling. "There." He gestured at the Buddha on my altar, which Ishtar had festooned with a garland of silk poppies. "Now it's not a bordello, it's a monastery."

Ishtar shrugged and flopped down on the bed next to me, extending her long legs and bare feet, tipped with scarlet nails. "Nursery, bordello, monastery. What's the difference? They're all portals to the Divine."

"So you're saying that those ten years I spent at the Zen center, I might as well have been at a whorehouse?" Ernie was sitting cross-legged on the floor by the Buddha, filling out paperwork. "Why didn't someone tell me that *before* I wrecked my knees meditating?"

"Cheer up," said Devi Das brightly. "We're sure that *many* people wreck their knees in bordellos." He picked up Ishtar's foot and began to massage it.

Lori reached into her backpack and pulled out an eggplant. "Well, I have to say that for me, *this* is the portal to the Divine." She sat down on the foot of my bed. "It's the one thing I can trust. You put the seeds in, you give them water, and the plants come up." She leaned over and set the eggplant in the Buddha's lap. "You can have faith in some guy who sat under a tree twenty-five hundred years ago if you want. I have faith in vegetables."

"So have you thought about what you're going to name the baby?" Ernie asked me.

"I'm still trying to decide. I just keep thinking of him as Noodle."

"You'd better be careful," Lori warned. "One of my landscaping clients is an actress and a single mom. She called her baby Oscar all through her pregnancy, just because she said that that's what she was *really* going for when she slept with the casting agent. After he was born, it stuck."

"He definitely needs a name with some kind of spiritual meaning," said Ishtar. "It's too bad that Prana Ma was wrong about him being a girl. Aradhana would have been perfect."

"No—nothing Sanskrit. No one will know how to pronounce it. I think you should go with something nature-based," said Lori. "Like River or Redwood."

"Come on, give the kid a break." Ernie set down his pen. "Suppose he grows up to be a Republican. Suppose he wants a career in investment banking."

"Then he can change it, just like we did," said Devi Das. "He can devastate his mother by changing his name to Chip and running away from home to get an internship at JP Morgan."

Lori picked up the baby name book off the floor by my bed. "Okay, I'm just going to read off a bunch of names. See when he starts to kick." She opened the book in the middle and began to read: "Jaspar. Jedediah. Jeremiah. Jerry. Justin."

"Jerry—now there's a good basic name," said Ernie. "You can't get into trouble with something like that."

"That was Amanda's father's name." My mother set the bottle of polish down with a click. "And believe me, he got into plenty of trouble."

"Woops, scratch that. That would be almost as bad as naming him Matt." Lori kept on reading. "Kianu. Kory. Kristopher."

But I wasn't listening any more. I was remembering a dream I'd had a few nights ago that I'd forgotten until this moment: a variation on the dream I'd been having about my father my whole life.

*I AM AT an airport. A voice comes on over the loudspeaker: "Amanda, please come to the baggage claim area. Your father is waiting for you." I run through the airport trying to find the escalators. But wherever I turn, I am stopped by airport security guards who insist that I take off my shoes and walk through a metal detector. "No," I keep telling them. "You don't understand. I'm not trying to catch a flight to somewhere else. I'm just trying to find my way home."*

"LINCOLN. Larry. Leonard," read Lori. I looked around the room. Ishtar's eyes were closed as she wiggled her red-tipped toes in Devi Das's palms. Ernie was chewing on his pen as he studied his paperwork, oblivious to the fact that he had a long ink stain running down his bald head and around his cheek.

Did my father ever dream about me, the daughter he never saw? Maybe not. Maybe it was possible to seal off a secret chamber of your heart, lock it with a bombproof metal door, and never open it again. Maybe, after a while, it was as if it had never existed.

AT THE BEGINNING of May, when I was almost thirty-three weeks pregnant, Lori drove me and Devi Das to my first birthing class—the only time, other than my weekly doctor visits, that I was allowed to leave my house.

The Great Expectations third-trimester birthing class was held in a cheery, white-carpeted room in the UCSF Women's Health Center. Lori had a gardening job and couldn't stay. So she just dropped us off at the front door and kept going, calling last-minute advice over her shoulder: "Be sure to request a birthing room with a bathtub!

Find out where you can get a doula!" Devi Das and I mistakenly spent five minutes in the Managing Menopause class instead, listening to a lecture on the pros and cons of hormone replacement therapy. By the time we got to the right place, my five pregnant classmates were already lying on their sides on pillows on the floor, practicing their breathing. "In through the nose, out through the mouth," the teacher was saying, a woman all belly and breasts, like a statue of a fertility goddess. "Ooh. Aah. Ooh. Aah." The pregnant women's partners sat behind them, cradling their heads in their hands, puffing along with them.

I hadn't missed much, the teacher assured me. But for the rest of the class, I couldn't shake the feeling of being *too late*. Most of the other women had also taken the first- and second-trimester pregnancy courses, as well as some Infant Care classes and—for a couple of high achievers—an infant CPR intensive. They spoke with fluency of phenomena I was only dimly aware of—mucus plugs, meconium, Pitocin drips. One woman—a slender blonde in a pinstriped maternity business suit who introduced herself as a CPA for an Internet services corporation—mentioned that she'd been rubbing her nipples with a washcloth for fifteen minutes a day to toughen them up in preparation for breast-feeding. I thought she was joking until I saw all the other women nodding their agreement. "And have you or your partners been massaging your perineums every night?" the teacher asked. "It's important if you want to avoid an episiotomy." More enthusiastic nods. I avoided looking at Devi Das. All I knew about my perineum was that it was in a place that I could barely even *reach* anymore.

Most of the other women had come to the class with their babies' fathers—dazed but game-looking guys who eyed their women's bellies with wary pride. Looking at them, I felt a pang of longing so strong it took my breath away. It wasn't the men themselves I coveted—they all struck me eminently forgettable, especially compared to the fecund radiance of their wives. What I yearned for was the sense of casual coupleness that the women rested in: their affectionate, proprietary irritation toward their clueless but well-intentioned mates. I even envied the lesbian couple, two women in their early forties who held hands throughout the whole class: the pregnant woman short and chubby, with a long brown braid; the not-pregnant partner lanky, with short, gray-streaked hair and a T-shirt that read, "Ban Republican Marriage." They inseminated through a sperm bank, the lanky woman told the group proudly. They shopped around for months to find just the right anonymous donor, an antinuclear activist with a Mensa-level IQ who had been raised on a feminist collective in Ontario. I was astonished by the thoroughness of their planning. By contrast, my own pregnancy seemed random, as if my baby were a stray kitten that had followed me home.

All the other women also seem to have planned every detail, from their maternity workout clothes to the CDs they'd selected to play during labor. Three of them had already put their unborn children on preschool waiting lists. Two had arranged for au pairs from Chile and Sweden. The bricks of their lives were cemented into place. Whereas my life was tacked together from scraps of driftwood. The slightest breeze could bring it crashing down.

"Now we're going to practice our partner massage," our teacher told us. "Especially in the early stages of labor, this can be a wonderful way to relax the laboring woman and take her mind off her discomfort. So ladies, why don't you lie down on your sides and have your partners put their hands on your upper back . . ."

For a moment, I allowed myself to imagine it: *What if Matt were putting his hand on my shoulders, his hands kneading my back. What if Matt were breathing along with me, in through his nose, out through his mouth.*

I looked at Devi Das. The tip of his nose was chapped and red. His knobby, calloused knees stuck out from under his lungi. He looked like a birthing partner I'd grabbed off the rack at the thrift store, hastily, on my way to class.

He smiled back at me.

"Shall we go for it?" he asked.

I took a deep breath. "Sure."

ONE MORNING IN the middle of May, Tom called and told me that he was going to stop by that afternoon.

I used his visit as an excuse to spend the whole morning washing and blow-drying my hair. Blow-drying turned out to be a big mistake—my hair flew around my head in a wild puff, like a dandelion about to go to seed. I tried on a vintage maternity party dress that Ishtar picked up for me at the Goodwill, with a neckline that showed off my hormone-enhanced cleavage. I hoped it would make me look like, say, the Naughty Debutante. But when I risked standing up to peek in the full-length mirror, I looked more like an elephant seal on her way to the prom. At the last minute, I yanked it off and threw on what I wore most days: a pair of stretchy leggings with the waistband cut, and a long, fuzzy, golden brown maternity sweater that Lori told me made my eyes look topaz. I didn't want Tom, I told myself. But I definitely wanted *him* to want *me*.

But the first thing that Tom told me—after the initial hugs and hellos—was that he'd started seeing someone. Her name was Rebecca; she was a few years older than he was, and taught art in a private high school a few miles from his new house.

"Well, that's convenient for you," I said, brightly. To my surprise, my stomach was sinking. All along, Tom had been my emergency fallback plan. He was like the box of canned food and bottled water Ernie insisted we keep in the basement in case there was an earthquake—we hoped we never needed it, but it was comforting to know it was there. I tried to arrange my face into an enthusiastic expression. "She can just drop by your house for dinner right after work!"

"Well, actually—I think she's going to move in next month. She might as well. We're spending every night together anyway."

*Move in? Into our house?* "Wow! How terrific!"

"Yeah. There's even a spare room she can use for an art studio."

*You mean, my yoga studio???* "Yeah. I remember from the pictures."

"That's right. I forgot I showed you those." Tom pulled out his Treo. "Want to see some pictures of Rebecca?"

*Sure. And then I want you to jab toothpicks under my toenails.* "I'd love to."

He handed it to me. I looked down at a woman with straight, shoulder-length red hair, translucent skin, luminous gray eyes, and a warm, shy smile.

"Isn't she great?" Tom looked at me eagerly.

I remembered how unfailingly kind he had always been to me; how willing to forgive me for bailing out on him to chase after Matt. *Come back!* I wanted to tell him. *I've made a mistake! I do love you, after all! Dump Rebecca! I'm the one you really should be with!*

I handed the Treo back to Tom. "She's beautiful," I told him. And as I said it, I knew it was true: "I hope you guys are really happy."

*Friends, I know nothing which brings suffering as does an un-*
*tamed, uncontrolled, unattended and unrestrained heart.*

—The Buddha, *Dhammapada*, ca. 500 BC

## CHAPTER 25

WHEN I HIT THIRTY-EIGHT weeks, Dr. Pat informed me
that I could get off bed rest. My cervix was 50 percent effaced, three
centimeters dilated, she told me, pulling off her rubber gloves. The
baby was full term. It could be born any time.

"Wow. Should I stick kind of near the hospital until it comes?" I
pictured my uterus unzipping like a flimsy purse, the baby tumbling
out of me while I walked down Mission Street.

"No, don't worry. Believe me, you'll have plenty of warning. Just
time your contractions the way they taught you in your childbirth
class. When they're about ten or fifteen minutes apart, just come
on in."

Out in the waiting room, Devi Das sat reading an article called
"Pumping Breast Milk at the Office" in *Working Mother* magazine.

He'd been planning to give me a ride home in Lori's car. Instead, we decided to leave the car parked in the garage and take a celebratory walk over to Golden Gate Park.

After a couple of months on bed rest, it was exciting to be walking down the street, even if my walk was more of a waddle. It was a bright afternoon at the beginning of June, with blue skies and a cool breeze. I was wearing a red maternity sundress that Lori had picked out for me at the Goodwill, and my newly shaven legs were bare. At a corner deli, we picked up cheese and tomato sandwiches, which Devi Das tucked in his cloth bag, and made our way through the park toward Stow Lake. I didn't even realize myself where I was leading Devi Das, until I found myself crossing an arched stone bridge over a waterway dotted with ducks, their green heads glistening. Only then did I know where I was going: to the little dell by the pond where Matt and I had shot the cat calendar so many years ago.

We stopped by the waterfall and I sat down on a park bench, out of breath. After so long without exercise, my heart was pounding as if I'd just pumped through second series.

"Mind if we borrow your phone?" asked Devi Das. "We want to give Ishtar a call and tell her your good news."

"No problem." I handed him the phone and leaned back on the bench, watching a pair of ducks dive, tails up. A couple of teenagers rowed by in a flat-bottomed rowboat, their oars splashing. *I stood on the cobbled stones by the waterfall and dropped into a deep backbend. Matt knelt in the grass, his camera trained on me, his body still a mystery. Our romance stretched out in front of us, bright with promise.* It might as well have been a memory surfacing from a past life: *I was a queen in ancient Egypt. I was one of Jesus' disciples.* I wondered if Bigfoot still lived around here. No, he probably died long ago. I hoped he went out happy, his belly full of mice.

I looked across the water and saw, rising over the park in the distance, the highest windows of the UCSF Medical Center, where

I would be delivering my baby. How odd that I had literally been able to see, right at the beginning of my relationship with Matt, the place where it would ultimately take me.

Devi Das hung up and sat down next to me. "What are you thinking about?"

I sat up and put my hand on my belly. "I was just hoping that my kid doesn't have to struggle with his love life as much as I have."

Devi Das reached into his bag and pulled out our lunch. "There's a story we heard a long time ago about how the native people in South America used to grow hemp to make rope from the roots." He unwrapped the sandwiches and handed one to me. "They grew it in these really rocky fields, so they didn't harvest very much, but what they did was unbelievably strong. Then the Spaniards came. They decided it would be way more efficient to clear all the rocks out of the fields so they could grow more hemp." He took a bite and chewed, a bit of lettuce bobbing out the corner of his mouth. "They got more hemp, that's for sure. But guess what? It was useless. It turns out it was growing around all those rocks that gave the hemp its strength."

I took a bite of my sandwich, tasted the tang of mustard, the juicy sweetness of tomato. The closer I got to delivery, the more acute my senses became. The sandwich was almost psychedelic in its intensity. "So are you telling me that all my struggles have made me stronger?"

"Stronger. More flexible. More resilient."

"I don't know. I think I'd rather be weak and happy."

"Yeah. We know what you mean. Sometimes we think that all the bad things that have happened to us have just been life's way of hammering away at the armor around our heart. Other times we think we wouldn't have even needed all that armor if life hadn't been such a bitch." He paused, chewing. "We never would have gotten started on our spiritual path if our brother hadn't died. And our spiritual path is the greatest thing that ever happened to us. But still, we never would have chosen such a loss. Or wished it on anyone else, for that matter."

We finished our sandwiches in silence.

"Do you mind if we take off now?" Devi Das asked. "We promised Ishtar we'd meet her for coffee."

"Go ahead. You take the car. I'll just take the bus home."

"Are you sure? We don't want you having your baby on the Number 16."

"Don't worry. The doctor told me I'd have plenty of warning."

I watched him walk off. He had stuck a daisy in his dreadlocks; it waved like an antenna. But in San Francisco, he didn't even draw a second glance. I slid off the park bench and lay down in the grass next to a snarl of blackberry brambles, their white spring blossoms tangled with the glossy red of poison oak. The sun was warm, but there was a cool edge to the breeze, and the grass was slightly damp. I'd have grass stains all down the side of my dress. But who was looking?

I was just starting to doze off when I heard a plaintive meow. I opened my eyes to see a gray tabby cat picking its way through the grass. "Bigfoot?" But of course, when I looked more closely, I saw that it wasn't. This cat was smaller and more delicate, and its ears weren't tattered. Its eyes were golden, not green. It was looking wistfully at the remains of my sandwich.

"Here you go." I sat up and held out a scrap of cheese, which it took delicately from my fingertips. I rubbed its head, ran my fingers down its spine. It pushed its head against my hand, arching its back and purring.

"Still a cat person, I see," said a voice behind me.

I jerked around.

"I went by your house, and Ishtar told me you were here. She said if I drove right over I might catch you." Matt had a camera around his neck; except for his gray-streaked hair, he could have stepped straight out of my memories. But he stood a few feet away, looking unsure of his welcome—an unfamiliar look, as if he had borrowed an expression belonging to someone else. "I hope I didn't just scare you into premature labor."

"Too late for that. I'm already full term." My voice came out a little shaky. "You're not exactly early, you know."

"Ouch. I guess I deserved that." He took a tentative step toward me. "I would have called first, but I was afraid you'd refuse to see me."

"If I had any sense, I probably would."

He sat down on the grass a few feet away. His face was pale under his tan; there were circles under his eyes. "Look, it's not like I've been avoiding you. I just got back from Bangkok yesterday. I went to your house as soon as I got up the nerve. I wasn't even sure you were there. Next, I was going to call your mother."

"Not a good idea. For one thing, she's gone back to Hawaii until the baby comes. For another, she'd cut your balls off."

"She wouldn't be the first to try." Matt looked at my belly. "You look . . . amazing. You must be almost due."

I nodded. "Any day now."

"And . . . how are you feeling?"

"Great, now. But I've been on bed rest for the last two months."

"I know. Ishtar told me. I'm sorry I wasn't there for it."

I shrugged, tried not to sound bitter. "That's okay. I'm used to it by now."

Matt leaned his forehead against his knees. "I guess I deserved that, too."

"To be honest, you're lucky I'm even talking to you right now."

He looked at me. "Look. Amanda. I don't know any graceful way to say this. So you have to just let me spit it out somehow. I acted like a jerk last time I saw you. I know that. And I'm sorry. It's just that—I couldn't believe how angry I got when you told me you were pregnant. It was like a tidal wave. And along with the anger was this feeling like . . . like I was going to die if I didn't get away from you as fast as I could."

I watched a pair of seagulls dive-bombing a duck on the pond, trying to snatch a chunk of bread from its mouth. "You know what, Matt? I don't have a whole lot of energy for processing your fear right now. Given that I'm going to go into labor like, any second. So you better get to the point pretty quickly."

"So, anyway—I left. And I went back to Thailand and went deep-sea scuba diving. Alone," he added, reading my mind. "Or mostly alone, anyway. I was trying to get my mind off the whole thing by doing something as exciting and potentially dangerous as possible. But it didn't work. I knew I had to do something to get my head together. So I wound up in this monastery in Burma, doing a two-month meditation retreat."

"Great. Your girlfriend's pregnant? Join a monastery."

"The few weeks were hell. I spent most of the time in a rage. I went over the situation again and again in my mind, trying to think myself into some reality where this"—he gestured at my belly—"wasn't happening. Or wasn't my problem." The cat had climbed into his lap. He stroked its head with his hand. "But when I finally sat still long enough, what I got was that underneath all that anger was just sheer terror. You know, my parents were so screwed up that I never really got to be a kid when I was a kid. I've been making up for that my whole adult life. And now I was supposed to have a kid myself? I was terrified that I was going to lose everything I'd worked so hard to maintain over all these years. My independence. My ability to walk away from anything." He looked at me. "My freedom to never again care about anything so much that if I lost it, it would break my heart."

I shrugged, refusing to soften. "I guess that's the great thing about being the dad, not the mom. You have a choice about whether you're going to sign on."

"Well, you had a choice, too, Amanda."

I shook my head. "No. I didn't. Not really. Not if I was going to live with myself for the rest of my life."

He leaned toward me. His eyes were intense. With the pond and the sky behind him, the gray eye looked almost green and the green almost gray, as if the two sides of his face were finally melding into a unified whole. "But that's what I'm saying, Amanda. That's what I finally realized, too. That if I walked away from you—if I walked away from this baby—then all my precious freedom, my so-called autonomy . . . it would be totally empty."

Something twisted in my chest. "So what are you telling me?"

He reached out and picked up my hand. It was as if my heart had been plugged into an electrical outlet: Against my will, something lit up and began to hum. "I'm telling you that—I want us to get back together. I want to be here for you and for the baby. I want you to give us another chance."

"Oh, great, *now* he shows up." Lori set a bowl of guacamole down onto my kitchen table with a brisk *thunk*. "Waltzes in just in time for the birth." She sat down across from me, tore open a bag of tortilla chips, and dumped them into another bowl. Even in the midst of a crisis, Lori was not one to eat chips straight out of the bag. "He's like those guys who watch TV all afternoon while their wives slave away in the kitchen getting ready for a dinner party. Then, when the guests arrive, the guys toss the steaks on the grill and take a bow. I'd love to have seen his face when you told him to take a hike."

She snapped the plastic wrap off the guacamole and looked at me. "You *did* tell him to take a hike, didn't you?"

I picked up a chip, scooped it into the guacamole. "I told him I needed to think about it."

"What's to think about?" Ishtar plopped herself down in the

chair next to Lori. "He's your tantric *consort*. Not to mention that he's the father of your baby. It's incredibly romantic."

"Consort! Give me a break." Lori glared at Ishtar. "The consort who responded to the news that you were pregnant by going *scuba diving in Thailand*. What's he going to do when the baby's born? Go kayaking in Alaska?"

The guacamole was tangy with lemon and garlic. I fought the impulse to put my hands over my ears. *We lay on the grass together, talking, until the fog came in and I began to shiver. Matt's arm around my shoulder, the warmth of his hand holding mine as we walked to his truck; two puzzle pieces clicking back together. "Want to grab a bite to eat?" he asked. "Yes," I wanted to say. "Yes. And then I want to go back to your apartment, and never leave."* It had taken all the strength I had to tell him to drive me here instead.

"Well, technically," said Ernie, leaning back against the kitchen counter and frowning, "she can't just tell him to take a hike. Legally, he's still the baby's father. He does have certain rights."

"Rights come with responsibilities," Lori snapped. "Let's see how many he's willing to take on. Precious few, I'm willing to bet."

"Maybe he's changed," said Ishtar dreamily. "People do."

"Not that much. Don't you ever watch Dr. Phil? 'The best predictor of future behavior is past behavior.'" Lori turned to Devi Das, who was standing at the stove making a stir-fry. "What do you think, Devi Das?"

I look at him, my stomach churning. Matt and I were on trial, and this ragtag jury of friends got to decide our fate. I wasn't sure what I hoped their verdict would be.

"We think the eggplants are done." Devi Das peered into the pan, frowning. "But the broccoli needs a few more minutes."

"Great," I said gratefully, heaving myself to my feet. "I'll get the plates. I'm starving."

I didn't want to talk about Matt any more. I was regretting

telling Lori in the first place. I wanted to take my memory of the afternoon off to my room with me, alone, and turn it over and over like a glowing ruby. I didn't want to put it under a jeweler's microscope to see if it was a fraud.


LATE THAT NIGHT, I lay in my bed in the only position that was remotely comfortable: on my side, with two pillows wedged between my legs, two more propped behind my back, two more under my head. It took ten minutes to wedge myself into position; then I got up to pee and had to start all over. Only after I got myself settled did I allow myself to take out my fantasies, like a rich dessert I'd been waiting all evening to savor.

*You can move into my studio,* Matt had said. *Sure, it's small, but we'll make it work. I'll stop traveling and get a real job—maybe as a photographer for the* Chronicle. *Or doing graphic design for a small press. Once I'm earning some real money, we can get a bigger place.*

I closed my eyes, put my hands on my belly. *Me and Matt and the baby, cozied up in Matt's loft bed. Matt's workstation under the loft replaced with a ExerSaucer and a diaper changing table. Matt walks in the door, home from work, swoops the baby up off the floor and into his arms. "Honey! I'm home!" I'm at the two-burner stove in the kitchenette, stirring a pot of vegetable soup. "How was your day at the office, dear?" The baby goes to sleep, gurgling. Matt and I make love on the floor.*

The Photographer's Bride. The Naughty Yogini.

But against my will, the story in my mind kept shifting. *The baby is screaming and won't go to sleep. It's getting later and later, and Matt isn't home. The phone rings; when I answer it, the caller gives a little gasp—unmistakably a woman's—and hangs up. Finally, Matt walks in the door, smelling of cigarette smoke and Scotch. He's full of apologies: The art opening went later than he thought; afterward, he went out for drinks with the gallery owner. He doesn't say the gallery owner's name.*

My left arm was falling asleep. I heaved myself onto my other side, laboriously rearranged my pillows. I tried to see Matt working a nine-to-five job. It was like seeing a Thoroughbred racehorse pulling a plow. And as hard as I tried, I couldn't imagine living with Matt, not really. I could only imagine yearning for him.

*But he's changed. Or, at least, he's promised to change. And I'll change, too.* My right hip was aching; I turned to the left side again. Did I dare to base a relationship on two people promising to be different than they've always been before?

On the other hand, did I dare not to?

I rolled back and forth for hours. No position was comfortable for more than a few minutes. Finally, long past midnight, I fell into a fitful sleep.

*I AM CURLED up on my bed with a jaguar. My hand is under his heavy, furred paw. The jaguar tells me he loves me, but he cannot be with me. "Why not?" I ask, weeping, burying my face in his fur. He looks at me with slanted, sorrowful eyes. "Our relationship worked when I was a kitten and you were a little girl," he tells me. "But now that we're both grown up, it will never work. You are a woman. I am a jungle cat." "Please," I sob. "Please. We can work it out." But he just licks my forehead with his hot, scratchy tongue and leaps out the window.*

I OPENED my eyes and stared into the darkness. My hips were aching. The glow of a streetlight came in around the edges of my curtains, casting a faint light on the empty bassinet.

Matt's face had been awestruck as he put his hand on my belly and felt the baby kick. Tears had come into his eyes. He'd bent his face down over my belly, his lips a few inches away. His breath had been warm on my skin. "Hey, little guy," he'd whispered. "It's your daddy."

Lying in the dark, I cupped my hand over my belly again, a pulsating globe of life. I begin to cry, and cry, and cry.

*   *   *

ONCE AGAIN, he was late, of course.

I was sitting on the sand at Ocean Beach, nine months—and an eternity—after I'd last met Matt there.

June in San Francisco is famously cold and foggy. But as if to rub my face in the fact that nothing in life is ever predictable, today was glorious. The sun shone in a cloudless sky. Just off shore, a seal's head bobbed in the glittering waves, then ducked under. A container ship steamed slowly toward the Golden Gate Bridge. About twenty yards away from me, a man and his son, who looked about eight years old, were digging an enormous hole in the sand with shovels. The hole was already deeper than the man's head. They were going at it with fierce efficiency—the man barking orders, the mound of excavated sand looming higher and higher, as if they were constructing a bunker for defending the coast from invaders, or a home they expected to live in for the rest of their lives. As if it wouldn't just be filled with water and washed away when the tide came in.

"I'm sorry I'm late." Matt flopped down next to me, leaned over, and kissed me full on the mouth. "I had to swing by the *Salon* offices. They want me to shoot a story in Sri Lanka."

"Don't worry about it. I've been enjoying the sunshine." I felt the aftershock of his lips on mine, fought the impulse to lean over and kiss him again. Instead, I looked at him and raised one eyebrow. "Sri Lanka, huh?"

"Don't worry, it wouldn't be until after the baby is born. And I wouldn't stay too long. No more than three weeks. A month, max." He pulled out his camera. "You look incredible. I've got to get a shot of this." He lay down on his belly in the sand, looked at me through the lens, and clicked. "Check this out." He showed me the tiny digital image, shielding it from the glare of the sun with his hand. The mound of my belly filled the screen, echoed by the curve of the hill behind me. But what really jumped out at me was the look on my face as I gazed at the camera—a combination of love and wariness, as if I were looking at the jaguar from my dream, and I didn't know whether to fling myself into its embrace or run for cover.

Matt saw it, too. He clicked the camera off, snapped the lens cap back on. "You're not going to move in with me, are you."

I shook my head. I felt something ripping in my heart. "No."

He looked away. "I didn't think so."

My throat was tight. I swallowed, but it didn't help. "It wouldn't work, Matt. It would destroy us both. And I can't risk that. Not when there's . . . someone else to consider."

"But that *is* who I'm considering. He needs—" He picked up a stick of driftwood, snapped it in two. "Look, Amanda. You didn't have a father. And I might as well not have had one, for all the time he spent with me. I've spent most of my life pretending that's no big deal. That I'm not walking around with a hole inside me the size of . . . the size of that sandpit they're digging over there." He nodded toward the father and son up the beach.

I looked at them. The man was standing on the edge of the hole, leaning on his shovel, looking into it. The boy was standing beside him, leaning on his shovel, too, his posture a comically precise mirror of his father's. "I *want* you to be the father. I want you to be as involved in the baby's life as you want to be. I just can't be your girl-friend again."

"I recognize this speech." He tossed the pieces of driftwood onto the sand. "It's the 'can't we just be friends' speech. I should know. I've given it enough times myself."

"Look. I've spent most of the last year getting over you, trying to fill up my own giant sandpit. I don't want to go back to hoping you're going to fill it for me."

"I know. I guess I just hoped we'd be able to be on the same beach while we shoveled."

"We can be on the same beach," I said. "Just maybe not on the same blanket."

We looked at each other. I wanted to sob. I wanted to run away. I wanted to throw my arms around him and never let go. I wanted to grab him by the neck and shake him until he turned into the person I wanted him to be. *Breathe. Feel the stretch. Hold the pose.* And then, for just a moment, I saw him as he really was: Not my father. Not my guru. Not the guy who was going to take away my loneliness by loving me. Not the guy who was going to take away my happiness by leaving. For a moment, he was just an ordinary human being: Like Lori. Like Devi Das. Like Ernie. Like Ishtar. Like my mother. A complex package of brilliance and idiocy, gifts and wounds. An ordinary person stumbling along a rocky trail in the dark, hoping the moon would come out.

"You're not going to be able to get rid of me, you know," he said. "I'm going to be over at your house all the time."

"Great. Because there'll be a lot of diapers to change." And then I said, involuntarily, "Oof!" Because the baby had taken his head like a battering ram and slammed it up against the inside of my cervix, as if he were breaking down a door. There was a stabbing pain, and my uterus clenched as if it were trying to crush a watermelon. "Oof!" I said again.

"What's up?" asked Matt.

A gush of liquid rushed out between my legs, soaking the sand as if I'd just peed in my maternity jeans. My whole belly clenched again. I grabbed Matt's arm.

"Here comes our baby," I told him.

# pose dedicated to the monkey god hanuman (hanumanasana)

*Kneel on the floor in a low lunge. Step your right foot forward about a foot in front of your left knee. Slide the left knee back as you drop the right thigh toward the floor. Now gradually begin to extend your right heel away from your pelvis, dropping your pelvis toward the ground in a deep split. Feel the burn of your hamstrings and groin as you challenge the strong and stubborn muscles that lash your thighbones to your pelvis.*

*So great was Hanuman's love for his masters, Rama and Sita, that he tore open his chest with his claws to reveal their image engraved on his heart. To rescue the kidnapped Sita from her bondage to a demon king, Hanuman leaped through the air from India to Sri Lanka and stole her back.*

*Now you ask your body to split its legs wide in a human imitation of the god's great leap. You claw open your heart and reveal the Divine etched upon it. You launch yourself over the ocean that separates the person you think you are from the person you can become.*

*Listen, my friend, this road is the heart opening, kissing his feet, resistance broken, tears all night . . . Mirabai says, "The heat of midnight tears will bring you to God."*

—Mirabai (1498–1565)

CHAPTER 26

Eleven hours after Matt and I had left the beach—speeding up Fulton Street and across Golden Gate Park in the battered old truck on which I blamed my entire pregnancy—I was pacing around my private birthing room on the fifteenth floor of the UCSF hospital, trying to jog my uterus into high gear.

I was wearing a white hospital gown tied at the back, with a fetal monitor strapped around my waist that broadcast every contraction in squiggly lines on a roll of paper unfurling by the side of my hospital bed. Lori was walking with me, her arm tucked under mine, so I could grab her whenever another contraction hit. Matt was stretched out on the bed, flipping through a copy of *The Birth Book: Everything You Need to Know to Have a Safe and Satisfying Birth,* as if cramming for an exam in a course where he'd skipped most of the lectures. Devi Das and Ishtar were squeezed into an armchair on the other side of the room, eating cherry Popsicles from the minifridge.

From the big picture windows at one end of the room, I could look out over the nightscape of the city, twinkling with lights, all the way to the distant arc of the Bay Bridge. When I'd arrived, I'd found the view inspirational. Now I just wanted to bang my head against the glass.

"You're doing great," said Lori for the twentieth time, as I dug my nails into her arm and whimpered.

"I'm *not* doing great. Eleven hours into this, and I'm only six centimeters dilated!"

"That was forty-five minutes ago. I'm sure you're farther by now."

Matt looked up from his book. "It says here that an increase in pain means that your labor is progressing."

"Ah! Pain means progress! Just like in spiritual practice!" Devi Das waved his Popsicle at me.

"Actually, it's only the internalized patriarchal terror of women's bodies that makes childbirth painful," said Ishtar. "I've heard of lots of women who experienced their labor contractions as being like giant orgasms."

I wanted to rip her eyebrows out with my teeth. "Well, guess what? I'm not one of them."

"Don't feel inadequate," Devi Das reassured me. "We're sure half those women were just faking it."

Another contraction seized my belly and I gasped as I grabbed Lori's arm. "Ouch. That was a big one."

"You can moan if you want to," said Ishtar. "Don't be inhibited."

"I'm NOT inhibited! Why does everyone think I'm inhibited?"

"Well. All I'm saying is, don't be."

"Would you like another Popsicle?" asked Devi Das. "The lemonade ones are quite good."

"No. I would *not* like another Popsicle." I looked at Lori, telegraphed an urgent message with my eyes: *Get them out of here before I do something bad.*

THE FIRST SIX or seven hours of labor had actually been quite festive. Ishtar had brought her iPod to plug into the birthing room's sound system, programmed with a selection of soothing, spiritual music: Tibetan refugee nuns chanting the Heart Sutra. Native American drumming. Five versions of Pachelbel's Canon. She'd even loaded in the CD I'd picked up in the Kerala ashram of Prana Ma chanting the 1,008 names of the Divine Mother. "Your birthing room should be like a temple," she'd said, switching off the overhead lights and plugging in a nightlight in the shape of a Tara. Devi Das had brought some sandalwood incense we'd picked up at the Satyanam Ashram and stuck it into the empty water glass on my bedside table. Sitting in the dim light squeezing Matt's hand—just a little more often than the pain actually called for—I'd imagined the nurses whispering to each other in the hall: "Have you been in Room 5? It's better than going to church." I'd done so much yoga for so many years—this baby was going to just slip right out, with just enough discomfort that I'd have a good story for my book tour.

But eleven hours into it, I was as sick of the labor as I was of the Heart Sutra CD. I was out of incense. Matt had put the lens cap back on his camera. Everyone else had eaten pizza and burritos and ice cream, while I'd had nothing but Recharge, ice chips, and Popsicles. I'd been in and out of the bathtub so many times that my fingers were wrinkled and puffy. The pain had been growing steadily worse, but not dramatically enough for me to feel like anything interesting was going to happen anytime soon. I wanted to fast-forward to tomorrow morning, when presumably I'd have an actual baby in my arms. But I had no idea how to get from here to there. I knew I shouldn't have skipped that last birthing class. That must have been the one where they gave us the secret trick for *getting the baby out.*

Now Lori snapped into sheepdog mode and herded Devi Das and Ishtar out of the room, ordering them to go home and get some sleep so they'd be able to help out the next day. Dr. Pat came in, and I lay down on the bed so she could check my cervix. "Still only seven centimeters. Your labor may be stalled. If it goes on like this for much longer, we'll need to give you some Pitocin to get things going."

"No! I don't want any drugs. I'm doing natural childbirth, remember?" Great. First my cervix was opening too soon. Now it wouldn't open at all.

"Mmmph. I'll check back in an hour or so. Then we'll see." Dr. Pat walked out.

Matt was starting to pace the room like a caged tiger. "Mind if I step outside and take a little walk? I need some fresh air."

*Oh, God, he's headed straight for the airport. Next I hear from him, it'll be a phone call from Bali.* I took a deep breath. "Go ahead."

As soon as he was gone, Lori sat down next to me and took my hand. "Listen, Amanda. I think you're going to have to let things get a lot more intense."

"You mean, with Matt?"

"*No,* not with Matt. Jesus. Could you maybe stop thinking about Matt for one second, seeing as how you're in the middle of having a baby and all? I mean with your *labor.*"

"That's not up to me."

"It *is* up to you. That's what I'm saying. I think you're shutting things down."

The last thing I needed right now was another lecture from Lori. "Why would I do that? Believe me, I want to get this baby out more than anybody."

"Part of you does. But part of you is terrified of letting things get out of control."

My uterus clamped down again. I grabbed the rail on the side of my bed. "Um, Lori? I'm kind of busy right now. Could you save it for later?"

"Amanda. Listen to me. You've always tried to control everything, to figure everything out in advance in your head. You like to wrap everything up into tidy little packages, like you do in your guidebooks. But this isn't *Childbirth for Idiots*. You're going to have to let go."

That wasn't fair. Which of us was the world's biggest control freak? And besides . . . "I *don't* control everything!" I protested. "I can't control *anything!*" The list of things I'd failed to control scrolled through my mind: *Matt. India. Enlightenment. My book. My mother. My father. Even my own thoughts.*

"But you try. And I think everything—*everything*—would go better if you didn't."

I closed my eyes. "Okay. I'll let go. There. Are you happy?" Maybe if I let go, the gods would reward me by making everything go the way I want. I'd let go, and then I wouldn't *have* to let go. *Here I go. I'm letting go, and surrendering, and softening, and . . .*

"I'm back." Matt walked in the door. "It's an awesome night out there. The whole block smells like jasmine." I opened my eyes. And as I did, a wave of pain crashed through me that was bigger than anything I'd ever felt, bigger than anything I'd ever imagined.

"Oh God." I grabbed onto Matt's arm as he sat down on the other side of my bed from Lori.

"Are you *okay?*"

"Yeah." *No.* The pain had passed, but I kept my grip on his arm. "Matt? Could you tell me a story? Just to kind of take my mind off . . . everything?"

He puts his hand over mine. "Sure. I'll tell you the story of how we first met."

"I already know that story."

"No. You know the story of how *you* met *me*. But you don't know how *I* met you."

"Okay. Whatever. Just keep talking." I was trying to keep breathing.

"I walked into the studio and spread out my mat next to yours. That first time, it was just because it was the only space in the room that wasn't taken. You were this twig of a girl, all arms and legs and the biggest eyes I'd ever seen. You were the only woman in the room who didn't look like she was auditioning for a part in a yoga video. You weren't wearing any makeup, and your hair was pulled back in a ponytail, and you were wearing sweatpants and a ratty old tank top. But once you started moving, I couldn't keep my eyes off you. Your body was like water."

My nails dug into his arm. "Keep going."

"I remember we were practicing second series that day. You were working on putting your leg behind your head. You kept your eyes closed, like you were off in some world where I would never be able to follow you. I remember the way the smell of your sweat mixed with the smell of the incense. A few days later, you left your red sweatshirt behind in the yoga room. I picked it up and took it home with me. I meant to give it back to you at the next class. But instead I just kept it under my pillow. It gave me the craziest dreams."

"So that's what happened to that sweatshirt! I liked that sweatshirt." I rolled onto my side. "Oh, shit. Here comes another one."

"Okay. Breathe. Focus."

"Just *please* keep talking."

"I think I knew, even then. I didn't want to know, but I did. I knew that there was something between us that would be there forever. Yes, of course, there have been other women. There probably will be again. But—"

"Excuse me, but wasn't the point of this story to get her mind off the pain?" interrupted Lori. "Because I don't know if this is exactly doing the trick."

"It's doing the trick for me," said Matt.

"For once, can it not be all about you?" She was glaring at him across my bed.

"It's not about me. It's about *us*. Me and Amanda." He leaned over me, cupped my face in his hands. "What I'm trying to say is—I love you. I always have loved you. I always *will* love you. Whatever else happens, whatever ways I've let you down, whatever way I let you down again, I want you to know that this is true."

"Aaaaaaaargh." It was a long, animal snarl I didn't even recognize as mine, emerging from somewhere deep in my gut. I stuffed the corner of the sheet in my mouth, tore at it with my teeth. I grabbed onto Matt's hand and squeezed it as if I wanted to break every bone.

"Breathe," he said again. "Just breathe."

"Matt. I don't think I can do this."

"You can do it. I know you can. Just pretend it's a really intense Ashtanga practice. Every contraction is another pose. Just breathe from one to another like you're doing vinyasa."

I growed again, gnawed at the sheet. I groaned. And that's when I saw him: Mr. Kapoor. He was standing at the foot of my bed, dressed in his yoga shorts, his bare chest swelling. His face was fierce. "Do your breathing and all will follow!" he roared. "One breath only. Then one more. A little pain—no problem."

I shut my eyes and begin to do *ujayii,* that deep, familiar, sibilant hiss in the back of my throat. I cling to the breath like a life rope as another wave of pain crashed over me, then another. *In. Out. In. Out.*

Mr. Kapoor kept shouting. "Every cell of your body is intelligent! Liberate its wisdom."

*I'm trying to. It hurts too much. In. I want it to stop. Out.*

"Feel the pain as sensation, mate, not as pain." Now Harold was there, too. "Is it pressure, or tingling? Is it moving, does it stay the same? Don't add to your suffering by resisting what is."

*It's burning. It's ripping. In. It's splitting. It's tearing. Out. Oh, I can't do it. I can't.*

"Who is the I who cannot do it?" Saraswati's eyes were piercing blue. "Show me that I."

*I don't know, I am gone, the person I thought I was is shattering into a thousand pieces . . .*

"The Divine Mother comes in many forms." Prana Ma's voice was tender. She wrapped me in her arms. "And one of those forms is you."

And then a tornado of pain blew through me, so huge that it spun all the gurus out the window. I was roaring, and spitting, and drooling, and tearing my nails down Matt's arm. This wasn't a quiet ashram temple. It was a sacrificial altar, with priests slaughtering goats to wild drumbeats. I was Kali with her tongue hanging out and blood dripping from her teeth. My pelvis was a ring of fire.

"Mmmm, hmmmm." At the foot of my bed, Dr. Pat was sliding her hand inside me. "You're ready to push."

"Matt," I hissed. "Get me out of here. I've changed my mind. I don't want to have a baby. I want to be a Tibetan nun. I want to be a yogini. I can't do this."

He put his hand on my heart. "You're already doing it."

And it was true. All on its own, my body was heaving, my belly rippling. I was turning myself inside out. The earth was cracking open.

"Here comes the head," said Dr. Pat. I heaved again. Something heavy and soft was sliding out of me, with a sucking feeling. Somewhere, someone was starting to wail. And then Dr. Pat was setting a slippery bundle onto my chest, and wrapping us both in a soft blanket. I saw a wet, dark head, a red face, a squalling mouth. Matt was bending over me. Forget our past lives: We had all three just been incarnated.

"Here's your little girl," said Dr. Pat.

It didn't register, at first. Then I heard Matt's voice. "Our *girl?*"

*For all things born in truth must die, and out of death in truth comes life. Face to face with what must be, cease from sorrow.*

—Bhagavad Gita, ca. 300 BC

# CHAPTER 27

W E BROUGHT THE baby home from the hospital the next morning just after breakfast. Astoundingly, we were allowed to just walk out of there with her, without even passing a basic burping-and-diapering exam. Matt and I sat on either side of her car seat in the back seat of Lori's VW. I held my breath over every bump, gripped the edge of her car seat so tight it left red marks on my palms. When we finally pulled up to my house, I couldn't figure out how to snap the portable car seat out of its base. So I scooped the baby out of the seat instead, sliding one hand under her head, the way we'd practiced with rubber dolls in my birthing class. She was floppy and soft and unbelievably small. I was terrified that I would break her.

My housemates had festooned the front hall with Tibetan prayer flags and blue banners proclaiming "It's a Boy." "Gender is just a societal construct, anyway," Ishtar said, as she followed me up the stairs to my room, trailed by Ernie and Devi Das. I set the sleeping baby in her tapestry-draped bassinet and curled up on my bed, as close as I could get to the bassinet without actually climbing in it myself. Matt and Lori headed home to get some sleep, both of them promising to come back later and help out. I was dizzy with hormones and exhaustion. But I was afraid that if I didn't keep watching the baby, she'd stop breathing.

"So Prana Ma was right, after all." Ishtar sat down cross-legged on the foot of my bed, her wildest faiths vindicated. The baby was a girl: hence, lighting candles in your ears drained the toxins from your brain, amethyst crystals could predict the outcome of the presidential elections, space aliens killed JFK. "And you even named her Aradhana, just like she said you would."

"I still might change the name. It's just that they wouldn't let me take her out of the hospital if I didn't give them something for the birth certificate, and all the names I'd thought about were for boys." An enormous bouquet of gladiolas sat on the bedside table. I picked up the card from my mother and read it: "Welcome, Aradhana dear! I'll be on the next plane from Hawaii to meet you. Just please don't call me Grandma. I prefer something like Nona, it's so deliciously Italian."

"So all the ultrasounds were *wrong?*" Ernie peered into the bassinet.

"Dr. Rao must have misread the early one. She did tell me it wasn't a hundred percent accurate. And as for Dr. Pat—she was just having a little joke, I guess. I told her she didn't need to tell me the baby's sex, because I already knew. So she never told me that I was wrong."

"You won't change her name," said Devi Das. "You can't. It's karma."

"It does sort of seem to be sticking." I couldn't stop staring at her, as if she were a drug I was already hooked on. Her tiny face was red and slightly squished, the nose flattened in transit. Her mouth was definitely Matt's: a pouty bow, pursed in concentration. Her tiny fingers clutched at a blanket printed with dinosaurs. Her brow was furrowed in a worried look, even in sleep, as if she were already starting to suspect that if anyone around here was going to get it together, it was going to have to be her.

"I think I'll take a nap," I told my housemates. But really, I just wanted to be alone with the baby. As soon as I was sure they were all the way downstairs, I scooped her out of the bassinet. I felt like I was doing something illicit, as if I needed someone else's permission to pick her up: but whose permission would that be? I lay down on my back and placed her on my belly, her head nestled just below my breasts. I had a feeling we would both sleep better that way. It was more what we were used to.

Her face was working in her sleep, as if she were dreaming. What could she be dreaming about at less than a day old? My breasts? The unfamiliar tug of the diaper around her thighs? The long, squeezed passage down the birth canal? The liquid darkness of the womb? Dread, surprise, joy, and awe flickered over her face, a preview of a lifetime of pains and passions. I wanted to wrap her up and put her in a cardboard box somewhere for the rest of her life, so nothing would ever harm her. In my dreamy, half-drugged state, it almost seemed like that would be a workable strategy.

"Aradhana," I whispered, trying it out. Was the name random, like so much else in my life? Or was it destiny? And how would I know the difference? More and more, it seemed like "it was meant to be" was just another way of saying "it's what happened."

# E P I L O G U E

From: Amandalayahoo.com
To: Maxine@bigdaybooks.com
Re: Enlightenment for Idiots

Dear Maxine:

You'll be happy to hear that I just FedExed you the final manu-script for *Enlightenment for Idiots.* I'm sorry it's a few months late. I'm sorry, too, that the first few pages are a bit crumpled. Aradhana got hold of it while I was trying to find the napkin where I'd written down your FedEx number, and her way of appreciating fine writing is to chew on it. Also, please ignore the typos in the last couple of chapters—Aradhana spit up on the keyboard and the "m" stopped working. I'd never realized how important the "m" is when you're writ-ing about spiritual awakening. I mean, there's *meditation,* and *mantra,* and *metta,* and—well, you get the picture. I called tech sup-port and got connected with this Indian guy in Calcutta, who didn't know a thing about yoga, although he said that he'd really like to move to Los Angeles and get into it. I told him that a liquid had been spilled on the keyboard, and he asked what liquid, and I said partially digested breast milk, and he got really embarrassed and put me on hold for over an hour.

Anyway, I would have cleaned things up a bit more, but I was afraid I'd miss the last FedEx pickup. And I know you said that this was absolutely the last extension you were going to give me, and that if I didn't get the book to you by tomorrow at noon I was going to have to pay back the money you'd already given me, and I could just forget about getting the rest of the advance. And if I don't get that advance I won't even have enough to pay the diaper service.

Am I telling you more than you want to know? It's so hard to tell. One of the side effects of sleep deprivation is that I never know when to stop talking. Earlier today, I heard myself telling the FedEx guy that I'd been putting garlic mashed potatoes in my bra. It's not a kinky thing—it's for cracked nipples—but he kind of seemed to take it the wrong way.

Anyway, if I'm remembering right, the last time we talked was a few months ago, when you and I had that little dispute about whether I could just split the book into two parts and turn in one now and one when Aradhana starts preschool. Well, you wouldn't believe how much Aradhana's grown since then. Back then, she was just this drooling colicky bundle who couldn't even roll over. And as I tried to tell you before I accidentally dropped the phone in the Diaper Genie, it turned out she was what my parenting books call a "fussy" baby—which is basically just a nice way of saying she screamed *all the time*. She couldn't sleep unless I was holding her, and even then she woke up as soon as I put her down, which meant that I did everything—ate, slept, checked email, whatever—with her in my arms. I even *peed* with her in my lap. My whole bed smelled like baby poop and sour milk. Every now and then, Lori or Devi Das or Ishtar or my mom would hold her so I could take a shower, and I'd stand there under the hot water pretending I was on a vacation at a spa. Once Ernie even offered to take her while I went to yoga at The Blissful Body. But my milk let down in Downward Dog, and I had to get out of there before I started dripping all over the mat.

Devi Das kept telling me that I'd feel calmer if I meditated, and when I told him I didn't have time, he asked, "How do you have time to do anything else?" I think that's when I threw the diaper at him.

Of course, I still loved her more than I'd ever have believed possible. And even when I didn't, I just did what they told me at the Parent's Support hotline and pretended I did until the loving feelings came back again. "Just fake it till you make it," the woman who answered the phone kept telling me. It was two in the morning at the time, and I kept wondering if she was faking it, too—using this sweet, compassionate voice, like she was just so *present* with me, like she cared so *much,* when really she was clipping her toenails and thinking, *What a loser. Why doesn't she just hire a nanny?*

But I have to admit, that "fake it till you make it" attitude has turned out to be helpful with all kinds of things (including writing my book, although maybe I shouldn't tell you that). And things are finally getting easier. Now Ari's turned into this gorgeous, happy girl with great big eyes—one green, one gray, just like her dad. She laughs all the time, like bubbles coming up from her belly. She's even starting to crawl, except so far no matter how hard she thrashes she can only go backward. I definitely know the feeling. But instead of getting mad or giving up, she just starts to chortle, like it's just a total gas that she lives in a world where everything she reaches for just gets farther and farther away.

Matt is madly in love with her, too—although that doesn't necessarily mean that he's around all that much. That's not entirely his fault, I keep reminding myself. Right after Aradhana was born, he landed a gig shooting a series of brochures for the San Francisco Zoo. It helped pay off Aradhana's birth expenses, but it meant he had to spend pretty much every day in the African Savanna, the Lemur Forest, the Australian WalkAbout, and Penguin Island. He'd blow in at random times to snatch Aradhana up from my arms, cover her face with kisses, and tell her all about rhinoceros courtship behaviors. Then he'd hand her back to me when she started to scream.

Anyway, when she was two months old, he left for Sri Lanka for three weeks, and he's pretty much been in and out of town ever since. "I wish you had a man you could count on," my mother keeps saying. But I keep telling her that I *can* count on him. I can count on him to be Matt.

Before he left on his last trip, he gave me a photo album he made. I flip through it whenever I start to feel a little low. The pictures are amazing; maybe someday I'll show them to you. Aradhana nursing, her mouth pressed wide against my breast. Aradhana asleep in a tangle of blankets, her arms flung out. A close-up of her tiny hand wrapped around my finger. Me rocking her in my arm, my hair a riot of curls, and a look on my face I've never seen before. You wouldn't recognize me, Maxine. I look tender, and soft, and hopeful. I look . . . happy.

It's strange—my memory of those first few months of her life is one long, demented blur. But when I look at the pictures, I can see the joy in every frame. It's as if Matt's camera was fitted with a special lens that filtered out the surface insanity and let what was underneath it shine through.

The picture I look at most often, though, wasn't taken by Matt. It was taken by Lori when she stopped by one afternoon and found me and Matt and Aradhana sprawled on my bed, fully clothed, all of us sound asleep. In the picture, I'm turned toward Matt, with Aradhana tucked in the curve of my body between us. Matt is half on his back, one hand reaching toward us, his head turned away.

I remember that Matt had gotten off work at noon that day— the macaw expert had called in sick, so his shoot at the South American Tropical Forest had been canceled. He'd come over to find me walking up and down the hall, sobbing, with Aradhana screaming in my arms. He'd bundled her up and taken her out to the park, still screaming, while I passed out on the bed. When I woke up, the sun was starting to set. Matt was lying on the bed next to me. Aradhana was nestled between us. In the soft, gray light I could see her long eyelashes brushing the curve of her cheek. Matt's face was a few inches from hers, his mouth pursed in dreamy concentration, exactly like hers. It felt so right, for us all to be sleeping there together. The love between us felt so simple and clear. I thought, *It's too bad we can't just stay asleep forever.*

Now, whenever I look at the picture, I see that the three of us are a family. But I also see how, even in sleep, Matt is turned halfway away from me and Aradhana. Even as his arms reach toward us, part of him is pulling away.

The picture breaks my heart. But I keep it. To remind me of everything that isn't possible between us. But also to remind me of everything that is.


Okay, okay, I can feel you getting impatient, Maxine. You're wondering, What does all this have to do with *Enlightenment for Idiots?* I'm getting to that. I really am.

You see, I thought I was going to India to find the path to enlightenment—and that when I found it, I'd turn into a whole new person. But what if enlightenment really *is* for idiots? Idiots like you, and me, and Matt, and Sri Satyaji, and Mr. Kapoor, and everyone else I've met on this amazingly screwed-up journey? What if when all those spiritual teachers kept talking about the present moment, they really meant *this* present moment, not some better one? *My* present moment—with me typing in a spit-up-stained nursing shirt while Aradhana naps, and desperately needing a drink of water but afraid that if I cross the creaky floor to get it I'll wake her up and this email won't get done? Or *your* present moment, with you drinking a latte and reading my message, wondering if I've lost my mind?

I mean, sure, my life is a mess. There's this family I see at the park sometimes. The mom has a fabulous haircut and she always has makeup on, the really expensive kind that looks like she's not even wearing any. And she looks like she's getting plenty of sleep, even though her baby is just about the same age as Aradhana. She already fits back into her skinny jeans, and her baby wears these frilly pink dresses, and neither of them ever has pureed bananas stuck in the creases of their necks. On weekends, her husband comes to the playground with her and swings with the baby in his lap. He's a big, good-looking guy with a great laugh, and he obviously adores them both. I look at their perfect family and I feel like . . . well, like I belong in the diaper pail.

But then I remember—I've got Lori and Devi Das and Ishtar and Ernie. I've got my zany, flaky mother. I've even got Matt, as much as anyone can have him. It's not the family I imagined. But it's real, and that counts for a lot. Because up close, nothing looks like it does when you're imagining it from a distance. Not a family. Not India. Not a guru. Not a yoga pose. Frankly, I'm starting to think that even enlightenment probably isn't everything it's cracked up to be. I wonder if you don't just sit there, at one with the universe, thinking, *Is this what all the fuss was about?*

Speaking of enlightenment, I've started teaching yoga. I teach a couple of morning classes, plus a mom-baby and a prenatal. They're going pretty well, especially since The Blissful Body started promoting me as "a senior student of the greatest yoga gurus in India." Devi Das and Ishtar are going back to India next month—to Khajuraho, to start a tantric healing center for yoga students. Ernie's going to take over Ishtar's room as his office—amazingly, his business has really taken off since his clients started hearing Ari crying during their consultations. And Lori and Joe are getting married right after Christmas.

A few weeks ago, I went to a support group for single parents and met this guy named Jacob. He has almost-two-year-old twins, a boy and a girl, and he looked like he hadn't shaved or showered in a little too long. He told us that his wife had had severe postpartum depression, and he ended up doing pretty much all the child care while she lay in bed and cried for the first six months. Then she started to go to this meditation group that her Jungian therapist recommended, and things seemed to be looking up for a while. But right after the twins turned one, her meditation teacher went back to Nepal, and she went with him. She's decided she wants to be a nun. Jacob's still in shock. He says it would be easier if she'd run off with another man. Because how can you compete with the promise of nirvana?

Our first date was at the park across from Grace Cathedral. We sat on a wooden bench eating Pirate's Booty and watching the twins on the teeter-totter. Aradhana sat in the sand squealing and beating her shovel on her bucket, like she was watching the Cirque du Soleil. When I told Jacob I was writing a book about enlightenment, he got a little freaked out. But I told him not to worry, I'd had enough India to last me for a long time.

Sometimes, I have to admit, I do find myself dreaming about it. I'll be pushing Aradhana in her stroller through Golden Gate Park, watching a guy in a baseball hat throwing a tennis ball for a Labrador—and suddenly I'll be sitting by the Ganges in Varanasi, watching the sun turn the river gold, breathing in the scorched fat of burning corpses. I'll be standing in the produce section picking out cabbage, and I'll be blasted by longing for smoky, sweet Indian chai, drunk from a unfired clay cup on the platform of a train that's about to take me a thousand years into the past.

But then Aradhana will bite my ear or yank on my hair, and I'll come back.

I'm not saying that you can't find enlightenment in India. Maybe it was all around me the whole time. Maybe it was there in the bicycle-rickshaw driver fixing his wheel with a piece of twisted coat hanger, or the fruit seller slashing the top off a coconut with a machete, or the smell of the sewers, or the dripping juice of a mango. Maybe it was in the eyes of that dog I didn't let myself rescue.

And who knows? Maybe it's here, too. That's what my book says, anyway. On a good day, I almost believe it myself.

I don't know how you're going to market "right where you already are" as a For Idiots destination. But I'm sure the PR department will come up with something. In the meantime, the fog is rolling in. My breasts are starting to tingle, which means that in a moment Aradhana will wake up and want to nurse. In about an hour, Lori is going to pick us up, and we're going to have dinner at her house, along with Jacob and the twins.

I don't mean to give you the impression that I've worked everything out. I'm actually still worried about a lot of things. For instance, I'm worried that you won't like the manuscript and I will have to take over Ishtar's night job on the sex hotline. I'm worried that I'm going to screw things up with Jacob—that he's just too nice and treats me too well, so I'll break up with him to go out with someone who's more like Matt. Or that secretly he *is* like Matt, and that's the only reason I'm interested in him at all, even though I haven't found that out yet.

But right now, everything's okay. There's just the glow of the screen and the touch of my fingers on the keys. There's a car alarm going off down the street and banana bread baking in the kitchen. There's my mother downstairs, flipping through the pages of a magazine, dreaming of the lives she never lived. There's Aradhana waking up, bubbling over with laughter, flapping her arms and legs and getting ready to crawl into her future.

Okay, so I haven't found enlightenment yet. But for now, maybe this is good enough.

With best regards,
Amanda

# ACKNOWLEDGMENTS

MY DEEPEST THANKS TO:

The members of my writing group—Katy Butler, Doug Benerofe, and Stephanie Vollmer—for their encouragement and feedback. Shoshana Alexander, the grand guru of writing coaches. Rachael Adler and Janice Gates, for cheering me on through chapter-by-chapter installments while we raised our children together. My big sister, Kathleen, for her inexhaustible support and wisdom. Vikas Rustagi of the Indian Department of Tourism, for empowering my research. My agent, Lisa Bankoff, for her skill and vision. Shaye Areheart and Peter Guzzardi, my editors, for slimming down the manuscript so it fits into its yoga pants. My dharma friend Carole Melkonian ("Sister Bliss"). My beloved son, Skye. Lou Hawthorne, for being the world's best father to Skye. And all the wonderful yoga and dharma teachers—too many to name—who have inspired and guided me on my spiritual path.

# ABOUT THE AUTHOR

ANNE CUSHMAN is a contributing editor to both *Yoga Journal* and *Tricycle: The Buddhist Review* and the coauthor of *From Here to Nirvana*, a seeker's guide to spiritual India. Her essays have appeared in the *New York Times*, the *San Francisco Chronicle*, and *O, the Oprah Magazine*, and on Salon.com. They have been anthologized in *Best Buddhist Writing 2004* and *2006*; *A Woman's Path: Best Women's Spiritual Travel Writing*; and other books. She codirects the Mindfulness Yoga and Meditation training program at Spirit Rock Meditation Center in California. This is her first novel.